PALADINS OF VALOR

Book 5 of
Libri Valoris

Edited by
Rob Howell

New Mythology Press
Coinjock, NC

Copyright © 2023 by Rob Howell.

All rights reserved. No part of this publication may be reproduced, distributed or transmitted in any form or by any means, including photocopying, recording, or other electronic or mechanical methods, without the prior written permission of the publisher, except in the case of brief quotations embodied in critical reviews and certain other noncommercial uses permitted by copyright law. For permission requests, write to the publisher, addressed "Attention: Permissions Coordinator," at the address below.

Chris Kennedy/New Mythology Press
1097 Waterlily Rd.
Coinjock, NC 27923
https://chriskennedypublishing.com/

Publisher's Note: This is a work of fiction. Names, characters, places, and incidents are a product of the author's imagination. Locales and public names are sometimes used for atmospheric purposes. Any resemblance to actual people, living or dead, or to businesses, companies, events, institutions, or locales is completely coincidental.

Cover Art and Design by J. Caleb Design (https://www.jcalebdesign.com/)

Ordering Information:
Quantity sales. Special discounts are available on quantity purchases by corporations, associations, and others. For details, contact the "Special Sales Department" at the address above.

The stories and articles contained herein have never been previously published and are copyrighted as follows:
FAMILY HEIRLOOM by HOWARD ANDREW JONES © 2024 by HOWARD ANDREW JONES
PALADINS OF THE UNBROKEN LIGHT by D.J. BUTLER © 2024 by D.J. BUTLER
HIGH WATER MARK by CHRIS HEPLER © 2024 by CHRIS HEPLER
THE PASSING OF THE MANTLE by DAVID BIRDSALL © 2024 by DAVID BIRDSALL
THE PURLOINED HEART by CHRISTOPHER G. NUTTALL © 2024 by CHRISTOPHER G. NUTTALL
APPRENTICE IN TROUBLE by CHAD BOYER © 2024 by CHAD BOYER
SEALED WITH A KISS by C.V. WALTER © 2024 by C.V. WALTER
ROMANCING SOME ROCK by EDIE SKYE © 2024 by EDIE SKYE
SPACE MAGE SECRETS by DANIEL M. HOYT © 2024 by DANIEL M. HOYT
VALORS WIRTH by JON R. OSBORNE © 2024 by JON R. OSBORNE
THE OATHS THAT BIND by H.Y. GREGOR AND DAVID SHADOIN © 2024 by H.Y. GREGOR AND DAVID SHADOIN
WELCOME TO DETROIT by NATHAN BALYEAT © 2024 by NATHAN BALYEAT
THOSE WHO WENT by GLEN COOK © 2024 by GLEN COOK
A TALE OF THE MUSES' DARLING by SARAH A. HOYT © 2024 by SARAH M. HOYT

PALADINS OF VALOR/ROB HOWELL -- 1st ed.
ISBN: 978-1648559914

Get the **free** Four Horsemen prelude story ***Shattered Crucible***
and discover other titles by Seventh Seal Press at:
chriskennedypublishing.com

* * *

Get the **free** New Mythology collection of short stories, ***Mythos*** at:
chriskennedypublishing.com/fantasy-mailer/

* * *

Discover other titles by New Mythology Press at:
chriskennedypublishing.com/new-mythology-press

* * * * *

Dedication

To the crew at FantaSci

Thanks for being awesome.

* * * * *

Preface by Rob Howell

What a ride this has been.

At LibertyCon 2019, I asked Chris Kennedy when he was going to do an anthology of fantasy stories. He said, "When you do it."

Then Joel Lyons and his crew offered to make it a thing at FantaSci. Now the *Libri Valoris* weren't just anthologies, they were an opportunity for new writers to get recognition and a membership to a con.

This is the fifth Book of Valor, and I'm immensely proud of what we've accomplished. Over seventy total stories. The twenty stories chosen out of the open calls were tremendous, and we've had the honor of publishing the first published work from several authors who are already going on to bigger things.

We've had some of the best writers in speculative fiction contribute, as well, including names such as Larry Correia, David Weber, Jody Lynn Nye, Jason Cordova, and a bunch more. D.J. Butler has been a rock star for me, having contributed an Indrajit and Fix story to all five anthologies, including this one.

This volume is stacked, actually, with contributions from Butler, Sarah A. Hoyt, Edie Skye, Glen Cook, Chris Nuttall, Howard Andrew Jones, Daniel M. Hoyt, and C.V. Walter. It's been an honor to work with all of these folk.

It's also been an honor to work with all the folk from Chris Kennedy Publishing. Mark Wandrey, Kevin Steverson, Bill Webb, Jon R.

Osborne, and Chris Kennedy himself have all contributed, among others.

Jon, in particular, has filled in quite a few corners in his Milesian Accords universe. He's got another in here, along with another Milesian story from H.Y. Gregor and David Shadoin that starts off a new thread in that world.

Our open call produced great stories again. David R. Birdsall gives us a paladin from the Ozarks. Chad Boyer provides a spacefaring one. Chris Hepler gives us a French paladin at the Battle of Gettysburg. And finally, Nathan Balyeat has one fighting an ancient evil in Detroit. That's a pretty interesting collection, if I do say so myself, and they were all fun to read.

We've been blessed with great editors to catch all the stuff I missed. Tiffany Reynolds and Zach Ritz were the team this time, but thanks to all who've helped along the way.

J. Caleb Design has provided all the cover art. Each time, I've given him three of my favorite characters from the anthology, and he's given us really fun covers. He's a great guy to work with, and I can't recommend him enough.

Thanks again to Chris and Joel for the opportunity. Thanks to all who contributed. Most of all, thanks to all the fans who've been here along the way.

– Rob Howell

* * * * *

Table of Contents

Dedication 5

Preface by Rob Howell 7

Family Heirloom by Howard Andrews Jones 11
   A Chronicles of Hanuvar Story
   Chapter I 12
   Chapter II 19
   Chapter III 27
   Chapter IV 31
   Chapter V 43
   Chapter VI 49
   Howard Andrew Jones Biography 65

Paladins of the Unbroken Light by D.J. Butler 67
   A Tales of Indrajit and Fix Story
   D.J. Butler Biography 98

High Water Mark by Chris Hepler 99
   Chris Hepler Biography 134

The Passing of the Mantle by David R. Birdsall 135
   A Fractured Brotherhood Story
   David R. Birdsall Biography 163

The Purloined Heart by Christopher G. Nuttall 165
   A Schooled in Magic Story
   Christopher G. Nuttall Biography 187

Apprentice in Trouble by Chad Boyer 189
   A Chronicles of the Dimensional Mage Story 189
   Chad Boyer Biography 211

SEALed With a Kiss by C.V. Walter 213
   C.V. Walter Biography 266

Romancing Some Rock by Edie Skye 267
   A Titan Mage Story
   Edie Skye Biography 308

Space Mage Secrets by Daniel M. Hoyt 309

Daniel M. Hoyt Biography 339

The Oaths That Bind by H.Y. Gregor and David Shadoin 341
   A Milesian Accords Story
   H.Y. Gregor Biography 383
   David Shadoin Biography 384

Valor's Wirth by Jon R. Osborne 385
   A Milesian Accords Story
   Jon R. Osborne Biography 417

Welcome to Detroit by Nathan Balyeat 419
   A Powers of the Night Story
   Nathan Balyeat Biography 450

Those Who Went Before by Glen Cook 451
   The Black Company on the Long Run
   Glen Cook Biography 476

The Muses Darling by Sarah A. Hoyt 477
   A Tale of The Muses Darling
   Sarah A. Hoyt Biography 506

End of Book 5 Libri Valoris 507

About the Editor 509

Excerpt from *A Reluctant Druid* 511
   Book One of The Milesian Accords

Excerpt from *The Chimera Coup* 517
   Book One of the Heirs of Cataclysm

* * * * *

Family Heirloom
by Howard Andrews Jones
A Chronicles of Hanuvar Story

When their walls were breached at last, the people of Volanus fought block by block, house by house, until most fell with sword in hand. Only a thousand or so survived to be led away in chains.

The city's treasuries were looted, its temples defiled, and then, to sate their emperor's thirst for vengeance, the mages of the Dervan Empire cursed Volanus and sowed its fields with salt. Their destruction was complete, apart from one detail: the greatest Volani general had escaped alive.

Against the might of a vast empire, Hanuvar has only an aging sword arm, a lifetime of wisdom, and the greatest military mind in the world, bent upon a single goal. No matter where his people have been taken, from the furthest outpost of the empire to its rotten heart, he will find them. Every last one of them. And he will set them free.

— *The Chronicles of Hanuvar*

* * *

Chapter I

Killian had come to hate being seen with the blade. It was a gladius, the short, stabbing sword worn by most in the legion, manufactured to a high standard by an old Birani smith. He'd purchased it from a retiring centurion when he himself had been appointed optio, and he'd treated it well from that day forward. Any smart soldier took good care of his weapons. That he'd wielded it to deliver Adruvar Cabera's death blow should have been happenstance, but his companions had made more of the weapon than they had his own prowess. So had his commander, Flaminian Marcius, who'd borrowed the sword and then "restored" it with fine new wraps and a gem-encrusted hilt, thinking to please Killian with the gift.

From then on, it had been too beautiful to wield, and Killian had to purchase an unadorned replacement, consigning Adruvar's death weapon, with its ridiculous jewelry, to his campaign chest until the end of his service. Then it had hung on pegs in his study near the books he'd never gotten around to reading.

He would rather have left it on the wall for the rest of his life. Now, though, the weapon swung on his belt, and owing to the damnably pleasant weather, there was no need for a cloak, which meant everyone spotted the gaudy hilt. If those who noticed hadn't happened to have heard what he'd done with the sword, his comrades obligingly told them.

They were fools, and he'd long since tired of them. All eight were legionaries, but four had never been deployed beyond Tyvol, and all had spent the bulk of their service posted in Derva itself until reassignment with him. The route to their destination required them to travel mostly through tiny farm villages, where they took meals from roadside taverns. Once the novelty wore off, the common fare and the dearth of female company left the men ill-tempered. They were too used to the capital's luxuries.

In addition to these complainers, the revenants had saddled him with a wizard, and a green one at that. Ilarius was a thin, young, scholarly sort, lacking the arrogance of his order, quiet unless someone made the mistake of asking him how his sorceries worked. Killian had committed that error only once, and been deluged with a wave of words that might as well have been a foreign language. He'd had to order the boy to shut up. The only thing Killian cared about the young man's magics was that they worked.

Thankfully, Ilarius mostly kept to himself, poring over scrolls in the evening, and even sometimes during their travel breaks. He'd claimed to be glad to be away from the revenants, and it might even be true, for he didn't speak to anyone about bloodlines or witches or the heresies of barbarians.

The revenant legate had the sense not to place the boy in charge of the expedition, even though the legate claimed it was the young wizard's powers that would get them to their goal. He'd selected Killian to lead, and had wanted to supply a guide as well, but Killian insisted on bringing his own, an unassuming fellow who'd once been a wine merchant and knew much of the Turian countryside. Though Killian didn't know him well, the man had a quiet competence that reassured him at least one aspect of this assignment would succeed—they'd get where they needed to go.

It had been a long, dull, irritating trip by horseback so far, but Killian forced them on. Life hadn't been easy after his army days.

He'd generally failed as a farmer, and even his generous pension had run through his fingers.

Still, this commission could set things right. Maybe he could finally hire an overseer to manage the slaves so he and his nephews could spend their time hunting in the woods instead of fighting the soil.

He thought about that future as he led the way across the countryside, consulting sometimes with the guide. A day out from Turian lands, they reached a sizable roadside inn, and Killian announced they'd stop for the day. This cheered the legionaries, who'd had to camp out the night before. They anticipated not just wine, but women, and traded boasts about their stamina with both in phrases ages old.

Ilarius seemed delighted for reasons of his own, and immediately requested he have his food served in a private chamber, so that he might study in peace.

Killian made the arrangements and passed over some coins to the innkeeper before settling into the common room in a corner far from the locals, some of whom bet on arm wrestling, and distant from his own boys, who thought themselves charming and amusing as they joked with the local harlots. He ate a decent meal and watched. Surely, the soldiers weren't so young they didn't know whores were predisposed to laugh at their jests, but then, they *were* idiots.

The guide disappeared somewhere. Killian didn't mind. He liked to be alone, which was why he wasn't especially happy when an old man in a worn, gray tunic came to his table and stood across from him.

Killian fixed him with a glare before returning to the mutton and lentil pottage. "Whatever you want, I'm not interested."

The old fellow placed his brown knapsack on the table, then rested his hand on it as he sat down at a bench on the other side of the battered wooden surface. The man's face was seamed with sun and dirt. The hair was shaggy. The nose was slightly hooked, the eyes a bluish gray. A scraggly beard hung down from his chin, but his face was otherwise clean-shaven.

"I've been waiting for you," the fellow said ominously. His voice was less weathered than his attire.

Killian's sigh was more a growl. "I'm really not in the mood."

"You're hunting Caberas, aren't you?" The old man leaned forward. "You're the man I foresaw. You bear the sword."

While Killian was processing that, the stranger whipped a dark brown object from his bag, displaying it with a flourish. Strange symbols, wandering lines, and a mystic Hadiran eye all drawn in black decorated the top. Killian didn't recognize the grisly thing for a skull until the old man turned its empty sockets to him and planted it on the table.

Killian pushed back, snarling. "I'm eating! Put that away!"

"Adruvar Cabera can't hurt you," the man said with a chuckle. "You already killed him." But he slipped the skull back into its bag.

"How do you know what I'm hunting?"

"I could tell you I've dreamed of it. I do have dreams, Centurion. But there's a simpler explanation. I have a relative high among the revenants, and word was passed along to me."

"And who are you?" Killian took a second look at the old man's stained tunic, coming to the belated realization he spoke with a priest of Luptar, lord of the dead. Between that and the skull, Killian felt his annoyance ebb before a sense of foreboding.

"I'm Brencis. And I, too, hunt Cabera. I'm told you have a tracker in your midst, but all I saw when you came in were these soldiers and the reedy one. Surely, *he's* not your tracker?"

"I don't see what business it is of yours."

"Those with you may be good soldiers, but it takes no skilled eye to see they're Dervan boys. Do any of you speak Turian?"

"Our guide has some," Killian admitted. "You don't look Turian."

"But I speak it well. And I can help you locate the Cabera."

The man's abrupt approach surprised him, but Killian had met clever conmen in his time. "I assume you want pay?"

"No."

"Attention, then."

"I want blood, Centurion. It's as simple as that. I've seen Narisia Cabera. I know what she looks like. Can any of your people say that?"

The old man spoke with such an air of conviction that Killian studied him anew. "You've dreamed of her?"

"Yes, but more than that, I've seen her with my own eyes. I was on the docks in Ostra where the Volani slaves were first delivered. I marked her well. You may say that her identity wasn't verified when she reached Tyvol, but she was pointed out to me."

Killian grunted at this news. On hearing it, he wondered why Legate Aquillius hadn't sent someone on this quest who'd recognize its main target. It seemed a foolish oversight.

"You might have started with that, instead of the hoary skull," Killian said. "What's the point of carrying it around?"

"The point of the skull is to bring me closer to anyone of their bloodline. This skull was bathed in that blood. It can help me find others who bear it, living or dead."

"My wizard says he can do something similar." Killian nodded his head toward the staircase up which Ilarius had retreated. "If you can find Hanuvar's daughter or any other Cabera with your skull, why haven't you?"

"I have limits. Bring me within a few miles of one of them, and I will feel them. Bring me within a few hundred paces, and I can practically smell them."

Over the course of their conversation, the man's words and quiet intensity had convinced Killian he was an unlikely charlatan. He put down his spoon. "You say you want blood. Why?"

"My brothers died in Hanuvar's wars." Brencis looked as though he might have said much more, but his mouth thinned, and he fell silent.

Killian had heard enough to take a risk. "I'm charged with helping the boy find Narisia, or Hanuvar Cabera himself. Or both. I'm told my tracker has the best chance the revenants can muster, but I'm always willing to improve my odds."

"Do you want them alive or dead?"

Killian concluded the eager old man would prefer the latter. "I get paid more if alive, but I'm sure they won't be that way long, no matter what condition we bring them in."

Brencis' mouth thinned disapprovingly, but he acquiesced. "Fine."

"We travel light, and we travel fast. Have you a horse? Travel gear?"

"I do."

"We leave at dawn on the morrow. Ride with us if you will. If you trouble me, I'll dismiss you. If I find you're a spy, I'll cut you down."

"I'll be there." The old man bowed his head to him and slipped away. Killian watched him go, wondering why there was something familiar about him. He then realized the intensity in his eyes was reminiscent of the kind of hunger for vengeance he'd seen in some old veterans.

At the least, it would help to have someone else along who knew how to talk with the Turians. And if the priest should prove untrustworthy... well, Killian was no stranger to eliminating problems.

* * *

Chapter II

Last winter, Hanuvar had observed the revenant mage from a rooftop while the young man labored over a kind of portable wooden platform holding spell ingredients, carried through the streets of Derva by a pair of assistants. Unlike the vast number of those claiming magical provenance, Ilarius' powers actually worked, and he'd doggedly pursued two men Hanuvar had freed from captivity, up until Hanuvar's snowball had disrupted the mage's tracking spell.

How Ilarius planned to locate Narisia, Hanuvar hadn't yet learned, but he wished to be on hand when the mage threw his spells. Apparently, the sword that had dealt Adruvar's death blow was to be somehow instrumental in the spellcasting, though Carthalo hadn't yet learned the details.

In his identity as a guide, Hanuvar's chief intelligence agent had worked partly into Killian's trust, and was consulting with him that morning in the pre-dawn glow while each held the reins of their mounts. Carthalo pointed south along the road, his finger moving as though delineating points ahead.

The rest of the men stretched and complained and tightened saddle girths while their horses snorted. No official introduction was passed along about Hanuvar's position in their party, but word had been disseminated, for the soldiers took him in. Hanuvar noted the surreptitious inspection the skinny young mage gave him.

Killian led the way, with Carthalo riding alongside. After him came the scholar, and then, in four pairs, the legionaries, though they'd dispensed with leg greaves and heavy armor. Hanuvar brought up the rear, eating their dust.

Riding to the rear was a necessary evil. Hanuvar wished neither to be examined closely nor to appear particularly clean. The dirt would continue to disguise both his appearance and his age, for it emphasized his creases.

On they rode through the green lands south of Derva. Little of the Tyvolian countryside was flat, but this rolling farmland was more level than usual, and tenant farmers and slaves worked the fields for rich families ensconced in country villas beyond the road, or absent entirely. The green bulk of the worn down Acanthes rose to the west, usually blocking sight of the more rugged and distant Vertigines. The sun was warm against his neck and shoulders, and he smelled of his own sweat and that of his mount.

The road they traveled had been old when Derva was just a little hill village and Turia waxed mighty from the coast to the rugged western highlands. Later generations had bricked the road with great care, but the route was unchanged.

Hanuvar himself had traveled it more than once, long years before. Had he been inclined to do so, he might have maundered on about the changed circumstances of his life, or the irony that he should be traveling in the company of Dervans to hunt for his own blood.

Instead, he was watchful. From time to time, one of the soldiers would glance back, and he hoped all they'd ever see was a strange old priest of Luptar. He dreaded them growing more inquisitive and dropping back to ask suspicious questions of him.

It wasn't the soldiers who eventually fell out of formation to join him, but Carthalo. The spy would never deliberately draw a connection between them, so Hanuvar knew there'd be a reasonable explanation.

Carthalo coughed a little and waved his hand in front of his face. "You seem to have found all the road dust, old man," he said.

The spy had an astonishing ability to blend into his environment. He was sturdily built and ordinary, and his appearance could be affable and unassuming, or stern and certain. Under the identity of a guide, he looked more the latter, a seasoned man of middle years. He'd chosen a tunic that emphasized his powerful arm muscles and chest, the better to suggest fitness for work, then topped off his dark head with a straw hat, worn and stained from much use.

"Brencis, is it?" Carthalo asked.

Probably the others couldn't hear, owing to the *clop* of the hooves and the low mutter of conversation from some of the soldiers, but Carthalo liked leaving nothing to chance.

"That's my name," Hanuvar answered coolly.

"I'm your guide, Silvio. I'm told you speak Turian." Carthalo then switched to that language.

Hanuvar had a good grasp of it, having spent years in the lands south of Derva, though it was haunted by an accent that wavered toward Dervan. Someone truly astute might have been able to detect the ring of Volani among certain words, but recognizing one accent in the speaking of a foreign language was likely beyond their companions.

"Killian sent me to speak to you in Turian and gauge how much of a liar you are."

"I'm a grand liar, as you well know," Hanuvar answered quietly.

Carthalo smiled tightly.

"What would you report?" Hanuvar asked.

"Two of our soldiers have served on the Irimacian border. They've been in a few skirmishes, but aren't what you'd call truly seasoned, although they like to pretend it. The others are more recent hires, who've won various awards for horsemanship and target spearing, but have never seen combat. I think the esteemed legate evaluates the worth of these men by how much they brag."

Hanuvar had encountered other commanders like that—usually men without much experience on the front line themselves. "There's a kind of soldier that usually travels in threes." Like Carthalo, Hanuvar didn't use certain names or titles, the better to disguise their topics of conversation.

"I've been watching for that. None show the mage particular deference, and all of them are a little arrogant. But I've got my eye on one who's more outspoken. He's younger, and his self-assurance could just stem from his upbringing."

"But it might be from the order, and the company he keeps."

"Yes."

"What have you seen of the wizard?"

"He's studious and dedicated. Ask him about his craft, and he'll spout a bunch of esoteric things he seems to believe."

"Trying to impress?"

"A little, but he's mostly a lonely enthusiast eager to talk shop."

"And what of our leader?"

"I don't think he wants to be here. I don't think he likes the job, but he's determined to see it done. He's a professional."

"What are they using to track the daughter of the dread general?"

Carthalo shot him a wary look. "We're not supposed to know that, but the mage talked a little in my earshot."

"And I'm not going to like it," Hanuvar guessed.

"I don't like it either. Part of the scalp of the general's father."

"The general," meaning him. Hanuvar stared into the distance, trying to keep the terrible detail remote from him, and not quite managing it. He remembered his brother Melgar saying in his later years the Cabera family line had only bad fortune, starting with their mother's death, then their sister's, but that their father had been the unluckiest of them all, dying with so many plans unfulfilled, most of his children half grown, and then being buried with part of his body missing.

"I haven't seen it," Carthalo added. "Is that even possible?"

"Yes. Yes, it is." Himli Cabera's body had been so badly treated by his murderers, there'd been almost nothing left to recover. Part of his scalp could well have been shorn free as a grisly memento and passed on to Dervan hands.

"What do you want to do about all this?" Carthalo asked.

"I've seen this mage at work. He actually can track people. He might well direct us to my daughter at last, and then we'll improvise. If not, we'll simply have spent some time in the Turian countryside."

"A relaxing vacation amongst the men who hunt for your blood," Carthalo said darkly.

He'd confessed that, when his agents had gotten wind of the revenant search, he'd hesitated to present Hanuvar with the information, fearing what he might do. In the end, Carthalo had agreed this might be their best chance for finding Narisia, risky as it was, and in any case, they had to disrupt the mission. He hadn't liked the idea of Hanuvar being personally involved from the very start, and his warning look now was a reminder of it.

Hanuvar understood his worries, but he'd made his choice. "Now we should briefly cover what you'll tell our leader we spoke about, so our tales agree."

"Of course."

That they did, and then Carthalo bade him farewell, cantered up past the string of soldiers, and fell in beside Killian.

Hanuvar was left alone to contemplate the existence of a final, physical remnant of his father, dried and held like a prize by a Dervan sorcerer for the purposes of hunting Himli's son and granddaughter and bringing them to their enemies for exhibition and execution. His hands tightened on the reins even as his father's words echoed in his ears. *Master your emotions, lest your foes use them against you.* From an early age, Hanuvar had been taught that those who let themselves be ruled by their reactions might as well turn control of their life's path to a wild horse.

He'd thought his father an old man, and it was strange to think Himli had been younger than Hanuvar was now on the night of his betrayal. He wondered how old he himself would be before his father no longer seemed more seasoned and wiser.

Never, he thought.

At midday, they halted in the shade of some oaks. To judge by ashes and blackened ground, and stones gathered about makeshift firepits, the stopover was put to frequent use, and sometimes doubled as an overnight camping spot. It even came with a designated waste area about thirty paces beyond the oaks themselves, where flies and stink were thick.

Hanuvar sat apart from the others on a weathered log. He was halfway through his hard roll and dried meat when Ilarius sidled over.

Up close, the mage's thin face was dotted with freckles. His eyes were dark and strangely hopeful. "I'm Ilarius. Do you mind if I join you?" His voice was mild and betrayed the same wary eagerness visible in his gaze.

"As you like," Hanuvar said coolly. He drank from his wineskin, and the young man sat down, studying him.

"It's Brencis, right?" He didn't wait for an answer. "A priest of Luptar."

"Yes."

"Killian says you're a magical tracker yourself. Are you an astronomer? Or are you a sympathetic magic user? Or a talismantic one?"

"I have some knowledge of many different schools," Hanuvar answered mildly. "I understand you're a talismantic practitioner."

"Yes. Killian said you have a talisman yourself, and that there are symbols upon it."

"That's true."

"I wondered if I might—"

"No."

Ilarius' expression fell, like a puppy denied a treat. And like a pup, he swiftly resumed his begging after a brief delay. "You mustn't think I'm after your secrets. I wish to share—"

"You'd be wise to share nothing," Hanuvar said. "You may understand that when you're older."

"I'm more skilled than you think," the young man said. His cheeks were flushed. "What symbol system do you use to draw your power?"

"I use a blend of them, but mostly I focus through my connection with blessed Luptar and the moon and stars."

"Not the planets?"

"Only as they're conduits for the power of Luptar himself."

"We should be allies."

"I should trust revenants?" Hanuvar asked. "Who lure sorcerers in for advice, then try them for crimes once they steal their secrets?"

"I'm not like that."

"I don't intend to chance it. I know too well what the other side is like. You think I want to risk my death to give you a little glimpse at my life's work? Begone."

The boy opened his mouth to say more. He pushed angrily to his feet, hesitated as if debating saying something more, then stormed away.

Hanuvar understood he hadn't made a friend, but he knew his façade would almost surely crack if Ilarius were permitted to examine the alleged skull of Adruvar and its particular symbols. The browned bone was a tool for a single purpose, and its time had not yet come.

* * *

Chapter III

When the sentry came to wake him at the start of second watch, Killian was already upright and putting on his boots. Mazentius, the youngest and burliest of the soldiers, tried to make a joke of Killian's readiness. "You have a date, sir?"

Killian grunted. "I'm going to check the perimeter. Keep an eye on things while I'm gone."

The younger man didn't know what to make of that, and retreated to the fire, moving a little stiffly, as if irritated Killian hadn't smiled at his jest.

Killian stood, shifting shoulders and neck. He buckled on the sword belt, listening to the *chirrup* of crickets in the cool night air and the snuffle of one of the horses, hobbled in a dark group.

The rest of his men lay twisted over their blankets about the fireside. Some were bundled against the night like children, and others slept without covers, pillowed on their rolled cloaks. He wished some men from his own unit were with him. If this lot had to rouse in the middle of the night to fight, could they even find their swords?

He shook his head in disgust. His eyes strayed over to where Brencis lay, curled far to one side of the camp, then he looked up to where the stars shone brilliantly through the clear heavens, including the great, shining bridge of them in a band above the moon, halfway to full.

There was no sign of the guide, but that didn't surprise him.

Mazentius frowned at Killian as he headed out. He probably wondered who'd bother walking the perimeter in peacetime, in friendly territory, when they had an armed and good-sized party. Killian didn't care enough about the man's good will to explain.

He strode away from the hill and into the rolling fields and brush surrounding them. After a quarter mile, a figure slid out of a copse and lifted a hand. Killian grasped his sword hilt until he was certain it was Silvio.

"Anything?"

"Not so far. Did you expect anyone in particular?"

"No."

The guide had claimed to have scouted for the legions in Herrenia, and watching him at work as they explored the surroundings reassured Killian that he'd spoken the truth. The man knew how to move, what to be alert for, and how to approach hill tops.

After a half hour circling, Killian stopped the guide by the little stand of trees where they'd rendezvoused. "You talked with the priest for a while. What was your take on him?"

"He knows Turian fairly well, though he speaks it with an accent. Like me," Silvio added. "What to make of him… well, he's a priest who doesn't like to talk much about magics. He's protective of what he knows. He doesn't want to share it."

"Did he say where he got the skull?" The head of Adruvar Cabera had been tossed into Hanuvar's camp, and then his body was recovered by another of the Cabera brothers. Killian had assumed the family would've interred the body parts in the Cabera family crypt or buried them in the lands they were occupying in Tyvol at the time.

"It didn't come up. I can ask him directly if you want."

"I may." It didn't really matter. "If he didn't talk about the skull, his magics, or his past, what did he talk about?"

"Phases of the moon and signs from Luptar. I don't pay much attention to that kind of thing. I'd rather not know about the lands beyond death. He also talked about his brothers, and how they'd been killed by the Volani. I've never heard a priest so obsessed with vengeance before. Is that common?"

"They're as human as the rest of us, I guess," Killian said. "To me, they always seemed most interested in the quality of the meat they can get off the sacrifices."

"Or arguing among themselves about signs and scriptures," Silvio agreed.

"Exactly. But priests of Luptar tend to be kind of loners anyway. Especially country ones."

"Loners are good at nursing grievances."

He had a good point, but Killian wasn't worried about it. "So you think he can do what he says?"

Silvio fell silent.

"What, you don't want to say?"

"I'm just trying to decide if you want a real answer, or if you've already decided, and you're testing me."

Killian frowned at that.

Silvio looked sidelong at him. "I think he's a lot more interested in finding Caberas than your mage."

"You doubt the mage? The revenant legate himself sent him. We're lucky the boy's not in charge."

"I just think that one's like a young tribune in love with his own armor. Ilarius doesn't give a damn about the battle, he just wants to look good doing it."

Killian nodded to himself. He knew the type.

Silvio asked a question of his own. "Do you really think this magical stuff is going to turn up Hanuvar or his daughter?"

"You were in the legion," Killian answered, saying nothing more.

"I've spent most of my life not getting paid to think," Silvio said. "I guess I can do it a little longer."

"Oh, I want you to think. I count on it. But that part's above our pay grade. If the magic works and hunts us up some fugitives, we get covered in glory." He felt his mouth twist. "It's overrated."

"So you're just here for the coins, but you want to see the job done right."

"Habit. Come on, I've seen enough. Let's get some sleep."

Silvio nodded, and they headed in together. Killian fell silent, thinking about his little troop. He didn't like them very much, but if they found a Cabera, he'd have to count on them to watch his flanks. He could probably stand to work harder to win them over.

At least he knew he could count on Silvio.

* * *

Chapter IV

Hanuvar woke before the dawn, though he didn't rise until the camp stirred. By this, the third morning of travel with Killian in command, he was used to the man's routines, so he was surprised when the taciturn leader stood before his team at breakfast.

"We'll reach Turian lands before midday, and not long after that, we'll close on the last reported point anyone saw Narisia Cabera. That's when our mage is going to throw his spell. If we find a living Cabera, do you realize how famous you're going to be? No door will be closed to you. You'll be getting free drinks in taverns for the rest of your lives."

The soldiers had been talking about varied permutations on an idyllic future where they were showered with money and affection, and their eyes shone to hear an aspect of it specified by their leader. His discussion of their potential prestige seemed to have made it more real for them.

Killian thumped his chest. "I know you all long for the kind of glory I've had in my career. Well, you lot are lucky. Most people don't get a chance at the kind of prize we're after."

One of the soldiers muttered a fervent, "Yes," and the others nodded vigorously.

"I don't know what we're going to find, but if there really are Caberas out here, it's not going to be simple. They'll have had months to prepare. You can't count the men who thought they were better than Hanuvar. They overflow the graveyards. And he may be old, but you ought to know there're some centurions old as him still in service, and they're hard as nails. You can bet he'll be just like them."

"Hanuvar's really alive?" One of the legionaries' voices came close to trembling. "I thought we were just after his daughter."

"The revenant legate says he is. And even if he isn't, the daughter's probably no pushover. She was an Eltyr. They're fast and deadly, and they go down hard. Some of the worst fighting of the war was at the Volani River Gate. The water foamed red with the blood of our men." Killian surveyed them. "You scared yet?"

"No, sir," Mazentius said.

"I can't hear you!" Killian growled.

The men got it then, and answered as one, a crisp shout. "No, sir!"

"That's better. You're Dervans. You're tough, and you're trained, and you've got me. But take off your dresses, boys, and get your eyes and your swords sharp. Vacation time's over. If we're going to stay alive, we need to stay alert." He sucked in a breath and gave them a final onceover. "All right. That's all I've got. Let's get packed and get hunting."

After their leader's speech, the men's spirits were high, and they were eager to be on. The horses sensed the excitement, and even they moved with more energy.

Shortly before midday, they reached the little river Elathri and crossed a worn stone bridge over the ancient border into Turian lands. Roadside villages here looked little different from those to the north, save that occasionally ancient walls were incorporated into buildings, and the tired old hills that rose beyond the towns were studded with old white stone mausoleums and cliffside tomb doors.

Long centuries had passed since the Turians had been the dominant culture of the region. Many nationalities walked their lands now. Despite the introduction of people from across the peninsula and beyond, many of the travelers still possessed the distinctive black eyes, wavy dark hair, and clear, pale olive skin so often seen in ancient Turian mosaics. The people looked out from their shops or up from their plows, observing Killian's expedition with little warmth, as though the Dervans were interlopers, even after all this time.

Despite their antipathy for the Dervans, Turian support for Hanuvar's invasion had never been as overt as those from southernmost Tyvol, though many Turians had joined his ranks as informers and scouts, and even infantrymen. Some walled towns had opened their gates to his forces. Hanuvar doubted any of his former allies would have survived a Dervan purge, but he kept his head bowed as if in weariness whenever passing through settlements here, hoping no one would look close at a dirty old priest.

Two hours after midday, they arrived at faded green hills scattered with abandoned walls built from the gray volcanic stones common to this area. Decrepit archways that must once have led to garden paths or mansions now fronted only dark forests. The wind was light, but often thick with the scents of lavender and rosemary.

The road wound in and out of ruins for another hour until Killian led them to a hilltop overlooking a valley. Here, he said, a patrol had followed Narisia Cabera and her two companions before the three disappeared into morning fog more than a year ago. A rainstorm had swept up and obscured their tracks, and no Dervans had seen the women since. Nor, so far as Hanuvar had learned, had anyone else.

With some eagerness, Ilarius went to the goods secured on one of the pack horses, carefully unwrapped the contents, and began to assemble them. Hanuvar pretended to perform his own spell preparations, and drew a circle of charcoal that he filled with moon phases and images of eyes and open hands. He then lit a nub of a candle and placed it within the brown skull, festooned with images the more artistically gifted Izivar had drawn upon it. Carthalo had recovered it from a big revenant they'd had to make disappear.

Hanuvar sat down within his circle, put his hand upon the skull, and began to mutter, his gaze mimicking inward absorption. In truth, he carefully watched Ilarius. Carthalo lingered near the mage, as if curious, though he was ready to strike. If Hanuvar's preparations failed, enemies would outnumber them very quickly.

Nearby, Ilarius finished assembling a small portable table—an improved design over the last one Hanuvar had seen him with. It had been crafted not only with high, ridged sides, but walled compartments for a variety of dark powders that Ilarius arranged before carefully covering them with squares of finely cut glass he removed from leather holders. Some symbols he drew upon the wood in dark charcoal; others had been burned into the platform's surface.

Even with some of the work prepared beforehand, it took the scholar almost half an hour to arrange all of it to his liking. When he was finished at last, he mumbled over Killian's sword for a time, then opened another leather container and reverently removed what looked like a small, dark brown wig.

Hanuvar's chest tightened at sight of his father's hair, and he continued to observe through slitted eyes.

Ilarius placed the scalp in the center of his legless table, sprinkling it with red powders and dried green herbs he had to lift one of his glass panes to procure.

Finally, he slid the table about on the ground with great care, eyeing the angle of the sun, reached within a pocket of his robe that lay just over his heart, and produced what Hanuvar first took to be a blackened, gnarled stick suspended by a black thread.

Most of the soldiers were watching, though they were supposed to be standing guard, and three of them gasped. Their proximity enabled them to understand more swiftly than Hanuvar that Ilarius had produced a mummified human finger. Once, twice, three times Ilarius dipped it against the scrap of Himli Cabera's scalp, then he whispered to it, sprinkled it with blue powder, and held it just above the table's middle.

Hanuvar rose to a kneeling position, the skull facing him in his left hand, as though he were engaged with it in silent dialogue. If he had to move fast, he could spring and strike in a single blow.

For a long moment, the finger was still. It swung a little to the left, though Ilarius seemed not to have touched it at all. And then, of its own volition, it turned half its circumference and pointed unwaveringly at Hanuvar.

"It works!" Killian cried.

"I shall have to adjust the spell to ignore the nearest Cabera," Ilarius said, his smile revealing that he wasn't irritated, but pleased. Hanuvar then understood the mage himself had doubted whether the spell would work. Possibly, he'd been hoping that he'd detect the nearby skull purported to be Adruvar's.

And then Ilarius said something that caused Hanuvar to tense once more. "There's a pull beyond the close one. A Cabera is somewhere along the road, beyond Adruvar's skull."

Hanuvar's own pulse leapt at this news, though he betrayed no outward sign of his excitement. He lifted the skull to his ear and narrowed his eyes in concentration.

Killian grinned. "Then get your finger more certain, mage. What does your skull tell you, Brencis?"

"He whispers that it's not Hanuvar who lies ahead."

"No?" Killian's hard eyes were alight with interest. "Does he say who's up there?"

"He taunts me," Hanuvar said. "He doesn't want to aid me."

Carthalo still waited near the mage, hand on sword hilt.

But Ilarius either couldn't perceive their trickery or wasn't suspicious enough of him to probe more closely. He bent and whispered to the finger. Once more, it swung and pointed left, down the road.

"So a Cabera is here? A living one?" Killian prompted. He sounded excited in spite of himself.

"I can't tell if she's living or dead," the boy admitted, "but I can tell she's within an hour or two of us."

Killian frowned and turned to Hanuvar. "What about you, priest?"

Hanuvar set aside worries for his daughter and freely improvised. "Adruvar worries, though it's the sleepy, wormy worry of someone who thought themselves beyond cares. And I think then that a Cabera must live."

"All right then. You two—help Ilarius get that conjuring table up on his saddle like we talked about. Stop staring, boys! Glory's coming your way!"

Hanuvar rose and wiped away his circle before the mage could pay its pictures any mind. He then put the candle flame out with his fingers, and pressed the smoking wax to his head and his heart. All the while, he forced himself to concentrate on the task at hand rather than the powerful emotions roiling within. Could his daughter truly be so close?

The soldiers proved so cautious with the table that Carthalo stepped forward to assist, helping Ilarius bear the thing with the tender care employed by a wounded nobleman's servants. As was his inclination, Ilarius overexplained the steps, and how the straps had to attach to the specially constructed saddle in just this way to keep it steady.

One of the older soldiers, Nelius, spoke to Hanuvar as he placed the skull in his pouch. His voice bore a hint of awe. "That's really the skull of Adruvar Cabera?"

"It is."

"Where did you get it?"

"I bought it from a Herrene, who said he had it from a tomb robber. It didn't take long for me to confirm it was genuine."

The platform holding Ilarius' sorcery was firmly affixed to the mage's saddle, between the horn and the horse's neck, but even so, the mage couldn't ride at any great speed for fear of disrupting the spell, and Killian chafed at the plodding progress. As the afternoon wore on, he rode up and down the line, twice demanding from Ilarius and Hanuvar if they had more to say. Hanuvar told him Adruvar was silent but brooding, and Ilarius simply said south, along the road, but that he thought the Cabera was close.

And so they traveled, on and on. So slow was their progress, they were passed by a wagon convoy bearing horse fodder and a whole pack of farmers and farm boys, as well as two buxom young women in old-fashioned Turian farm dresses. They raised their heads and coolly ignored the whistles and invitations, as remote and removed from the soldiers as the stone doors built into the distant cliffs.

Just before evening, they passed another low line of hills and looked down on a little town.

Ilarius straightened in his high-backed saddle. "Here! The Cabera is up ahead. Very close! Probably in the village!"

"Keep your voice down." Killian rode closer. "What do you need to do to find her?"

"I just need to hold steady for a moment. I'll adjust the spell a bit."

Killian was visibly irritated, then nodded tightly and pointed off the road. "All right. Let's move over there. How long will this take?"

"Less than a quarter hour."

Killian waved everyone to a little clear spot. A brook ran along the road, and the men dismounted and led their horses to drink, while Ilarius hunched over his table and shifted powders around.

Hanuvar dismounted with the soldiers. He tucked the skull back into his satchel and let his own animal drink.

Killian frowned at him. "Adruvar's not saying anything?"

"I'll have to pray again. And I won't waste my own spells until we're closer."

Mazentius lowered his waterskin. "Centurion, what was it like? To kill Adruvar Cabera?"

Clearly, all the soldiers had been wondering that, because all eight fell silent, listening keenly.

Killian's frown deepened, and Hanuvar felt certain he'd tell them to mind their own business. But he held to the friendlier demeanor he'd settled on this morning.

"He knew he was going to die," the centurion said finally. "We'd hit both flanks, and the center had crumbled, so it was only a matter of time."

So far, this perfectly matched what Hanuvar had been told of the battle. Flaminian Marcius' scouts had intercepted a letter from Adruvar, and he'd marched his legion double-time through the night to link up with the legion that had been following Adruvar's army. When Adruvar woke, he faced a force twice as large as the one he'd prepared to fight.

"Adruvar didn't want to be captured alive—or maybe he just wanted to take as many legionaries as he could with him when he went down—so he charged into a line of us. We cut his horse out from under him, but when he hit the ground, he just kept coming." Killian mimed rolling his shoulders and standing upright.

The men listened, spellbound, and Hanuvar realized he was doing the same. He wondered if the priest he pretended to be would look as fascinated, and he supposed he would.

"He was already bleeding, and his helm was off, and in we came." Killian swung an imaginary sword. "Zip, zip. He cut them down. He was a big man, and he had one of those curved Volani swords, heavy on the business end—falcatas, they call them. They can take a man's head off in a single blow if you've any strength. And Adruvar Cabera was strong. Seven men he brought down, and a couple of others he crippled. And then I was up in front of him. He'd just lopped off my optio's arm, and it was up to me."

Hanuvar couldn't have turned away now had he been told his daughter waited just behind him.

"Adruvar's left arm was hanging useless, and his armor was rent, and he bled from a dozen places. Those wounds would probably have finished him pretty soon anyway, but he was still up and killing, and I had to stop him. So I did."

"How?" Mazentius asked, guileless and enraptured as a boy listening to a bedtime fable.

Killian shrugged, seeming embarrassed to add details. "I ducked his swing. It took off my crest and pushed the helmet up so the strap was over my chin. But you know what it's like in the middle of a battle. I didn't even feel that it'd gouged my forehead."

Probably most of his listeners likely *didn't* know what it was like in the middle of a battle, but they listened silently.

"I drove the sword up through a big tear in his armor and found his heart. I heard the breath leave him, and he sagged. I kept hold of my sword, so when he dropped, I fell with him, trying not to land on his blade or a sharp gash in his armor." He looked at his audience as if measuring them. "You ever kill a man?"

None of them wanted to say they hadn't, and Killian had the grace not to wait too long for them to admit it. "It's true, what they say about how a man's eyes glaze when they die. But first, you see the strength of their life in their gaze. How much they want to hold onto it." Killian's jaw firmed.

Hanuvar imagined the scene then, the centurion on the ground, suspended on one hand over Adruvar, eyes locked, close as lovers. Such a moment was always disturbingly intimate. If you stared too long, you saw too much.

"Their fear, you mean?" Mazentius asked. "Was he afraid of dying?"

Killian shook his head, his disappointment in the question manifest. "It wasn't like that." This man had met Adruvar's gaze in his final moments and experienced the death lock prior to that glazed loss of focus. Some men reveled in it, or claimed they did. Killian, though, had clearly been affected by it. And it came to Hanuvar that his brother had fully planned to die, and that in a strange way, his death by this centurion had been a mercy. Adruvar had fallen to a man who'd respected him.

Ilarius called from where he sat hunched in his saddle over the table. "I've got her! She's really close. I think I can find the way!"

With that news, Killian ordered them back into the saddle, riding at the mage's side as they headed down the brick road and into the little farm town.

Hanuvar knew the place; Melgar had fought a skirmish here against a Dervan scouting party, and Hanuvar had looked down on it from the south while listening to his brother's report.[1] Once, he'd stood on that very ridge two miles beyond the other side of the town, standing not just with Melgar, but with their brother Harnil and the commander of cavalry, Maharval.

That friend and all three of his brothers were dead, but the town still lived. It appeared much the same, with its wide fields spreading out across the hills to east and west, and the tidy square houses with

---

[1] Antires doesn't name the town, but from this description, it must be Mertosa, close by where both the first and second battles of the same name were fought.
— Silenus

their green tile roofs standing along winding streets, built to follow the roll of the land.

More than ever, it came to him that this was a mission of the dead. Why would Narisia shelter here, so close to where she'd last been seen? It made no sense, not if she lived. Perhaps she'd been wounded during her escape, and her friends had tried to nurse her to health in these hills.

Might it be that she'd succumbed and had long since been buried along some lonely ridge? That would certainly explain why no one had been able to find her.

There was a fine line between anticipating outcomes and worry. Hanuvar had schooled himself toward the former, so that he might be ready for the vicissitudes of fortune. He knew that a man who'd considered outcomes and determined reactions slept more soundly than a man who worried over them. He wondered how well a man would sleep once he'd stood before his daughter's grave.

* * *

Chapter V

Only the central street ran relatively straight through the village, and those who worked or purchased at the shops and tavern counters turned to stare at Killian and his troop as they passed through. They were keenly aware of Ilarius and the narrow wooden platform stretching from his saddlehorn to his horse's mane. They pointed at the dried finger he dangled on its string and whispered among themselves.

Killian didn't care. For the first time since they'd begun this journey, that old, keen sense of excitement burned in his blood. He was on a hunt, and his hounds had scented quarry.

The men had felt it, too, and paid no mind to taverns or women they passed. Even the priest seemed keyed up, though his mien remained grim.

They passed into the village's outskirts, where wider spans of ground separated tidy old villas set down shady lanes lined with ancient Turian stone pines. Ilarius seemed untroubled by their course, and focused ever more hungrily upon the terrible finger he held over his board with his right hand while his left held the reins stretched beneath the platform. "The villa ahead, on the right. We're very close!"

A trio of children roamed the villa's grounds. The youngest, a little girl in a long, blue double tunic, jogged along the road at the side of a large metal hoop, which she rolled with a stick. Another girl of ten or twelve brushed the mane of a bored gray pony, while a teenaged boy bent low to cinch its saddle.

Once it was clear that the troop of soldiers was riding down their road, the boy called to the smallest, shouting her name, Drusilla, twice, before she ran to him. He pointed her to the house, handed the pony's reins to the elder girl, and pointed her on as well, then stepped into the road.

Peeping constantly over their shoulders in curiosity, the girls walked toward the white, two-story villa four hundred feet further back, the pony clopping after.

Killian rode at the mage's side and didn't miss the anticipation manifest on his face. The mummified finger continued to point straight ahead.

"We're very close now," Ilarius said tensely. "Practically on top of her."

The boy waited in an ordinary tunic and sandals, but he carried himself like someone who expected obedience. Tall and slender, his arms and legs were gently muscled. He had a Turian's dark, wavy hair, and a narrow, pleasant face with a slightly hooked nose. His eyes were dark and alight with intelligence.

Killian drew to a stop before him. The boy's brow furrowed when he noticed the strange contraption affixed to the front of Ilarius' saddle, but he addressed Killian.

"Greetings. You're on the land of Senator Clemens Horatius Marcellus. Do you seek him?"

Marcellus was more than a senator. He'd been a general in the Second Volani War, and one of the few to survive successive engagements against Hanuvar himself. Killian knew he'd been forced from active service after taking a wound that should have killed him. Instead, it had left Marcellus in recuperation for more than a year. By reputation, he was a soldier's soldier. He held senatorial rank, but was almost never to be found in Derva itself.

Killian eyed the boy, debating how exactly he should answer.

"It's him," Ilarius said in a low voice. Perhaps he thought it wouldn't be heard by the boy, whose brow wrinkled further.

"What are you talking about?" Killian asked.

Ilarius had lowered the finger so it wasn't visible over the rim of the platform. He raised it now and it could be seen pointing directly at the youth.

"It's him!"

The boy proved to be remarkably well possessed. "Gentlemen?" His voice was firm, but polite. "What brings you here?"

Killian bowed his head. "I'm Killian Pullio Vicentius. We're on an errand for the state. Are you... the son of Marcellus?"

The youth answered without hesitation. "I am. Tiberius Paulus Marcellus, sir."

Far behind him, the front door of the villa opened, and a white-haired patrician emerged, closely followed by a sturdy retainer. Both strode in haste. Drusilla had vanished, but the older girl looked anxiously back from beside the door, the pony at her side.

"How old are you?" Ilarius asked.

The boy's gaze drifted to the mage, and a flicker of disgust briefly touched his features. He'd noticed the mummified finger. "I 'm fifteen."

This wasn't going at all as Killian had expected. He searched for the priest, but didn't spot Brencis at first. The older man had dismounted to lead his horse up one side of the lane. He stared at the boy's face with such intensity, Tiberius sensed it and returned the scrutiny.

Marcellus shouted as he drew closer. He would arrive in only a few moments.

Killian motioned Ilarius to move the finger, but the mage only stared blankly. "Break your charms," he snapped, then turned to the priest. "Well? Does your… advisor say anything? Is this boy one of them?"

"Adruvar does not know him," Brencis answered.

Killian cursed under his breath, reflecting then that the priest had earlier said only that the person they traced was not Hanuvar. It was Ilarius who'd promised Narisia.

Marcellus halted before them, a dour, broad-shouldered manservant at his side. The senator was a hawk-nosed older man, vigorous, though his face was florid from his swift-paced walk, and he carried a layer of fat.

"Senator Marcellus," Killian said, then introduced himself. "You must pardon us. I was… hoping we might have the chance for… a conversation."

He was stumbling badly, but he wasn't entirely sure what he should say or do. He needed time to consider the best course of action. "Your son is a fine young man. Is he… yours by blood?"

The senator's brows had ticked up at mention of Killian' name, though he didn't acknowledge recognizing it further, and his reply was coolly formal. "I adopted him when he was an infant upon marrying his mother."

"Ah." Killian didn't follow politics; he had little to no interest in the lives of the famous, and was aware of Marcellus only because he'd met soldiers who'd spoken well of him. "Who's your wife?"

This was clearly the wrong question to ask, for Marcellus' heavy brows drew closer. His retainer stiffened.

"What's this really about?" the old soldier practically growled. "Who sent you?"

Killian cleared his throat. "Perhaps... perhaps this might all be cleared away if we could speak privately."

"I'm in the midst of other duties at this time." The old man's voice was steely.

"Your pardon. This evening, then?"

"If that's your wish." Marcellus' glance passed darkly over the rest of them. "Leave your entourage behind."

"Of course." Killian bowed his head.

The senator motioned his son to follow, then about-faced. Tiberius glanced back at them dubiously and followed. The retainer stared warning for a moment, then fell in after.

Killian spoke quietly to Ilarius. "So it was him. Definitely him, the youth?"

"I'm certain of it."

Mazentius spoke to him from behind. "You saw Adruvar's face. Does this kid look like him? Maybe it's his son."

The soldier didn't have the years right. Killian shook his head. "He's too young. Adruvar's been dead eighteen years. And this doesn't help us at all, anyway. The boy's too young to have been at war against Derva, and he's been raised by a Dervan senator."

He licked his lips and spoke to the priest. "What of you? Anything to report?"

Brencis' eyes were a peculiar gray as they caught the light, and the sad, determined expression was so similar to that upon Adruvar's face as he died, it was momentarily startling.

Killian's impression of the priest's power had increased, but only now did he understand how truly magical the man must be. "Could the boy be Hanuvar's son?"

"He's no child of Hanuvar's," the priest answered, "but for answers, I must speak with the spirits and coax more from them."

"Is there another possible Cabera around here?" Killian demanded.

"Only the skull and the boy," Ilarius said, looking as though he expected a dressing down.

Killian turned their column, moving through the others to lead them back into the village. He supposed they'd have to find room at one of the inns. What could he even say to Senator Marcellus? Was there any point left in talking with him?

* * *

Chapter VI

There was no mistaking the young man for anyone other than a child of Harnil Cabera. It wasn't just the shape of his face, it was the way he tilted his head to one side while questioning, and the burning intellect in his gaze, not to mention the incredible self-possession.

Another Cabera lived. Hanuvar had thought himself an uncle only once, to Edonia, wherever she might be, for Adruvar had sired no children, and Harnil had never married. But this boy, no matter the darker coloration, was unquestionably his brother's child.

What he was doing here, in the family of a Dervan general driven from this very village by Melgar himself, was the least of the mysteries before him. The greatest of them was what he was to do with the knowledge. The young man had been raised as a Dervan. How might Hanuvar even approach him?

He wasn't the only one befuddled by their discovery. Apart from selecting an inn for them and delegating Carthalo to arrange for rooms, Killian had nothing to say, and headed off for his inn chamber with a bottle of wine and an order for a meal.

Hanuvar retreated to a room of his own. He opened the shutters and leaned out to face south, where it was just possible to see a tree on the edge of that distant property. An oak his nephew might have looked upon every day of his life. The tree and this village were more familiar to the young man than his own bloodline. What did he know of Volanus?

Someone rapped at his door.

"Who is it?"

"It's me," Carthalo answered.

"Enter."

Carthalo opened the door. He bore a wash basin and pitcher. He was followed by a plump Turian woman and her wiry son, both carrying platters they set on a scarred table near the window. Carthalo thanked them and sent them away.

"Why are you here?" Hanuvar asked.

"Killian is sulking in his room, and most of his men have wandered off." Carthalo poured water into the basin. "I thought you might want to freshen up."

"Harnil preferred the company of men," Hanuvar said, moving over.

"But not exclusively," Carthalo pointed out. He dipped his hands into the water and scrubbed his face. He stepped back and pointed to the basin, but Hanuvar demurred. The role Hanuvar played was uninterested in cleanliness.

"At least wash your hands."

He looked down at the foods—dark bread with nuts and seeds baked in, smoked trout, and some particularly pungent garum, a Dervan fish sauce rendered more fragrant owing to the Turian preference for strong flavors. He dipped his hands into the basin, scrubbed the worst of the dirt from them, and then broke off some of the flesh from the fish.

"You wish to speculate," Hanuvar said.

"Harnil sometimes served with Cordelia. She was sly, witty, and capable. Tall, and dark-eyed. Turian."

Hanuvar hadn't known everyone in the intelligence network. "Go on."

"She was pregnant before the end of the war, after Harnil's death. She returned to my service, but gave the child over to a sister in Turia."

"A sister married to Marcellus?"

"Not that she mentioned." Carthalo broke off a slice of bread. "Cordelia didn't survive long after the war, so we can't ask her. What do you want to do?"

"I don't know." Hanuvar was seldom at a loss for a course of action, but so far, he hadn't developed one, and the halting course of his speech betrayed his confusion. "I want to speak with the boy, find out what he knows—about his family, and his past."

"Cordelia was smart, so he probably knows nothing. For his own good. He seems happy here."

"Happy among people who killed his own." Hanuvar chewed the fish, though he wasn't hungry. He barely registered its taste, despite the spices.

"You don't sound like yourself."

He lifted his other hand, showing an empty palm.

"You know Dervans can be fine people, and Marcellus was one of the better commanders. Melgar thought him honorable."

Melgar had arranged a prisoner exchange with the general, and had even briefly spoken to him in person.

"I don't understand why Cordelia didn't pass her son along to you. To us."

"She probably intended to raise him as her own. I doubt she meant to die."

"No," Hanuvar agreed. He realized the fish he clutched was disintegrating in his fist. He relaxed his grip. He was reacting with the emotional equilibrium of a teenager in love.

"No," he agreed with a deep exhalation. He thought then of the young woman, leaving perhaps on some scouting foray or courier mission when the Dervans were overrunning the countryside, turning the care of her son over to her sister, and wondering if she'd see him again. "I doubt she intended that."

They heard the unmistakable sound of hobnailed boots in the corridor. Someone delivered a hard rap against their door.

Hanuvar shot Carthalo a warning look, but the spy shrugged, as if to ask what did it matter now if they were together?

"Who is it?" Hanuvar asked. He didn't have to feign the priest's irritation this time.

"Killian. Is there anyone in there with you, priest?"

"I am," Carthalo answered.

The officer pushed open the door and stepped in, his expression somber.

"What's this about?" Carthalo asked.

"All the men have left. Even Ilarius."

That the reclusive scholar was involved told Hanuvar all he needed to know.

Carthalo swung his feet off the bench and reached for his weapon belt. "They're going after the boy, aren't they?"

"They think they're due some glory."

"What are you going to do?" Carthalo asked.

Killian breathed out in resignation. "Marcellus has pull. If the jackasses upset him, it could make trouble all the way to the emperor and Legate Aquilius. And I don't want the revenant legate mad at me."

"Not if he's the one paying us." Carthalo buckled on his weapons belt.

"That, too." Killian's gaze shifted to Hanuvar. "I need every man I can get, Brencis. I could use the help."

And Hanuvar wanted to protect his nephew. He just wasn't sure how the character he played should act, so he was a moment answering.

"I know you want a Cabera," Killian continued, "but the boy's as Dervan as me, raised by a senator and general."

The soldier had bluntly stated the same truths Hanuvar had been wrestling over. Killian misunderstood the furrowing of Hanuvar's brow. "You don't believe me?"

"I believe you," Hanuvar said finally. "What's in it for me?"

"I'll get you the pay due an officer for a month, and a bonus to boot, same as these bastards were getting."

Hanuvar pretended he was mulling it over, although he was aware of the press of time. His brother's son might be facing eight angry soldiers and a mage at this very moment. He drawled out his answer, as though reluctant. "All right."

Killian must have sent word to the stableboys, hoping both men would help, for all three horses were saddled. The trio was soon mounted and moving out at a canter.

Evening was nearly come, and the light through the trees was muted. This time, no children were visible in the villa's yard. This time, a string of horses cropped grass in front of the open villa door.

They left their mounts with the others. There was no question which way they should go. Shouting echoed through the halls and led them to a wide courtyard with a central rectangular pool. Harnil's son stood with Marcellus and his man; they were all but ringed by legionaries, with the heavyset Mazentius at their center point.

The young soldier pointed to Killian. "Are you here to help?"

Killian put a centurion's snap in his answer. "Our investigation's over. We were hunting fugitives. There are none here."

Mazentius shook his head. "We were hunting Caberas, and we found one."

Marcellus turned to Killian, hand thrust angrily toward Mazentius. "This man has invaded my home and pawed over my private papers. He has no business here. Will you please remove him?"

"You want to remove me?" Mazentius' voice rose mockingly. "You're harboring a Cabera!" The soldier shook the scroll, then addressed Killian. "First thing I found in his document chest—adoption papers. Then this!"

"You have no right!" Marcellus roared.

"But I do!" Mazentius said, almost crowing. He smiled as he returned his attention to Killian. "When the senator's wife fell ill, she left this letter for her husband, to be opened on the boy's sixteenth birthday." He waved the scroll at the boy. "He's the son of Harnil Cabera, brother to Hanuvar!"

"None of that matters," Marcellus snapped. "He's *my* son now."

Mazentius laughed, and his companions looked smug. "Cabera blood matters a great deal."

Hanuvar checked the boy for reaction, but Tiberius' grave expression hadn't changed.

"It's a curious coincidence, isn't it, that Marcellus spoke out against the Third Volani War?" Mazentius asked. "Just like Ciprion. Makes you wonder what little secret Ciprion might be hiding, doesn't it?"

"Are you aiming for a job in the revenant corps?" Killian asked. "You don't want to make trouble for them."

"He *is* a revenant," Ilarius spoke up. "Did you think they'd send one of their best mages out without a guard?"

Hanuvar put his hand to his hilt. Violence was imminent.

"That's enough!" Marcellus declared. "No one has authority in my villa but me!" He pointed at Mazentius' group. "I'll report your conduct to the emperor himself! Now give me back my property!"

Marcellus strode forward, hand outstretched for the scroll. As Mazentius backstepped, one of the others raised a palm as if to stop the old general, who swept it aside. The soldier grabbed his arm, and the two tussled.

Marcellus still knew how to fight. He slammed his elbow into the legionary's nose. Blood sprayed. Marcellus' attendant shouldered in, immediately opposed by a pair of soldiers drawing swords.

And then the senator stumbled back. The opposing soldier held a bloodied knife, and a crimson stain splattered the old man's side.

For the briefest of moments, the only sound within the courtyard was the sigh of the breeze through the decorative trees. Then Marcellus gasped.

The boy cried out, and the soldiers moved on him and his father both.

"Protect the boy," Hanuvar ordered Carthalo, and started in, one of his secreted blades in hand.

Killian moved at the same time. One soldier came at him with bared blade but dropped after a savage hack drove through his jaw and sprayed a mass of teeth. Killian cut off the howl of pain by slashing deep through his opponent's forehead.

Tiberius bared a knife and shielded his adopted father. A slim legionary advanced on him, sword raised. Hanuvar's throwing knife embedded deep from such close range, and the soldier crumpled with the hilt protruding from his eye socket.

The boy spun in surprise, staring briefly at Hanuvar before another man advanced on Marcellus' retainer and crossed blades with him.

In one hand, Hanuvar carried the gladius he'd hidden in his robe; with the other, he drew another knife.

Carthalo advanced to protect Killian's flank.

Hanuvar winged his second throwing knife toward Ilarius, who chanted and sprinkled black powder. His spellwork stopped abruptly as the knife planted itself firmly just above his collarbone. He choked, flailed his arms spasmodically, and ripped the weapon out. He patted feebly at the spurting blood, swayed backward, and then Hanuvar could spare him no more attention, for Mazentius had left his last three soldiers to run interference against Carthalo.

The disguised revenant turned on Hanuvar, his bared sword streaming black goo. From previous revenant encounters, Hanuvar knew poison had coated the blade the moment it was pulled from its sheath.

Hanuvar ducked the high strike; poison droplets spattered the floor. He parried the backswing and slashed down into Mazentius' sword arm. The younger man screamed in pain, freezing with his head raised and mouth parted. Hanuvar had plenty of time to slice through his face, but then had to let go of the blade jammed into his adversary's skull to duck a swipe from the brown-haired soldier on his left.

He slid on blood-slick pavement. Mazentius' body thumped to the ground beside him, and Hanuvar snatched the still steaming sword from limp fingers.

He swayed his head away from brown hair's thrust and felt the legionary's fist, clenched about the hilt, punch past his cheek. Hanuvar drove the smoking revenant sword up through his loins, and the legionary stumbled past Harnil's son, teeth parted in a silent scream. He splashed into the pool.

Hanuvar scanned the area. A paling Marcellus had balled up his tunic to protect his side. The retainer warded the old man and his adopted son, but no other opponents advanced against them. Killian and Carthalo dueled the final pair.

Hanuvar was readying to assist when the centurion dropped his man. Carthalo finished his own opponent with a jugular slice. The soldier put hands to the blood gushing from his neck, accidentally gashing his own face with his sword, then folded.

Killian stepped back to watch, his blade dripping blood. He swayed, glassy-eyed, and Carthalo reached out to steady him. He was too late—the veteran sagged, and Carthalo helped guide him to the ground.

"Brencis," he called weakly.

Hanuvar would rather have joined his nephew, watching with wide eyes, but he still hadn't decided what he'd say to him. So Hanuvar walked through the carnage to reach Killian, realizing when he saw the white face and the blood pooling on the stone beneath him that the soldier didn't have long. Carthalo's glance showed agreement.

"Cut by a revenant blade," the spy said. "There were three in all. The tall, quiet soldier," he added.

The dying man's eyes held the sharpness of a healthy man suddenly facing death. His gaze seemed to probe deep, touching Hanuvar's soul. There was recognition there. From seemingly far away, a voice called for bandages and aid, and a little girl cried out for her father.

Killian's mouth moved, and Hanuvar had to strain to make out his words. "I thought you were just a Volani hater. When we met the boy, I saw you staring at him. Intensity."

He paused to try for a breath he couldn't catch, then pushed on. "I get it now. Recognition. The way you moved—" almost, he laughed "—just like Adruvar." He smiled weakly and let out a cough. "Clever. Looking for... daughter?"

Hanuvar nodded once.

"Your brother died bravely," Killian whispered.

"So have you," Hanuvar assured him.

Had someone ever told him he'd speak kindly to Adruvar's slayer, or grip his forearm as he passed, Hanuvar would never have believed it, but this he did. When Killian stilled, he closed the man's eyes himself. He then wiped the soldier's jeweled blade clean and passed it on to Carthalo.

Only then did he turn to see what had befallen Marcellus.

The old general sat on a bench, his tunic torn open along the left. A pair of slaves had arrived with a pungent cask of vinegar and bandages, and must already have cleaned the wound, for the retainer was sewing up a short gash along the senator's sturdy side. Marcellus held his lips clamped shut while Tiberius looked on.

A matronly older slave had hands about the shoulders of both of Marcellus' daughters, watching open-mouthed from a doorway to the courtyard.

There was no scent of digestive fluids from Marcellus' wounds, so the slice had probably missed organs. The old soldier watched their approach from under drawn, heavy eyebrows, then nodded to them, waiting to speak until the final stitch was pulled taut. A deep, white scar puckered his abdomen a little lower down.

"I don't think this one will kill me if that one didn't," Marcellus said, having seen the direction of Hanuvar's gaze. "I'm indebted to you men for your help. I can recognize a legion man when I see one. You handled yourselves like seasoned skirmishers, not line men. Who did you serve under?"

"Ciprion," Hanuvar answered.

"And now you're a priest of Luptar," Marcellus said. "Well, I'll need no rites performed for me today. The revenants hire you?"

"The revenants hired Killian," Hanuvar explained. He couldn't keep his eyes from tracking to Tiberius. It was almost like looking at Harnil again.

The boy returned his careful scrutiny without understanding it. There was gratitude there, and curiosity, and shock. He'd seen brutal death this day, and his father wounded, and maybe feared he'd be hauled away by revenants.

"And he hired us," Carthalo finished. "But two of the 'normal soldiers' they sent with him were revenants."

"He should've seen that coming," Marcellus said. "I always hated those bastards."

The manservant finished tying the threads and turned, breathing heavily, to consider Hanuvar and Carthalo.

Marcellus' gaze grew hard. "What the revenants were saying about my son... Am I going to get trouble from you?"

Hanuvar had a hard time answering, but not for the reason the old man probably thought. Finally, he shook his head. "No, General."

"We're very good at keeping secrets," Carthalo promised.

"I've a question for your boy, though," Hanuvar said, "if you don't mind me asking."

"You risked your life to keep him free," Marcellus said. "I think you've the right, but it's up to Tiberius. What's your name?"

"Brencis," Hanuvar said. "This is Silvio."

"Well, the least we can do is host you this night, but I'll see you're both rewarded."

"We didn't help in hope of a reward," Carthalo said.

"Any man could see that," Marcellus replied gruffly. "You fought for the right of things, like we're told good Dervans do. Precious few of them. All right, Priest, what's your question?"

Once again, Hanuvar studied the slim young man before him, remembering Harnil at a similar age. Perhaps he'd been a little taller, and his hair hadn't been quite as curly, but they were close enough in appearance, it was like peering back through time. The boy's expression grew more and more perplexed, and Hanuvar realized he'd stared too long.

"When the revenant told you your origin, you didn't act surprised at all. Did you already know?"

"I've known for years my blood father must have been a Volani officer. They occupied nearby lands during a lot of the war." Tiberius looked to the old general, watching closely. "Father told me one day I might learn I wasn't who I thought, but that I should be proud of my heritage. He said I came from a line of warriors."

"I was supposed to wait to read the letter," Marcellus explained, "but I didn't want any mysteries about my son to turn up and surprise me. If she'd lived, my wife would have told me. Three wives I've lost now," he added. "Each one young and vital. And look at me. I keep collecting scars, and somehow, I keep going. Life's just not fair sometimes."

"No," Hanuvar agreed, "but I suppose we have to thank the gods for the blessings we receive, and find a way forward when their reasons leave us in darkness."

"Just like a priest," Marcellus said, although not unkindly. "I'll have my people tend to you. I should have a word with my daughters now. They've just witnessed things I never wanted them to see." He groaned as he pushed to his feet.

"We left much of our gear at the inn," Hanuvar said. "We'd best go gather that."

"Well, don't be too long about it. We'll pull down some fine wine, and you can tell me about your campaigns." He took in the mass of bodies and shook his head in disgust. "My poor slaves are going to have to clear all this up. And I'm going to have to report this. I don't even know what I'm going to say."

"Tell them an agent of the revenants foiled an assassination attempt," Carthalo suggested.

Marcellus' chuckle at his cleverness died as he felt his side and groaned. He then walked toward his daughters. "No, don't come in here, girls. No need to come any closer. Your father's fine. It's just my clothes that need to be thrown out, not me."

His retainer walked with him, watching as if he expected the old man to faint.

Tiberius remained.

"Gather our weapons," Hanuvar suggested to Carthalo.

His friend absented himself.

Hanuvar knew he didn't have long, so he spoke quickly, with quiet confidentiality. "I met your blood father. You resemble him strongly."

"Do I? What was he like?"

"He was a brilliant man, and a brave one, but what I remember most is what a fine laugh he had. He was one of the funniest men I ever met, and very charming. He was a natural storyteller. He loved plays." He was probably saying too much, but the boy listened raptly. "Do you like plays?"

"I always have," he answered eagerly, "and books."

Hanuvar nodded. "He was always reading."

"Did you know him well?"

Hanuvar knew now he'd said too much, but he couldn't help himself. He wanted the moment to last, for he knew there'd likely never be another.

What more could he say? Should he ask the boy about his favorite books, the foods he liked, the places he'd been? What his childhood had been like, and when he'd learned to ride? Was a marriage arranged for him already, and did he like the girl? What did he hope to accomplish?

How might he squeeze a life's worth of encounters and connection into the course of a single conversation?

Sadly, he knew it couldn't be done.

"In coming years," Hanuvar said, "this evening may be a blur, in which only a few terrible scenes stand starkly. Hold to the brighter ones. Recall how bravely your adopted father faced the men who wanted to take you away. Know that the dead man there killed your uncle Adruvar, but he died defending you. He acted with honor in both instances. A man's life can take strange directions, but if he models himself after people of character, and acts accordingly, he can lift his head high even in the bleakest of circumstances."

The boy seemed to be listening, but who could ever really tell how much the young took from the old?

Carthalo drew up beside him, waiting at his shoulder. Marcellus, leaning now against the older daughter while the younger clung to his good side, was directing slaves into the room, apologizing to them for what was sure to be a terrible effort, even as they affectionately chided him and told him he should get to a bed.

He was apparently one of those like Ciprion who treated his slaves as valued employees, a Dervan ideal more the exception than the reality.

Hanuvar extended his hand to Tiberius, who took his arm a little questioningly.

"I'll remember your counsel, Priest Brencis."

"Don't think of me as a priest of Luptar. I'm just a gray-eyed man who's lost a lot of people he loved. I'm glad you didn't lose your father this day. May you live long and well."

"Thank you. I hope the same for you. Are you not coming back?"

"I don't think that'll be possible. Someday, you'll understand."

The young man looked at him strangely, then bowed his head. "Thank you again."

Because he had trouble letting go, Hanuvar held the clasp a moment longer than he should have, and then he and Carthalo walked past the rectangular pool with the floating body and its billowing blood, and on out to the road, where they collected their horses. Hanuvar delayed briefly to scatter Ilarius' powders and retrieve the small bag with his father's scalp.

Carthalo didn't speak until they were in the saddle once more, riding side by side down the roadway. "You didn't tell him about yourself or our people."

"No." They'd left no gear at the inn; it was time to start the long journey back to Apicius.

"I heard a lot of what you said. He seems a smart lad. He'll probably figure out who you are, someday."

That had been Hanuvar's intent, although what he'd really like to have done was sweep him into his embrace—to take him on with them to Apicius and raise him the rest of the way as a proud Volani. He could hear about his uncles and aunts, and his ancestors. He could sit at Hanuvar's right hand and help to build New Volanus.

Maybe, in some better world, Hanuvar had ridden off with Harnil's son to shape the future. As long as he was dreaming, though, why not imagine a world where the child had grown up in Harnil's company, and where father and son might have joined Hanuvar at the table for dinner every week, where his cousin Narisia could have taken him riding along the shore, and when he might have grown up playing board games with little Edonia?

These seemed simple wishes, and he hoped that, somewhere, they were true.

"If I live long enough," Hanuvar said, just before they reached the end of the lane, "maybe I'll send him a letter and tell him more about his father."

"Maybe?"

A long moment passed before he found the strength to answer in a normal voice. "It might be best to leave him to this life. It could be he's ended up the luckiest Cabera of them all."

* * * * *

Howard Andrew Jones Biography

Howard Andrew Jones' new sword-and-sorcery series debuted in 2023 from Baen, starting with Lord of a Shattered Land, and continuing with The City of Marble and Blood. Book 3, Shadow of the Smoking Mountain, will be released in October of 2024. His Ring-Sworn trilogy, beginning with For the Killing of Kings, was critically acclaimed by Publisher's Weekly. His debut historical fantasy novel, The Desert of Souls, was praised by influential publications like Library Journal, Kirkus, and Publisher's Weekly. Its sequel, The Bones of the Old Ones, made the Barnes and Noble Best Fantasy Release of 2013, and received a starred review from Publisher's Weekly. He's the author of four Pathfinder novels, numerous short stories, and has assembled and edited eight collections of Harold Lamb's work for the University of Nebraska Press. He served as managing editor of Black Gate magazine from 2004 until 2018, and is managing editor of the sword-and-sorcery magazine Tales From the Magician's Skull, published by Goodman Games.

* * * * *

Paladins of the Unbroken Light
by D.J. Butler

A Tales of Indrajit and Fix Story

"I've heard this called the Notaries' Reef," Indrajit said. "I can't imagine what the name means."

Indrajit sat at the rear of the little boat, one hand on the rudder. The sail, set by his experienced hand, bowed out with the breeze, and pulled the vessel quickly toward the line of rocks. The clouds overhead bellied down gray and heavy, spitting fat, cold raindrops onto his back and neck. The absence of hair on Indrajit's head let him feel the chill, but the long, bony ridge of his nose tended to wick the water away from his eyes and send it dripping off his chin.

All the Protagonists wore wool cloaks against the weather.

"A notary is a sort of legal professional," Philastes Larch mused. The wiry Pelthite curled up in the bow, grinning back at the rest of the Protagonists. He was dark, with thick, curly hair. He'd been a shepherd in the Paper Sultanates of his youth, and a junior diplomat, but he seemed completely at his ease on the water, as well. "A notary creates and authenticates legal documents. Perhaps the name refers to the reef's function of sheltering Kish's ships from the worst of the sea's waves, as a notary protects his clients from the excesses of law and the vicissitudes of private life."

Munahim the Kyone, the tall, dog-headed archer and swordsman from the King of Thunder Steppes, leaned over the ship's gunwale and vomited.

"I might have guessed the same, once," Fix replied. Indrajit's partner was short and copper-skinned, with broad shoulders. His wide belt rattled with knives, a falchion, and an ax, and he braced himself against the action of the waves with his feet spread wide apart and the butt of a spear planted firmly on the wood between them.

Fix looked as if he could walk through a brick wall when he was angry, but his voice was high-pitched and musical. "Now I wonder if the reef isn't named for notaries because of the tendency of notaries, advocates, and other legal professionals to rip the hulls from their clients' undersides. The reef protects ships from mild waves, but in a storm, it sends sailors to the bottom."

"But the chasuble is here?" Philastes asked.

"That's what the fence said. Apparently, he heard it from some Grokonk who owed him money and couldn't afford to pay. He offered this secret instead."

"I notice the fence isn't here," Philastes pointed out, "or the Grokonk."

"We know where to find him," Indrajit said, "if we need to."

Fix nodded. "The information's good, or at least the fence believes it is."

"Maybe it's a notary's chasuble," Philastes said.

"It's the Chasuble Radiant, formal vestment of the Hierophant-Lucent," Indrajit said. "Keeper of the Eternal Northern Eye, High

Priest of Sheleg, Footman and Herald of the House of Hort, Lightbearer for the Living and the Dead."

"Is that in the Epic?" Philastes asked.

"The fence told us." Indrajit shrugged.

"There was a lighthouse out here," Fix said. "That was also a temple, maybe. Or a magical laboratory. Or some kind of weapon."

"Maybe a ship full of notaries sank here." Munahim pulled himself back within the boot and wiped his mouth with the back of his forearm. "Maybe the Hierophant-Lucent was the one who sank them."

"I think a story that cheerful would be more widely known," Indrajit countered. "We'd have a Notaries Day on the calendar, or a Feast of the Hierophant-Lucent. We'd all come down to the harbor and throw congratulatory flowers to the reef."

He scanned the ragged scythe of rocks around which the sea frothed and hissed.

"I've never heard of Sheleg," Philastes admitted.

"Gods die," Fix said. "They die when their people are gone, or their function isn't needed, or when their sites and memorials are obliterated. If the lighthouse/temple was destroyed, I'm not surprised Sheleg was forgotten."

"The Hort-worshippers still remember him," Indrajit said, "and there's an epithet for Sheleg in the epic: 'lofty Sheleg, in gold shining, knows the paths of the dusty sleepers.'"

"You can see how the 'in gold shining' part got us thinking," Fix said.

Philastes looked ahead. "Maybe the name's aspirational. Someone placed the rocks there, hoping to sink a ship full of notaries."

"That might be why it isn't on the charts." Indrajit sniffed. "Hiding the trap, as it were."

"Charts?" Fix sat upright. "Are you telling me you *read* a *document* before coming here?"

"I looked at a map. It was just a picture. There might have been words on it, but I didn't *read* them. Obviously."

Fix frowned. "So if you didn't read the words, it's possible you were looking at a city map. Did it show individual streets in the city?"

"It did." Indrajit found a little cove he liked and leaned on the rudder to send them in that direction. "So?"

"So a map of the city's streets wouldn't show reefs, just like a pilot's nautical chart wouldn't list street names."

"The map had a mermaid on it," Indrajit recalled.

"Not dispositive," Fix said. "Mapmakers are forever throwing doodles into the corners of their work."

"Maybe the notaries own the reef," Philastes suggested.

"Which notaries?" Indrajit asked. "All of them?"

"The notaries in the lighthouse?"

"Maybe it's not a trap," Munahim offered. "Maybe it's a curse. May notaries wreck their ships here!"

The boat bumped against the rocks, and Philastes leaped out. Despite the shelter of the reef, a wave seized him, and would have dragged him away if Indrajit hadn't caught him by the arm. Philastes took a coiled length of rope stapled to the bow and climbed onto the reef to tie it.

Indrajit gathered another massive coil of rope and followed Munahim and Fix onto the rocks. They were slippery under his feet, but he found that comforting and home-like. "As long as it's not a curse that turns us into notaries."

He found he had to raise his voice. The waves that had swelled silently in the bay crashed on the stone with a deafening furor.

"Maybe it's a mistranslation of an older name," Fix wondered. "Maybe 'notary' is another word for 'lighthouse-keeper.' Maybe 'notary' sounds like something different in Pre-Imperial Kishite, or sounds like the name of a favored concubine of one of the emperors."

Munahim announced, "When I have concubines, I shall name a rock after each of them."

"More likely, it's a corruption resulting from putting the name into writing. Or it's just a bad joke." Indrajit loped his way up the rock with long, dignified steps. Fix followed, harrumphing.

At the top of the rock formation, the storm hit Indrajit full in the face. He stopped and inhaled, sucking the salt and moisture into his lungs.

"We could invoke Hort Stormrider," Philastes suggested.

"What for? Is this not enough storm for you?" Fix asked.

"We could placate his wrath and avert this storm. To summon his aid in finding the temple of his dying footman." Philastes shrugged. "As one does."

"Hort isn't mad at us," Fix said. "Winter is coming."

"Don't mind Fix," Indrajit said. "He has no poetry in his soul."

"Don't mind Indrajit. He doesn't know the difference between poetry and religion."

"There's no difference," Indrajit said.

"See?"

"Maybe we should find this hole," Munahim growled. "I feel fine, but you're all going to feel chilled."

Indrajit said, "I'll outlast you, Kyone. This is practically home to me."

Still, the Kyone was right. Indrajit stalked about the rocky ridge, letting his head dangle slowly back and forth, as if he were lying on his belly in a boat, scanning for fish. The trick was not to focus, to let the corners of his eyes and the unseen parts of his mind do the work, to just stay relaxed and wait for the answers.

He found the hole.

"Stay back," he warned his comrades.

The curious structure described by the fence did indeed exist. Hunkered down among the wet black rocks, a ring of stone surrounded a shaft. Edging to the very precipice, Indrajit looked down and saw stone walls descending into darkness.

Darkness, but also, perhaps, a tiny glint of light down there in the abyss?

The shaft was circular and twenty cubits across. It might have been a well, only it was too wide, and the descent was broken by the sagging partial remnants of floors, clinging to the walls.

The rest of the Protagonists joined Indrajit. Each man had a rope slung over his shoulder. Philastes peered down the shaft and whistled. "It does sort of look like we're standing at the top of a ruined lighthouse looking down. But the Earth has swallowed up the lighthouse, leaving it a shaft that descends into the netherworld."

"Poetic," Indrajit said, "and unsettling."

"Why isn't the shaft full of water?" Munahim asked.

"Something down there is drinking all the water." Philastes shuddered.

"Pumps," Fix suggested. "Has to be."

"It could be pumps," Indrajit conceded, "but if so, they're pumps worked by demon servants, or ghosts, or sorcery. No jobber crew is out here on the reef, squeezing water out by hand at all hours."

"It needn't be sorcery. The work could be accomplished by mechanism."

"A more respectable word for sorcery." Indrajit inclined his head.

"Mechanism is part of the natural world," Fix said. "Mechanism is real."

"Magic is part of the natural world. Nothing is more real than magic. It's been with man since the time of the gods, and it'll always be with us."

"Mechanism works," Fix insisted.

"The universal testimony of mankind from the very beginning," Indrajit said, "is that magic gets the job done."

Philastes interjected, "Right now, what's going to get the job done is rope."

Indrajit tied one end of his length of cord around a sturdy fang of black stone and tossed the remainder down the shaft. "I'll go first."

"I'll go last," Fix suggested. "If Munahim and Philastes stay in the middle, they can cover both of us."

"Best if you stay up here," Munahim suggested.

"And miss any fighting?"

"If anything happens to the rope, we'll all die," Munahim pointed out. "I can stay if you prefer, but if you want me to give Indrajit cover, I probably need to follow him down the hole."

Fix granted the point, brow furrowed and lips pursed.

Indrajit lowered himself into the pit. The sound of the waves disappeared, and with it another sound Indrajit hadn't realized he'd been hearing, the steady hissing of the rising storm. The shaft had its own noise, though—a steady *hum* came from below and from the stone walls at the same time.

He slid down to the first partial floor, a shelf of buckled stone slabs that blocked only a third of the tunnel. Holding tight to the line, he stomped on the stones until he was confident they'd hold his weight, then waved to summon the next two Protagonists to the descent.

His eyes adjusting to the gloom, he studied the depths below him as Munahim and Philastes came. The next shelf was a bare lip on one side of the shaft, no more than a pace or two wide. He thought a faint glow emanated from beneath it.

The rain fell harder. At the top of the shaft, Fix wrapped himself in his wool cloak and disappeared, looking like one of the rocks of the reef.

"I don't know what a chasuble looks like, to be honest," Munahim said.

"It's a vestment," Philastes told him. "Something like a tunic or a toga. It doesn't have sleeves."

"It'll be made of gold," Indrajit said, "apparently." He listened, but couldn't hear the rain striking bottom.

"I thought it was supposed to be 'radiant,'" Munahim said.

Indrajit sighed. "Sheleg is the one in gold."

"So you said. I'm not familiar with the ways of gods."

The Kyones claimed they'd killed their own gods millennia ago.

"A priest who dresses up in liturgical clothing is taking on the role of his god," Indrajit continued, "obviously."

Munahim scratched himself under the chin. "Is that so?"

"That's so." Indrajit swung the tip of the rope out and found it wouldn't reach the lip he'd aimed for next. He took Philastes' line and tied it to a rocky outcrop. "Lighthouse—golden god—radiant chasuble... it all fits."

"I see," Munahim said, nodding. "What does it fit?"

"The chasuble will be gold. Worth money. So we'll be able to pay some bills and maybe hire a new man."

"We should hire a Thûlian," Philastes suggested. "The powder priests are fearsome."

"More fearsome than a female Grokonk?" Munahim asked. "More fearsome than a Gund? And a powder priest is all but useless in weather like this."

"You want to hire a Gund?" Philastes asked.

"I think we should buy mounts. Horses or Ylakkas. Or maybe a Drogger to carry treasure on expeditions such as this."

"Our treasure will be a vestment," Indrajit pointed out. "And how would you expect a Drogger to climb out of this pit?"

"An Ylakka, then," Munahim persisted.

Indrajit went down the new rope. His grip became more difficult as rain soaked the line, but he slithered down to the height of the crescent lip, and then pushed himself a few paces to one side until he could get the ledge under his feet. Warm air rose from below. Holding the rope in one hand, he walked to the widest part of the stone lip, then laid on his belly to look down.

He could see nothing over the bulk of the stone. He felt the warm breeze on his face, and smelled an oily, metallic tang, while cold drops struck the back of his head. But holding the rope loose and dangling it down like a plumb line, he could see a golden glow limning its wall-facing side.

The *hum* was louder, almost a growl. If there were indeed demons at the bottom of this pit, bailing out the water with all their otherworldly might, he didn't want to meet them. He continued to lie flat and consider as first Philastes, and then Munahim took the rope and made their way painstakingly down and over to join him.

"If there's a beast living at the bottom of this well, I fear it," Munahim said gravely.

"What if it's a notary?" Philastes asked.

"I fear notaries of ordinary size." Indrajit searched the ledge for a rock to anchor the next rope and didn't find one. "I think the way forward is for me to swing out to the other side of the pit, and then swing back, lowering myself on the rope."

"You're confident there's another ledge directly below this one?" Munahim looked over the lip of stone into the abyss, and his face expressed anything but confidence.

"There's something," Indrajit mused. "It could be a lamp. In Underkish, there are green lights that never stop glowing. It could be a light like that, fixed into the wall."

"In which case, you climb back up here," Philastes said.

"Yes."

"Then we knot another rope to the bottom of this one and keep climbing."

"Hmm." Indrajit stretched and gripped the rope, leaving a little slack, and then wrapping the cord around his forearm. "The fence didn't make it sound as if we'd have to descend all that far."

"Are we in Underkish?" Munahim asked.

Indrajit considered. "I suppose we might be. I suppose we might find tunnels that connected us to the sewers and underground ruins we know and love."

"At some point, if we keep going down, we'll reach the netherworld." Philastes frowned.

"Surely, it won't come to that." Indrajit pressed himself against the wall, then strode boldly to the edge and threw himself into space.

He dropped and bounced, feeling the rope stretch, and experiencing searing pain in his forearm as the line ripped skin away, and then he was floating across the shaft, spinning as he went.

He handed himself down quickly, focusing on the rope so as not to lose his grip. Beyond the ambit of his control, he saw a golden light. It seemed to orbit around him and beneath him, and then to rise as he fell, until it revolved at the level of his feet, then his knees, then his waist, and then his chest.

He struck the wall on the far side, bounced off, and came spinning back. The light opened like a flower in the morning sun, growing from a spinning dot to a blotchy cloud, and then solidifying into an alcove. The rope bumped against the stone lip over his head and bent, and Indrajit slipped into the golden light.

He relaxed his grip, let himself slide, and landed hard on his back.

* * *

Indrajit awoke.

He lay on stone, groaning. He felt alternating currents of warm and cold air, and his vision was a golden blur. His mind spun, but when he collected himself, he found he'd retained control of the rope, mostly by virtue of the fact that he was lying on it, pinning it to the floor beneath him. He carefully collected it in his left hand and rose, wobbling to his feet, drawing his legendary sword, Vacho, with his right.

The alcove was a hallway that proceeded forward toward a figure at a crossroad. The golden light emanated from glass baubles affixed on short arms to the walls at intervals of ten paces. Indrajit lurched to the nearest and wrapped the end of the rope around the metal arm.

"Indrajit!" Munahim yelled.

"I'm here!" Indrajit's voice was an unsteady croak. "I'm here, I'm fine!"

"Is there a chasuble?" Philastes called.

"Should we join you?" Munahim asked.

"Wait for my word!"

Indrajit advanced along the hallway. It was unfurnished, uncarpeted, and unpainted. The stones the floor, walls, and ceiling were built of were smooth, flat, polished, and round, with a gray, fine-grained mortar holding them together. Twenty paces in, the passageway split into three, and a man waited in the center of the junction.

He stood very still, hands hanging at his sides, but a hand's width away from his hips. His skin had a metallic sheen to it, and his hair, coiled in tight, spring-like loops, was bright orange. His eyes were closed, long, dark lashes resting on his cheeks, and his head bowed. He appeared to be unarmed, and his only garment was a sleeveless vestment like a smock, red in color.

"Are you a statue?" Indrajit asked.

The orange-haired man raised his head and opened his eyes. His irises were a piercing blue, so bright they seemed to shine.

"Or maybe a notary?" Indrajit added.

"Are you the Paladin of Sunless Radiance?" the man asked him.

Radiance? Indrajit didn't dare answer either yes or no. "I've come a long way."

The orange-haired man nodded. "Through great darkness and famine."

"Enemies dogged my path," Indrajit told him. That, at least, was true. "But I'm here now."

"In time to do battle with the Boy in the Storm."

"… yes?" Indrajit tightened his grip on his sword hilt.

The orange-haired man nodded again. "Very good. The actor must know when the real thing is here." He extended a hand.

Indrajit took the offered hand and was rewarded with a peculiar, complicated grip. He struggled to reciprocate, shook the orange-haired man's forearm vigorously, and finally saluted. The other man saluted back, then walked down one of the passages until he disappeared.

Indrajit stood at the crossroads, rubbing his chin. He could follow the orange-haired man, but there was no guarantee his path would lead anywhere interesting, including to the chasuble. Really, he should summon the other Protagonists.

"Paladin!"

Indrajit turned to face the source of the new voice and saw a yellowish-green, froglike man, only three and a half cubits tall, holding a short spear. The frog man wore a plain white tunic and was barefoot, with long, wide toes splayed on the stone.

"Grokonk," Indrajit murmured.

"I was warned you were a mighty warrior," the frog man said in a voice that glugged like water. "I was not warned you were haughty."

Indrajit stepped back and raised a hand. "Not Grokonk, then?"

"You insult me," the frog man said. "A hero must win by valor as well as by self-sacrifice. Prepare to fight."

"I'll fight you if you want, but first, I need to know a few things."

"I was told you were a riddler." The frog man tightened his grip on his spear. "Go on."

"You're not a Grokonk," Indrajit said. "So... what are you?"

"I am the Boy in the Storm."

"You've come to do battle with the Paladin of Sunless Radiance," Indrajit said.

"Prepare to die," the frog man said.

"We can fight to first blood."

The frog man hesitated, then nodded curtly. "Prepare to be wounded."

"You haven't answered my riddle," Indrajit said, "so I won't permit you to pass. Or to win. Honestly, look at you; I'm twice your size. Just answer the question."

The frog man frowned. "My name is Fthim."

"And what race of man are you?"

"Ssilibip." Fthim sniffed. "Not a Grokonk. Grokonk can barely jump at all."

"Fthim the Ssilibip." Indrajit nodded. "I only wish your language had more sibilants. And what do you know about Sheleg?"

"Footman and Herald of the House of Hort, Lightbearer for the Living and the Dead. I seek his paths."

"Ah, good. Our way lies together."

"You are the Paladin of Unbroken Light," Fthim told him. "You stand in my way."

"I will stand aside. You can lead both of us to the... paths of Hort. What do you know of the Chasuble Radiant?"

"You can't stand aside. I have to slay you."

"Defeat me," Indrajit said, "in a battle to first blood."

"Fine," Fthim said.

"It doesn't have to be a lot of blood," Indrajit pointed out. "A scratch would do."

Fthim lunged forward, stabbing his spear at Indrajit's chest. Indrajit stumbled back, managing to batter the attack aside several times, until he'd retreated out of the hallway and into the wider alcove.

"I have more riddles!" Indrajit yelled.

"You are a deceiver!" Fthim screamed. "You delay me, and the sun rises!"

"Where's the Chasuble?" Indrajit bellowed.

"The Hierophant-Lucent has it!"

Indrajit sidestepped another attack and grabbed the haft of the spear in his left hand. He yanked, pulling it away from the Ssilibip, and sheathed Vacho.

Fthim trembled and fell to his knees. "I have failed."

"Shut up." Indrajit poked the tip of the spear into the palm of his hand, drawing blood. "There. Is that enough?"

"I must smear your blood on my face."

"I suppose I'm just grateful you don't have to drink it." Indrajit grabbed Fthim's forehead, wrapping his fingers around the Ssilibip's cranium and smearing a blot of blood on the frog man's forehead. "Will that do?"

"You are indeed honorable," Fthim said.

"Look..." Indrajit said. "I am the Knight of the Unbroken Light."

"The Paladin."

"Paladin. And in your journey, I'm a foeman. A troll on the bridge. But I'm the hero of my own story, and I'm trying to find something."

"I will not tell you the road to my village."

"Fine." Indrajit nodded. "Are you going to find the Chasuble Radiant?"

Fthim's lip quivered. "I must wear it for my people to shorten the winter."

"Right. I'm coming with you."

Fthim looked down at Indrajit's legs and then up his tall frame. He snorted. "You can try."

"That's all I can ever do, Boy in the Pond."

"Boy in the Storm."

"Lead on."

Fthim led Indrajit to the mouth of the alcove, where it opened into the immense shaft. He squinted into the gloom, searching the opposite side of the abyss.

"The Chasuble Radiant will end winter?" Indrajit asked.

"The Chasuble Radiant will imbue heat into my body." Fthim's voice caught as he spoke. "My body will radiate heat for my people and drive winter away. There, do you see it, Paladin?" He pointed across the shaft with his spear.

At first, Indrajit saw nothing. He narrowed his eyes, cocked his head, and finally took a step to one side before he could make out what Fthim was talking about.

There was an opening on the other side of the shaft. It was dark, and the irregular shape of its mouth threw shadow over the whole thing, concealing it.

"Indrajit!" Philastes called from above, unseen. "Who are you talking to?"

"His name is Fthim!" Indrajit called back. "He's guiding me!"

"I'm not guiding you," Fthim said. "You're following me."

"Fine," Indrajit said. "So some of my friends are also going to follow you."

"You're bandits."

"We're the Paladins of Unbroken Light," Indrajit told him.

"There's more than one of you?"

"A paladin travels alone if he has to, but if he can, he prefers to share the road."

Fthim glugged wordlessly to himself. "Well," he finally said, "I hope you can keep up."

The Ssilibip crouched and sprang forward across the shaft. He shot like a dart straight into the shadowed maw of the entrance on the other side, and when he landed, golden lights in the space activated, illuminating a smooth-floored tunnel.

Fthim turned and shook his spear at Indrajit.

"Indrajit," Munahim called out, "shall I shoot him?"

"No!" Indrajit snapped. "He's a friend! Look, just… watch me and try to follow."

Taking a deep breath, he recovered the end of the rope from the light fixture. Eyeballing the distance across the shaft and down, he measured out the slack he thought he'd need, then wrapped the line around one arm, behind his waist, and then around the other arm. Standing at the lip of the shaft, he waved Fthim back. The Ssilibip scurried back into the passageway, hunkering down beside one wall.

Indrajit ran and jumped. His long strides and his best leap carried him halfway across the pit. He arced and dropped, and the angle of his descent very nearly brought him into the open tunnel mouth, falling short just a handful of cubits, and then the rope caught. His descent was arrested with sudden pain in both forearms, and his downward momentum became abrupt forward thrust. He yelped, and then he slammed into the mouth of the tunnel, scraping along the wall and being pulled up into the ceiling before he crashed to the floor.

"Ouch," he said. His head hurt, and the air was knocked from his lungs. He kept his eyes closed.

"I was warned the Paladin of Unbroken Light was fearless," Fthim said. "I was not told he was mad."

"The distinction isn't as great as you might think." Indrajit grunted.

"Are your arms broken?" Fthim asked.

"They might be," Indrajit admitted. "Give me a minute."

Eventually he rolled to his side and climbed to his feet, releasing the rope. "Come down!" he called out.

"Do all the Paladins look like you?" Fthim asked.

"The other ones aren't as handsome as I am, but they're fierce warriors, and true." He stretched and shook himself, trying in vain to dispel the ferocious ache in both his forearms. "How far do we have to go?"

"I've never walked this road before," Fthim admitted. "The Boy in the Storm wears the Chasuble Radiant but once."

Indrajit frowned. "Why don't you bring it back to your village and just keep it?"

Fthim pointed down the smooth-floored, smooth-walled passage. "This is the way."

"Are we close?"

"You are but the first of three guardians. I don't know how far we must walk, but we must defeat the Fire Serpent and the Rainbow Sorcerer."

"I suppose I should have expected that." Indrajit took a deep breath. "Lead on."

Fthim padded forward. His feet slapped the floor with a sticky sound. Glass globes affixed to the walls on either side of the passage illuminated as they came within ten cubits, but continued to glow behind them. Indrajit drew his sword and held it ready as they walked. At a crossroads, Fthim muttered wordlessly to himself and counted off on his fingers before turning left.

Indrajit kept an ear out and thought he heard Munahim crashing into the tunnel behind him, growling and yipping under his voice. The Kyone had a sense of smell as good as any hound, and would be able to follow Indrajit even if the lights went out.

"Here," Fthim said.

The corridor ended in a featureless door.

"The Fire Serpent is next," Indrajit remembered.

Fthim said, "You can't kill the Fire Serpent, and it isn't worth trying. We must get past it. The great secret is that it must rest to the count of five after exhaling fire before it can do so again."

"Sorry," Indrajit said, "I think you just said that the thing on the other side of this door exhales fire."

"It jets flaming oil, actually."

"Much better." Indrajit took a deep breath. "What's your plan?"

Fthim said nothing.

"Your plan is to open the door, jump, and hope it misses."

"I can jump far and fast," Fthim said.

"I've seen that." Indrajit shook his head. "What about a decoy?"

"What do you mean?"

Indrajit shrugged out of his cloak. It felt good to get out of the scratchy wet wool, and the air here was warm and dry anyway. "We open the door a crack and poke this through on the tip of my sword. If we're lucky, it's not very smart, or its eyesight isn't great. It spits flaming oil on this cloak, and then you and I have to the count of ten to rush in and kill the serpent."

"The count of five," Fthim said.

"Fine."

"If you're still running when you get to ten, you're probably dead."

"I understand."

"It's not even a slow count," Fthim said. "You have to count at a brisk pace. Like this: one, two…"

"What do you think of the plan?"

Fthim nodded. "It's a good plan, Paladin. A hero must win by cunning as well as by self-sacrifice."

"Any idea what's on the other side of the Fire Serpent?"

Fthim blinked. "Stairs down."

"Have you memorized a map or something?"

"Last year's Boy in the Storm," Fthim said. "I'd already been selected for this year's honor, of course. So part of my task was to welcome him back and make him comfortable. I listened to his account, before he lost his voice. I was also taught from the records of what happened in earlier years."

"Last year's Boy in the Storm lost his voice?"

"He barely outlived his winter." Fthim looked down at the floor.

"That's too bad." Indrajit chuckled grimly. "Otherwise, maybe he could have been here."

Fthim looked at the floor and said nothing.

"Fine," Indrajit said. "Get ready."

He hung the cloak on the tip of his sword, grateful that the wool was thick enough to resist immediate slicing. The smell of the wet fibers seemed stronger now that the cloak wasn't wrapped around him. Positioning himself against the door, he leaned against it quickly but gently. The door gave, opening a crack, and he shoved the cloak through the gap, dangling it like a dancing marionette.

Sudden flame engulfed the cloak. Flaming liquid spattered Indrajit, striking his tunic in two spots, and burning his shoulder. He dropped the cloak and slammed the door open.

"Run!" he roared.

Fthim sprang past him into a large open space and almost fell through the floor.

The chamber beyond the door was vast. It had no floor, only a grid of metal beams, spaced far enough apart that a drogger could plunge between any two of them and disappear into the darkness below. On the other side of the chamber, a platform clung to the wall, and behind it waited an open, visible passage, apparently descending again, though Indrajit couldn't yet see the promised stairs. Light came from two long, luminescent beams overhead.

On the platform, an enormous serpent reared up. It lacked the smooth, sinuous shape and movement of a serpent, but resembled the puppet of a serpent, built of sheets of steel, bolted together. Its joints were visible, massive steel balls. Its mouth was a simple open cone with a black cylindrical tongue in its center. On the serpent's neck was mounted a saddle, and sitting in the saddle, Indrajit saw a man with orange hair and metallic skin.

Fthim hurtled past Indrajit and nearly fell through the floor, but managed to grip one of the beams. From there, he leaped forward again, and Indrajit saw that the frog-man was going to cross the chamber well before he did.

But the Chasuble Radiant was real.

Indrajit broke into a run. He didn't dare sprint, fearing he'd miss his step on the beams and plunge into the dark depths below, but he ran at a steady pace and counted. *Two... three... four...*

The serpent swung toward Fthim, but seemed to give up on the Ssilibip immediately, and then swiveled back to glare at Indrajit. Indrajit focused on the platform and the tunnel at the far side, but they seemed farther away than when he'd started.

Five.

Indrajit heard a hissing sound and a squeak. Though he looked past the serpent, he saw from the corner of his eyes a jet of liquid spray from the cylindrical tongue, and he leaped forward.

Missing his footing, he fell.

Flame crackled the air above his head. He felt blisters rise instantly on his cranium, and then the fire shut off again.

Indrajit struck a beam of the floor with his chest. He bounced and would have fallen into darkness, but managed to wrap his arms around the steel. He clenched his fist and managed not to drop his sword, but his legs dangled.

One...

He scrabbled, trying to get his feet on anything that would give him purchase and failing to find anything.

"Paladin!" Fthim yelled.

Two... Indrajit ignored the searing pain on the back of his head and the pounding in his lungs. He swung one leg up onto the beam, focusing on keeping his grip on his sword.

Three... Indrajit heard a repeated clanging sound and the Ssilibip's yell. He dragged himself up onto the beam, knowing that at best, by the time the serpent was ready to spit fire again, he'd be exactly where he'd been before, exposed and vulnerable.

Four...

Indrajit stood, tottered, caught his balance, and lurched forward, focusing on his footing. Maybe the serpent would miss.

Five. Indrajit heard an elastic *twang* and a crisp sound like a thin sheet of metal being punctured. He braced himself for the flame, but it didn't come.

Then the Ssilibip yelled again. "Paladin! Your friends have come!"

Indrajit lost his balance again and slipped. This time he caught himself on his knees at the intersection of two beams. Kneeling, he looked up at the Fire Serpent. It slumped still, its conical mouth sinking slowly downward with a metallic groan until it came to rest against a beam at its feet. The rider in the saddle on its neck sagged backward, a long arrow in its chest.

"Indrajit!" Munahim called from the door. "Do you live?"

"I live!" Indrajit chuckled weakly and steadied himself with a hand on the beam. "I live."

Munahim took the time to sink another arrow into the serpent-rider's chest, and then he and Philastes crossed the network of beams. They picked Indrajit up when they reached him and carried him across to the platform on the other side. He slumped where he stood. Munahim leaned against the boxy, metallic base of the Fire Serpent.

Indrajit's arms, knees, and chest all hurt. Having managed not to lose his sword by sheer force of will, he slid it carefully into its sheath.

"Sometimes a hero must win by having friends," Indrajit told Fthim, who stared with gaping mouth.

"As well as by self-sacrifice," Fthim said.

"The Rainbow Sorcerer?" Indrajit asked. "Is that what's next?"

Fthim nodded. "And then the Chasuble Radiant."

Munahim made a satisfied growling sound in the back of his throat.

"I'm beginning to have doubts about this chasuble," Philastes said.

"The Chasuble Radiant exists." Fthim glared at the Pelthite. "The Chasuble Radiant saves my people every winter."

"Those aren't my doubts. What does it look like?"

Fthim licked his lips and shrugged. "The guardians will show it to me."

Philastes met Indrajit's gaze and raised his eyebrows. "I see."

So there was a Rainbow Sorcerer, and then something called guardians to deal with. Indrajit straightened his back, twisted a kink out of his neck, and pointed at the exit. "Stairs down, you said. And then what?"

"The Rainbow Sorcerer kills with light," Fthim said. "The way past him is to swim underwater, where the blessings of Hort deflect the sorcerer's evil."

"You probably swim underwater just fine. Can you breathe underwater?"

Fthim nodded. "Maybe I should go on alone."

"Have we not become friends? Have we not been good allies?"

"You almost died."

"What's that thing you say?" Indrajit cleared his throat. "A hero has to win by self-sacrifice."

"I know a trick, if we had a reed," Philastes said, "or a length of pipe."

"I don't have either of those," Indrajit said. "I know a trick, if we had a mirror. Or rather, the Epic tells the exciting tale of Prince Chiranjivi, who battled a demon that fired beams of light from its eyes."

"That's very like the Rainbow Sorcerer," Fthim said. "What did Prince Chiranjivi do?"

"He deflected the beams of light with a mirror," Indrajit said. "But we no more have a mirror than we have a reed."

"Yes we do." Munahim banged a sudden fist against the steel base of the Fire Serpent, which answered with a resounding *boom*.

"The Fire Serpent is attached to the floor. It won't come with us."

By way of answer, Munahim attacked the serpent. With bare hands and with the pommel of his sword, he knocked and tore at the steel until he managed to peel away a sheet of it. The metal was thin, almost as thin as foil, and as large as a shield, albeit a ragged and rectangular shield.

Munahim handed the sheet to Philastes. "Polish that." Then he returned to his work.

It took the Kyone fifteen minutes, but by then he had three large, irregular chunks of steel, more or less polished by the action of Philastes rubbing them vigorously with a rag.

"This may be a bad idea," Munahim said. "I'll do it."

"It's a terrible idea," Indrajit said, "but I'm the Paladin of Unbroken Light. I'll do it."

Each Protagonist carried a sheet of steel, gripped with two hands. Fthim led the way, down stairs, through two more crossroads navigated with finger-counting and silent recitations of his litany of travel. Glass bulbs in the walls lit their steps. Fine mist and a huge grinding sound warned Indrajit that they were close, and then the passage opened into a chamber full of water.

They stood on a shelf above a churning lake. Light emanated from strips in the walls, spaced irregularly and arranged according to no obvious aesthetic principle. From unseen gaps in the ceiling above, water poured down in cascades, crashing onto the surface and roiling it.

To the left and right, enormous cylinders rose and fell, climbing along transparent pillars they encased at their core. As they rose, the waters of the lake seemed to drop slightly, and when the cylinders shot back down, the transparent pillars filled with water.

"What Druvash devilry is this?" Indrajit asked.

Philastes laughed. "I think those are the pumps."

Fthim pointed. Beyond the falling water and the pumping cylinders, across the lake, was a similar shelf to the one they stood on. Warm yellow light leaked from a doorway in the wall.

"Where's the Rainbow Sorcerer?" Munahim sniffed the air and squinted into the dim corners of the room.

"He'll come if I dive into the water," Fthim said. "Last year's Boy in the Storm told me so before he died. Also, there are monsters below the surface. They will try to suck me in, but they lie still, so all I have to do is swim straight through the middle."

"That's the pumps," Philastes said. "Do what he said, you'll be fine."

"What did last year's Boy in the Storm die of?" Indrajit asked.

"You test me, Paladin." Fthim shook his head. "I'll dive in. Be prepared."

Indrajit, Munahim, and Philastes crouched defensively near the entrance to the room, raising the steel sheets. Fthim rushed forward and dove headlong into the water. As he sliced neatly into the frothy lake, a beam of light cut through the dim air and nearly touched his foot.

"There!" Munahim barked, and then a flying thing fell upon them.

Indrajit never saw the Rainbow Sorcerer clearly, but in the brief glimpses he did get, it seemed to be a globe. The globe was the size of a large man's chest, and it flew through the air, changing direction and speed effortlessly. Nozzles protruded from its surface, and beams of colored light erupted from the nozzles, aimed at the Protagonists.

Munahim yelped, and Philastes roared. They ducked and held up their sheets, adjusting the angles based on where the reflected beams of prior attacks struck. They hit the ceiling, resulting in sparks. They destroyed two light strips. They struck a pump.

And finally, Philastes managed to angle a red bolt of light back at the sorcerer, knocking it to the ground.

Before Indrajit could even draw Vacho, Munahim rushed forward. He bashed the globe repeatedly with his long sword, drawing sparks and metallic whines of protest, and then he kicked the globe into the lake. With a flash of light, an angry hiss, and a bitter cloud of smoke, the Rainbow Sorcerer sank into the water and didn't resurface.

They followed Fthim, splashing across the water and making their way to the door. Before entering, Philastes looked back. "Is it my imagination, or did one of the pumps stop working?"

"They aren't pumps anyway," Indrajit said. "You heard Fthim. They're monsters."

Beyond the doorway waited a room bathed in soft golden light. The light emanated from the walls, which appeared to be featureless stone, but glowed. In the center of the room, a glass tube, ten cubits tall and four across, hung from chains above the floor. Fthim stood beneath it, his spear cast aside and lying on the floor.

Beside Fthim stood a man with metallic skin, curly orange hair, and bright blue eyes.

"You!" Indrajit drew his sword.

"Wait!" The orange-haired man raised a hand. "We have not met. You met one of my brothers."

"I killed one of your brothers," Munahim said.

"And I do not hold it against you." The orange-haired man smiled.

"This is the guardian," Fthim said. "He will put me in the Chasuble Radiant."

Indrajit frowned and looked about the featureless room. "Where is the Chasuble Radiant?"

Fthim pointed at the tube over his head.

"I don't understand," Indrajit said.

"I'm afraid we don't have time to explain," the orange-haired man said. "You've destroyed one of the pumps, so we already run the risk that your road will be flooded before you return. If you wish the Ssilibip to live, you must stand aside."

Indrajit muttered, but didn't see any other course, so he got out of the way. The orange-haired man raised his hands and the glass tube descended until it enclosed Fthim and rested on the floor. Then the glass burst into brilliant white light, obscuring Fthim entirely.

"What's that doing to him?" Philastes asked.

"It will save his people this winter," the orange-haired man said, "and his journey will remind them that they must continue to seek excellence and generate heroes."

Indrajit said, "And then he'll die. This thing will save his people but kill him."

"He'll die a hero." The orange-haired man smiled. "He'll be remembered as such."

"Who are you? By what right do you do this thing?"

"We're the keepers of the Ssilibip. We were made to do this."

Suddenly, the orange-haired man's gaze seemed a thousand miles away, and Indrajit wondered whether those blue eyes even saw him at all.

"Do they agree to it?"

The orange-haired man shrugged. "Do any of us agree to the conditions by which we live? I did not choose to be their guardian. I do it because it is my lot."

Indrajit wanted to drag the orange-haired man out into the lake and drown him, but he resisted the urge. "That's the Chasuble Radiant. That enormous thing. There's no treasure here."

"I never said there was." The orange-haired man shook his head. "You may leave. Fthim will make his way home well enough. He won't feel sick for many weeks. In fact, for a time, he'll feel extremely vital. He'll be strong and fast, and attractive to the females of his village. And he'll radiate the heat they need to survive the winter. When the end comes, it will be fast."

"And painless," Indrajit said.

The orange-haired man didn't respond.

"You're supposed to say it'll be fast and painless," Indrajit prompted him.

"Fthim's end will be fast. It will not be painless."

"There has to be another way for Fthim's people. This is madness."

"This is the way the world is," the orange-haired man said. "You can complain to the gods, if you like. You can wish the ancients had made other arrangements. But here we are."

Indrajit ground his teeth, and for a long time said nothing. "We'll take him home," he finally said.

When the light of the Chasuble Radiant abruptly stopped a few minutes later, the orange-haired man raised his hands again, and the tube rose off the floor on its chains, allowing Fthim to emerge. He walked with a spring in his step and a gleam in his eye.

Heat radiated from his body. Indrajit felt the heat standing two paces away.

"Let's hurry," Fthim said. "I can breathe underwater, but if we don't cross the lake soon, your road will be cut off."

They sloshed across the shelf in knee-deep water, and then swam. Halfway across, Indrajit thought he caught a glimpse of the Rainbow Sorcerer, lying in the depths of the lake, coughing out sparks. Crossing the beam floor of the Fire Serpent's room, he kept a careful eye on Fthim to be certain the Ssilibip didn't slip or stumble, but Fthim seemed hale and nimble. As he crossed the beams himself, Indrajit heard water flowing below.

When they reached the shaft, Fthim found the end of the Protagonists' rope and handed it Indrajit. Their hands touched slightly, and Fthim's skin burned. Pointing across the shaft and up at the alcove on the other side, the Ssilibip said, "I'll just jump from here."

Indrajit finally found words. "You knew."

"I thought you did, too," Fthim said. "I met you as the Paladin of Unbroken Light, an obstacle on my journey. Only later did it turn out that you were the Paladin of Unbroken Light, my companion."

"You didn't need us," Indrajit said.

Fthim shrugged. "Who knows how it would have turned out had you not been there?"

"And now you'll just die?"

Fthim shook his head. "*Now* I'll save my people for the winter. *Then* I'll die. I wish you an end that glorious."

Then the Ssilibip turned, leaped across the shaft, and disappeared.

Philastes shook his head. "What are we going to tell Fix?"

Indrajit took a deep breath. "The truth, of course. He won't be disappointed. Fix understands love."

* * * * *

D.J. Butler Biography

D.J. (Dave) Butler has been a lawyer, a consultant, an editor, a corporate trainer, and a registered investment banking representative. His novels published by Baen Books include the Witchy War series: *Witchy Eye*, *Witchy Winter*, *Witchy Kingdom*, and *Serpent Daughter*, and *In the Palace of Shadow and Joy*, as well as *The Cunning Man* and *The Jupiter Knife*, co-written with Aaron Michael Ritchey. He also writes for children: the steampunk fantasy adventure tales *The Kidnap Plot*, *The Giant's Seat*, and *The Library Machine* are published by Knopf. Other novels include *City of the Saints* from WordFire Press and *The Wilding Probate* from Immortal Works.

Dave also organizes writing retreats and anarcho-libertarian writers' events, and travels the country to sell books. He tells many stories as a gamemaster with a gaming group, some of whom he's been playing with since sixth grade. He plays guitar and banjo whenever he can, and likes to hang out in Utah with his wife, their children, and the family dog.

* * * * *

High Water Mark
by Chris Hepler

On little things like that—a cup of water—battles were decided.

— Michael Shaara, *The Killer Angels*

Miri prayed under her breath the entire night she, Jessie, and Séraphine stole out of the Confederates' camp, convinced they'd be shot as traitors before they reached the Army of the Potomac. Séraphine's patron angel might make her bulletproof, but God had never prevented Miri from getting hurt before, and if the scars she'd seen on Jessie's back were any indication, her mortality was just as certain. As blessed a warrior as Séraphine was, a dozen rebel soldiers would suffice to kill all three women, and as of tonight, this Pennsylvania backwater was host to seventy thousand.

It had been Jessie's idea to bring buckets and pitchers, and that probably saved their lives. They hadn't hidden in the tree line, instead taking the road into town on foot as if they were authorized. While the other two cast their eyes down, Séraphine walked proudly, adding to the illusion.

When stopped by perimeter guards, she did the talking. "Fetching well water, sir. For Longstreet's men." Longstreet didn't command these guards, so the order couldn't be immediately verified.

"I ain't seen women armed for carrying water," was the response. Séraphine's breastplate and saber were hard to miss.

"It prevents desertions. In Yankee territory, they think they can escape." She indicated Jessie, then the revolver on her hip. "I'm tired enough without having to give chase." Séraphine masked her accent as best she could, but a lifetime in France slipped out.

"You foreign, Miss?"

"No longer. I came to Virginia last year, to walk with your army."

Unsure what to make of that, the guard glanced among the three women. One tall and proud; one petite but sturdy; the last a slender figure in long skirts with a skin tone that overrode any other opinion he might have of her.

"You get back as soon as you can. She gives you any trouble, one shot in the air, and we'll be there."

Miri glanced at the mounted men, their eyes always searching. There'd be no outrunning them if it came to that, but Jessie's plan of hiding in plain sight had worked. A rider followed them toward the well from a distance, and as soon as another traveler needed interception, that set of eyes was off them.

The trio hurried into the grayness of the twilight, passing by the dark blue of the bodies on the field, stripped of weapons and shoes by rebel scavengers, to the Union ranks.

* * *

"I'm sorry, ma'am," General George Meade said, "but I don't have the foggiest fucking idea who you are."

Séraphine didn't miss a beat. "I am Séraphine Léonin de Lorraine, *chevalier* of the Order of Jeanne la Pucelle. I came to the United States by way of Virginia to answer a prayer."

The officers around the room—a tiny one, inside some family's farmhouse—shared glances. It was spacious enough that they could lay a map on the table, but everyone had to stand close, breathing each other's air.

Miri was no stranger to body language and guessed they were predicting a venomous response from Meade.

But Séraphine held up a hand, anticipating him. "You gentlemen will ask why I was within the Confederates' ranks."

"It was my understanding that when a paladin makes a vow, they pledge their life and honor, yes." Meade looked like a snapping turtle focused on the hand of some fool who thought to tease it. It wasn't unheard of for paladins to request duels of enemy commanders, and though the women had been disarmed for the meeting, it wouldn't be far from his mind.

"Are you familiar with the holy entities that speak to us?"

"Miss Sarah, I've heard many tales of paladins' powers, but I've also heard the quotation of your countryman Napoleon. I believe he said, 'God tends to fight on the side of the heaviest artillery.'"

If the phrase amused Séraphine as it did the men in the room, she didn't show it. "If Napoleon said such a thing, I haven't heard. But as to your aspersions, I didn't come here as a matter of survival. I came because the *Shekinah* said a noble soul traveled among the Army of Northern Virginia, and when I came to free her, I saw the horrors of her enslavement."

She pronounced it *horreurs*, and Miri hoped the soldiers understood her correctly.

"You're a man I cannot shock with detail," she continued. "I'll only say, when men take up arms to set other men free, warfare no longer stains the soul, but cleanses it. I've brought these women to your army, where we belong."

Meade rubbed his nose, setting his mustache aquiver. "Why do you think I need you to win this scrap?"

Miri sucked in a breath, waiting for Séraphine to go off about what they'd read in the newspapers, that Meade had only been in charge for three days.

Instead, she uttered a single word. "Precedent."

A soldier snorted. Miri only had time to look in his direction before Meade's words hit like punches. "Major Biddle, if you have an opinion to share about the wins and losses of this army that I'm not already *keenly* aware of, by all means, voice it *now*. Do you have such an opinion?"

The chastised major looked straight ahead. "No, sir, I do not."

"Then you're invited to *review* your goddamn *troops* and send me a report of their readiness in an hour, without which I'll have to assume you've rendered them unable to fight and inform your commanding officer of such. Understood?"

Biddle saluted. "Yes, sir."

"You're dismissed." Meade turned back to Séraphine. "You. Are you bulletproof?"

"I can be."

"But another paladin can counter that. The... dispelling."

"Correct."

"And in your time amongst Lee's men, did you see paladins who would fight for him?"

"See? No. But General Longstreet knew me for one immediately. He'll have some, but no more than the fingers on one hand. We're rare."

"What's the difference between them and you?"

"We speak to the powers above. They speak to powers who *pose* as the powers above. The invisible world is full of deceivers. One can only tell by the deeds they perform."

Meade's face seemed etched into a permanent scowl, but the silence stretched on long enough, Miri thought her mentor had satisfied him.

Then he turned on her. "You. What can you do? Heal the wounded or suchlike?"

Miri felt every set of eyes in the room on her. She reflexively curtsied before remembering she was dressed in boys' trousers, so she doffed her cap. "Begging your pardon, sir, I'm the lady's novice. I can't, um... I'm training to fight, but I have yet to receive an annunciation. That's the time when one works... miracles."

Meade's glare was disgusted. Miri had seen that look on her father's face.

"And you?" Meade addressed himself to Jessie, who inclined her head.

"Sir, the other side had me carrying water for cannon swabs, and tending the horses that pull artillery. I imagine with your folk, the work ain't too different."

This seemed to mollify Meade. "Cadwalader, our paladin will require a horse, and she's going to need it where the fighting matters most. Get all pertinent intelligence about the enemy forces from her. Then have a man guide her down south to the line across from Longstreet so his boys can't work any surprise voodoo. Keep the three of them together. Miss Sarah, it's on your head to keep these two disciplined. Is that a task you're equipped for?"

Séraphine stiffened. "Sir, my novice Miriam excels at following orders. This other soul, Jessie, braved death and worse to allow us to slip past hostile forces. Their courage shall be sufficient for your needs."

The skeptical mask slipped for a moment, but just a moment. "Then as a proud son of Pennsylvania, let me welcome you to—" he glanced at the map "—Gettysburg. Dismissed."

* * *

That night, Séraphine met with the commanding officers of a regiment camped in a field studded with boulders.

Miri soon recognized that the regiment was shorthanded. Their welcoming smiles and introduction to the gun crews were entirely too friendly. A dozen of them showed Jessie and Miri how to serve water to the gunners properly. After a half hour, they stepped back and watched them mime the actions. Once the instruction stopped, Jessie snatched up a ramrod and took the lead.

"Here they come," Jessie barked. "Cannon just fired; what happens first?"

Miri pointed. "Vent gets cleaned and covered. Big debris cleaned out with the coil tool. Sponge goes in the water bucket. As soon as that sponge lifts out, I fill the bucket."

"Good. What happens next?"

"Dry sponge in the barrel. Powder in the barrel. Call for ammo. Ammo carried from the ammo chest to the muzzle. Load, round gets slammed down the barrel."

"*Wadding* after the powder. Then load."

"Powder. Wadding. Round. Gun aim. Powder gets pricked. Ears covered, mouth open, order to fire."

"Order to *clear*, then fire. You stand behind that cannon, you'll be eating metal."

"Right."

There were chuckles and murmurs among the cannon crew. There were only two still paying attention, while the rest ate or wandered off to relieve themselves. Miri knew what the remainder were saying, and her ears burned. She was getting shown up by a slave—or more correctly, a woman who'd been one until tonight.

Jessie heard them, too, but her eyes were hardened by punishments unknown to the novice.

"I thought paladins knew war," Jessie said, "or at least learned it fast."

Miri lowered her lamp, hoping Jessie wouldn't see her face redden. "Lady Séraphine thought I could."

"She wrong?"

The question was so simple, it cut through a year's worth of misgivings. Two hundred and fifty miles of traveling. Endless lectures. Drills of swordplay and bayonet. All because Séraphine claimed she could see a mark on Miriam Campbell no one else could.

"She ain't," Miri said defiantly. "The annunciation will fix a lot. A baptism by fire might spark it. It happens that way to some."

If skeptical glances were a contest, Jessie would have won it. "And if it don't, you... got a plan?"

"If it don't, I'm dead. So, it's this or nothing."

"You got a home you can go to? Family?"

The novice's voice grew quieter, but urgent. She spoke for Jessie alone. "No. Not any more than you."

Jessie pursed her lips. "That bad?"

Miri nodded. "If I don't see my parents again, I'll call it sign enough that heaven listens."

Jessie had been hard to impress—she'd said her masters prevented runaways by taking revenge on their loved ones when they fled. They'd miscalculated when they broke her family up, as fear for herself didn't hold her back. But she seemed to chew on the thought, no doubt aware there was enough cruelty to go around.

"Well, you stick with me. I been in this war two years now. This ain't my first time around twelve-pounders. We stay near them, we got a good chance of seeing the next day."

Miri gave a small smile. "Appreciate it, I do, but I ain't a coward."

Jessie grinned back. "I know, but ease into that fire baptism a little bit at a time, just for the sake of us standing next to you."

* * *

Miri didn't sleep for more than an hour that night, and when the sky began to lighten, she heard the crunch of old grass under Séraphine's hard leather boots.

Miri was on her feet immediately. The world swam a little.

"What do they plan for you?" Séraphine asked.

"Water carrying, ma'am."

"Then you should be ready with it before they wake. The regiment will want to eat early."

"It's for the cannons."

"Have you made allies since I saw you last?"

Miri hesitated. Could she rely on the cannon crew if it came to it? There'd been more jeers than smiles. They might defend her, but she wouldn't gamble on it. Camp followers were only prized for ability.

"Just Jessie."

"Make friends this morning. Today will be battle."

There was little Miri could do but nod. She hadn't been among the whistling bullets as the other two women had, only seen the bodies on the battlefield afterward, the washes of red on the long, dead grasses of the plains that made good killing grounds. Miri's father had introduced her to violence, yes, but war was something else. It turned humans into small things: water for a cannon, a shape in a gunsight, a source of shoes.

She grabbed two buckets and a pitcher. After getting her bearings, she found a rocky creek and filled all three containers. Back and forth she went until dawn became morning, and a crowd had gathered around her campsite to drink their fill. Some washed. Many ate cherries from a pail. Then Miri spotted a familiar face from the gun crew, the ammo runner.

"In all the work last night, I forgot to ask. You boys all from Pennsylvania?"

The artilleryman made a face. "This is the 20th Maine under Colonel Chamberlain, ma'am. Heard there are Pennsylvanians and New Yorkers up and down the line, though. Where you from?"

"Fairfax County, Virginia," Miri answered.

"Ain't that Johnnie territory?"

"It's a stone's throw from the Potomac. If land were destiny, I coulda gone either way."

"Something change your mind?"

"That French woman, there. Only one in my life who said if I applied myself, I could amount to something. You got a name?"

"Clark," the ammo runner replied. "Me and Richard, here, we signed up together. Got dared into it. Stayed in... out of orneriness, I guess. Last battle, we didn't even get to fight."

A report sounded in the distance. Another, farther off.

Clark's face hardened. "Speak of the devil. Sounds far up the line. Twelve-pounder, I think."

"Ours or theirs?" Richard asked.

"Have to see. Half of theirs used to be ours before Hooker." There were grunts. No one thought much of generals who lost battles.

The men stood, some putting down cups, others wolfing down everything on their plates. Their clump made its way to a ridge where they could get a look at the road. It ran past the rocky hill to their left across their field of view and north to the town on the right. The cannon smoke came from the north.

The chatter came fast. "Think we're going that way?"

"Can't be, Longstreet's across from us. Look down there. I think that's Sickles' boys gone to fight 'em." The cannoneer pointed at a distant line of Union blue, advancing well beyond the advantage of the ridge and into trees. Not a forest. An orchard, farmland.

The air split with the loud cry of a bugle. Near the bugler, not far away, officers fell in, and gradually, the entire company. The baggage crew wasn't present, but Séraphine was, mounted and ready to move out. The young officer who spoke had a bird insignia on his shoulder bars: Colonel Chamberlain. Rather than sit astride a horse, he stood with his soldiers.

"I've just been informed Sickles has engaged Longstreet directly across from us. In his infinite wisdom, he left that hill there uncovered. As most of you can guess, the enemy corps are numerous, and they'll do everything in their power to flank the Union left. As of this moment, we *are* the Union left."

There were mutters, nearly all curses. The faces of the soldiers by Miri were grim.

"Our orders are to hold and deny them. If we retreat, this army will be enveloped. I don't see a scenario that doesn't lead to a complete rout of all our divisions at their greatest strength." The colonel paused. "Cannons can't make it up that rocky hill there, so the artillery is to take targets of opportunity and secure this ridge from an advance. The infantry will make a line up to the top of the hill, dig in behind those boulders, and hold it against the Rebs. We cannot yield. Understood?"

There were scattered cheers, but not many.

How many soldiers does the regiment have? Miri thought. She'd heard a thousand was normal. This was less than half that.

"You're likely wondering who the new girl is. Ma'am, want to introduce yourself?"

Séraphine regarded the troops. They knew her for what she was. The paladin's breastplate caught the orange sun coming over the camp like a relic of another age. Her autumn-maple hair blew in the wind, but the back didn't come out of its braid, and what few strands crossed her face did nothing to mar the cold steel in her eyes.

"I am your guardian angel."

The cheers were louder that time.

* * *

"*Pitcher!*"

Miri scrambled from the side of the sixth gun's wheel, where she'd poured a gallon or so into its bucket. As its crew immersed the sponge, she glanced down the line. A man at gun four seemed frustrated, stuffing his sponge repeatedly into what had to be a low fill. She ran, hunched over, because somewhere out there were sharpshooters who'd picked off their first mounted observer.

The world trembled again, a huge *thump* that shook Miri deep in her chest every time one of the battery's guns fired. When she got further back behind the safety of Cemetery Ridge, she broke into a sprint. In seconds, she'd reached the lines of buckets Jessie had set up and refilled her pitcher. She heard a curse before she saw anything, as the now-freewoman set down two more punishingly heavy loads of water.

"What's happened?" Jessie asked.

"They been bashin' each other in the peach orchard and among those rocks down the way," Miri reported. "I can't see the battery helping much but warning Johnny Reb not to come further."

The world shook again.

"*Pitcher!*"

"Come see." Miri handed Jessie a second pitcher, and they hustled to the front. Miri practically dove to the fourth cannon's bucket and sopped the sponge right. A cannon away, Jessie did the same, and poured her remainder into the canteens of the thirsty crew. The July sun was merciless, not a cloud near—

Wait.

One cloud, swirling and growing, not in the firmament of the sky, but somehow low, on the far side of the rocky round hill where the infantry had dug in. It wasn't natural, and that meant one thing.

"Jessie!" Miri dashed to her, trying to keep low. "Take over here. I have to warn Séraphine. They've got a paladin."

"You think she don't know?"

"She's going to be looking at the Rebs down a gunsight. Take over, and I'll never ask you for anything again."

Jessie's eyebrows went up. "I'm "I'm 'a hold you to that. You run now; I got these boys."

Miri ignored the call of "*Pitcher!*" and started the longest sprint of her life. One hand on the pitcher, one hand on her cap.

Dressing like a pageboy was fine when in camp, but out here, she'd be a target. As she ran, she couldn't see the sharpshooters in green taking pot shots at her, but the men in gray were to her right, a thousand yards off or so. Then five hundred. As she reached the men in blue, the bullets zipped past, sounding like she'd hit a beehive.

"You the 20th Maine?"

"155th Pennsylvania, boy!"

She ran on, uphill, continuing to hunt. New York 146th. A bullet cracked the tree next to her. Crouch. Hustle. Pennsylvania again, the 91st. Many bullets now, too many to stay standing. New York again, 140th. She gave up asking and crawled on all threes for what seemed like an hour. Finally, at the end of the line, with her heart in her throat and her cap in her teeth, she saw the colors of the battle standard. Maine.

"Séraphine!"

A high-pitched rebel yell drowned out any reply. The Mainers fired from behind rocks and brush, blunting the advance with blood and gun smoke. The paladin was off her horse and had a rifle in hand, and only dimly did Miri remember to look beyond, to the left.

"Séraphine!" She crawled to her. "*Paladin!*"

The battle maiden turned where she was pointing and saw the cloud through the trees. It could easily have been mistaken for rifle smoke, hovering over the southwest.

"Get down!" she shouted at her squire, fired one shot from the rifle somewhere unseen, and drew her saber. She touched it to her forehead.

The world went still. The air around Séraphine shimmered, not so unusual in the July heat, but Miri knew better. It was the blessing of the *Shekinah*, the angel said to be the bride of God in the Zohar and books of Enoch. Séraphine stood, and a bullet glanced off her shield.

In answer, the tree nearest them exploded in fire and light. A *boom* greater than artillery deafened the men and silenced the rebel yell. The flaming debris of the shattered tree tumbled down the hill.

Miri gaped. "What the hell was that?" Was it a new weapon? No. It had come from above.

"Baraqiel," Séraphine growled. "Before he fell, he was the lightning of God."

As the dust cleared, the shine of a helmet was visible first, then a figure clad in argent mail. Chain armor. A revolver in the left hand, a saber in the right. Behind the paladin were gray and green uniforms. Not many. Just enough, if you came from behind.

"How do I help?" Miri's voice was low. If she drew attention, she was meat.

Another bullet glanced off Séraphine. As if it were the most natural thing in the world, she drew her own pistol. "Aid Chamberlain. The Maine need ammo."

And with that, she stalked toward her opponent.

Séraphine shot steadily with the cavalry revolver, not at the paladin, but at the men behind, downing one, two, three. Their return fire had no effect, and they broke.

That confused the paladin, offended him. He whirled back and forth, incensed at being ignored. He fanned his pistol's hammer with his wrist, blazing away.

Then she was on him. Their blades and feet moved too fast for Miri to follow.

Séraphine gave ground at first, dancing back to see if he'd overcommit. He didn't. She subtly switched her avoidance to sidesteps, letting her blade retaliate and pressure him without wasting movement.

Above them, his personal cloud became a shape. The shape became the face and torso of a being. It was no man, no woman, for they were born of clay. Baraqiel, if that was its name, was light and sparks of the divine—or at least the infernal. A second shape coalesced rapidly, anger burning in its face as the two guardians seized one another by the wrists.

Miri feared for Séraphine and her protector, but what could she do? They'd live or die as the Creator willed.

Sudden urgency shot through her. The colonel. She crawled back toward the 20th Maine, toward the man with gold braid on his shoulders and a pistol in his hand.

Chamberlain was behind a rock, his face white. His voice was a ragged gasp—he'd been hit somewhere. "Pitcher! Is that flank covered?"

"For now, yes, sir." She held out the pitcher, but could feel there wasn't much left in it.

The colonel looked as if he could hardly believe his eyes. He took a few seconds to drink as a gray-bearded soldier limped over next to him.

"Ammo's dry, Colonel. Up and down the line."

"No relief from New York or Penn?"

"They ain't exactly going to stand up and invite us over."

"Can't retreat or resupply."

The aide shrugged. "That fact hasn't changed all day, good sir."

Miri didn't say a word. This was it. *I'll either receive the annunciation or die.*

A glance over at the ringing swords. Lightning arced down at the combatants, and Séraphine whipped up her saber in a roof-block. The lightning split to either side of her, sending fire up from the dried leaves. She fired her pistol into the face of the enemy, another distraction to keep him from finding her weaknesses.

Séraphine's guardian blazed with a fire that set the trees alight with one hand on Baraqiel's neck. Just as the scent of burning pine joined that of all the black powder, the two entities glistened in a light on par with the sun flashing on metal. Then the light was gone.

The dispelling, Miri thought.

A sudden *click*. Enraging the other paladin had caused him to waste ammunition.

A report—Séraphine had conserved hers.

As he reeled, bleeding, her blade came down on his wrist. Yes, he had chain armor. No, it didn't prevent a break. His weapon dropped from his nerveless hand, and then her pistol had a stationary target. His forehead.

Miri, in awe, watched him fall.

Séraphine, exhausted, sank to one knee. She saluted Miri with the blade. No, not her. Chamberlain.

The colonel didn't celebrate, even for a moment. He addressed his aide. "Fix bayonets."

The old man whistled. "How you figure, sir?"

"They can't have much left in them, either. Send the order down the line. Fix for a charge. The center goes straight at 'em. The far left will swing to envelop. Like a closing door."

Miri saw a body sprawled out on his back near her, some boy with his blond mustache fringing a red hole in his face. She took his rifle and checked it. Empty.

Chamberlain looked at Miri. "Ma'am, I suggest you keep your head down."

In a casual motion, Miri plucked the boy's bayonet from its side mount, slipped the ring over the barrel, and locked it in place.

The colonel opened his mouth. For a second, nothing came out. Then, "How many times have you trained that?"

"Lost count a few months back," she replied. "Sir."

Chamberlain shook his head, but he was grinning. "Guess it's a day for miracles."

A Union bugle sounded, but inexpertly. The standard bugler had probably been hit.

She crouched behind Chamberlain as he drew his sword. Men clutched their rifles. The gray monstrosity was emerging from the tree line below. The time was now.

Another blast of the bugle, and Miri screamed along with the 20th. Down they went, close enough to see the rebels' looks of astonishment. The backpedaling. The aiming of the rifles, the eruption of fire trying to create a thin shield of lead.

Pain flared in Miri's side, like a stitch, but there was nothing to do but the simplest thing she could.

A cannon. A shape in a gunsight. A source of shoes.

Later, she couldn't describe the man in front of her. Tall, wide, armed, skilled?

It didn't matter.

The bayonet went below his arms, into his gut, and she knocked him off his feet. Her weight, barreling down the hill, nearly tore the rifle from her hands.

She'd done it. If there was a time for the hosts to mark her, surely it would be now.

Nothing came.

She gasped for air. It had been slammed out of her as much as him.

Her victim stumbled. She pulled the weapon free and tore her throat with another scream. In went the bayonet again, and out with a great gout of blood and stench.

She whirled to meet a second gray uniform. The reb was dropping his sword. Kneeling. She raised the bayonet.

"*Miriam!*" Was that her name? She didn't turn at the sound. Eyes on the kneeling one.

"They're running! They're running, don't kill your prisoner!" It was Séraphine. Her hand touched Miri, and Miri startled, like a woman suddenly awoken. "You did it. Maine did it, they're retreating."

"Oh." Miri risked a look. Hair and sweat stuck to Séraphine's forehead, but her eyes, gray as hammered pewter, shone with joy. Chamberlain limped along the line, checking his soldiers. He touched his cap when he neared them. As she saluted, Miri realized she'd lost hers.

"Ma'am, that was fine swordplay up there. If I had a regiment of you, I dare say we'd chase Lee all the way back to Richmond."

"Unfortunately, it cannot be taught," the paladin said.

"Then your apprentice has got battle in her blood." He looked at Miri and shook his head. "Let me get an escort here for your gentleman."

Séraphine looked at the punctured man near Miri. "Baptized by fire, Miriam?"

Miri didn't absorb the question at first. She touched her side, and it came away wet. She felt tendrils of pain there, yes, and her breath came ragged from running all day. Sweat slicked her body, and her nose itched from smoke.

She fell to her knees and vomited onto the forest floor, the wracks of her muscles grinding the pain of her wound.

When she could speak again, she asked, "Séraphine, what's it supposed to feel like?"

"The best day of your life."

* * *

Séraphine examined Miri's wound while New Yorkers and Pennsylvanians herded the prisoners away. "Your ribs, they deflected the bullet. If it were an inch further sideways, you'd be breathing bone and blood."

Chamberlain had been right. There was no shortage of wonders. The Mainers had held off four Rebel regiments, two from Alabama and two from Texas. Her cause was righteous.

If not this, what glory will satisfy the heavens? Miri wondered.

Séraphine stripped the enemy paladin of his ammo satchel, unbuckled his weapon belts, and handed the sheathed sword to Miri.

"I shouldn't," Miri said.

"Just hold it; I've enough to carry."

Miri spotted her pitcher and brought it on their long limp back to Cemetery Ridge. They found Jessie at a field hospital, scrambling to keep it stocked with water.

Sickles' corps had been torn in half, and though the Union had held Little Round Top, as locals called it, the price had been high. The cries of the dying and those receiving field amputations were constant. The wind would sometimes shift, changing the smell of ragweed to the stench of death.

Séraphine spoke with some officers while Miri filled her pitcher. When the paladin returned, Miri removed her coat and shirt to let Séraphine wash and dress her wound. She returned the favor as best she could. The paladin's hair was burnt, singeing her scalp.

"Do they reckon on another attack tomorrow?"

Séraphine betrayed no emotion. "Lee may fight, or he may fear failing again. All we can do is fortify the hill. Are you prepared?"

"I think I'm no good for much but cannon water now, and that only if Jessie can help."

"Then I'll find us a place. Perhaps one closer to the ammunition."

Miri nodded. "Good."

Séraphine jogged off to the command tents, somehow still energetic. Miri watched her go, wondering if, after her annunciation, the heavenly host would make her as resilient. Squinting at the sun, she picked up a lost blue cap off the battlefield, wondering if any soldiers would begrudge her this part of the uniform of the Union. None did.

Her eye fell on the dead paladin's sword in its sheath. He'd scratched words into the flat buckle: Tristan Henry Tyrell, 15th Alabama, and below that: 4 Smithfield Road, Birmingham.

A long way on foot, Miri thought.

Did he know Baraqiel's nature? How hard a glance had he given it when it was offering him the power of the lightning and the feeling of righteousness? It was said the Devil could quote Scripture in the service of lies, and she herself didn't know the book well.

Perhaps he'd run from his family to the first person who gave a damn.

Miri pulled the saber a few inches out. It was grooved, like the bayonet had been. She hadn't seen bayonetted men before. Plenty of rifle butts, sabers, shootings. But she… she hadn't hesitated. Yet the heavens were unimpressed.

A cannon. A shape in a gunsight. A source of shoes.

Nausea rose in her, an echo of before.

If not fighting, what am I doing here?

* * *

When the morning came, so did the orders. The 20th Maine was pulling back. Casualties had been too heavy. Pennsylvanian reserves would defend their home state. As the troops passed each other, Miri marveled there were still so many men ready, even eager, to walk past the dying and step foot into the exact same spot. They believed the same wouldn't happen to them.

But then, what was the alternative?

They spotted Jessie driving a wagon, dozens of buckets sloshing in the back, and a youth riding next to her.

"Moving up in the world!" Miri called. "Where you going with all that?"

"Middle of the line. Safest place to be."

"They need more hands there?"

"Don't doubt they do. I saw at least fifty guns. You coming along?"

In answer, Miri swung into step next to her.

Séraphine rode off to find a messenger to inform Chamberlain of their absence. They passed up the long, thin line of troops before arriving at a mass of cannon batteries overlooking the ridge, and a great field of knee-high grasses, yellow from the July heat. Meade's headquarters—the little white farmhouse—was within view.

They'd no sooner joined the cannon crews and started distributing water than Séraphine found them.

She opened her saddlebags. "Eat. Compliments of the 15th Alabama." They had hardtack, same as everywhere, but also cornbread, peaches that might have come from the orchard-turned-battlefield, and, amazingly, coffee beans they brewed with the cannoneers over a fire. A soak of the hardtack in the coffee, and it became warm and palatable.

Cannon fire began, though it was distant. Gobbling their food, Jessie and Miri carried an arm-aching number of buckets. When the wagon's supply had been exhausted, Miri felt as if she'd marched to each regiment's home state personally, and that included the Minnesotans.

She found Séraphine down by a low stone wall, next to a soldier whose field glasses she'd borrowed. "Any storm clouds over there?"

"If I were Lee, I'd consider losing a *chevalier* an important mistake. He may conceal them today." Séraphine's attention never wavered from the tree line in the distance. "They're massing across from us. If you want safety, go far from here."

Miri shrugged. "Can't imagine anyone becomes a paladin by running."

"It's not so simple," Séraphine said quietly. At Miri's look, she elaborated. "When I was a novice in '48, I stood at the Chateau d'Eau with the 14th Line Regiment. When the revolution came, I stepped aside. For that, the *Shekinah* appeared. I thought, 'What devil is this who says I'm a hero? I chose the maddened mob over my brethren in the nobility.'"

"But the people were right, weren't they? That was the test."

"Only in schools does a teacher say, 'Study, then test.' When God tests you, you pass or fail, and only after do you study for answers."

Miri looked at the dust beneath her feet. Pale brown, trod and dried so much, it wasn't even good soil. "Well, at least we're on the right side. Those others... do they even know they're wrong?"

Séraphine took the field glasses back. "They have certainty. It would be a poor bargain without it. To feel purpose, to say 'here walks a paladin, and in his wake is naught but victory'—men will lose their lives for that feeling." She searched the far-off greenery for signs of gray. "Certainty is good. But clarity is better. I think it'll be some time before the attack. Drill with Jessie, and rest if you can."

Miri had barely slept over the last three days, and her whole torso ached—the right side where some muscle was torn, and the left side that had to compensate to keep her standing and hauling water. A little rest was a blessing.

The *thud* of far-off cannons disturbed her sleep. Then, a horrific noise. Sitting up, she searched for the sound, only to see men running toward the farmhouse headquarters. A cannonball had hit a horse. Its scream went on until a rifleman ended its suffering.

"If they were trying for our guns, they sure overshot," Jessie commented.

Miri frowned, once again feeling like an amateur. "If they hit General Meade, I'd call it on target."

A sudden blast from overhead made her flinch. The Union cannons had fired exploding shells yesterday, but being targeted by a Confederate one felt altogether different.

The world devolved into shouted orders, spraying dirt, and—mercifully—a deafening volley of return fire. The comforting line of blue faded into white smoke, its acrid stink eating away at Miri's nostrils.

There were a few seconds when she thought the rebels in the woods might have been scared off.

As if in answer to her fancies, a distant rumbling sounded, and then the world caught fire. Shells hammered the air and earth, and she flattened as fragments came down. Her eyes squeezed shut to keep out the plumes of dust, but there was no escaping the sounds of the screams, the curses, and yes, more horses by the farmhouse that had never seen war before, but had seen their brother die.

"*Pitcher!*"

Miri opened her eyes. Dust rose next to a Vermont cannon crew scrabbling to load their gun. Their bucket had spilled, not from an impact, but from a human trying to find cover and tripping over it. Without water, the cannon wasn't safe to use.

You have to be joking.

Cannonballs thudded against the dirt road. The rebs were inaccurate, but they'd learn the proper range unless given something else to think about.

Miri snatched up her pitcher. The wagon was empty, but she had an idea. Dashing to a second gun, she scooped a little from its supply over the protestations of the crew. Then she ran to the gun in need and righted the bucket. Miri poured the pitcher over the sponge, wrung it by hand into the bucket to avoid waste, and flattened at the *crunch* from the northeast.

There was a hole in the roof of the farmhouse. Bluecoats scrambled out of it like a kicked anthill. A tap on the shoulder reoriented her, and Miri scrambled away from the cannon before a crewman slammed home the pricker. A yank and then the blast, the blast you couldn't get used to. Her ears whined at the punishment.

The thumps of war continued. It was a duel of artillery, a game of nerves. Spot the enemy among the smoke. Swab. Clear. Dry. Wad. Load. Duck. Aim—hastily, but well, or it'd be all for nothing.

Miri didn't know how long it lasted, only that she and Jessie bet their lives on keeping the sponges wet. There were screams of man and horse, and some dud shells, but never did their crews shout *misfire* or see a ramrod accidentally fly at the enemy.

Finally, a hand signal went down the line. The Union guns stopped, one at a time, like the silence was picking them off.

Miri's stomach seized. *Are they giving up?* Meade's headquarters was battered. Could a lucky shell have killed him?

Séraphine rode through the smoke down the line with other commanders. *Load and hold*, they signaled. The sponges plunged; the barrels readied. "*Here they come!*" Séraphine shouted. "*Pick your targets!*"

Miri focused on the tree line, where the orange and blue of the Army of Northern Virginia's flags punctuated the gray masses and the fierce shine of bayonets. They must have stretched a mile across, and to the north, another mile began. Behind both, a second row.

The 20th Maine, when they'd assembled yesterday morning, had numbered in the hundreds. Here, there must have been fifteen thousand, marching deliberately toward the chance to end this war. When they were close, they'd charge.

"Dumb fucks must think we're out of ammo," a cannoneer said. "No way would they march a mile over open ground like that."

Séraphine gave the man a withering stare. "If you would, sir, put a shot into their front line. I want to see what happens."

The aiming specialist cranked the elevation screw to lower the angle of attack, got clear, and the cannon shot a solid round short of the first row, skipping the ball into the line at waist height.

A green flash sparked, and for an instant, Miri saw the arms of some luminous being interposing itself. The cannonball hurtled up into the air as if it were rubber, bouncing free in some child's game. It would have landed in the second row, but two more figures flashed, as if lit by sparks. They protected the lines with an amber glow overhead, like a turtle's shell.

"Guziel," the paladin reported. "Arakiel of the earth. And Kurteel. This will not be easy."

Miri's dread grew. The Virginians drew fire from up and down the line now, and she saw a bevy of flashes, but no gaps in the ranks. "Do you need me? To help kill them?"

"The host, fallen or otherwise, are beyond human weapons." Séraphine's face was grave. Then, seeing the effect on Miri, she warmed. "But as Jacob discovered, angels can be wrestled."

"What are you going to do?"

"I'm being tested," she said. "Don't worry. Everything is clear."

The paladin raised her sword, and the air heated around her. She put spurs to the horse, riding forward down the ridge, across the road. One leap, and they were over the fence to the battlefield.

The Virginians saw her charging at them, and once she was a few hundred yards away, succumbed to the temptation to pick her off. Rifle fire popped, but neither Séraphine nor the horse gave any sign of injury.

The bayonets leveled at her as she galloped toward them. Then she stood in the saddle and slipped one foot out of a stirrup, then the other, to land in the tall, dead grass.

"What's she doing?" Jessie asked.

Miri feared to speak the truth as she saw it.

Séraphine's saber came down through the air, and the shimmer around her revealed the invisible world. The *Shekinah* grasped the fallen angel to its left by its hair. Its second hand grabbed the one to the right by the throat.

Then the marching army was upon Séraphine, and she disappeared into the hole she carved in their ranks. The last angel converged. A clump of soldiers turned. A mounted officer tried to maintain order.

Jessie urged the spotter. "Sir, you better load."

He just watched.

Like the hand of a drowning woman beneath the waves, Séraphine's saber jutted up from the morass, and her angel burned like a tornado of fire. Then, for a moment, all four otherworldly beings vanished, and the front line of the Rebel army was just a confused mob standing in a field.

With no cover.

"That's four hundred yards," the spotter reported. "Load canister."

The ammo officer pulled out a shot that looked like a tin can, rattling it once to check it before they jammed it down the throat of the gun. The can held deadly metal balls that would spray holes in anything standing near the target.

You'll kill her! Miri wanted to scream. With her blessing extinguished, Séraphine was no more than a single woman with a sword amid thousands of enemies.

But for a moment, she'd delayed the charge.

The cannon fired, and Miri's whole body shuddered. She couldn't see the blood from here, only the gap in the line.

A cannon.

The Union riflemen fired in a staccato ripple, as the rebels were within range now.

A shape in a gunsight.

The Virginians had lost discipline, pausing to fire, pausing to reload, but there were so many, they continued to fill the gaps in the line, a line that kept advancing, double-time now, trying to make it across the killing field.

A sudden cry. The wet-sponge swabber jerked, then dropped to his knees. His hand went to his back and came away bloody.

"*Sponge!*"

Miri grabbed the implement from his hands and stuffed it down the barrel. A twist, a yank, and she was out of the way.

The man across from her had the dry sponge. He jammed, swabbed... and his hand went to his hip. "Get down! They're targeting us!"

The pops of rifle fire couldn't be distinguished as friend or foe. Miri crouched, straining to see anyone aiming for her amid the smoke, if it was safe. She saw nothing. Nothing was safe.

Jessie grabbed the rod from the barrel. "*Powder!*" she shouted.

The powder officer was crouching, and he threw the bag to her. Her hands full, it flopped against her chest before she pinned it, and her face blazed with anger. She stuffed it down the barrel, grabbed wadding, and reversed the sponge-stick to drive both home.

"Ammo!" she cried, and looked at her skirts. Miri wasn't sure why until she saw the spreading red from the back of Jessie's thigh.

The ammo officer was on Miri's side and crawled to her. Whatever he thought of Jessie giving orders didn't matter. He knew the drill, and he clung to it like a man climbing a mountain's face. He gathered his courage, stood, and dunked a canister round in before Jessie stuffed it.

Another bullet. Blood sprayed from Jessie's back. Miri looked for the gunner to aim but saw no one. The bodies were piling up, and the gunner might have been one of them, or he might have rabbited.

Jessie sank to her knees and stumbled to Miri's side.

"*Vermont!*" Miri yelled. "*Aim this gun! There ain't enough women here to save you!*"

She locked eyes with a gunner from the cannon next to her.

"Like this!" he yelled, grabbing the elevation screw on his own weapon. Miri twisted it until the gun leveled its barrel at the fence by the road. The charge had gotten held up there, as the rebs had to pick their way over it while Union rifle fire kept pummeling them. Some shot to provide cover, while others picked off cannon crew, still others reloaded, and the ones in front advanced. It was a ragged mess.

The pricker. Miri searched the ground. It was shiny metal, not hard to spot by the bodies in the dust. She scooped it up, slammed it into the vent, and forgot entirely about standing clear of the cannon.

* * *

Miri didn't know how long she'd been out. Her elbow and her chest hurt, and she remembered the metal axle driving one into the other. Her head and neck throbbed—she'd fallen on them—and her sides felt no better.

Still hearing shots, she rolled to her knees and blinked. The fence where she'd aimed was blown to flinders, and the Virginian infantry that had been there…

… no longer stood there.

The Confederates hadn't reached them. Vermont bluebellies surrounded her, swabbing down the cannon, grabbing the tools, readying another round. But they didn't need it. The onrushing wave had washed up to the infantry line, but no farther. Stabbings. Surrenders. The shooting of those who ran.

Miri looked for Jessie. She wasn't here, nor the dead and wounded gun crew.

"Where'd everybody go?"

"Hospital crew came with a wagon. Filled up, though. They're coming back for you."

Miri said nothing, her eyes focused on a bucket ten yards back. It was a spare, kept nearby for refills. She found her pitcher and dipped into it, thinking it wasn't here by chance, but some kind of design.

"You. Miss. Can you help a man with that?" It was one of the new cannon crew, hand bandaged, but standing. Miri settled near him and let him drink.

"*Pitcher!*" came the call, and she responded. Another three men by the guns. A refill of the pitcher. Another two. Then down to the battlefield.

Her steps came quicker. She could reach Séraphine, and nothing would stop her.

Offal overpowered the scent of blood, as canister and shrapnel had shredded the bowels of the bodies. Gray uniforms were stained like butcher paper, the walking wounded and walking dead trying to hobble away from Union soldiers taking prisoners. In the distance, Miri saw a breastplate, reddened and glistening in the afternoon sun.

Séraphine was missing pieces. Her hair was matted with blood and bone. Her broken sword lay in a hand only attached by a thread, and the canister had punctured her breastplate. Her eyes were open and staring, the whites turned crimson from burst vessels.

Miri washed gore stains from her mentor's face before opening her mouth and pouring water in. She hoped for a cough, or perhaps for Séraphine's lips to latch like an infant on its mother. Neither happened. The only woman who thought Miri was worth anything had been reduced to… this.

Pain pricked Miri's eyes, and her nose clogged as her cheeks became wet. *Shekinah*, she thought, *what kind of test was this? I'm no replacement for her.*

She shut Séraphine's eyes.

A wheezing sound made her turn. A thin body in gray lay buried under the mass of another twice his size. Miri pushed the weight off, and a dozen black flies flew up, their investigations disturbed. The larger man was missing half his head.

The formerly pinned one had holes in his guts and sat in grass thick with blood. He opened his mouth, but only a croaking sound came out.

Miri knelt next to him and let him drink.

He didn't even have the strength to wipe his face, having exhausted himself struggling. But he lay back in the grass with fewer lines on his forehead, easing into a rest.

"Can see your mark," he rasped.

Miri tensed, unsure what she had just heard. "Are you... one of the blessed?"

"Figured I was, but you know what they say about God and the heaviest artillery." His eyes narrowed into a squint, from effort or pain, she couldn't tell. "Didn't think your kind would help me any."

"I'd say the same, but maybe I'm supposed to change that."

"Pretty thought." He coughed. "What's a paladin... without a quest?"

His cough got wetter. His head lolled aside. When it didn't straighten, Miri folded his hands on his chest.

You, General Meade had said. *What can you do?*

And everything became clear.

Nothing spoke to her, at least not in words, but her feet took her back to the Union lines and the hospital tents. Marching. Then double-time. Then sprinting. The smell was as bad as that of the battlefield, but here she could shout Jessie's name until she heard a response. Her sister-in-arms lay on a door supported by sawhorses, a barnyard equivalent to a hospital bed.

Miri embraced Jessie, held her normally strong arms. They felt terrifyingly limp.

"I've got you," Miri murmured. She repeated it, hoping Jessie could hear her, because she could barely hear herself. "All you gotta do is live."

Jessie mumbled something.

Miri shook off the haze, placing her ear to Jessie's mouth. "Say that again?"

"I thought you weren't going to ask me anything anymore."

"Before you become a paladin, you're still allowed to lie."

Jessie smiled, but there was bright blood on her teeth. She coughed, and it became a wracking fit. Miri turned her, trying to let her get the fluid out so she could breathe. Then her gaze lit on the pewter pitcher she'd set down. It had a little left in it.

She lifted it to Jessie's lips. Jessie swished and spat out the first sip, no doubt getting rid of the tastes of blood and gunpowder. The second was a long pull to relieve her parched throat. Miri wet her hand and wiped it across Jessie's forehead.

"Did they stop?" Jessie asked. "When we got them?"

"As far as I know, you saved the whole damn army," Miri said. Jessie scowled, unbelieving. "You kept that cannon going…"

A cannon.

She fought off the image. Jessie was more than that. "You were the reason Séraphine was here, you got us safely to the Union lines, and without her charge—"

Jessie's eyes fluttered.

"—aw, hold on, don't leave now. She was the only person who believed in me and you. And you ain't even tasted real freedom yet. You gotta stay!"

She wet her hand again.

You. What can you do?

Miri searched for the exit wounds on Jessie's body, where the bullets had struck bone or irregular meat and leapt off in directions as traumatic as they were random. She found one on Jessie's torso and sprinkled water on it, washing away the blood. Beneath it, the wound washed away as well, the skin whole again.

"What…" Jessie's face scrunched. "Something just happened."

Miri moved down to the thigh wound, dripping the last of her water on it. She brushed the blood with her fingertips, and they came away sticky. Jessie wiped the area with a fold of her skirt, and it was clean. She stood shakily to her feet.

Miri clasped her hand. "I was hoping to hear trumpets or something, but… an answer's an answer."

"You got your 'nunciation thing?" Jessie looked incredulous, but then she gestured at the teeming field hospital. "Not much point in wasting time. Can you save all 'a them?"

"I'm not a prophet," Miri said, "but if you ain't giving up, I don't see how I can."

She took her pitcher and went to work.

It wasn't as simple as the miracles she'd heard of in Scripture. No more wounds closed at a touch. But amid the horrors of surgery and infection, Miri cooled fevers and moistened parched throats. She took the letters they'd pinned to their uniforms and handed them to the couriers to notify their families.

They died, and sometimes they died painfully, but they died *comforted*.

That night, General Meade, having survived the shelling of his headquarters after all, came and watched her labors, saying nothing until it was time to go. Miri saw him make an aside to his officers, but she couldn't make out the words.

It didn't matter, for she knew the essence of what he said. It was the same as the voice she heard, more authoritative than that of generals or presidents, whispering, *There walks a paladin, and in her wake is naught but mercy.*

* * * * *

Chris Hepler Biography

This is Chris Hepler's second story in the *Libri Valoris* series, the first being "The Torturer of Camelot" in *Keen Edge of Valor*. Previously, he created the comic *Mythkillers* and the novel *Civil Blood: The Vampire Rights Case That Changed a Nation*. He has contributed to the universes of *Mass Effect*, *Star Wars: The Old Republic*, *Pirates of the Caribbean*, *Shadowrun*, and *Wayfinder*. His most recent projects are crafting the sequel to *Civil Blood* and surviving the plague of layoffs that has been synonymous with the last year of the video game industry.

Chris has been to Gettysburg twice, but has never wrestled an angel, preferring martial arts that focus on striking.

- Website: https://www.christopherhepler.com
- Twitter: @theotherhepler
- Bluesky: theotherhepler.bsky.social

* * * * *

The Passing of the Mantle
by David R. Birdsall
A Fractured Brotherhood Story

Acrid smoke billowed from the muzzle as the old shooting iron bucked in Unc's hand.

A sharp pain shot through his left shoulder. In the old days, he could've cleared leather and fanned three shots into the fiend before they even managed to grip the butt of their shooting iron, but times and shots had taken a toll on him.

Maybe the creature lying on the ground had once been a man, or maybe it had always been this way. It was impossible to know for sure.

Mantle Bearers like himself were a solitary sort, so knowledge didn't get passed around like it should. At least not now, not since their reputation—and by extension, the order itself—had been ripped asunder.

The creature bucked a few times and pulled Unc from his musings. Looking closer, he could see black liquid soaking into its clothes. One of the pools spread from its chest, and another puddled on the stomach.

The beast hissed at him as he approached. Unc kicked the creature's shooting iron farther from its hand. Standing over the creature, he leveled his antique black powder revolver at the beast's forehead.

Inky black foam frothed from its mouth as it gurgled something in its infernal tongue. It was probably some type of curse, because it punctuated its speech by spitting the filth on Unc's boot. Amazingly, despite the greasy black blood, the beast's fangs seemed pearly white in the moonlight.

"Tell them Unc sent you." He fired one last round through the center of its face.

The body twitched a couple of times before the arms and legs shot out straight. It was nice that the vital areas were the same as humans. He just wished it didn't take some of his own life to end one of theirs.

Unc had made a practice of destroying or hiding the fiends' weapons, just in case. It never ceased to amaze him how icy the beast's firearm felt, even though it had just been fired. He opened the chamber and pulled the rounds. They felt sticky because of the human blood smeared on the bullets.

They took blood from innocents, wove magic with it, and then smeared it on the damage-dealing parts of their weapons. The more life they could pull from the victim, the more damage the weapon caused. Bearers healed faster, were immune to diseases, and their muscles grew denser after taking on the Lord's Mantle, but hemo magic negated all those benefits.

He reached under his waxed canvas jacket and felt the dampness where the creature's shot had hit him. *Only grazed, thank the Lord*, he thought.

Thankfully, Bearers healed very quickly. Still, he needed to stop the bleeding and give it time to heal.

After a quick look around the area, he found some yarrow. He wadded up several handfuls of the medicinal plant, soaked them with water, and pressed the handfuls to his wounded shoulder.

Now to hightail it outta here.

It wouldn't be long before some of the townsfolk followed the gunshots up here, and then there'd be trouble. These creatures had gotten good at manipulating townspeople. They brought convenience to small towns. Before Unc knew it, he'd gone from being the hero dispatching the forces of evil to the bad guy who destroyed what the town saw as their easy meal ticket. They never even realized they were the ones literally being fed on.

Unc hadn't traveled very far through the forest before a vision raced through his mind. That was one of the ways the Lord guided him from one mission to another. They normally came in the way of flashing scenes complete with sights, sounds, and sometimes smells.

The visions always ended with a quiet, peaceful feeling. In those moments, everything in him came to the briefest of rests. They were glorious respites in an otherwise chaotic life—always being driven to an encounter, and then having to fight, and eventually flee to the next.

This vision was of a train rolling through a lonely, dark wood and a small campfire near the tracks with two slowly shifting shadows. Stories and laughter filled the night. The feeling wasn't just of peace, but of coming home.

When the vision ended, Unc felt a single tear roll down his cheek. Having a place to call home was a dream he'd given up on long ago.

The lonesome whistle of a train in the distance pulled him from his treasured moment of peace.

He trudged toward his next task.

*　*　*

"Hello there," Unc called out to the small campfire in the woods. He could see two shadows, one larger and another smaller.

"I'm not here to harm anyone. I was walking the rail and saw your fire," he said. "Is it okay if I share it with you?"

He waited a little bit, but no reply came.

"I don't really want to intrude on any of the activities here. Like I said, I saw the fire and just kind of hoped to take a bit of the chill off, but if you're not too keen on that, I'll just go ahead and carry on."

He heard wracking coughs from the other side of the camp outside the firelight.

A child, coughing something fierce.

A large shadow crossed the firelight and headed in the direction of the coughing. Before Unc realized it, he was rushing toward the child as well.

A girl in her early teens was doubled over, her entire body clenched with every wet cough. When she looked up at Unc, fear and tears filled her eyes, while crimson blood tinged her lips. Blood stained the simple handkerchief clasped in her hands.

An older man, presumably her father, knelt next to her. One arm patted her back, the other hand clutched an old shovel. He looked at Unc with concern and determination in his eyes.

Unc put both hands out in front of him. "I'm not going to hurt anyone. I just want to help."

The father pointed the shovel at Unc. "Stay back for your own good. She's got consumption."

"I've been around consumption before. If I didn't catch it then, I'm not likely to catch it now."

With that, the young lady went into another coughing fit. The father laid the shovel down and cradled his daughter.

Curing consumption was beyond Unc, but he did know something about easing a cough.

"I'll be right back," Unc said, and then moved into the woods.

The surrounding was a mix of evergreens. Pine, cedar, and the goal of his search—eastern hemlock. He cut a few of the newest twigs, careful not to do too much damage to the trees.

After a brief search, he found a small creek. He scooped water up in the old tin coffee can he used as a pot and headed back to the small camp.

The young lady hadn't stopped with her body-wracking coughs.

Unc put the tin coffee can with water on the coals at the edge of the fire. He laid out an old bandana and used the handle of his knife to grind the hemlock into small pieces.

"What are you doing?" the father asked.

"I'm making a medicinal tea," Unc answered. "It can't cure her, but it'll ease the cough."

After the twigs were ground up, he dumped them into the water, which was coming to a boil. While the tea brewed, he set an old tin cup with a broken handle on the flattest rock he could find. Next, he wrapped the bandana over the top of the tin cup. After the boiling water took on a well-tinted appearance, he used an old pair of metal pliers to pick up the coffee tin and poured the tea through the bandana into the broken cup.

"This will help," Unc said, then added apologetically, "I'm sorry, it's hard to handle the cup. It's too hot to hold by hand, and the handle broke a long time ago, but it's all I have."

"I got something." The father retrieved a ceramic mug from a satchel and handed it to Unc.

Unc poured the hot tea into the mug and handed it to the father.

The father gave him a suspicious eye as he took the cup.

"I'm not out here trying to poison the sick, sir."

The father nodded and gingerly coaxed his daughter to take a small drink of the hot liquid. As she sipped the tea, her cough began to lessen. The father wiped the last traces of blood from his daughter's face and lips. She rested against him as she sat holding the cup.

He looked back at Unc. "I appreciate that, sir. There's not a lot of people around who'd show kindness to someone with consumption anymore."

"It's all right. I've been around it a few times. I'm sorry your young one there has to go through it."

"Well, I still appreciate it. My name's Michael Cornwell, and this is my daughter, Mary."

"Pleasure to meet you. I'm Unc."

"Unc?" Mary lifted her eyes from the cup to meet his. "Short for Uncle?"

"That's right."

"How'd you get that name?" Michael asked.

"A long time ago, I worked up north at a school just off the Missouri River. The young ones couldn't say my name, so they started calling me Uncle. If a child calls you Uncle, that does it, you're Uncle evermore. They eventually shortened it to Unc. It just stuck. I'm proud of it, and no one knows me by anything else now."

Mary said, "Thank you, Unc, for the tea. It doesn't taste really good, but it makes me feel better."

"Sometimes, that's what counts," Michael said as he draped one arm over her shoulder.

"I'm glad it worked for you," Unc said.

The three sat for a few moments.

Unc looked around the meager camp. "I couldn't help but notice you all don't have much in the way of food. I got a couple cans of beans you can have." He pulled the last cans of food from his bindle and set them on a rock.

"What if we say we want you to leave?" Michael asked suspiciously.

"That's fine. I was just kind of looking for a little company and a warm fire for the night. But I understand."

Michael nodded toward the food. "You're just going to leave your food here and walk away?"

"Yes, sir. You all need it more than I do. I can find plenty out here in the woods to sustain myself." He nodded over to the small pile of food they'd foraged. "That there's not enough to keep yourself going, much less a growing one. So, you keep the food, and I'll be on my way."

Mary looked up at her Pa, then looked over at Unc, and back at her Pa. She nodded her head. Michael seemed to understand some sort of unspoken language between them.

"It's okay," Michael said, "you can stay."

"If you're sure. I don't want to be imposing on your comfort."

"I think it would be nice to hear a few new stories."

"You can teach me how to make this tea," Mary added.

"Well, I can definitely regale you with a couple of stories," Unc said. "As you could probably tell by the gray in my beard, I've been around a-bit."

The evening passed with easy conversations. Michael explained that they were waiting for the next train to stop at a water refill station a short way down the track. They'd hop the train and head to the next town, where they'd restock their supplies.

In the morning, Unc brewed coffee with the dawn, and some more tea for the small band of travelers. Unc poured the steaming liquids into the family's cups and handed them over, then set his broken tin cup aside to cool.

Mary looked at his and asked, "Why do you set your coffee aside? It'll get cold. Won't that make it bad?"

"I'd love a hot cup of coffee, too, but I broke the handle off my cup a long time ago, and I ain't always so smooth with my pliers in the morning."

She gave a brief nod of understanding before going back to sipping her tea.

That day, Unc gave them some medicinal recipes they could use on their travels and showed them how to find the right plants for them. Then the band spent the daylight hours foraging for wild, edible plants and anything they could use to make their little hobo jungle more like a home.

As the sun set, they fixed a meal from what they'd found. While their little stone soup cooked, the men took turns telling tales, each trying to outdo the other. The winner was whoever got the biggest laugh from Mary.

After they'd eaten, Mary pulled out a ball of yarn no bigger than her two fists and began crocheting. Her nimble little fingers were doing what honestly looked like a little bit of magic to Unc.

At a closer look, he noticed she didn't seem to be concentrating or even really looking at her hands while she worked. She just did it without even appearing to try.

Finally, after she'd completed several rows, and probably half the ball of yarn was used up, she pulled it all loose and started over.

Unc finally had to ask, "Mary, why do you tear your crocheting all apart and do it all over again?"

"My ma taught me how to crochet before she got sick. After the Good Lord took her, and Pa got back, we started on the road. This was all the yarn I had left. If I just used it up, I wouldn't have any more to keep practicing."

"She gets really nervous sometimes," her pa added. "Without the crocheting, she'll tear up the skin around her fingernails until she bleeds something fierce."

"It's all the images and sounds and stuff that runs through my head. I get this urge to just go someplace, and I can't, but the images won't stop. Keeping my hands and mind busy constantly helps keep the thoughts at bay."

All Unc could do was swallow and nod in understanding.

"I was down south working on the oil patch in Corsicana, Texas," Michael said. "There's some good work down there. I was sending money to take care of them, and I hoped to save enough to bring them down with me."

He tossed a small stick into the fire. "Then I got word that her ma had consumption, so I jumped some trains to get back, but I didn't make it in time. Mary was the one who took care of her ma in the last days. Stayed next to her ma even when townsfolk were telling her she needed to stay away."

"I wasn't going to let Ma go through it alone." She went back to crocheting.

"We had to sell off everything we had up there to pay for doctor bills and funeral arrangements. What was left just wasn't enough to get a proper ride back to Corsicana. So, we took what we could carry." Michael nodded toward the ball of yarn. "That's all we could manage."

"I'm sorry you two have to go through this," Unc said.

"Things will be better in Corsicana. I can find work there, and the doctors said the weather there might help Mary's consumption."

Unc reached to drink his now cold coffee.

Mary nodded toward his hand. "Did you burn your hand on your cup?"

"The scar?"

"Sort of a triangle with a circle. That one."

He took a deep breath.

"No, I got it when the Mantle was passed to me."

The father squinted, trying to make out the brand. "What's your real name?"

"Avodah the Mantle Bearer. Taken into service in the year of our Lord 1869."

"I figure if you were looking to hurt us like everyone says you Bearers do, you'd've done it already," Michael stated flatly.

"Thank you."

"You seem to be on the back side of sixty. It's 1895 now. Did you get started late?"

"No, not really. I became a Bearer the day after I graduated primary school. I got this watch as a graduation present." Unc handed a wind-up watch from his coat pocket to Michael, showing an engraved date of 1869.

"You can't be that young," he protested.

"A Bearer needs to put some of his life force into weapons so he can dispatch a fiend. We age every time we kill one of the evil things. Some do it by putting some of their own blood on the weapon, but that's a crude and unskilled method. I use meditation and prayer to put some of my soul into my attacks."

"How do you become a Bearer?" Mary asked.

"God chooses you. The Bearer's Library in Chicago used to keep detailed records of the Bearers—how they took up the Mantle, when they passed it on, who took up the Mantle after them, and a full lineage of the order. Unfortunately, the entire library was lost in the Chicago Fire of 1871."

"I was told the fire was started by some cow kicking over a lamp in a barn," Michael said as he handed the watch back to Unc.

"That's the story, all right. That's not what happened, though. Fiends of all sorts laid siege to the library. When they couldn't break in, they set fire to a nearby barn. They destroyed a lot of Chicago and killed most of the order in those few days."

Unc took another mouthful of his cold coffee and grimaced. "We lost good people, all the information we had on where Bearers were on a mission, the different ways the Mantle is passed on, even the different types of fiends and the best way to defeat them. All gone in one attack."

"That's terrible," Mary said.

"That's not even the worst part. While we were trying to recover, the fiends figured out if they moved into poor areas and offered things people wanted, the people would turn a blind eye to the evil they brought with them. They'd give favors, money, health, or other valuables in exchange for the life force of the victims. Now when we come in and kill the beast, the townsfolk get upset because they see their easy life being taken away. It's hard to fight the good fight when the ones you're trying to save don't want to be saved."

"Are you all trying to rebuild or something?" Michael asked.

Unc pulled out a small, leather-bound journal. "A friend of mine who goes by the name of Cuz is trying. He's set up a camp hidden in the Ozark hills. He's tasked me to make a journal of everything I learn. As other Bearers find him, he's telling them to keep journals of their own. The hope is for these journals to be passed down to new Bearers, and eventually we'll build the knowledge again, but it'll still take generations."

"What's in your journal?" Mary asked.

"How I've dispatched every one of the fiends I've crossed, what types they were, and how I found them." Unc flipped through his journal, pausing briefly on pages. "There's medicinal recipes, how to care for and use my revolver, the process to melt lead and cast bullets, and what it takes to make black powder while on the road when you can't buy it. How the Mantle was passed to me. How to put your life force into a weapon so it's sure to dispatch a fiend. All sorts of useful information."

"Does it show how to get to this Cuz you mentioned?" Michael asked.

"No, that it doesn't. His mountain is a secret between us Bearers and the Good Lord Almighty. We don't want fiends to find him by getting ahold of one of our journals."

"Then how will new Bearers find him?" Mary asked.

"God gives Bearers visions that drive us where we need to go. When Bearers need to find Cuz, God will lead them to him."

"Kind of like a shepherd does."

"Yep," Unc answered as he slid his journal back into his coat pocket, "just like a shepherd."

"How do fiends keep people keen on them if they take some of their life?" she asked.

"Some fiends postpone the actual spending of their victim's life until they use it, just like us Mantle Bearers do. We do it so we can stay alive until we have our final battle. They do it to lull their victims into thinking they haven't lost anything. Nothing immediate happens, so they think everything's fine and keep making deals with the beast. Then one day, the beast spends that life force. If the victim is lucky and has enough life left, they just age and keep going. If they gave over a lot, they fall over dead."

"That's awful," Mary protested.

"Sure is, but Mantle Bearers spend their own life force in the same way. That's why we only use those weapons when necessary, and in as small a quantity as we can get away with."

"Makes sense," Michael said. "How'd you get your mantle?"

Unc tossed the last few drops from his tin cup into the fire, adding a sizzling sound to the night. "I left the day after I graduated to go to the seminary. On the way, I came across an old man fighting the town doctor on the road. I tried to intervene, because I just had this pressing urge to help the stranger."

Mary leaned forward. "A pressing urge?"

"Yep. Can't explain it. Anyway, while trying to break it up, I picked up the stranger's cane and hit the doctor in the face. Black blood sprayed from the wound."

"Black blood?" Michael asked.

"I'd never seen anything like it. Anyway, then the doctor snarled at me with huge fangs I hadn't noticed before. I hit him again, and he fell to the ground. As I turned to the old man, I felt a searing pain in my hand."

Unc showed the scar. "This was burned into my hand. The stranger was dead. I got intense visions telling me to go to Chicago. At first, I tried to ignore them and go on with my life, but eventually, I couldn't resist anymore. That's when I started my duty as a Mantle Bearer."

The silence of the night grew uncomfortable.

Mary went back to crocheting. She asked Pa for a knife to cut the yarn.

"I haven't sharpened my knife in a while, Honey. I don't know if it'll do a clean cut like you want."

"If you want, you can use mine," Unc said. "Be careful, it's sharp."

"Yes, sir."

After cutting the yarn, she held the knife up to show the handle to her father. "Look, Pa, it's got a triangle with a circle in it scratched on it, just like his scar."

"That's nice looking." Michael handed it back to Unc. "You do that yourself?"

"Yep. It's a bit of scrimshaw. I must keep it hidden, now that Bearers have a bad reputation, but before, it was something I could show off."

Again, they were quiet.

"The next train heading south should be here tomorrow," Michael said. "Then it's a day's ride to the little boomtown of Beddington Valley."

"A boomtown?" Unc asked.

"It used to be nothing more than another refill site, a couple of buildings, and a family-run bunkhouse, but in the last year, they've grown." Michael chuckled. "Now they've got a mercantile, telegraph office, stables, and even a saloon with rooms for rent. All that carved into a narrow little valley with nothing but rocky hills on each side."

"Maybe I'll just mosey along with you, if you don't mind. Boomtowns are always interesting."

* * *

Early the next morning, the train stopped to refill its water tank. While it was stopped, the travelers snuck into one of the cargo cars. As they got close to Beddington Valley, Michael shouted, "We can't wait until the train stops!"

"Why?" Unc asked.

"Beddington Valley has a real mean marshal now. He arrests any hobos he finds on the train. More than a few have died in the jail overnight."

"How did you hear about it?" Unc asked.

"A fella I worked with stayed the night at Miss Kitty's Saloon on his way back home. He grew sweet on a girl who worked there, and she told him."

"Did they get married, Pa?" Mary asked.

"When he stopped again to take her back to Corsicana, he found out she'd gotten sick and passed away."

"That seems to happen a lot," Mary said.

"That's not going to happen to you. We're going to make it to Corsicana, and everything will be fine."

"Yes, Pa." Mary took his hand. "We'll be fine."

"A mean marshal in a boomtown," Unc muttered. He took a deep breath and reached out with his soul. The darkness clutched for him in return.

"What did you say?" Michael asked.

"Okay, you all need to remember something. You two can't act like you know me in town. No matter what happens, you can't come near me."

"If that's the way you think it needs to be," Michael said.

"It's to keep you safe," Unc said while holding Mary's eyes with his own. "Do you understand?"

"Yes, sir," Mary replied.

"Thank you." Unc grimaced. "In fact, I don't think it'd be good for all of us to walk into town together."

Michael said, "Surely nothing's going to happen as soon as you walk into town."

"If there's the type of powerful fiend I think is there, it's going to be drawn to me very quickly."

"How do you know there's one there?"

"Because I can feel it drawing me to it from here," Unc explained. "I don't want either of you getting caught in the middle of what I need to do."

"I don't want this to be goodbye." Mary's eyes welled with tears. "I'm always needing to say goodbye. No one ever stays."

"I know, little one," Unc said while crouching so he could look up into her eyes. "I really don't want this to be goodbye, either, but this is something I need to do."

The train whistle signaled its approach to the town. They opened the cargo door and moved to the edge.

"Okay," Michael said as he leaned out the door, "it's almost time to jump. There's a field coming up that's got a little slope away from the tracks and tall grass. It'll cushion our fall."

"Will Mary be able to handle it?" Unc asked.

"Are you kidding?" Michael rolled his eyes with a big smile. "She *loves* it."

Just then, as the field was passing by the open door, she flung herself out, squealing with delight.

All Unc could do was shake his head in disbelief, pick up his bindle, and perform his own leap of faith.

The sun hung low over the trees as the small group of travelers dusted themselves off. "I have to ask you, Mary," Unc said, "why do you get nervous sitting around the campfire, but you've got no fear of throwing yourself from a moving train?"

"I don't know why for sure. When I'm doing something dangerous, my mind gets quiet. All the images and urges go away, and things are peaceful in here." She tapped the side of her head.

"I think I understand," Unc said with a hint of sadness in his voice as he patted her on the shoulder.

Mary gave him a confused look, and then just shrugged. "What now?"

"Beddington Valley is just around that bend." Michael pointed down the tracks. "It's less than a mile from here."

"Don't let it be goodbye," Mary said suddenly while grabbing Unc's hand. "We can skip this town and keep going. We can be a family. You can be my real uncle. We can all go to Corsicana. Right, Pa?" Mary looked over her shoulder to her father with pleading eyes.

"That's fine with me," Michael answered.

"I'm sorry, Little One, but I can't."

"Why not?" Mary cried.

"You know what it's like to have somewhere to go and something to do, but you can't, right?"

"It hurts your brain, bad."

"I have to go through that all the time. The evil will still find me, and that'll put you and your pa in danger, too. Now that wouldn't be the right thing to do, would it?"

"No, I guess not," she replied while wiping the tears from her face.

"I appreciate everything you've done these past couple of days," Michael said.

"I appreciated the company. You showed what having a family was like. I'll always cherish that."

The young girl reached into her little pouch and removed the project she'd been working on and handed it to Unc.

He looked at it closely. It was a long potholder of sorts, the right length and shape of his hand.

"What's this?" Unc asked.

"It's a special holder," she answered, "so you can hold your tin cup with hot coffee in it without burning your hand."

Unc turned the potholder over in his hands. It fit his hand with a loop for his finger and thumb to slide into so it would stay in place as he opened and closed his hand.

"I'm sorry if it's too small," she said apologetically. "I'd have made it bigger, but I only had enough yarn to make that."

"It's the most beautiful thing I've ever been given, but I can't accept this. You need that yarn to keep your hands and mind busy."

"I made it for you," she said with steel in her voice. "You can't give it back. When someone, especially family, makes you a gift, you must take it."

"Family?"

"You're my uncle, which makes me your niece. You can't give it back."

Her father put one hand on her shoulder and looked Unc in the eyes. "It's true. It'd be an insult if a family member doesn't accept a gift from another family member."

"I guess you're right," Unc finally answered, still admiring the gift in his hands.

"Good," Mary said with a smile.

"That means you have to take gifts from me, too." Unc handed his pocketknife to Mary. "Here. It's very sharp, and you need to keep it that way."

"You can't give me this," she protested. "It's too valuable, and you didn't make it for me."

"That's not true. I carved that symbol into the knife. I just didn't know it was for you until now. As you said, a handmade gift given between family members must be accepted, so you take it."

"Pa?" Mary looked up at her father.

"Unc has you there. I think you need to keep it."

"Okay," she answered as she deftly flipped the blade open and closed with one hand.

Unc smiled. "Good. Now remember to keep it hidden. I don't want anything bad to happen to you because of it."

"Yes, sir." She slipped it into a pocket.

Unc stepped to the side with her father and handed him the old wind-up pocket watch. "Take this into town, trade it for the supplies you need, and make sure to get her a full ball of yarn. I can't do what I need to if I don't know she has her crocheting to fall back on."

All he did was nod and shake Unc's hand.

The three stood in silence for a few moments as the sun sank lower, and the shadows lengthened.

"You two had better get going now," Unc said. "You still have time to make it into town before sundown."

"We could spend one more night together," Mary said hopefully.

"Sorry, Little One. We're close enough that whatever lurks there can feel me. It could come looking for me, and I don't want you two around if that happens. I'll need to do a lot of praying tonight to be ready for tomorrow, anyway."

"There's a bunkhouse where railroad workers stay in town," Michael volunteered. "I've stayed there on the trip before. The family that runs it is good people. They'll let us stay the night if we agree to cook and wash the dishes for them."

"That's good. God go with you."

* * *

Unc was tired.

He'd led a hard life, and he felt like it was coming to an end. No new images raced through his mind showing what his next stop would be.

This is the end, he thought. *Good. Time to lay this burden down.*

A fire warmed him in the brisk night air. He'd made no attempt to hide the fire from sight. It was better to have the showdown out here, away from Mary and her pa.

Smiling, he wrapped the cup holder around his battered tin cup full of hot coffee. It couldn't have fit his hand any better. That little girl truly had blessed eyes and hands. *Such a nice, simple pleasure.*

The evil in the town felt like something pulling on his skin toward the source. Another Mantle Bearer had said the moon pulls on the ocean, causing the tides, and that's how it felt now. This evil could wait a little longer.

Besides, hot coffee, the clear sky full of stars, and the time with Mary and Michael are my reward. I get to cherish them for longer than I deserve. Tomorrow'll sort itself out, anyway.

* * *

He wasn't sure whether he ever actually fell asleep or not. He broke camp and gathered his bindle together. The last thing he did was load the last of his blessed bullets into his antique revolver.

Beddington Valley seemed like a happy town, a prosperous town. All the buildings looked to be in good repair. Storekeepers swept boardwalks in front of their stores. People waved and talked to each other as they passed.

Unfortunately, the town was in the middle of the foothills. There were no signs as to why it should be prospering. No industry, no farms, no logging, nothing. Miss Kitty's Saloon and Kitty's This That and the Other Thing, the general mercantile, sat near the railroad tracks. Clever names meant there was a clever creature involved, and he guessed it was Miss Kitty herself.

The pull on his skin nearly dragged him down the center of the main road. He expected it to lead him into either the saloon or the store, but instead, it led him toward the end of town near the stables.

As he passed the mercantile, he caught movement out of the corner of his eye. On the boardwalk stood Mary, with her pa standing behind her, one hand resting on her shoulder protectively. Both had genuine smiles on their faces, and in the girl's hand was a full roll of the prettiest blue yarn.

The girl started to pull away from her pa, but Unc shook his head no, and made a shooing motion with his hand. She looked at her pa with confusion, then back to him.

Michael placed both hands on her shoulders and pulled her close to him.

Unc had made it about halfway down the street toward the stables when he heard the thundering of hooves roaring into town. His skin nearly pulled from his body in that direction.

Two riders galloped up. A man and a woman swung off their mounts, and despite their casual demeanor, they were obviously looking for something.

The man was dressed in jeans, a white shirt, and a short buckskin riding jacket. A pearl-handled revolver hung low in a gun belt at his side. The woman wore a short crimson satin skirt with a ruffled petticoat peeping out underneath. Light from the streetlamps danced off the sequins sewn on the matching bodice.

To Unc's surprise, the woman slid a shortened lever-action rifle from a saddle scabbard smoothly. She spun the lever action weapon deftly, chambering a round before stepping away from her mount. Its shortened barrel and sawed-off buttstock made it easier to conceal and fire quickly in small areas while still packing a lot of deadly lead.

This situation had just gotten a lot more complicated. It was always preferred to only harm the beast and spare any bystanders.

While the Mantle's gift told of the presence of evil, it didn't single the actual evil out.

They could both be beasts. It was unlikely, but not unheard of. Most times a beast had an ego bigger than Texas, and they didn't get along with each other routinely. When they managed it, though, things went bad in big ways.

The two moved cautiously down the street toward him. They still seemed to be uncertain of the exact danger. It probably felt like a predator was stalking them from some unseen place.

Some of the town's folks picked up on the tension building and moved into the buildings.

The man left his gun in the holster, but had his hand looped in the belt near it. His eyes scanned the faces of the people on the boardwalks, streets, and even in the windows.

The woman, on the other hand, had her weapon at the ready. Her eyes never fixed on the faces of the people until they fell on Unc's. When her eyes locked with Unc's, the corner of her crimson-red lips twisted in a smirk.

So she's the beast.

Unc cleared leather, thumbing the hammer back in one smooth motion and firing. Before the thick smoke blew away in the breeze, he'd instinctually fanned the hammer back with his now free hand and fired four more times.

He paused, holding his breath, waiting for the smoke to clear. The couple stood less than twenty paces away.

Somehow, the man had ended up in front of the beast. His pearl-handled revolver still hung in its holster. Her arm was wrapped around his neck, holding him up as a shield.

She released her consort, and he flopped unceremoniously to the ground. Unc lost control of his discipline and allowed his eyes to follow the body as it toppled to the ground.

Artificial thunder rolled through the town. A trickle of smoke rose from her shortened rifle.

Unc felt his knees fold under him. He started to raise the old revolver.

In a flash, she was in front of him, and kicked the antique weapon from his stiffening hand playfully. She grabbed his face by the jaw and sneered in his face, "Who sent for you?"

Unc tried to speak, but no air entered his lungs. He wadded his old shirt up and pushed it into the bullet hole. This time a little more air entered his starving lungs.

She screamed, "Who?" She released his jaw from her grasp and backhanded him. Her small, delicate-looking hand struck with the force of a steel ball peen hammer.

Blood and teeth erupted from his mouth, and he fell to the ground. He heard her yelling something to the groups of people scattered around the boardwalks that lined the street. He lifted his eyes, and for the first time, he saw a group of people huddled around an old man lying on the boardwalk across from him. The man was finely dressed in new clothes, but his hair and beard were shaggy and unkempt. An old woman knelt next to him, crying, and shook him, apparently trying to get him to respond.

With one arm, Kitty hoisted Unc from the ground.

"Who called him?" she screeched to the onlookers. "This is my town now, and one of you thought this old piece of trash—" she shook him like a rat in a terrier's jaws "—could just walk into my town and kill me?"

With that, she tossed Unc with little effort toward where the young girl and her pa stood.

Kitty slowly turned in a circle, with arms outstretched, her gun hanging clipped by the scabbard ring from a sling that crossed her body from shoulder to hip. "I brought money to this God-forsaken little hole in the wall. You finally got a saloon with real booze instead of that rot-gut persimmon wine you all brewed. So what if your daughters must work for me to service the railroad workers and businessmen I bring through. You've got a store, and I see to it that it's always got whatever you want. Who cares that you have to pay with your life force? It's not like *you're* doing anything with it."

Through his blurry eyes, he could see the townsfolk scratching their heads sheepishly and looking at the ground. His head turned to where Mary was. Her pa held tight to her arm as she pulled hard against him, trying to get to Unc.

It was all Unc could do to shake his head no.

The young girl's actions must have caught Kitty's attention, because she laughed. "Awww, isn't that sweet. Let her go to him."

He prayed, *Please, God, don't let her go.*

"I said let her go!" Kitty shrilled.

Startled, Michael let go, and she rushed to Unc's side. As she fell to her knees, dust from the street billowed around her, sending her into a coughing fit. Blood streaked her lips, mingled with her saliva, and slipped from her mouth in small droplets onto Unc's prone form. Self-conscious, she tried in vain to wipe them from him with her hand before clasping his bloody hand.

Kitty sauntered over to the other side of Unc and squatted down across from the girl. "Is this your grandpa?"

The girl shook her head. "He's... my friend," she got out between the coughs that wracked her body.

Kitty lifted the young girl's head with her hand so she could see her face fully. Kitty dragged one thumb slowly over the girl's bloody lips, and across one cheek, leaving a crimson smear. "Really?"

The girl stared into Kitty's cold blue eyes defiantly. "Yes."

"I don't think so," Kitty replied and then licked the blood from her thumb.

Kitty stood in a flash and stepped over Unc, grasped the girl by her arms, and spun her around in a circle, displaying her and her dirty, blood-speckled dress and face to the surrounding crowd.

The crowd instinctually stepped back, knowing the signs of consumption. Some crossed themselves, while others pulled their fascinated children back from the scene.

"See," Kitty hissed, "sick people like you don't have friends. They'll never accept you. Even him."

She punctuated the statement by kicking Unc in the side. "You'll die horribly and alone."

Unc tried to gasp in pain, but his lungs wouldn't fill. He rolled over. As he did, he ended up on something hard.

The attack dislodged his hand and the wadded-up shirt he was holding against the hole in his diaphragm. Struggling, he tried to bundle some of the shirt back up to try and plug the hole. In the process, his fingers brushed against hard, smooth steel.

Kitty set Mary back on the ground, and then sank to her own knees in front of the girl. She leaned in and purred, "But I'll be your friend."

She brushed Mary's hair back from her face and let her hand rest on her cheek. "I can cure you. All you must do is ask. In return, you agree to stay with me. You'll live a healthy life, free from disease. From time to time, I'll take a little of your blood—far less than you were just coughing up—and a little of your life."

Need a clear shot, Unc thought.

Mary quickly looked over to where the fine-dressed older man now lay motionless on the boardwalk, his new widow weeping across his corpse.

"Oh, come now—" Kitty chuckled "—it'll just be a little of your life. You'll still live far longer than you will with consumption, and you'll be disease-free for all of it."

Mary looked back up at Kitty. "No."

Kitty snarled, wrapped her arm around the girl's waist, and hoisted her into the air in front of her like a shield. Then she strode toward Unc. "Whether you like it or not," Kitty screamed, "you're going to help me!"

Lord, give me that shot, he prayed.

Kitty halted right over Unc's body. Still holding the young girl in one arm, Kitty unclipped the lever-action weapon from its sling with her free hand, spun it in the air to make sure a round was chambered, and pointed it at Unc's head.

"I tire of this game, Mantle Bearer," Kitty sneered. "Your time is over."

Before Kitty could pull the trigger, the girl drew the folding pocketknife from inside her dress. Her small hands that had built up so much strength and dexterity from years of crocheting deftly flipped the blade open and slashed the wrist of Kitty's gun hand. The blade might have been small, but it was enough to cut clear to the bone of Kitty's wrist, severing the tendons and causing the fiend's hand to open and drop the gun.

Kitty threw the girl to the side, reaching for her injured hand.

Thank you, Lord.

Unc rolled back over toward the commotion, his old .32-caliber friend gripped in his hand. The shaved blade of the front sight was clearly nestled in the shallow vee machined into the top strap of the firearm. Beyond the blade was the side profile of Kitty's head. Time slowed down, giving him an instant to savor his final hunt.

The gun danced one last time in his hand, and smoke bellowed from it.

He rolled onto his back. The gun fell from his hand at his side. Pain wracked his body as he struggled to hold the shirt on the wound to his stomach so he could breathe while the pain in his chest increased.

He was ready to slip into the darkness when a scream of pain jerked him back from the brink.

Struggling, he turned toward Miss Kitty, but her body lay still on the dirt road.

Well, that's no surprise, I suppose, he thought.

He turned toward Mary, who'd somehow made it to his side, and his fears were confirmed.

She clutched her bloody hand, a confused look on her face. When she opened it, he saw the unmistakable symbol of a Mantle Bearer burned into her palm. The small pocketknife lay in the dirt in front of her. Mary's red blood and the fiend's inky blood on the blade were mixed across the etched symbol on the handle.

Unc pulled the journal from his coat pocket and, trembling, handed it to Mary. "I'm sorry," he whispered.

* * * * *

David R. Birdsall Biography

David R. Birdsall has always made his way in the world using his hands and his mind. His passion is in learning about the people often overlooked by society across history. With a formal education that ranges from Human Services to building maintenance, he's used every opportunity to experience everything life has offered him.

Now with the support of his family, he uses those skills and experiences to craft fictional stories that showcase the common person and their triumphs over adversity. His stories are available to the public through the fine publishers of New Mythology Press, Raconteur Press, Saddlebag Dispatches, Dragon Soul Press, and Amazon.

Currently, he lives in central Missouri with his wife of more than 25 years, a daughter, three dogs, and three cats.

* * * * *

The Purloined Heart
by Christopher G. Nuttall
A Schooled in Magic Story

I knew she was trouble the moment I saw her walk into the bar.

She was tall, with long, red hair tied neatly back in a ponytail, wearing leathers cut to reveal her curves without interfering with her movements. Her short-sleeved shirt exposed a hint of cleavage and two tanned and muscular arms, one carrying the scars of an adventurer's life. A sword hung from her belt, an expensive pistol resting right beside it.

She looked around the bar, saw me, and walked toward me with the air of someone who wouldn't be denied. A drunkard grabbed her arse, and she punched him out without even looking at him. I guessed she had knuckledusters under her gloves. Or magic.

I studied her thoughtfully as she sat down facing me, her eyes studying me with equal interest. There was a tiny hint of magic surrounding her, far less than I'd have expected from a female adventurer. They tended to have magic of their own, or paid a sorcerer to layer protection spells over their bodies, or their adventures would come to a short, sharp, and humiliating end when they encountered a rogue magician. The basilisk scales woven into her leathers would give her a certain degree of protection, true, but any capable magician could easily work around them to swat her like a fly. Or turn her into one.

Her voice was calm and focused. "Quinn?"

I looked back at her. "Who wants to know?"

"My name is Starlight," she said, "and I want to hire you."

I raised my eyebrows. "Starlight" sounded silly, the type of *nom de guerre* an innocent or inexperienced child would adopt before having the naiveté knocked out of them. I'd have laughed, except she didn't *move* like an inexperienced kid. The way she held herself, her awareness of everything around her, spoke of a person with as much experience as me, perhaps more. It was hard to place her origins, but I'd have bet good money she was noble-born, perhaps on the wrong side of the blanket. That would certainly explain how she had enough money to go adventuring, and the freedom to do so.

"I see." I cast a privacy ward. The rest of the customers turned their attention back to their drinks and stopped pretending they weren't trying to listen to us. "What can I do for you?"

Starlight eyed my drink, then shrugged. I passed the glass to her. I don't know what the bar put in its alcohol, but I had a sneaking suspicion they should've poured it back in the horse. If there was another bar in town that served magicians, I'd have been drinking there, but magic and alcohol rarely mix. A drunk magician is a danger to himself and everyone within a mile or two.

"I've been hired to rescue a kidnapped girl," she said. "I need your help."

"And why do you need me?"

"The girl was kidnapped by Lord Dragon," Starlight said. She looked down at the table just long enough for me to notice. "I need a magician to help me rescue her."

My eyes narrowed. I've never met Lord Dragon personally, but I knew him by reputation. Most independent sorcerers adopted a nom de guerre of their own—they were just as bad as mercenaries and adventurers when it came to renaming themselves—yet their names were often talismans. A man who called himself Lord Dragon was almost certainly a pretentious git, a complete idiot, or a dangerously unhinged maniac. The fact that he was still alive after taking over a tiny lordship for himself suggested very strongly he was the latter.

The stories about him didn't make the prospect of *facing* him any more attractive. He lived on the fringes of magical society, doing things most magicians would shun him for doing, and his isolation from his own people made him all the more dangerous to anyone who crossed him. If the stories were true, Starlight was asking me to take a horrendous risk.

"I was offered five hundred crowns for the girl's safe recovery," Starlight said quietly. "I'll split it with you if we rescue her."

"Five hundred crowns?" I stared at her. "Are you sure?"

She nodded. I was astonished. That was enough money to buy a house, or the magical education I'd been denied since my expulsion from school.

My mind raced. If someone was willing to pay that much, the girl couldn't be a commoner. An aristocrat's daughter? I felt a stab of pity. Lord Dragon was reputed to be a slaver, crafting slave collars to keep his victims in helpless bondage for the rest of their lives.

I suppose that explained why the girl's father had hired Starlight, rather than asking for help from a magical ally. If word got out that the girl has been held prisoner by a slaver, even briefly, she'd be unlikely to make a good match. She might never marry well. Or at all.

I considered it, unwilling to admit to myself I'd already made up my mind. On one hand, trying to break into a magician's home was a good way to get killed, or worse. On the other, two hundred and fifty crowns would go a very long way. I had some money stashed away in a safe place, but the life of an adventurer doesn't offer many chances to save. And in truth, I didn't want to leave a young girl in a slaver's hands. The magical community shunned enslavers. It was just a shame they couldn't be bothered to actually do anything about them.

"Very well," I said after some haggling. "I'll do it for half the reward money."

Starlight looked relieved. I guess she'd been having trouble finding a magician to accompany her. It wouldn't be easy to find a magician willing to burgle another magician, and most of those magicians would be reluctant to risk challenging a dark wizard on his home turf. I hope she wasn't planning to try to cheat me of my reward, if I did as she wished and helped her save the girl. It would be the last thing she ever did, if so. She had so few protections against magic, I could strike her down with a wave of my hand.

"We need to move quickly," she said. "When can you leave?"

"This place?" I stood, brushing down my tunic and trousers, and picking up my knapsack. I carried everything I owned with me. Travelling light was a lesson I'd learnt the hard way. "Now, if you want."

Starlight smiled, then stood and led the way outside. I had to admire her movements as she walked. They spoke of very real experience; experience gained the hard way. She was attractive, no doubt about it, but she was attractive and alluring as a tiger. I knew better than to try my luck, not with someone like her. I'd already seen how she handled unwanted male attention.

"I have a horse," Starlight said. "You can ride behind me?"

I nodded. I knew how to ride, of course, but I've never been particularly fond of horses, and I'd never bothered to purchase one for myself. If I needed to ride somewhere in a hurry, I'd rent a horse or simply travel by stagecoach.

Starlight, by contrast, looked like the kind of aristocratic girl who'd have grown up surrounded by horses, and who'd been put in the saddle almost as soon she could walk. I'd often thought those girls silly, but they did have their uses. A girl who'd consider washing dishes to be beneath her would have no qualms about mucking out a stable.

Starlight's mount was a small warhorse, another sign she came from serious money. The beast eyed me sardonically, but made no objection as I scrambled up behind her. Starlight reined the horse out of the stable and onto the road, the beast picking up speed as we cantered north. I carefully kept my hands to myself, mentally considering what I'd need to break into a magician's house. I hoped to hell the girl hadn't been enslaved already, even if she hadn't been sold on to her final buyer. A slave collar could be removed, but the former slave would never be quite the same afterward.

"You never said," I said. "Who is she?"

"Lady Carolina Lacy," Starlight said. "A daughter of Lord Lacy of Alluvia. Under the circumstances, her father has very limited choices."

"And far too many enemies who'd pay good money for his enslaved daughter," I said, trying not to shudder. "If it becomes public that she was enslaved…"

I scowled. It was worse than that. The Alluvian Revolution had shattered the established order, slaughtering most of the aristocrats and sending the remainder running for their lives. A handful had been smart enough to send their children and disposable wealth out of the country, and Carolina's father might have been one of them, but even if he'd saved *some* money, he wouldn't have the resources to hire more than a handful of adventurers to rescue his daughter. If word got out, it would be impossible to marry her to a foreign nobleman who might use his influence to assist her family.

Probably. One could overlook anything if the dowry was high enough, but Lord Lacy probably didn't have enough money to convince someone to overlook *that*.

Poor girl.

We rode for hours, found an inn to spend the night, and then travelled onward. Starlight was a good conversationalist, I discovered, although she was reluctant to talk about herself. I'd have admired that in her if it didn't make it harder to understand why she'd chosen the adventurer's life. She was young and pretty, and clearly of good family; she could've been almost anything, and yet she'd chosen to be an adventurer. I supposed I couldn't really hold it against her. I'd never been keen on talking about myself, either. Far too many people assumed I'd been expelled for being a dark wizard, not being scapegoated for another student's behavior.

"This town is the nearest one to Lord Dragon's territory," Starlight said as we looked for another inn. "Do you need anything?"

"I should have everything I need here," I said, tapping my bag. "If we need specialist tools, we can come back and purchase them."

That wasn't a pleasant thought. Lord Dragon had had plenty of time to fortify his territory against intruders. The simple fact that the aristocrat who owned the land hadn't managed to evict him was clear proof his territory was well defended, or—I supposed—that Lord Dragon had an agreement with his overlord. It was rare for a magician to pledge himself to a feudal superior, but Lord Dragon had already discarded so many customs, I couldn't imagine him being reluctant to discard one more. He was a slaver, after all. I could easily imagine him trading a handful of spell-controlled slaves for territory and freedom.

We spent the night in the inn, then set off on foot the following morning. The landscape was rough and patchy, dominated by tiny farms run by peasants eking a living from the soil, but it grew wilder as we made our way toward his territory. There were fewer and fewer peasants living close to the magician—a bad sign. The road was surprisingly decent, for a place so far off the beaten track, but the trees grew so thick, it was hard to see a path through them.

I spotted the beggar's mark on a stone at the edge of the territory, and frowned. The mark was a clear warning—to those with the eyes to see—not to cross the line. I guessed something bad had happened to the first beggar to visit the magician, and the others had taken heed.

"We need to get off the road," I said. Any magician worthy of the name would have dozens of spells woven into the road to sound the alarm when unwanted guests entered his territory. "Stay with me."

Starlight snorted. "What do you think I was planning to do?"

I smiled—I'd had a few partners who'd gotten themselves into trouble by wandering off—and led the way into the thicket. It was difficult to pick a path through the trees. They were so close together, I had no idea how they survived.

I stopped as I sensed a flicker of magic ahead, and reached out with my senses, parsing out the first set of traps. Lord Dragon wasn't taking anything for granted. There were dozens—no, hundreds of spells littering the landscape, from simple repulsion spells and nightmare hexes to change and paralysis curses, the latter designed to inflict as much pain and agony as possible.

I had no idea how he powered them all. Constantly replenishing the spells would be an utter nightmare, even for an entire team of magicians, and it should've been impossible. The area wasn't known for being tainted with wild magic, and only a fool would risk trying to use wild magic to power regular spells. There were easier and less painful ways to commit suicide.

We inched forward, careful not to touch any of the spells. Some were relatively harmless, even to a powerless mundane; others would've killed me as easily as they'd have killed her or any wanderer who took a wrong turning and found himself walking blind into a magician's territory. I could feel a web of magic flickering through the trees, powering the charms—

A nasty thought crossed my mind, and I pressed my ear against the nearest tree, looking back in shock as I heard a psychic scream. Horror washed through me as I realized what Lord Dragon had done. He'd turned every intruder who'd entered his territory into a tree, their life force and magical potential channeled into the defenses. I'd seen some horrors in my time—man's inhumanity to man was always shocking—but this... Lord Dragon might not be a necromancer, but he was still a monster. I shuddered to think how many people had been sacrificed to power his defenses.

"I think we're nearing the house," Starlight said. She'd been so quiet that her voice almost made me jump. "Can you get inside?"

"We'll see when we get there," I said.

So far, I hadn't seen much to impress me. Lord Dragon had a surfeit of power, but he didn't seem to be using it very imaginatively.

I could think of several ways to improve his defenses, to make it impossible for anyone to get inside without sounding an alarm. Our path through the deadly network of traps was a winding one, but so far, we'd avoided triggering any alarms or being turned into frogs. Or trees. The forest came to a dead stop, revealing a mansion hidden within the trees. It was smaller than I'd expected, although that was meaningless when magic was involved. Whitehall was far bigger on the inside, and I'd seen other magical buildings that were very similar. Lord Dragon certainly had enough power to craft a pocket dimension and keep it from collapsing indefinitely.

I peered forward, looking for possible traps or watching eyes.

There were none.

The lawn was overgrown, and the flowerbeds crammed with herbal ingredients. I couldn't help thinking no one was bothering to take care of the gardens.

That puzzled me as I inched forward, carefully probing the mansion's defenses. There was a cluster of heavy spells around the back door, and I guessed there were more around the main entrance, but far fewer around the windows. I glanced at her—she looked pale, yet determined—and darted forward, crossing the lawn and inching up to the wall.

The charms around the window were nasty, yet weirdly independent, as if the designer had never seen the need to weave them into a single pattern. I touched the wood gingerly, carefully channeling my magic into the window frame.

"Odd," I muttered. Lord Dragon *knew* wood channeled magic. He'd set up a defense network that relied on wood to channel power from his victims into his spells. I couldn't help wondering if I was being tricked, lured into a trap. It was a very strange oversight. There was a reason most magical households were built of stone. "What in the world is he doing?"

"Hurry," Starlight hissed. "We don't have much time."

I nodded curtly, although I refused to risk speeding up. It would've been impossible to try this if he'd woven the spells together, and it was quite possible he had an inner network monitoring the outer spells. It would be astonishingly paranoid, but even paranoids had enemies.

If he'd kidnapped an aristocratic girl, I was entirely sure he'd taken girls from the neighborhood first. It wasn't as if the local gentry would've cared as long as he left their children alone. No one would pick a fight with a sorcerer over a commoner.

I shoved the thought out of my mind as I worked my way through the network, disabling his spells one by one. There was no alarm. I built my spells up carefully, then opened the window and scrambled inside. The air was heavy with magic, pressing down on my senses and making it hard for me to feel anything beyond a few meters, but there was no alarm. Starlight followed me into the room, one hand on her sword. She'd have been better off with the gun. She didn't seem to be a blademaster, and it was rare for a magician to be killed by a swordsman.

"Be careful where you put your hands," I said. "Don't touch anything unless I check it first."

Starlight nodded, keeping her hands to herself.

Lord Dragon appeared to have scattered traps everywhere, even within his own home. There was no shortage of cautionary tales of magicians who'd accidentally killed themselves after booby-trapping their own house, but our unwitting host didn't appear to have heard any of the stories. I wondered, idly, who'd taught him. There were more efficient ways to defend his territory than scattering hexes seemingly at random.

I sent a handful of recon spells moving through the door and into the corridor beyond and waited to see the results. The corridor appeared to be empty, although the spells couldn't reach very far beyond the door. I opened it carefully and peered into the corridor.

Portraits lined it, the eyes charmed to follow us as we walked out of the room. They didn't seem to be linked to any defensive spells, but it was hard to tell. There was so much magic in the air that it was growing increasingly hard to pick out Lord Dragon's charms. He had to be damaging his own spells.

I shivered, my earlier thoughts mocking me. Perhaps he was a necromancer after all. If he'd found a way to make necromancy practical...

Something moved ahead of me. A door opened, and a serving girl—naked, save for the collar around her neck—stepped into the corridor. I stared, distracted for a few vital seconds.

I was torn between astonishment at her perfect body, her nakedness drawing my eye, and horror at the spells woven into the collar. Looking at them was like looking at something fundamentally wrong, something so horrific, it shouldn't exist. I'd seen the aftermath of mercenary raids, or the twisted remnants of people who wandered into wild magic regions and came out *changed*, but this...

The girl raised her eyes, saw me, and screamed. And charged.

I swore and cast a freeze spell. The slave collar was designed for a single purpose. The wearer would follow instructions given to her by her master, including standing orders to attack intruders on sight.

Her eyes were wide with horror even as she stopped in her tracks. I could sense the slave collar struggling against my spell, pushing her to keep fighting even though she was hopelessly frozen. She had no magic of her own, no way to free herself.

I leaned forward, trying to find a way to remove the collar. I'd never made a slave collar myself, but I knew enough to be wary. The slaver might well have keyed the collar to kill the wearer if someone tried to free the slave without the owner's consent.

Starlight hit me.

I jerked forward, twisting automatically, since she'd hit my shoulder.

I turned and saw her staggering toward me, her fist swinging at my jaw. She wasn't moving like herself. She moved as if she were drunk—or as if she were being puppeted by an outside force.

I swallowed hard as I realized she was no longer in control of her own body. Her face was a rictus of pain and regret, and something else, as if the force controlling her was not wholly used to manipulating her body.

She took another swing at me, telegraphing her move so openly, I had no trouble dodging it.

My magic sparked, casting a spell to stop her. The magic flickered and died before it even touched her bare skin. I gritted my teeth and punched her in the nose. Blood stained my hand, but she kept coming. I guessed whoever was in control of her had made sure he wouldn't feel her pain.

Starlight drew her sword and hacked at me. I turned and ran, moving down the corridor as fast as I could. I was completely confused. I hadn't sensed any spell capable of taking her over so completely, so quickly, yet she was clearly not in control of herself.

I could hear her chasing me, the magic in the air making it difficult to cast a spell to slow her down. A dozen options ran through my head, all certain to work, but at the cost of hurting or even killing her outright. I wasn't sure what to do. If she wasn't in control of herself...

I glanced back and saw her face, twisted unnaturally. *What the hell happened to her?*

I shaped a spell—the most powerful cancellation spell I knew. It would disrupt, if not destroy, every spell within reach—including the one controlling her. There'd be no hope of hiding our presence if a sizeable chunk of Lord Dragon's spells vanished in a single catastrophic moment, but I suspected our presence was no longer secret, anyway. The serving girl had screamed, and something had overwhelmed Starlight.

I grabbed all the power I could muster, channeled it into the spell, and—

Something wrapped around my ankles and yanked hard. I fell to the ground, the magic dissipating as I landed badly. I could feel something slithering over my body and realized, to my horror, that wooden vines were growing out of the floorboards. They grabbed my hands, pulling them behind my back and wrapping around my wrists to keep me immobile.

I heard a grunt and looked up. A middle-aged man was looking back at me. I knew without a shadow of doubt that it was Lord Dragon.

"I wouldn't try to cancel any spells," he said in an oily tone that made me want to hit him. He spoke like a man so assured of his own superiority that he could play with his captives all day. "I've got your friend's heart."

I stared at him. Lord Dragon was surprisingly fat—unusual in a magician—with greasy black hair, a fleshy face, and beady dark eyes.

He wore a purple toga long enough to cover everything below the neckline. A single jewel hung around this neck, glowing with magical power. His fingers rested on the gem as he stared down at me, magic glittering around his fingertips. Up close, I could see threads of magic linking the gem to Starlight.

I glanced at her and shuddered. She was standing there helplessly, slumped over like a man-sized puppet whose strings had been cut. I swallowed hard as it dawned on me what had happened to her. Lord Dragon had warped his power into her heart, taking her so completely that he could do anything to her. I didn't know if I'd ever met the real Starlight. The person I'd met might be—

No. That couldn't be true. Starlight had presented herself as an experienced adventurer, and I didn't think that could be faked. She'd been real, and yet… she'd also been under his control. How much of the story she'd given me had been true? She hadn't come across as a liar, yet most unsuccessful liars tended to be killed very quickly. I wondered, suddenly, if she'd been sent to bring a new victim to her master or… or what?

Lord Dragon kept speaking, prattling on like a man impressed by the sound of his own voice. I knew the type. It wasn't enough to be rich or powerful, handsome or strong; they wanted to gloat, to make sure you knew you were screwed, and how badly you were screwed. I'd met mercenary captains who were happy to boast about the number of towns they'd sacked, or women they'd taken.

Perversely, it was almost a good sign. A man who wanted to gloat was almost always insecure, wanting to hide his lack of confidence under a show of strength. I reminded myself not to take it for granted. Lord Dragon had enough power to be extremely dangerous.

"She thought she could best me," Lord Dragon said. He walked up to Starlight and grabbed her breast. Hard. She made no visible response, but I'd have bet half my fortune she felt it. "Churlishness like that deserves a special punishment, don't you think?"

I kept my voice even. If he wanted to talk, I had no intention of stopping him. "What did you do to her heart?"

"I took it out of her and placed it in this gem," Lord Dragon said. "She's mine now."

I forced myself to think. There were a handful of sorcerers who'd removed their hearts and hidden them somewhere on the theory it would grant a kind of immortality, but it never ended well. A single cancellation spell could break the link, killing the sorcerer instantly. I've known a few sorcerers who were heartless—metaphorically speaking—but none would actually survive losing their heart. It could easily happen by accident. A sorcerer who walked into the wrong household might discover the connecting charm coming apart, sentencing him to death. If Lord Dragon had done that to Starlight...

My mind raced. He could hold that over her head for the rest of her life. No, he'd done worse. He'd woven his charms into her helpless heart, giving him complete control over her body. I feared he might also have control over her mind... or did he? He hadn't made use of her undoubted fighting skill when he'd taken over. Could he? I didn't know. It was easy to use blood to influence someone's behavior, or to insert suggestions into their head, but to do that with a heart? I couldn't see why not, yet he clearly hadn't.

Unless he wants to be sadistic, I thought. A person as individualistic and independent as Starlight would hate the thought of being turned into a puppet, her entire body controlled by a man who wanted to use her and humiliate her. Even standing helplessly would be humiliating beyond words, unable to keep him from playing with her body as he pleased. *As long as he has her heart, she'll be at his mercy.*

"I told her to recruit a sorcerer I could use," Lord Dragon continued. "What did she offer you?"

I scowled at him. "Half the reward money for your captive. Or do you even *have* a captive?"

Lord Dragon giggled. It was a disconcerting sound. "She brought you to rescue herself. That was a damp squib, wasn't it?"

He reached out and pinched Starlight's breast. "As if I would ever let her go…"

I cursed under my breath as a trio of servants arrived, hauled me to my feet, and half dragged me down the corridor. Up close, I could feel the spells keeping them enslaved. They were profoundly unnatural, their mere presence making it hard to concentrate. And yet I had to.

Starlight had been ordered to find a magician, and she'd done so by recruiting one to save an innocent girl… to save herself. Had she hoped I could free her from the ghastly trap, or kill her to spare her from further torments?

If I'd paid more attention to her as we made our way into the mansion, I might've realized she was no longer in control of her body before it was too late. No wonder the defenses had been so ineffectual. Lord Dragon had been toying with us, probably watching through Starlight's eyes. The pervert had probably been disappointed she'd hired me rather than seducing me. And then he'd lowered the boom.

Think, I told myself. I had no idea why Lord Dragon wanted a magician, but I was sure it wasn't for anything good. Perhaps he intended to add me to his forest of magic sources, or even use my body in a ritual, or...

I didn't want to know. *There has to be a way out of this.*

My knuckles ached. I'd hit her hard enough to make her nose bleed, and yet it hadn't been enough to put her down. Any adventurer would have shrugged off the blow and kept coming, and in her case, she wasn't even in control of her own body. I could see her blood on my skin, and that meant...

A thought ran through my mind. I could use the blood to link to her mind and... the thought cut off sharply as the servants toss tossed me into a cell. It wasn't the worst cell I'd ever been in, but I couldn't move. They left me lying on the floor as they walked away.

I gritted my teeth and pushed magic into the wood. It shivered against my skin and splintered. I grunted in pain as I pulled my hands free, then did the same to the bindings around my ankles. My blood mingled with hers, creating a link I could exploit if I had time. The cell was designed to make it *almost* impossible to use magic, but it was very difficult to suppress a blood link.

I forced my thoughts into the link, trying to reach out to her mind. There was no sense of her awareness, nothing that suggested she was awake inside her own body. I couldn't tell whether he'd switched her off or buried her so deeply inside her mind that she had no awareness at all of the outside world. My thoughts kept moving, expanding further as I tried to see through her eyes. There were no spells barring my way, as far as I could tell, but I still couldn't see through her eyes. It took me too long to realize her body was still linked to him through her heart.

Bastard, I thought. I'd never been a healer. I knew the basics, of course, but putting someone's heart back in their chest was beyond me. I didn't even know what spells he'd used to keep her heart—and her—alive. They had to be incredibly fragile. The merest disruption would kill her instantly. *What did you do to her?*

I allowed my thoughts to wander onward, into the spells binding her heart. They were fantastical, and yet they could be broken—if I was willing to kill her in the process. I wasn't, even though I feared she'd rather be dead than a slave.

And she *was* a slave, as much a slave as the poor collared girls I'd seen earlier. I had to free her without killing her. I forced myself to stand and staggered over to the door, pressing my hands against the stone. This door wasn't wood, and the lock was charmed against lock-pickers, but I had no trouble opening it with my tools.

I smirked as I stepped outside. The overconfident ass had thought to relieve me of my knapsack, but he hadn't bothered to actually search me. It made a certain kind of sense—most magicians relied on their own powers rather than weapons or tools—yet it was still an oversight. A very careless oversight.

My mood darkened as I slipped through the corridors. The building didn't seem to be bigger on the inside, but I still had no idea where to find anything. The blood link should've drawn me straight to Starlight, wherever she was, yet there was so much magic in the air, I was reluctant to go straight there.

I walked downstairs into the basement and looked around, noting the workshop and enough tools to outfit an entire crew of magicians. Did Lord Dragon have apprentices? I found it unlikely, but stranger things had happened. There were quite a few low-powered magicians who had just enough power to know what they lacked, just enough power to make them useful to someone with low scruples and lower morals. I'd met a particularly nasty young man who'd been the brunt of his village's jokes until he'd developed enough power to make them suffer. They'd stopped laughing when they'd realized how dangerous he'd become, but it had been too late. If Lord Dragon had an apprentice...

It didn't look as though he did, I decided. There was no rhyme or reason to his layout, suggesting he lived and worked alone. Taking an apprentice would've forced him to adapt to the newcomer and lay out his supplies so anyone could use them. I shuddered as I saw the pair of charmed collars on the workbench, the spells emplaced and waiting for a victim. They felt worse, somehow, than the spells I'd seen earlier. If I put the collar on, it would be the end. And I felt a compulsion to do just that.

I ground my teeth, biting my lip to remain focused. The spell was a powerful compulsion. No doubt the slavers salved their consciences by telling themselves the slaves put the collars on willingly. Nonsense. The slaves weren't remotely willing to go into slavery.

I picked up the first collar and fiddled with the spells, erasing the compulsion text while strengthening the identification charm. I had no idea what sort of security spells Lord Dragon had set up near his inner sanctum, but it should help keep me from being detected if the spells took me for one of the slaves.

I briefly considered walking out of the mansion and escaping into the woods, perhaps going for help, yet I couldn't bring myself to leave Starlight behind. There was probably no one who *would* help. It wasn't as if anyone in the magical community owed me enough favors to come save her, or do something about Lord Dragon.

The collar opened a handful of doors for me. I spotted a number of slaves—all naked girls—but none of them paid any attention to me. That puzzled me for a moment before I worked out that their collars recognized the collar I was carrying and thought I had every right to be there.

I wanted to tell the girls that I'd free them, and I intended to do so, but I dared not do anything to break cover. I didn't think their collars could read their thoughts, yet it would be child's play to program a slave to report any attempt to free them or confess to any plans they might have to free themselves. I didn't think many of them would get so far. The collars would make sure of it.

I touched the blood link again and let it lead me up to the inner sanctum. Lord Dragon seemed to want to impress, although I had no idea who was visiting. The decor was unbelievably garish, glittering golden statues and artworks scattered everywhere. If there was any pattern, I couldn't see it. It looked like one of the mansions built by the new rich, a place owned by a man who'd made it and feared he hadn't, a man who showed off his wealth in a manner that also showed off his insecurities.

I leaned against the door, pressing my fingers against the wood, and feeling at the charms. The collar made it easier. It was literally impossible for one of his slaves to plot against him, so he hadn't bothered to take any precautions against it. I picked up a piece of wood—let him think me a weak wand wizard if he wished—and infused a handful of spells into the stick, then kicked open the door. I triggered the charms at the same time, steering his magic into harmless spells that were astonishingly distracting. I didn't care what happened to the magic as long as he wasn't trying to use it on me.

Lord Dragon whirled around as I crashed into the room, moving with surprising speed for man of his bulk. I saw Starlight right behind him, standing against the far wall like a piece of wood. Her face was slack, utterly blank. I grimaced, then aimed the wand at Lord

Dragon, unleashing a hail of spells. He shielded himself with an effort. I guessed he was far too used to drawing on the magic in the wood, the magic I'd channeled elsewhere. The sudden lack of power meant he had to focus his mind on me. I had to admit, despite being caught by surprise, he actually did a pretty good job.

I cast a shield to protect myself, then reached out through the blood link. My magic ran to Starlight and through the link from Starlight to her heart, which was linked directly to Lord Dragon's magic. He had powerful wards protecting himself, but I was already inside his defenses. There was no time to be clever. I cast a spell that freed her from her trance, covering it with a transfiguration curse aimed at his brain. Turning half his gray matter into stone, even for a few microseconds, would be utterly lethal. He deflected the spell, somehow, and raised a hand to curse me—

His head exploded. Starlight had shot him in the back.

I didn't hesitate. I dived forward, catching the gem before it hit the ground. The spells around the heart were somehow both complex and surprisingly simple, but I managed to follow their logic and reinforce them—and subvert them—before they collapsed completely. The heart pulsed with a steady thrum… her heartbeat. I held her heart in my hands and felt, for an instant, the utter power of life and death. I could do anything to her; I could make her say or do or believe anything…

"Here," I said. I held out the gem to her. "I believe this is yours."

Starlight sagged as she took the gem. I could guess what she was thinking. She could easily have traded one master for another. "I… I thank you."

I gave her a considering look. "You *were* the girl who was kidnapped, weren't you?"

Starlight looked embarrassed. "I thought I could take him. He was kidnapping young girls from the surrounding area and enslaving them, and... it had to be stopped."

I understood. It was never easy to admit when you were outmatched, particularly when you grew up in an environment where you had to fight for each and every scrap of respect. Starlight couldn't have backed down from the challenge, even though she'd known how dangerous her opponent could be. I had to admit, she'd found a unique way to escape captivity. She'd hired someone to rescue her, and done it in a manner that gave her plausible deniability if her master asked pointed questions.

A low shudder ran through the building. I swore and turned to flee. Starlight followed me, shouting orders to the stunned and disoriented former slaves as they struggled to collect themselves after a long period of enslavement. The entire building shuddered again, then started to collapse as the magic woven into the walls faded away. I hoped—prayed—that all the slaves managed to get out before it was too late.

Starlight and I barely made it out before the entire building collapsed into a pile of rubble. Something caught fire a second later, and the entire pile went up in flames. I couldn't bring myself to care. Lord Dragon and all his works would be lost forever.

"So," I said. "Is there actually *any* reward money?"

Starlight grinned. "Yes," she said. "And more jobs, too, if you want them."

I smiled. "Sure."

* * * * *

Christopher G. Nuttall Biography

Christopher G. Nuttall is the writer of *The Empire's Corps*, *Ark Royal*, *Schooled in Magic*, *The Zero Enigma*, and over a hundred other novels, novellas, and short stories set in alternate history, fantasy, and science fiction universes.

Born in Edinburgh, Chris moves between Britain and Malaysia with his wife and two young sons.

* * * * *

Apprentice in Trouble
by Chad Boyer
A Chronicles of the Dimensional Mage Story

"How long we going to stay here?" Katie Calliston asked as she pushed the call button for the elevator.

Grayson Knight looked around the lobby. The bellhop had said he'd bring the bags up in a separate elevator. He tried not to lean on his staff. His teacher had insisted, "A mage doesn't look foreboding if they lean on their staff."

The rest of the clientele seemed to be the lazy rich, enjoying an island vacation from the mainland. Still, their contact wanted to meet close to here. Grayson's apprentice wore a practical outfit of shirt and jeans, but it was new and fashionable. She fit in here. Grayson's clothes were a little too worn to be welcome in the lobby.

"As long as the contract requires. Then we can move on to see about getting you back to your parents."

"You promised you'd teach me magic first."

"You're picking it up. Maybe not as fast as I did, but a lot faster than many I know." He pressed the fourth floor button. He checked the lobby one more time as the doors closed. Nothing out of the ordinary outside.

He turned to her. "Also, since we don't know where your parents are, we don't know how long it's going to take. I'll keep teaching you until we find them, but we aren't going on a long retreat out in the wilderness just to teach you."

"They had to have fled somewhere when the Union took over Trestesli."

"As you've said how many times before? And how many times have I told you, Karl's already done some research on that? You know how effective his contacts are. Of the six commercial ships that left the planet, none of them had your parents booked as passengers."

"So we can go back to one of the estates my parents own, and you can keep training me until they get there?"

"I got things to do other than just being a teacher. I only learned most of what I know in the last two years, so I don't have a large jump on you. By the time we finish Karl's contract, you'll probably be better than me."

Katie tilted her head. "You can't get out of training me that easy. You swore an oath."

"I did. And I'll honor that oath. Don't worry. You aren't rid of me that easy, either."

The elevator dinged. They stepped out into the hallway with Grayson leading. There were a couple of guys behind him just leaving the last door. A maid was in front, cleaning the farthest room.

"Do you have your key?" he asked.

"Yes." She pointed and slipped past him to open the door. As she reached it, Grayson felt movement behind him. He glanced back curiously.

The two guys were pulling pistols from behind their backs.

He pushed Katie forward as he tied magical threads into a spell. The barrage of bullets impacted the shield he put around them. His staff glowed as he connected the shield to it so he wouldn't have to hold the spell up all by himself.

"What?" She half turned back at the same time, hearing the guns.

"Just open the door. Take your time," he reassured her. Bullets from the maid's gun bounced off as the two men reloaded.

She turned back with trembling hands. It took her a couple seconds to open the door.

Grayson grimaced as the bullets continued to impact the shield, but the power stone in the staff could hold it for a while against these light attacks.

"Go to the left." He ushered her through the door, closing it quickly. Katie entered the master suite.

Grayson saw dark shapes on the balcony. He pointed to the bathroom. "Head in there, lock it, and hang tight. I'll get us out of here."

Grayson sensed the shield taking more rounds as he looked at the main room.

Three more shooters were firing submachine guns from the balcony. The shield was holding, but there was no way out.

With another gesture, he pulled a red thread of magic and wove it into a fireball. He saw the men change magazines at the same time. *Amateurs*, he thought as he threw the ball to explode in their midst.

The explosion reflected into them from his shield, and none of them got up. The door burst in at that point, and the three from the hallway entered.

He strengthened the shield into a larger dome and pulled more red energy to work on another fireball.

Two crashed through the balcony doors, swinging on harnesses, and he almost lost his fireball.

One fired a shotgun at him.

He was raising his hand to throw the fireball when the beanbag went right through his shield like it wasn't there and threw him back against the wall.

"Stay down," commanded the one with the shotgun.

Grayson tossed the fireball anyway. The explosion wrecked that part of the room, but the bathroom door was fine, so he didn't have to worry about Katie.

He groaned as he stood up. His chest felt like someone had kicked it in. With a quick flick of his hands, he tied another shield spell together. It came into existence just in time to send several bullets ricocheting off it.

Two more beanbags hit him before he could ready another fireball. It fizzled in his hand as one of the gunmen fired several shots into his chest.

Everything faded to black.

* * *

Ballistic cloth is one of the best inventions of modern times, Grayson thought. His armor had lost its illusion and looked gray with mottled spots where it had stopped the bullets.

Grayson sat up and groaned. His apprentice was gone. Bullet holes riddled the hotel room, and his fireball had singed what was left. There were no indications of where they'd gone.

But oddly, I'm not dead, he thought.

He pulled in mana, opting for healing mana's light blue hue to help ease his pain. Nothing happened.

Nothing.

He realized each wrist bore a bracer with intricate runes. He switched to magesight and saw the spells wrapped in them.

They were finely crafted. In fact, the craftsmanship was masterful. He traced the glyphs with his fingers and realized he only knew some of the glyphs. His heart beat faster. Unknown arcane glyphs were always a good find, even if they were completely shackling him at the moment. *Impressive. Very impressive. And annoying.*

He reached out again to pull threads of magic. They tried to respond, but they just drained into the bracers. *When was the last time I couldn't use magic?* he wondered. *Before I went to the academy. Better reset my expectations.*

He looked around to see if he could find any other clue to her whereabouts.

Through the opening where the balcony windows had been, he saw the glint of an air car speeding away to the south.

They'd taken his best magic items, but not his bag. He pulled out a small compass. It glowed with yellow magic.

At least I can track her, even if I can't fly.

As he pulled his backup ballistic vest from his bag, he sighed.

I guess there's only one thing to do.

* * *

"How long will you be renting the air car for, sir?" The receptionist at the rental counter beamed at Grayson Knight.

"Let's say five. I'm heading over to the mainland to see the sights."

"Oh, what fun. I'll make sure the nav system has all the local landmarks set up for you. Do you want the damage waiver?"

Grayson knew his apprentice was about the same age as the receptionist, but he'd have turned down her request to train her if she'd been this damn bubbly.

"Sure."

"Very good, sir. Your car is the white one out the side door here."

"Thanks. Have a good rest of your shift."

He jogged over to the sleek, white air car. It was an expensive model with several safety features that might prove useful when following his charge.

As he slid behind the wheel, his wrist comm beeped.

He saw who it was and sighed. "Yes?"

"Grayson, where are you? Where's Katie? Why is the room destroyed?"

"Hi, Karl. She was taken by unknown assailants. They destroyed the room when they kidnapped her." He gained altitude and turned toward the balcony of his room. "I'm in a rental car. Come to the balcony, and you can hop in."

Grayson piloted the car near the railing, and Karl jumped in, making the leap look like a hop onto a couch rather than a jump over four stories of empty air.

"Well?" Karl looked at him impatiently. "I don't understand how they found her. Or why they took her. Or *how* they took her."

Grayson grimaced.

"No idea on the first part. The second part has me stumped. She said she was just looking to learn magic, so I don't know much about her past. The third—well, they brought more firepower than I was ready for."

"Where are they taking her?"

Grayson put the compass on the dash in front of him.

"Somewhere over there. You have weapons?" Grayson shook his head. "Sorry, stupid question."

"I'll forgive you, since you haven't been in any dangerous situations for like three months. Do you have any?"

"No. They took everything but my bag." He gestured with his arms. "And these bracers are suppressing my magic."

"How'd they take her?"

"I was in the process of getting her down behind the bed when they took me from the balcony. My situational awareness was compromised. It won't happen again."

"How do you figure? She was your primary responsibility, so it makes sense that you were concentrating on her."

"Yes, but I should have checked and sealed the balcony before stashing her away."

"Run the whole thing through with me. We have time." He waved a hand forward at the vast ocean in front of them.

Grayson set the navigation to follow the compass' direction. He leaned back and shook his head. "After you and I separated, we got a room and went up to unpack. Nothing out of the ordinary in the hotel lobby. Nothing remarkable about the elevator ride. When we got out, there were a couple of people walking away from us in the hallway, but non-threatening. When we got to our door, they started shooting at me."

"How do you know it was at you?"

"Everything was aimed higher and toward me, away from her."

Karl nodded and gestured to Grayson to keep going.

"They were going for a grab the whole time," Grayson said.

"Okay. Why? Why take your apprentice?"

"'Cause she knows more about magic than anyone else on this planet besides me?"

"Because she's pliable, unlike you?"

"That's a good point. She knows some of our order's secrets—" Grayson shook his head "—but nothing critical."

"It brings you to them," Karl said

"I don't even know who 'them' is. All I know is, I'm going to rain down some destruction if they hurt her."

"That's a given for both of us. Lots of destruction and revenge, but we just know the vague direction they're going."

"They were professional enough to take the bodies with them."

"Bodies?"

"Karl, give me some credit. I took out some with fireballs."

Grayson looked at the dash where the compass sat. "The needle's flashing quicker. Looks like we're getting closer."

"Good call, picking the sports car."

"So what were you doing while I was doing all this dying? You're my bodyguard. You handle the mundane. I handle the mystical, right?"

"I found out that the request for you was bogus, and you were just lured here for no purpose. Though I guess now, the purpose was to steal your apprentice."

"All your famous contacts, and you couldn't have figured that out before now?" Grayson hit the steering wheel for emphasis.

"Well, I'm a little annoyed at Nathaniel, who told us about the contract and requested us to come. I think we might have some words after we get your apprentice back."

"I was thinking…" Grayson turned to look at his friend.

"Oh, do tell." Karl's voice picked up an octave.

"I think you should have an apprentice, too."

"I see how much trouble your apprentice causes you." Karl shook his head.

"Only because I didn't get to pick her." They were closing in on a beach city. Several hotels dotted the waterfront.

"Same difference. Even if you get to pick them, they're a hassle."

"You pick one, and we'll know."

"Too much trouble."

The compass flashed a little quicker, then beeped.

"They've landed." Grayson pointed ahead of them. "Over there somewhere."

Karl pulled a gun out from the holster at his side and checked the magazine.

"Is that an upgrade?"

"Yeah. I got it earlier when I found out Nathaniel betrayed us. I figured we'd need a bit more firepower. Are you mad that I didn't get you one?"

"A little."

"I figured you could use your magic, and I'll use this."

"But now I don't have magic." He waved the bracers again.

"You want a pistol? I got spares." Karl gestured at two showing in the holsters on his thighs.

"When we get out. No sense in juggling now."

He slowed the air car down, making some turns to figure out where the compass was pointing.

"Looks like the top of that building." He pointed.

"Gray, let's ease up to them from below," Karl said. "I'll scan, and then we can put it down on the pad."

"Do you think they have any defense?"

"Wouldn't you?"

"Yeah." Grayson pulled his left hand off the controls and made a few gestures. Nothing happened.

"No shield?" Karl asked.

"I'm afraid so. Looks like we're doing this the hard way."

"The hard way is flying an aircar into an ambush?"

"Attacking a position we knew nothing about."

Karl nodded. "Okay, I'll give you that."

Grayson looked out onto the open-air gardened terrace. There were no guards, just an air car sitting on a landing pad, and an open door on the far side that led into the building. The windows were all opaque. "Bring us to the other side of their vehicle, and we can go in on foot," Karl said.

"Sounds good." Grayson looped over the other air car and landed.

Nothing moved. There were no sounds except for the babbling of a small fountain water feature on the far side of the garden.

"Spooky," Grayson commented as he grabbed the compass from the dash. Karl tossed him a pistol. He checked the safety and load, then nodded to his friend.

Karl walked up the pathway to the open door. After a quick scan, he waved Grayson forward. "Clear."

Grayson stepped inside. Several lounge chairs and couches were scattered about the room, with a long bar on the far side. Two exits were on either side of the bar. The one to the south looked like a kitchen.

"Kitchen or main house?" Karl asked as he covered the south side.

"Main house." Grayson hugged the wall. "Looks dangerous. The guy with the gun goes first."

"We both have guns. Decoy goes first?" Karl countered.

Grayson snorted. "Very well, but if I get shot, I'm going to be very mad."

He pushed the door open and rolled left.

Karl rolled right.

They were in a long hallway with several doors exiting off the sides. They could see the rest of downtown through a window at the end.

"Let's head to the end and see what we get. The compass says she's down one level and toward that end."

Grayson moved quietly down the hallway. The second to last doors were an elevator. He pressed the call button as he continued to watch the last set of doors and the window.

"No bad guys jumping out at us yet," Grayson commented.

Karl just grunted.

"You think they're all down a floor?"

Karl grunted again.

The elevator opened. It was empty.

Grayson pointed at the camera in the elevator corner. "They know we're here."

Karl grunted a third time.

* * *

The elevator doors opened, and a voice called out.

"You may keep your weapons, but we'll kill the girl if you fire them."

Grayson looked at Karl and shrugged.

He let the weapon drop and stepped into the reception area. Four guards wearing masks and black armor held assault rifles pointed at them.

"Well, what are we going to do then?" Grayson asked.

"The boss wants to talk to you. Since you have no magic, he has a proposition for you."

Grayson gestured to lead the way.

Two guards led them through an electronically locked door.

Grayson grimaced when he saw Katie held tight against a minion. The minion had a gun pressed into her side, but at least she didn't seem hurt.

She saw him, and he saw the relief in her eyes.

"Hi, kid. Told you you aren't getting rid of me that easily. I'll get you out of here in a second."

"I doubt that," commented a man who stepped around a couch and stopped in front of Grayson. Just out of arm's reach.

"Who are you, and why'd you kidnap my apprentice?"

"I'm Dannen. We're humble servants of the Anarchy Corp, and we want you to do something for us." He sounded so smug, Grayson would've wanted to punch him in the face even if he hadn't kidnapped Katie.

"Have me do what? I can't currently use any magic, thanks to you, so what good am I to you?" Grayson looked around the room. Four flunkies stood in a semi-circle behind him and Karl. Three others guarded the far door.

"I need you to set fire to a building and ensure that a politician dies."

"I'm sure you have several people in this room who can do that. Why do you need me?" Grayson walked toward the windows on the far side, cutting the distance between him and his apprentice.

"Please stop walking, or I'll have them shoot her in the leg."

Grayson stopped and looked back at the scarred face. "Not kill her outright? Do you have plans for her?"

"They said they're going to ransom me to my parents," Katie called out as she tried to step farther away from her captor.

"Please be quiet." The man made a gesture, and the guard tightened his grip on her. "I need the fire to be started magically in multiple areas at once. Then I need you to ensure the politician doesn't leave, preferably by locking the building down with magic so no one can leave at all."

Grayson frowned. "Won't the politician have a mage protector to ensure their escape?"

The man pulled out a bean bag. "Don't worry about her mage protector. We'll take care of him. Once you get there, I'll have Violet get you into the reception and take off your bracers. Then you can do your magic, and once you're done, we'll release your two companions. Fair?"

Grayson looked at his friends. He shrugged. "Fair. The only problem is, I'll need my staff to generate enough power to do all the things you want me to do."

The man grimaced, and then shrugged. "Far be it from me not to give you the tools you need to complete the mission. I have your motivation here with me. You can have your staff after we remove the bracers there."

Grayson shrugged again. "Karl, take my pin. My order won't be happy with the events that are about to unfold." He tossed it over.

Karl grabbed it out of the air and pinned it to his combat vest. He nodded once.

"Mr. Grayson, enter the lavatory there. There's formal attire hanging from one of the stalls. Please put it on, and then return."

The suit was in a plastic protective bag. He pulled it out and whistled.

These people spent some money. I haven't had one so fine in a long time.

He found it fit him close to perfect. *Something else to remember.*

He stepped back out, and Katie whistled, while Karl chuckled.

Dannen looked at the only female gunman in the room, a smaller woman with purple hair wearing a long overcoat. "Violet, take Mr. Knight to the venue. Make sure you get the okay before unlocking his bracers."

"Yes, Mister Dannen," she replied as she picked up a small stone. Then she grabbed the staff. The staff's power stone glowed, and an arc of lightning shot toward her, then curved into the stone in her hand. Grayson flinched, as he'd expected the lightning to blast her, but she was unharmed. The stone clearly drained all magic aimed at it, similar to the bracers.

Dannen smirked. "The rest of us will wait here for your return. If you don't return with Violet, our agreement is off. If you don't complete the task, our agreement is off. If you fulfill the mission, we'll return your companions unharmed, and won't bother you further on this planet."

"If I return, will you give me the location of her parents?"

"We can do that. If you don't make it, they'll reunite, anyway. It'll just make us some money first. I'll give you a hint, though, so you have something to look forward to." Dannen's mouth twisted into a smile that made Grayson want to check his pockets to ensure he still had everything. "They're on the planet Lertiss."

Grayson nodded. "Thank you for that."

He then gestured for Violet to lead the way into the elevator. As they got to the exit, he turned back and looked at his friends.

"Prepare for my return."

Dannen laughed mockingly. "Prepare for my return. Who talks like that?"

* * *

Violet pushed the bottom floor and stepped back to keep an eye on him.

"How did you get looped into this?" he asked.

"I signed up just like everyone else. 'Sides, I get to wear pretty things and convince suckers to give me stuff. Not a bad life." She opened her overcoat and showed off the red satin floor-length dress. It hugged her curves, and if he weren't being blackmailed, he wouldn't have minded taking her to the bar for a drink.

"Not a bad life, until it goes wrong. Then pain and incarceration await you. Even death."

"They have to catch us first and, so far, Dannen's kept us ahead of the authorities. The Anarchy Corp is just too big an organization to let anyone rot in prison for long."

Grayson grunted. He'd figured Dannen had other plans, but no plan survives contact with the enemy. Grayson smiled.

Violet took a step back, seeing his expression, and shook the staff at him.

"Don't get any ideas. We have your apprentice and friend. Just follow the rules, and everything will turn out fine."

Grayson nodded and wiped the smile off his face. The elevator stopped. Violet wrapped the staff in her coat and gestured for Grayson to lead the way out.

He held the door to the street open for her. Wheeled traffic was light, though pedestrian traffic was a little heavier, and the flow definitely went to the east. He fell into stride with Violet as she held the staff like an umbrella against a shoulder.

"The Visneer. Up one block and to the left. We check in to room 212. There's a team there with our passes. Then we head across to the convention hall roof, and you can do your magic."

The Visneer took up a whole block. They entered the spacious lobby and circled up to the second floor. The hallway had lush carpet that devoured the sound of his brightly shined shoes.

Violet gave a sequenced knock on room 212's door. It was replied with a series, and she replied again.

The door opened to an armed man. He beckoned them in, and after checking the hallway, closed and locked the door.

The room was a typical hotel room. It could've been a mirror of the one Grayson had left seven hours ago, though this one was more opulent and didn't have a bunch of scorch marks and bullet holes.

Two men worked on laptops. They had the feeds of multiple cameras from the convention hall showing on their monitors. Two more were cleaning weapons at the dining room table.

"Hey, do something with this staff. And we need our passes," Violet commanded as she discarded her overcoat on the counter. She handed the staff to one of the men dealing with the weapons.

The left side man in front of the laptops handed her two big press passes and then returned to his seat.

"Are you watching what the security people are watching?" Grayson leaned back against the door.

The right-hand man said, "Of course. We hacked into the feed several hours ago. *Before* the politician's advance team did their checks so we were undetected."

"Okay, Gray. Time to get your game face on. Remember, you're doing this for your friends." Violet gestured for him to lead the way back out. A man handed the staff back to Violet. The staff had changed appearance into a cane. Violet held it against her shoulder and followed Grayson out.

What did they do to my staff? I didn't feel any magic. He looked back down at the bracers. *Never again.*

"Well?" Violet asked.

He shook off the distraction. "Ready."

They walked across the bridgeway to the convention center. The security detachment allowed the cane in without blinking. Grayson shook his head, as it was probably more powerful than a rocket launcher.

Violet smirked as they breezed through security. "Okay, magic man. Time to head to the roof."

There were cameras in the stairwell. "Is your team turning off the cameras in here? We don't want security knowing we're heading to the roof."

"They've already looped this section."

Grayson gestured at his bracers. "Okay, then, let me out of the bracers. I'm going to need to attune to my staff on the way up so I can cast this magic."

"Attune? Dannen didn't say anything about attunement."

"Of course not. You handle all your magic via items. In order to cast spells through items, you have to attune to them. Draining my staff of power means I have to reattune myself to it. I might as well do it on the climb up the stairs."

"Don't try anything funny. I can always put the bracers back on you." Violet pulled a small gray key out of her purse and unlocked the bracers.

He took a step back and could feel the magic around him again. It was exhilarating, like a light on after being in the darkness for hours.

"I won't try anything funny. It's only five flights of stairs, so I might need some time before we go out onto the roof to finish."

Violet gave him the staff, and Grayson started up the steps.

She quickly followed. "Hey, slow down. No funny stuff."

"I'm deadly serious. You're forcing me to kill thousands of people. There's nothing funny about tonight."

"I can put these back on if you don't slow down," Violet threatened as she fell a little farther behind.

Grayson sighed and waited at the next landing.

She pointed at him. "Thanks, but we still hold your friends hostage. Any false moves, and they won't like what happens to them."

"I *am* familiar with the situation."

They reached the roof access, and Grayson held out a hand before Violet could open the roof door.

"Hold on." Grayson pointed at the security camera on the inside, watching the door. He'd stopped before he entered the camera's viewing area. "Do your men have that camera circumvented, too?"

She pressed a hidden earpiece. "Do you have the security camera on the roof door compromised?"

She nodded. "We're good."

Grayson shrugged. "Just wanted to be sure we aren't going to be recorded when we leave and start causing mayhem."

They went out.

Grayson threaded a quick spell and disabled the camera permanently with an orange flare.

Her hand went to her ear. "Did you do anything to—?"

Grayson cast another spell to cut her radio as well.

She looked at him quizzically. "You don't think you can get back there before I can get to a radio and let them know you are coming?"

"Oh, I think I can. You see, while we were heading up the stairs, I've been pulling as much magic into my staff as fast as possible, and now I'm ready to start this fight again. Also, you'll be unconscious."

She grabbed for the gun in her purse as he snapped a spell at her head. The purple spell twisted around her, and she collapsed onto the roof. A bit of smoke coiled up from her pocket and the overloaded stone.

The door had closed behind him, but he wasn't heading back that way. He was going to his friends, and a tracing spell on the order badge pointed directly at them.

The next spell took a bit of time. Teleportation isn't something one rushes, especially when you're going someplace you haven't been before. He concentrated on the destination and the locus of his badge, a token of his oath of valor and honor.

He still needed more power since he only knew about where he needed to show up. The flows from the diamond on top of his staff were tinted yellow for the transportation spell, along with hints of the rest of the colors of the rainbow.

He finished the spell and snapped it down. He appeared next to Karl in the same room he'd left them in. Dannen was lounging on one of the couches. Karl and his apprentice were sitting on another. The guard beside him started to raise his gun.

Grayson slammed the butt of his staff down and thickened the air a foot away from him in a growing circle. The guard's hand slowed until it seemed to be moving through molasses.

He cast spells, but with slight delays to them so he could drop the slow spell before they'd go off. He tied them off with a magical slipknot he tied to his pinky. As he finished the last spell, he pulled the slipknot loose and dropped the slow spell.

Several things happened at once. A red shield appeared around Grayson and his friends. The gun pointed at him was suddenly encased in ice, and when it fired, it exploded, sending the gunman flying.

Thick ropes pinned Dannen to the couch. The rest of the gunmen were frozen in ice.

Grayson surveyed his handiwork. He slammed the butt of his staff down on the wounded gunman's head, silencing his screams. Then he stalked over to Dannen.

When he got there, he leaned on his staff as a wave of vertigo hit him from the expenditure of all that energy in a short period of time. His long stare allowed him to catch his breath.

Grayson looked at Karl. "Take Katie and head up to the air car. We can leave from there."

"You coming with us?" Karl asked as they moved to the elevator.

"I'll be along shortly. I want to have a quick conversation with Dannen."

Karl and Katie disappeared through the doorway. Grayson leaned in closer.

"So, Mr. Dannen, I think I'd like to know more about this organization you're a part of, as well as specifically where on Lertiss my apprentice's parents are residing."

"Mr. Knight. We know who you are and who you work for. You're making a dangerous enemy." Dannen continued to struggle, to no avail.

Grayson had to give it to him. All his men were down, and he was still struggling.

"I'm pretty sure I'm already your enemy, since you kidnapped my apprentice and my bodyguard." Grayson pressed the end of the staff into Dannen's stomach. "Do you want to tell me the answers to my questions?"

"My men will be here soon to save me."

"I have a few ways to get you to tell me. However, the easiest is just to get you not to think about it." Grayson spun white and purple threads together. He released the magic into Dannen's mind.

A moment later, Dannen said, "The parents are on Merthins. They're being hosted by the royal family there."

"I thought Lertiss was a lie," Grayson said.

Dannen looked at him in horror. "How'd you make me do that?
"

Grayson turned to follow his friends before reinforcements showed up. "Magic really is quite powerful. And to show you just *how* powerful it is, you can eat this fireball."

A fireball spell is easy. You mix red and yellow together and launch it at the target. The more of each you put in equally, the bigger the explosion. The only tricky part is guiding it to the target. If you flinch, such as when several henchmen come running out the far door and fire their pistols at you, well, the spell can hit the wrong target.

In this case, the couch Dannen was sitting on. It exploded, catapulting Dannen across the room.

Grayson didn't wait to watch him land. He just pried the elevator doors open with a quick air spell and floated up the shaft to the roof.

He raced out onto the terrace to see Karl already revving the engine of the air car. His apprentice was in the back, with her hands out like she was going to cast a spell at whoever was following them.

He smiled. *She always was a fighter.*

"Let's get out of here before the bad guys figure out there are stairs!" he yelled, jumping into the passenger seat.

Karl threw the car up into the air and pushed the throttle all the way forward to get away.

"Even if he does, he's half couch." Grayson shrugged. "Even so, he'll think twice before messing with a mage's apprentice."

* * * * *

Chad Boyer Biography

Chad Boyer is an avid reader of speculative fiction. He grew up reading Margaret Weis and Tracy Hickman on the fantasy side, while Weber and Gibson and Stephenson kept him turning pages on the science fiction side.

He currently has two books in print and a serial on Substack and Vella.

He lives in Southern California with his wife, three kids, and a dog. When he isn't writing or reading, he holds down a day job coding software.

Website: http://www.chadboyer.me

Twitter: https://twitter.com/ChadBoyer

* * * * *

SEALed With a Kiss
by C.V. Walter

"**T**hey used to worship us." The immortal who was going by Joe Severin gazed out of his tinted office window to the casino floor.

"What are you going on about?" his sister asked from the couch. She was going by Tanda these days, just the one name, but she was considering changing it when she changed her hair from an ankle-length silver to something short, curly, and darker. Marda? Marina?

"Humans," he said, his lips curled in disgust. "They used to pay us the tribute we deserved and worshiped us like gods."

"They still do." She was flipping through a glossy fashion magazine while she lounged on his soft white leather couch.

"Not the way they used to." His hair was black and fell just past his shoulders when it wasn't tied back with the leather thong that probably qualified as an antique. His fashion choices were always on trend for the time period, and they screamed wealth and taste—except for the hair. He hadn't changed it since he'd stepped into the mortal realm, and didn't seem likely to.

Tanda tossed the magazine to the other end of the couch. "And what do you call this? They pour tribute into your coffers and years of their lives into your service. I can feel the power you gain from each wager, every punch of the clock, every savings account drained to feed their dreams of avarice."

"Not like I used to," Joe said with a frown. He was too old and powerful to pout, but his sister could see the discontent at the corners of his mouth. "And the offerings are so small. Hardly a drop from each one."

"And you get millions of them a day. Stop whining because the source of your power is boring. I don't care how many temple virgins you consumed, you couldn't take enough in a day to compare to an hour in this casino. And half of them cost more in gifts and power to their families than they were worth."

His sister stood and stalked over to him, her heels muffled by the plush carpet, until she stood beside his shoulder. He met her eyes in the reflection from the window, then looked back down at the floor.

"They never understood why they had to want me, the purpose of me asking them about their every desire. The ones who offered themselves up to benefit their families and asked for nothing for themselves were the worst."

"You feed, brother dear, on the worst humanity has to offer and then complain when they offer you their best," Tanda said with a snort. "I, at least, can appreciate where my power comes from."

"And you spend it on frivolous things," he said with a derisive glance at her appearance.

They were both tall and lean—the one thing about their appearance they couldn't change—and Tanda loved soft fabrics against her skin. The few interviews she'd done had focused on her love of all-natural products like silk and fine wool, fabrics she'd been wearing since they first stepped foot into this realm, but they never mentioned how much they cost. The cost of her deceptively simple silk dress could have paid the wages of two of the fulltime casino employees for a year, with a hefty tip left over.

"Perhaps I should give my seamstress a raise," she mused.

"She won't appreciate it."

"No, but it'll keep her with me a little longer and make the major design houses green with envy. I might insist she take on an assistant and add a couple of your dancers to my retinue."

"You always did think of me," Joe said. "That flavor of greed can be intoxicating."

Tanda stiffened, and her eyes shifted from bored amusement to a focused hunt. "Can you taste that?"

"Taste what? I've never been as tuned to the subtlety of human emotions as you are."

"Hunger, greed, and lust," she said. "Over by the bar. With a heavy dose of fear and self-doubt."

He followed her gaze and found the couple she was focused on, then followed the swirl of emotions to the attentions of several hungry looking men staring at them. The man had the shoulders back, head up bearing of some kind of warrior, with short, curly, brown hair. His companion was soft and plump, with full, pink lips and dark brown hair that cascaded down her back.

"Newlyweds, do you think?"

Tanda shook her head. "Too brittle for that, but I suspect a few drinks might push them in that direction. If someone were interested in taking a personal hand in their destruction, I'd suggest they go and buy them a round and be friendly."

"Who'd want to destroy such a happy, beautiful couple?" Joe asked with a grin.

* * *

Violet shifted on her stool when the bartender put the drinks down—whiskey on the rocks and a daiquiri with a fancy name. She took a sip from her drink and glanced up to watch her boyfriend taste his. He put the glass down before she'd finished enjoying the view, and he caught her staring.

With a slight smile, he reached out to give her thigh a gentle pat. "Nervous?"

"A little. I really want your sister to like me."

"I like you," he said. "You make me happy. I can't imagine for an instant she wouldn't like you."

"You never know. I'm not exactly the active, outdoorsy type, and you're—well, you," she said and gestured at his body. He'd spent over a decade as a Navy SEAL and kept himself in mission-ready shape, even if he'd transitioned to support. "She might decide you need someone who can keep up with you."

"She doesn't get to decide that." He put a finger under her chin to lift her face so he could look in her eyes. "You're warm, and soft, and sexy as hell. And you look *amazing* with your lips wrapped around my—"

"Derek!" she gasped. Her cheeks flushed bright pink, and his wicked grin spread the heat to the tips of her ears and down her chest.

"What? It's true. I particularly like the little moan you make when you're enjoying yourself."

She glanced around at the other people at the bar and was relieved that none of them appeared to be close enough to hear. "I thought you didn't want to talk about that kind of thing in public."

"No, I told you you're not allowed to make that sound in public. Though I'm tempted to make it really difficult for you to resist."

He leaned in and kissed her gently, and she could feel herself smiling when he pulled back. With a grin, he raised his glass in a small salute and took a drink. She glanced down and returned his grin before taking a sip of her own drink.

The only hint she got that someone was approaching was a slight tensing in Derek's posture before the man stopped next to them.

"Are you folks having a good time?" he asked. The man was tall and slender, with light brown skin that could have been a mix of a dozen ethnicities, or simply a really good tan. His black hair was pulled back in a neat queue, and his all-black suit screamed expensive.

Violet nodded, and Derek answered, "Yes, sir, we're having a wonderful time. The drinks are quite good."

"Excellent," he said with a smile that showed a few too many teeth. "Did you two just come in for drinks and a little gambling, or do you have rooms in our resort towers?"

"Um…" Violet started and met Derek's eyes.

"Just drinks, for now," he said. "We're meeting someone before we decide on the rest of our plans."

"Well, I hope your plans include one of our excellent restaurants, though I'd understand if you stayed at the bar for a while. Mitchell pours a great cocktail. Allow me to introduce myself before I tell you the next round is on me. I'm Joe Severin, and I own the Portals to Paradise Casino."

"Oh!" Violet gasped in surprise.

Derek stood and stuck out a hand that Joe took with obvious reluctance. "It's great to meet you, sir. To what do we owe the pleasure?"

Joe's smile widened. "One of my floor managers mentioned there was a beautiful woman causing a disturbance. I thought I should come down here and see for myself and, I must say, I can see what they meant. Your wife is absolutely stunning."

"Oh, we're not—" Violet started to correct him, but Derek cut her off.

"Yes, she is."

Violet blushed, and Joe held his hand out for hers. He took it and held her gaze as he bent to press a kiss to the skin just above her knuckles. "When you're tired of playing with the boys," he murmured, so soft she could barely hear, "come find me, and I will show you paradise."

He straightened and turned to Derek with a flashy gold poker chip in his fingers. "Allow me to pay for your next few drinks and dinner. If you want a room, just show this at the registration desk, and they'll accommodate you. Mitchell, anything their heart desires, on me."

"You got it, Boss," the bartender said with a nod.

Derek took the poker chip and flipped it through his fingers a few times before putting it in his pocket. "That's very kind of you."

"Not at all," Joe said, and stepped away as quickly as he'd arrived.

* * *

Joe burst into his office, practically chortling with glee and the overflow of power from the emotions he'd siphoned off the people at the bar. Not just the couple he'd talked to, but everyone else who'd been sitting and watching them.

He'd forgotten how heady it could be to receive that much energy in person.

"Did you have fun?" his sister asked from the couch. She was typing on her phone and hadn't looked up as he came in.

"It was better than I hoped. Greed and envy from everybody watching them, anxiety, jealousy, and fear from the couple. And the seeds sown to create more, with a token to collect it all."

"Do you think the token was wise?" she asked.

He waved her concern away, his gaze fixed on the couple by the bar. "Humans these days don't recognize a token as anything more than a trinket. I doubt either of them would know how to use it to do anything even if they recognized the power in it."

"As long as you're sure the risk is worth it."

"And a third player enters the arena," Joe said. His hands were on the glass, his breath causing little bursts of fog with every exhale.

"Did you hire someone to try and break them up?" Tanda sounded a little more interested at the prospect of watching a relationship implode with a little help.

"No. I'm saving that pleasure for myself. There appears to be a rival for the man's affection. They certainly appear very comfortable with each other."

"Are you going to watch them all night?" Tanda had turned back to her magazine and flipped to the next page. "Because if you are, I'm going somewhere else."

Joe turned to her and smirked. "Am I not giving you enough attention, sister dear?"

She flipped him a gesture she'd learned from the humans and found very useful. "Hearing you narrate your latest diversion has already become tiresome. If that's what you're going to focus on tonight, I'm going to go find my own diversion and leave you to yours."

"Well, far be it from me to keep you from being entertained," Joe said with a scowl. "If you want to go, then go. I'm going to enjoy the possibility of getting very personal satisfaction from my newest little toys."

Tanda kicked her legs off the couch, turned, and stood up in one smooth, if overly dramatic, motion. She brushed imaginary wrinkles from her skirt. "I'll leave you to it, then, but remember, they're not your toys. Not yet, anyway. They haven't used the token."

"Of course they have," he said, then looked down at the bar where the three humans had been standing moments earlier. They were walking away, and the bartender had just cleared their glasses.

Joe stalked to his desk while Tanda smirked at him. He picked up the handset from the phone on his desk, punched his speed dial, and waited half a ring for the bartender to pick up.

"What's up, Boss?" Mitchell asked without preamble.

"You charged the couple I gave the token to," Joe demanded.

"They paid cash for their first drinks and didn't order any more after you'd left. I didn't have a chance to charge them for anything else. And I tried. Trust me."

"Who was the woman who joined them?"

"Dude's sister," Mitchell said. "Little sister, I think, though he wasn't explicit about that."

Joe snorted in disgust and hung up the phone.

Tanda laughed and walked toward the door. "Have fun with your playthings."

He ground his teeth in irritation. Until they used the token, they weren't his playthings, and she knew it. If he wanted to get what he was owed, he'd have to wait for them to use it. Or force them into it.

With a grimace of irritation, he pulled out a map of the local area and spread it across his desk. The Portals to Paradise Casino wasn't on the Strip, but it wasn't very far from it, either. Most people who wanted to enjoy the nightlife followed the same path out of the casino, and that's where he started the tracking spell.

It took a while to find them. The spell had trouble finding the token consistently, as though it was being hidden behind something every few steps, so he had to keep feeding it power every time he lost it.

They stopped at a popular restaurant, and Joe picked up the phone to call the manager.

* * *

"Sam, what have I told you about paying for dinner?" Derek asked.

"That you love it when your little sister is sneaky and manages to take care of the check before you have the chance?"

Derek's sister turned to grin at him as they walked back to the Portals to Paradise Casino. Her gaze flitted over Violet, and her smile dimmed slightly.

"Sam," Derek said, disappointment and amusement warring in his tone.

"Look, I'm sorry if you wanted to show off in front of your girlfriend, but I got a nice bonus, and I wanted to surprise you. Do some push-ups or something instead."

"It has nothing to do with that. You're my little sister. I'm supposed to be taking care of you."

She blew a raspberry at him.

Samantha Derring was the same height as Violet, but that's where most of their similarities ended. Where Violet was soft and rounded, Samantha was lean and firm. She was funny and vivacious in ways Violet never imagined she could pull off.

Violet had spent a decade in customer service. Sam was a pilot.

She was exactly the kind of woman Violet had expected Derek to prefer. Even her hair, the same shade of brown as her brother's, caught the light and seemed to shine. Night had fallen, and Violet could almost swear the bright colors and flashing lights ever present in this area of Las Vegas were designed to showcase all of Sam's beauty.

Derek's hand squeezed hers while he continued to argue with his sister. She looked up at him, and he smiled at her and winked.

Noise further ahead drew his attention before she could follow up on the wink.

"Sam, don't get too far ahead!" he called.

What had started as a shouting match turned into an all-out brawl that was spreading to the onlookers and heading in their direction.

"Detour!" Sam shouted back and ducked into a blocked-off alley that was obviously some kind of maintenance track rather than a path.

Derek and Violet hurried to catch up with her, only to turn the corner and see her backing up slowly with her hands raised. The lights from the street ended a few feet into the alley, casting the man threatening her in shadows that concealed everything about him but his build and the knife he was holding.

"Hand it over," the stranger growled.

"Sam, what does he want?" Derek stepped in front of Violet, his hands out at his sides, and she watched the confrontation around his bicep.

"You, too, dumbass; purse, wallets, cash. Empty your pockets. Now."

"I told you, I don't have anything on me," Sam protested, taking a step back.

Derek stepped forward. "I'm reaching for my wallet. You don't have to do anything rash. I'll give you what you're asking for."

The stranger reached out impossibly fast and grabbed Samantha's wrist, yanking her forward, and wrapping the arm with the knife around her neck. She let out a scream, and he pressed the blade of the knife against her throat.

"Shut up. Damn right, you'll give me what I want, and so will she," he said. "Throw the money and the goods on the ground and back out of the alley."

Derek threw a small brown wallet on the ground and put his hands back up. "Everything I've got is in there. Let her go, and you can have it. The women don't have any money on them."

The man holding Sam gave a chuckle that made the hair on Violet's neck stand on end. He moved forward, and the light caught on the back of his hand. Mottled green skin held a wicked looking dagger, the blade of which was still pressing against Sam's neck.

Her eyes were wide with panic, and she bit back a frightened yelp when the first drop of her blood slid over the knife.

"Let her go, we'll walk away, and you can have everything in that wallet," Derek said, his voice steady and deceptively calm.

Violet could see the tension radiating up his back.

Whatever fight had started on the street was getting closer. She could hear shouting, bodies impacting each other or their surroundings, and demands they stop. The alley itself, however, was strangely quiet.

The monster holding Sam took a few heavy breaths, then shoved her at Derek before scooping up the wallet, running down the alley, and disappearing into the shadows.

Derek caught his sister and, before he could do more than ask if she was okay, the fighting from the street was on them.

One of the combatants was shoved over the barrier to the alley and into Violet. She caught herself against Derek's back, and he pulled Sam into his arms and looked around.

"Doorway!" he shouted over the noise and pulled the women into a dark alcove further down the alley.

"Sam, you're bleeding," Violet said.

Samantha reached up to touch the shallow cut on her neck, and the door next to them slammed open. Instead of a surprised or angry employee telling them to move away from the door, they were enveloped in a vortex of light and sound.

Blind and deaf from the assault on her senses, Violet could feel the wind tearing at her hair and clothes, crushing her breath back into her lungs, until she folded in on herself to try to hide from the unrelenting noise and pain.

When it finally stopped, and she dared to open her eyes, the world around her was strange, the colors oddly muted, while scents threatened to overwhelm her senses. Violet could tell she was lying on some kind of grass, and it smelled amazing. She looked around for the others and saw Derek on his knees, shaking his head, and some kind of hawk lying dazed just beyond him.

Something—her scent? the color of her feathers?—told Violet that the bird was actually Samantha.

"Sam? Vi?" Derek asked, looking around.

Violet tried to answer him, but her voice wouldn't work. She managed a growl that shocked everybody. Samantha rolled over and, with a few powerful pumps of her wings, flew several feet away before she crashed back down into the ground.

Derek jumped up and ran after her.

Violet tried to do the same, but couldn't get all her legs moving the way she expected them to, especially the ones that used to be her arms. While she worked to get all her limbs coordinated, Samantha got her wings working and took off, Derek running after her.

"Wait," she tried to call. "Derek! Help!"

The only thing that came out was a series of barks even she knew weren't something he could understand.

* * *

Joe looked down at what was left of the goblin who'd brought him an empty wallet and snarled in disgust. Even though the ooze they dissolved into dried into a fine powder, cleaning them up was a nuisance. Worse, summoning another one would cost him more power than he felt like spending.

Everything he'd done to collect more power that day had cost him more than it was worth. Even dealing with his servant's inability to reclaim the token he'd given the ungrateful humans had cost him a useful servant.

He was getting annoyed.

The phone on his desk rang, and he stepped around the drying pile of ooze to get to it.

"What?" he asked.

"A couple of our guys are gonna need to be bailed out, Boss," the human voice on the other end of the line told him, "and we never did find that couple you were looking for. They were spotted on the street for a bit, but it looks like they decided to take one of the back entrances to the casino, or they went to another one."

Joe rubbed the bridge of his nose, feeling a headache forming between his eyes. "Send the details to the lawyers and have everybody keep a lookout. Let me know if anyone finds them."

"Will do, Boss."

He hung up the phone and took a deep breath. His office door opened, and his sister sauntered through, her nose wrinkling at what was left of his failed servant.

"I thought you were going out tonight," he said when she sat down.

"I was. And then there was a riot in front of my favorite restaurant that had your fingerprints all over it. So I decided to spend some time in, only to find my entrance locked."

"What are you talking about? The doors to the casino are never locked."

"Not the doors, brother dear, my *entrance*."

His expression of frustration was explosive. He started cussing in modern English and worked his way back through languages that hadn't been spoken in several thousand years.

When he'd wound down, she lifted an eyebrow at him. "I take it you know the cause of my inconvenience?"

Joe waved at the pile of drying ooze. "If I'd known how badly he'd screwed up, I'd have flayed him first."

"Your regret, then, is that you killed him too quickly?"

"And that I'll have to have the maid service in here in a couple hours. It would have been more convenient to do it somewhere he wouldn't have left a mess, but I saw no need to draw out his punishment."

"I see. I take it your plan isn't proceeding the way you'd prefer it to?"

"No," he huffed. "They haven't used the token once. Plus, they keep hiding it behind something that blocks my connection to it and its ability to collect the emotions of the people in the group. Oh, and they appear to have done something to your entrance."

"I thought you were sending people to encourage them to use it. Surely your professional temptresses were able to manage something."

"Nothing I've been able to verify. I don't think he even noticed some of them."

Tanda's lips twisted slightly. "Then what do you think they did to my entrance?"

"If they were still carrying the token, which by all appearances seems to be the case, I think they activated it."

She blinked. "But humans can't use it."

"Humans can't use it the way we can," he corrected. "If they have the magic and the blood sacrifice, they can absolutely use it."

"So we find out where they've gone, follow them, get the token back, and kill them there. It won't even be as hard as destroying them here. Your power in our realm is unmatched."

"Humans create more than a little chaos when they use magic they don't understand, and that's assuming I can get to our realm without any of our enemies finding me. We left for a reason."

Tanda shrugged. "If you want to leave one of your tokens running around, out of your control, that's up to you. I wouldn't want to, but I've always been the flighty one."

Joe ground his teeth.

* * *

Violet did her best to center herself in her new body. She could still smell Derek on the wind and hear him talking to Samantha. So many new things overwhelmed her senses that it took a while to sift through them.

When she thought she could, she tried walking toward the Derek smell—and promptly fell over. With a growl of frustration, she struggled back to her feet and tried again.

Eventually, she got all her feet and legs working in the right order and direction and set off in the direction of the smell. He was further ahead, and the scent was fading, but she was sure she was going in the right direction.

Then the wind shifted, and she lost the scent.

They'd moved from some kind of grass to a forest with large, smelly trees. There was so much information in every whiff she got from the trees around her except for which direction Derek had gone.

Tired and thirsty, Violet laid her fluffy head on her paws and whimpered. She wished she'd been more outdoorsy. Derek enjoyed hiking and camping and was probably doing fine in the woods. If he had Samantha, and she'd figured out how to fly, she was probably fine catching her own food.

Violet knew dogs could hunt. She was even pretty sure she knew what kind of dog she was. Why she'd been turned into a dog was still a mystery, along with why Derek hadn't been changed into anything.

Maybe whatever magic had brought them here had decided he was perfect the way he was. She might have even agreed—she'd certainly never had any complaints—but she wished he'd stayed with her. Or come back for her.

She sighed and pushed herself to her feet, sniffing along the forest floor for a hint of Derek's scent, when the wind brought her the distinct odor of stone, cinnamon, chamomile, and something indescribable that made her hackles rise.

She backed away from the scent, growling low, and crouched away when the source came into view.

An old woman was riding a mortar and pestle through the woods like it was a raft in a stream. She was sitting in the bowl of the mortar, her silver hair playing about her face in the wind, her hand on the pestle as though she was using it to steer.

Violet could tell the moment the old woman spotted her and adjusted her course to stop in front of her.

"Well, what have we here? A pretty girl lost in my forest while night is falling," the old woman said. "That won't do. No, that won't do at all. I think I'm going to have to take her home and make sure she's taken care of. Would you like to come home with me, Pretty Girl?"

Violet started to growl at her until she remembered the stories about the old woman who rode around in a mortar and pestle. She bit off her growl and stared at her warily.

She cackled, and it reminded Violet of every cartoon witch she'd ever seen. "Oh, you're a smart one, you are. Would you like to come with me and be my honored guest? I have a nice, warm fire, a big, soft bed, and a path that tends to bring wayward heroes to my door."

When she perked up at the mention of heroes, the witch cackled again.

"Yes, there's a young idiot chasing around my forest," she said, reaching out to pet Violet's ears, "and I suspect you're more than a little irritated at him. Why don't I take you to my home and see what we can do about getting you back where you belong?"

Violet stood up and shook herself before padding over to the witch's strange conveyance. Before she could jump in, the witch picked her up and lifted her in over the side. She scrabbled to get her feet under her while the witch jumped in after her.

The witch met her disgruntled *woof* with a cackle of delight, and they were off through the woods.

The wind brought every kind of smell into the bowl, and Violet suddenly understood why dogs stuck their heads out car windows. She was safe—for the moment at least—relatively comfortable, and able to enjoy all the smells around her.

The woman's house was less exciting than she was expecting, though something about it definitely smelled odd. The walls were slightly rounded, more like an over-stuffed chair than a building ready to fall over, with a scraggly, thatched roof, and windows set at odd angles.

Her door was set between two large, bare shrubs, with a twisted cobblestone path to get to it. The fence around her home was made of strangely shaped ivory posts that smelled oddly compelling to Violet.

Once the mortar bowl came to a stop outside the house, it tilted and let both of them walk out, before righting itself and going around behind the house.

Violet gave a curious *woof*, and the witch patted her on the top of her head.

"Not for you to know, Princess," she said. "Maybe someday, when your bones are brittle, your teeth are dull, and your mind is tougher than the mountains. But not yet."

The wind shifted, and all sorts of interesting smells washed across her nose. Violet found herself pressing her side against the witch's legs, her tail wagging, while she strained to keep from following the delightful scents.

"You're a good girl, Princess. Let's give you the tour so you can explore and get what you need while I'm gone."

* * *

Derek was exhausted when he found the gate to the witch's house. He held an angry hawk who'd finally figured out how to hold on to his hand without putting her long, sharp claws through his skin. Cuts and blood covered his hands and arms from her attempts to fight him, and then her attempts to secure herself to him after she'd gotten tired of fighting.

He thought it was near dusk, but the constant rolling, dark clouds overhead had made it look like dusk for hours. It was definitely getting darker, though, and he hoped it was nightfall instead of a storm.

Sam squawked at him and pecked his arm until he stroked a hand down her back.

"I found shelter," he told her. When she pecked at him again, he smacked her lightly on the back of her head.

"I realize it's scary, but we're here without food or weapons. We're lucky I felt my gun getting hot and got rid of it before it blew up. Unless you want me to be dealing with burns and shrapnel from holding on to it? You saw the hole it made when it exploded."

She shook herself in the way he'd come to realize meant he was right, but she wasn't going to admit to being wrong.

He sighed. "So, we're going to go up there and ask for help from the only thing resembling civilization. And then we're going to use that help to go find Violet."

Sam squawked and shook herself again, and Derek ran his hand down her feathers.

They'd been fighting since he'd managed to catch her, and he knew she was afraid. One of the things they had in common was a tendency to run toward the things that scared them. That had served them both well in their careers, but it made interpersonal relationships difficult.

"Once we have Violet, we'll look for a way home. Maybe whoever lives here can help with that, too."

Sam squawked, and Derek waited for her to peck at him. When she didn't, he ran a hand down her feathers again.

The fence made of bone didn't fill him with joy. Neither did the gate made of the same thing, nor the way the leafless bushes in front of the house moved without wind.

Everything about the house told him to stay away, but he knew when he needed local help. If Sam hadn't fought him every time he'd tried to help her, they might not need the help, but he didn't blame her. And he didn't blame Violet for running off because she was scared.

The *creak* as he pushed the gate open sounded like a scream, and Derek suppressed a shudder. It groaned when he closed it behind him, and he didn't like that sound any better.

None of the stones on the path to the door were set right, tilting one direction or another, but the grass on either side of it was long and tried to twist around his boots. By the time he made it to the porch, the door was open, and an old woman in a shapeless dress, wearing a colorful shawl, and leaning on a gnarled wooden cane was watching him.

"Why are you here?" she demanded. "I didn't invite you."

Derek squared his shoulders and nodded his head to the old woman. "I'm here to ask for help, ma'am. I was separated from one of my companions earlier, and I was hoping you'd seen her."

"Oh?" She cackled. "One of your companions, is it? You're the first man I've seen in weeks."

"I was traveling with a woman."

Sam fluffed at him, and the witch pointed at her.

"What have you got there? It's female, isn't it?"

"Yes, ma'am. I'm looking for another woman."

"One not enough for you?" The witch glared at him, and Derek had to fight the urge to look down at his feet.

"This is my sister. The woman who's missing is my girlfriend."

"Just a friend? Well, why are you sure she's missing? Maybe she decided to strike out on her own." The witch gave him a sly look.

"She wouldn't do that," Derek said. "She's not... this isn't the kind of place she'd be comfortable in."

"Oh? You'd be surprised what a woman who's been abandoned in a strange place can do. Did you expect her to wait for you until you came back and found her?"

"Yes, actually, or not to move too far away from where we were."

"So, you went back to find her? Did you tell her to sit? Stay?"

His gut jolted at the way she said the commands. "I didn't."

"Well, you can't expect her to follow directions you didn't give her, can you?"

"No, ma'am."

"I might be able to help you," she said.

"Thank you."

"And it won't even cost you much. That bird you're holding will make a very nice stew. I'll trade you information for her."

Sam squawked in indignation, and Derek shook his head. "I won't trade my sister's life for the information. What else do you want?"

"Hmm," the witch said, her expression calculating. "Perhaps something you don't value as highly. You have a shiny token in your pocket, do you not?"

Derek shoved his hand in his pocket and found the gold poker chip the man in the casino had given him. He'd actually forgotten he had it.

The way the old woman looked at it, her eyes gleaming with avarice, told him it might be worth more than he'd thought.

A dog barked inside the house, and the woman spun. "Hush, Princess, I'm talking to the nice young man at the door."

The dog whined, and she sighed. "Yes, I'll feed you soon. No hawk, though, he doesn't want to trade."

"I can't give up the token," he told her, "but maybe there's something else I can do. Do you need any work done? I'm pretty good with my hands."

The old woman looked him up and down, and the avaricious gleam in her eye turned calculating. "I'll bet you are. All right, work for me for three days, and I'll give you a hint to find your girlfriend."

"Help me find her first, and then I'll work for you."

"Oh, ho! You think to cheat an old woman? You'll work first, though I'll swear she's not in any immediate danger. Will that satisfy your mind?"

Derek struggled with the decision. He needed the help, or at least a place to rest, and he didn't trust that he'd be able to find Violet on his own.

"All right," he said. "I'll make that bargain."

The woman stepped out her front door and closed it behind her. "I'll show you where you'll be sleeping, then I'll put you to work."

* * *

The barn, as the woman had called it, was filthy. It held two stalls that hadn't been cleaned out in ages, filled with old, moldy hay, water buckets half full of stagnant water, and evidence of a leak in the roof near one of the walls.

One of the few things in good repair was a sturdy bird perch next to one of the walls. Samantha had regarded it with suspicion before taking her first step onto it, but settled quickly enough when it didn't shift under her.

"There's tools over there," the old woman said with a wave at a dark corner in the back. "Decide where you'll be the most comfortable, then come up to the house, and I'll get you some blankets."

She turned and left him staring at the space and the work that needed to be done. Obviously, the stalls were occasionally occupied, but he couldn't tell what kind of animal would want to live in that stable.

Derek found the tools and set to work cleaning out the stable. He had one stall done by the time night had truly fallen, and it was too dark to work without a lamp.

Samantha had occupied herself, following him around the barn and pouncing on what he suspected were vermin hiding in the old hay.

She was sleeping on the perch when he took himself up to the house, walking slowly as the ever-present clouds mostly covered the moon.

The old woman opened the kitchen door and gave him a disgusted look. "You are *not* coming into my kitchen smelling like that. Sit there, and I'll bring you some dinner. Or you can go bathe in the bucket and come inside."

"Where's the bucket?" Derek asked, more excited at the prospect of getting clean than a chance to go inside the house.

"Around that way," she said, gesturing with her cane. "I suppose you'll be wanting clothes, too, won't you?"

"If you have something I can borrow until I can wash what I'm wearing, I'd appreciate the kindness."

The old woman harumphed at him and shut the door. She came back with a thin towel, a stack of clothes, and a lantern.

"Leave your clothes on the stool next to the bucket, and I'll add them to the washing up tomorrow," she told him.

"I can wash them, ma'am. I just need more light to work by."

She harumphed at him again and shut the door. The dog barked inside, and she answered it, but he couldn't hear what she said.

Tired, sore, and anxious to get as clean as he could, Derek went in the direction she'd pointed. When he found the "bucket," he laughed. While it was built like a bucket, it was large enough to be a small pond, and low enough to simply step into, with a clever system coming over the roof to fill it with water, and another to take water down to the garden he could just make out in the dark.

It was the work of a moment to shed his clothes, which he dutifully put on the stool, and step into the water. While he hadn't expected the water to be hot, he also hadn't expected it to be as warm as it was, and he was grateful it wasn't freezing.

He'd found a sliver of soap in the pile of clothes, and he scrubbed himself as thoroughly as possible. His scrapes and cuts burned with the application of the soap, but he felt better after it was all done. The cuts didn't look as bad as he'd expected when he was toweling off, but he stopped inspecting them when a beautiful, massive, long-haired collie came running around the house and barked at him.

"Oh, aren't you a pretty girl!" he said, his towel forgotten. She walked over to him and licked his chest along his ribs. He let her, then brought his hand up slowly to pet her behind the ears, and she leaned into him.

He took a step back, and she leaned into him harder. He took another step back, and she jumped up, her paws against his chest, and licked his cheek. Her weight and the sudden movement sent him backward into the water.

Derek struggled to his feet, the soaked towel clutched in his hand, and ran his hand down his face to clear the water from his eyes. The dog was barking and prancing backward, showing her obvious enjoyment of the game. If he hadn't known better, he'd swear she was laughing at him.

"Princess!" the old witch called. "Don't bother the man in his bath! Come have your dinner."

The dog barked again, then raced off toward the kitchen door.

* * *

When Derek returned to the kitchen door, it was with a damp shirt in his hands, and wearing the pants the witch had given him. He'd done his best to clean his boots and socks and hoped they were up to her standards.

She opened the door and looked him over.

"Is there something wrong with the shirt I gave you?" she asked.

"No, it's working very well as a pouch," he said, and held it up so she could see it.

"That's not its intended purpose."

"And yet, that's how I'm using it."

"Why are you using it like that?" she asked.

"Because there are no belt loops or pockets on these pants, and I have too many things I keep in my pockets to carry them in my hands."

She harumphed at him, then turned and walked into the kitchen. He followed her and was surprised to see a place set at the table with a huge steak on it. The plates and utensils were gold, and the tankard of ale looked like it was covered with gold filigree and gems.

"There's your dinner," she said, pointing to the table. "Sit and eat so I can clean up and go to bed."

Derek moved to the table and saw the dog that had knocked him into the bath. She was lying next to the table and looking forlornly at a wooden bowl of unappetizing soup. He moved his chair to sit down, and her eyes turned to look up at him.

He sat, and she humphed, looking back at her bowl and pushing at it gently with her paw.

"Is your dog okay?" he asked.

"Oh, she's pouting because she doesn't like her dinner, but vegetable soup is good for her."

Derek nodded and cut into his steak. He picked up one piece with the fork and palmed the other one. While he raised the fork to his lips, he watched the dog, then dropped the other piece of steak near her head while he reached for his drink.

Out of the corner of his eye, he watched the old woman puttering around in the kitchen, and cut more pieces of steak. One more went into his mouth, and another went on the floor to the dog, who was watching him with rapt attention.

"Did you put your clothes on the stool?" she asked him.

"I did." He looked up at her. "I'll clean them in the morning when there's enough light to see."

"I told you I'd clean them. See that she eats while I do that. If she doesn't finish that soup, she has to sleep outside."

The dog whined and laid her head on her paws, the very picture of doggy misery.

"Yes, ma'am," Derek said and watched her leave through the door. Once she was gone, he cut the rest of his steak into big pieces and turned to the dog.

"Do you like steak?" he asked, and she sat up. "Will you bite me if I feed you?"

He held out a piece to her, and she looked at it for a long moment, then tried to take it out of his fingers without biting him but couldn't quite get her teeth on it. He moved it to the center of his palm, and she managed it better.

"Good girl," he said, patting her head. Then he placed the plate with the rest of the steak on the floor and took her soup. It was cold and lumpy, but he'd eaten worse. With only a small sigh of regret for the rest of his steak, he drank the soup out of the bowl, doing his best to avoid actually tasting it.

When he turned back to the dog, she was licking the plate clean, her tail wagging furiously behind her. He patted her head, and she looked up at him and licked his face. With a chuckle, he traded their dishes again, and then went back to petting her.

He'd never seen a collie her size before, but something about her coloring was familiar.

"Are you a good Princess?" he asked the dog, and she barked. Her tail stopped wagging, and she sat down. "You're a beautiful Princess. You sit so pretty."

She growled at him.

"Oookay," he said, drawing the word out. "I guess gratitude for my steak only goes so far. Are you going to jump at me if I stand up?"

The dog laid down again, her head on her paws, and watched him. Not quite the picture of doggy misery he'd seen earlier, but she definitely wasn't happy.

Derek finished his drink, then stood to take his dishes to the sink… where he discovered there wasn't a sink. He was standing there when the old woman came in and snatched the plate and tankard out of his hands.

"Finished already, did ya?" she asked.

"Yes, and I was going to wash my plate, but I'm not certain how you do that in your kitchen."

She scoffed at him and went to the door with the gold plate and the gem-encrusted tankard and threw them into the yard.

"What are you doing? I offered to clean them!"

She turned to him and shrugged. "Why bother? They're just plates."

He opened his mouth to protest, but couldn't. She wasn't wrong, but he had trouble understanding why she would do that.

"Did you get enough to eat?" she asked.

"Yes. Thank you very much for your hospitality."

"All right, out to the barn with you. I'll need you bright and early."

Derek grabbed his shirt bundle off the table and took the lantern she handed him to find his way down to the barn. The sky was overcast, so he had no idea how late it was, but he could feel the exhaustion of the day weighing on him.

He hoped, wherever she was, Violet was safe.

* * *

The only sign it was dawn was the muted glow of the sun behind the gray clouds that hung heavily in the sky.

Derek woke to the old witch knocking on the door to the barn with her cane. She pushed the heavy doors open and walked over to a squawking Samantha with a gold bowl that matched the plate he'd eaten off the night before.

Sam fluffed her feathers at the bowl, then dove in, only coming up long enough for Derek to see the red that covered her beak. Whatever she was eating was bloody, and she was enjoying it.

"Breakfast is on the table," the old woman told him. "Eat, then you'll work. Can't have you collapsing from hunger."

He walked up to the house, stretching his limbs to work out a long night of sleeping on packed earth, and secured the tie on the shirt bundle he was carrying. Wisps of fog lay along the ground between the barn and the house, and it got denser further away from the buildings. When he walked into the house, he saw a steaming mound of bacon, eggs, sausages, potatoes, and other things he didn't recognize on a large golden plate.

There was also a very dejected looking dog staring sadly at a bowl full of dried bread. Before he sat down, Derek handed her a sausage link. She gulped it down with a great deal of enjoyment, so he gave her another while he started in on the eggs.

When he'd made enough room on his plate, he took her bowl of bread and mixed it in with his potatoes, which had been chopped up and fried in grease. He lifted a piece of bacon to his mouth, and the dog whined.

A glance over showed her sitting very still and watching the bacon in his hand intently. He looked at the pile sitting on his plate and sighed.

"You can't have all of it," he told her, and handed her the piece he'd picked up. She took it gently, her teeth barely grazing his fingertips, and ate it delicately. She got half his bacon and a couple pieces of potato in her bowl when he set it back on the floor in front of her.

The old woman came in as he was finishing his meal and checked her bowl, which she was licking the bottom of.

"That's a good Princess," she said, patting the dog. "Now, Ivan, it's time for you to get to work."

"Yes, ma'am," he said and stood. "Except, my name isn't Ivan."

"Oh? Are you not Ivan the Idiot, then?"

"No, ma'am."

"Then, do you want to give me your true name so I can call you whenever I want you?"

He saw the calculating look on her face and hesitated. "Ivan will work just fine, ma'am."

"Ah, maybe he's not such an idiot, your hero," she said to the dog. The dog woofed and wagged her tail. "Come along, Ivan, we're going to start with having you fix the pen for my goat."

Derek was dubious about the goat pen, but he followed her out the door—wincing slightly when she threw his breakfast plate into the garden—and down to the fenced area behind the barn. The dog trotted happily alongside him, and he couldn't help but reach out and run his fingers through her fur.

Something about the dog was familiar, but he couldn't put his finger on what.

A thick fog lay about halfway into the pen she took him to, and he would have thought it had been built for a few cows or horses rather than a single goat. The fence was made of large wood posts and rails that looked like small trees.

Small trees that had been savaged by a beaver.

Large chunks were missing from sections all over the fence. Nothing had fallen off yet, but it was a near thing in places.

"Do you know much about fencing, Ivan?" the old woman asked.

"Yes, ma'am; I grew up on a ranch. How many goats do you have in there?"

"Just the one," she said, and whistled.

Out of the fog trotted the largest goat Derek had ever seen. Bigger than most horses, it pranced its way over to the old woman and leaned down to nibble on the top rail. Suddenly, the missing chunks made sense. Derek was surprised it hadn't managed to bite through them.

"She likes to sleep in the barn when it's cold," the old woman explained, patting the top of the goat's head, "but she won't stop chewing on the fence, so I need the damaged rails replaced."

"Are the fencing tools in the barn?"

"Yes. And the extra rails are in a pile behind it."

"I'll get to it, ma'am."

"I'll have dinner ready when you're done. And Princess will be out here to help you."

The dog barked and wagged her tail, and Derek was reminded of just how much bigger she was than other collies. Maybe the animals just got big here?

"All right, Princess, let's go get some tools." She ran over to him and bumped gently against his legs. He stroked her neck and back, more certain than ever that there was something very familiar about her.

They came back with the tools and the first rail to hear a great *crack*. The goat danced back, splinters of wood falling out of her mouth, and the rail she was chewing on fell to the ground. She bleated, kicked at the wood, and jumped over the fence.

"Shit!" Derek said, dropping the rail and the tools, his hands free to engage the giant creature.

Princess barked and ran at the goat, who bleated and backed up, then jumped back over the fence into the pen. She stood, focused and ready for the goat to try something, while Derek picked up the tools and rail.

"Good girl, Princess," he said. "You're going to be a big help with this project."

* * *

It took all day to fix the pen, and both Derek and the dog were drooping by the time they got back to the odd house. Princess flopped in front of the fireplace, but the old woman stopped Derek at the door.

"Bath," she said, pointing him toward the bucket around back.

He nodded and trudged around the back. His clothes were clean and folded on the stool, with a new pair of socks on top. It only took a moment to strip out of his clothes and step into the warm water with a sigh of relief.

What was left of the soap was where he'd left it on the side of the bucket the day before, and he scrubbed himself thoroughly. As dirty as he had to get for work, he enjoyed being clean when he could be, and this kind of bath felt like a luxury.

It was so relaxing, in fact, that he had to shake himself to keep from falling asleep. He got out and let the cool air wake him up enough to dry off and get dressed. It took a few minutes to unwrap the shirt bundle and move all his things back into his pockets, but he took the time to check everything and make sure it was in working order.

He flipped the gold token through his fingers. It was worth something in Vegas, or it was supposed to be, but he didn't know why the old witch would want it. She certainly didn't seem to have any use for actual gold, with the way she'd been treating the plates. If it would help get Violet back faster, maybe he should trade it.

With a sigh, he put it back in his pocket, though he continued to finger the ridges along the side.

"Where are you, Violet?" he asked out loud. "I wish you were here. I miss you."

Princess barked, and he smiled. He stepped away from the water and braced for her to come around the side of the house.

She was obviously tired, but happy to see him. Her tail swished back and forth like a fan behind her. He let go of the token, letting it fall into his pocket, and reached out to pet her.

"Come to knock me in the bath again?" he asked, ruffling her ears.

She barked and leaned into him.

"You did a great job today with the goat. Maybe you can help me find Violet once my three days of work are up."

Princess growled and shoved into him.

"Don't want to help me? I don't think she changed into a bird like Sam did. I just wish I had something with her scent on it so you had something to work with. Your owner said she wasn't in danger, but I'm worried that she's cold, hungry, and miserable."

She woofed and bumped against him again.

"At least I can make sure you're not hungry. Though how you got this big eating bread and vegetable soup, I have no idea."

They got to the kitchen door and went inside. Another steak on a gold plate and more soup in a wooden bowl were waiting for them.

"Leave your clothes on the stool again?" the old woman asked.

"Yes, ma'am," he said, cutting into his steak while the dog sniffed at the bowl of soup.

"All right, I'll go see to them while you finish your dinner and get to bed. It took you too long working on that fence today. I had other things for you to do."

"Yes, ma'am," he told her.

Once she was gone, Princess was sitting prettily next to him, doing her best not to beg for his steak. He laughed, speared half the steak on his knife and fork, then turned to put the plate down where she could get to it. Alternating bites of steak with the vegetable soup wasn't bad, and they were both finished by the time the old woman got back.

"You must have been hungry," she said, looking at his cleaned plate. "Well, you did a lot of good work today. Head to bed, and I'll see you bright and early tomorrow."

She walked him to the door, handed him a lantern, and threw the plate out into the garden. He didn't see the dishes from the day before, so maybe there was someone who came by and picked them up? He hadn't heard anybody during the day, but he'd spent most of it with a noisy, obnoxious goat and a barking dog.

When he got to the barn, Samantha flew over to him and landed, very carefully, on his shoulder. He waited for her claws to pierce through his shirt and was surprised when something solid pressed against his skin instead.

"Hey, Sam, did you miss me?"

She rubbed her face against his, and he stroked his hand down her feathers. "You landed very well; have you been practicing?"

Her head bobbed in an enthusiastic acknowledgement, and he smiled.

"Good. You know I haven't been neglecting you on purpose, right?"

She acknowledged him and rubbed her face against his again. He yawned, and she squawked in indignation.

"Sorry. I'm beat. Did you keep my bed clear?"

She bobbed again, then flew back to her perch and fluffed her feathers. He got the feeling he'd woken her up when he came in, but he was glad to see her.

* * *

It was certainly early when the old woman came to wake him up, but it definitely wasn't bright. The pale light of dawn struggled through the clouds and only just managed to create enough light to see by.

"Breakfast is on the table, Ivan," the old woman said, holding up the bowl of something bloody, which Sam attacked with abandon.

"Yes, ma'am," Derek said with a yawn. He stretched and felt the solid thing Sam had landed on the night before in his sleeve. He stood and felt for it, then realized a piece of leather had been sewn into the shoulders of his shirt. "Thank you for the alterations to my shirt. I appreciate it."

"You're welcome. Now hurry and eat. You have a long day today."

Derek headed to the house, and Princess greeted him at the door. She led him back to the table and looked pointedly at the bowl that had been put down for her. Without any preamble, Derek switched out the bread for his sausage and added a couple slices of bacon to it before he sat down.

Princess set about eating her breakfast with obvious delight while he tucked into his, and they were both done by the time the old woman got back to the house. She harumphed at his plate and threw it out the door into the garden.

"Follow me," she said, and led him deeper into the house, his lantern in her hand.

From the outside, Derek had assumed it was a one or two room hut, but her path wound through corridors and past impossible doors until they got to a storage room. She hung the lantern on a peg near the door and motioned him inside.

It was full, floor to ceiling, with shelves of silver plates, bowls, and other dishes he couldn't identify. Everything had such a level of tarnish on it that he could tell they'd been sitting in there for years without any kind of care.

"I understand you know something about polishing," she told him.

"I've polished a few things."

"Everything in this room will shine by dinner."

"It might take—"

"Dinner will not be served until it is finished. You may have Princess to help you, if you'd like."

Derek hesitated. "I'm not sure—"

"The tools are on the table over there. Best get started. It's going to take you a while."

The old woman pushed past him and went off into the rest of the house.

"This hut doesn't occasionally turn into a blue box, does it?" he asked Princess.

She woofed and wagged her tail at him.

There was a pile of cloth strips, a bag of powder, and a jug of water on the table. He took a bowl off the shelf, sprinkled some of the powder and some of the water in it, then grabbed a fork off another shelf and mixed them until he had a paste.

He started with the biggest pieces on the bottom shelves and got to work. Princess laid down next to the table and took a nap for a while. She woke up and trotted out to the rest of the house. When she came back, he was halfway through the second shelf, all the biggest pieces finished and gleaming on the bottom.

"Are you back for another nap, Princess?" he asked.

She woofed and laid down next to the table again.

"You're such a pretty dog, Princess. Your coloring reminds me of Violet's hair. Shall I tell you about her?"

The dog sat up and woofed at him, and he laughed.

"All right. We met while we were both traveling to see friends—different friends who knew each other, so we all ended up at the same bar. I couldn't keep my eyes off her, but she was focused on laughing with the people she knew and getting to know everybody else at the table. Eventually, she ended up sitting next to me, and I did everything I could to keep her there for the rest of the night."

Princess woofed and laid her head down on her paws.

"We'd both had a few drinks when I kissed her later, but it was like magic. She fit against me so perfectly, and her lips tasted like the honey whiskey she'd been drinking. I don't know which of us was more upset when we realized we lived on opposite sides of the country. But we made it work, even when I was deployed and couldn't contact her for days or weeks, or when she was super busy and fell asleep while we were talking."

He finished a bowl and got another one. "She's amazing and perfect, Princess, one of the kindest, prettiest, sweetest, sexiest women I've ever known."

Princess whined, and he looked over at her. She'd crawled closer to him, and he patted her.

"You're pretty, too, Princess, but she's my other half. I'm going to spend the rest of my life making up for not being able to find her right away, and I'm okay with that. Every day letting her know how much she means to me sounds like the perfect way to spend my retirement."

With a *woof,* Princess sat up and licked his hand, then put her paws on the table to reach up to his cheek. Derek scratched her ears and laughed.

"Do you want to hear more stories?" he asked, and Princess woofed. "All right, how about our first date? The one that took nine months to make happen and lasted almost an hour."

Derek talked about Violet and found himself smiling even as the ache of missing her grew. Princess was a receptive audience, and he talked until he was hoarse, the tarnished silver shining faster under his rag as he moved through the stack on the shelves… until he reached for the next dish and found he was done.

* * *

Dinner was the same thing as the previous two nights, but Derek was so tired, he could barely keep his head up enough to eat. Princess had followed him out to the bath and stayed nearby, her head on her paws while she watched him.

When the old woman dismissed him to the barn after throwing the gold plate into the garden again, Princess went with him out to the barn.

"If you're not back by the time I go to sleep, you're sleeping in the barn tonight," the old woman warned. Princess gave a brief *woof* in reply and kept following him.

"You have a nice, warm fire to sleep by," Derek told her. "You should go back."

She ignored him, and he was glad for the company. When he laid down with his blanket, she laid down next to him, and he was grateful for the companionship.

He woke to Sam squawking and the old witch tutting at her. Princess stretched next to him, and he realized he'd put his arm around her in his sleep. Since he'd dreamed about a mundane day with Violet, doing the dishes and organizing the pantry, he must have been comfortable. It was a welcome change from the ones where he was searching for her through an endless, foggy forest, but it didn't change how much he missed her.

He greeted Sam, and the old woman shooed him toward the house.

The sky was the endless overcast he was used to, with moments when a sunbeam almost made it through during his walk to the house. Only half his usual breakfast was on his plate on the table. The other was on a plate on the floor for Princess.

"I think we've been caught," he said, and Princess woofed in agreement. They both set to their meal with an appetite, and he waited for the old woman to scold them when she walked in. Instead, she repeated her pattern of the last few days, and threw the gold plates out the door before turning to him with his task for the day.

"Your sister tells me you're some kind of military man," she said.

"She did? How?" At her raised eyebrow, he nodded. "Yes, ma'am, I am."

"Can you use anything besides that toy you brought here with you?"

"Several things, and I'm pretty good at improvising if I have to."

"Well, you're going to need something when you leave," she said and started walking through the house. She followed a different route and ended up at the door to a room filled with weapons and armor in various stages of disrepair.

She tried pieces on him one at a time, discarding some for being the wrong size, the wrong shape, or too damaged to repair quickly. When they'd gone through the pile, he ended up with a battered breastplate that looked like it was actually made of plastic, a shield that had obviously been used as a pot lid at one point, and a helmet that could have doubled as a colander. She'd also come up with a compound bow that looked like it was about to snap, and a long stick she called a staff.

"They'll need some polish, of course." She chuckled. "Can't have a knight in shining armor without the shine, now, can we?"

"I'm hardly a knight."

"Oh? You don't fight for money or a king?" she asked, her eyes shrewd.

"I mean, I do get paid, and the commander in chief is the head of the country, but no, not for a king."

"A belief, then. With an oath to defend the principles of that belief and the people they protect. A paladin with a strange god, but I've heard of stranger. And you'll still need armor that shines. You can sit by the fire with the silver polish to see if it catches the light."

Derek followed the old woman and kept his belief that the plastic and metal would never shine to himself. He'd been wrong before, and this was his final day working for the old witch. If she wanted him to polish trash, he'd polish trash.

He took the polish she handed him and sat on a stool near the fire. Princess laid down next to him and let out a big yawn.

"No goats to chase today?" he asked with a laugh.

She woofed and rolled onto her back, her legs stretching while her tail wagged back and forth along the floor. Derek leaned over to scratch her belly, and her back leg started to kick.

"I'm happy for the company," he said with a final pat, and set to work on the armor.

He worked until his back and shoulders ached. First, the breastplate, until he got it clean enough that it might have been metal. Then the helmet, and he watched the paste patch the holes until it was a solid metal bowl. He poked and scratched at the dull gray metal, but he couldn't make the holes reappear.

The shield took the longest, and after several hours, he was convinced more than ever that it was, in fact, a pot lid. He stoked the fire to get as much light as he could, and there was nothing in his hand but pot metal.

The old woman came out to check on him and he showed her what he'd gotten done so far. "Though I don't know if there's much more I can do to make this shine."

She licked her thumb and bent to rub it against the metal. It shone just a little before her spit dried, and she shook her head. "No, it's there. I just don't think you're seeing it the way it needs to be seen."

Her gaze rose suddenly to his, and he found he couldn't look away from her. "Would you see the truth, or the possibilities?"

Derek couldn't blink. He wanted to, but his eyes refused until he opened his mouth and answered her. "Both, if I can, but the truth above all."

She broke the eye contact, and he closed his eyes as his heart pounded in his chest, though whether from panic or fear, he couldn't tell. When he tried to open them again, she licked her thumb and swiped across both of his eyelids.

* * *

Derek shivered and opened his eyes. He looked down at the shield in his hands and suddenly *knew* what it was. It had been a lid at one point, but it had also been picked up and used to defend the person using it from hot frying oil, wild animals, and humans looking to prey on the innocent. It had been a pot lid, but it became a shield, and it deserved to be respected for what it had become.

He looked up at the woman, and her face shifted so much that he had to look away after a moment before he became dizzy.

"What are you?" he asked.

"Many things to many people. A savior and a creature out of nightmare. Sometimes all of them at once."

Another shiver ran down his spine, and he nodded.

He glanced over at Princess, hoping to take comfort in her happy, furry presence, and saw Violet curled up next to him.

His breath rushed out of his lungs, and he struggled to breathe. She'd been here the entire time, and he hadn't noticed. Worse, he'd treated her like a dog, like a pet! A well-loved one, but still—his face burned with shame.

"Did you see her change when you came into this world?" the witch asked.

"No," he said, afraid to reach out for his sleeping lover. "I watched my sister turn into a bird that I would never be able to track, so I chased her. At first, I thought Violet was right behind me, but then I couldn't find her."

"She's loyal and brave and smart. There are worse things she could have become, and you appreciated those things about her, even when she couldn't speak."

"I've always appreciated those things about her."

"She could hear it more often," the witch said. "Now, get those shined. You're being hunted and must leave tomorrow. If they're not ready, I don't know that you'll survive."

Derek looked at the armor he'd worked on and saw what needed to be done. "I'll be ready."

She nodded and left him to his work.

He worked late into the night and stopped only when Princess/Violet nudged him off the stool and toward the table. The old witch served him quietly and sat down to eat with him. She served dinner that night on sturdy earthenware plates with plain carved cups for beer.

"What happened to the gold plates?"

"Refuse to eat off anything less than gold?" She cackled at his look.

"I thought the gold was over the top to begin with."

"We're done with the gold plates, though you'll need gold and your wits about you tomorrow. Get some sleep; you must wake early tomorrow."

She took the plate from in front of him and put it in the sink, along with her own. Derek nodded and left for the barn. When Princess/Violet followed him, he felt a pang in his chest, and turned to tell her to sleep in the house.

Instead, he saw how happy she looked, how much she enjoyed being with him, and he couldn't send her away.

"Violet." He knelt. She licked his face, and he smiled, burying his face in her furry neck. "Thank you for staying. I'm sorry I didn't see you. I'm sorry I lost you."

She whined and leaned into him, her tail waving like a fan behind her.

"I'd tell you that you don't have to stay with me tonight, but I'm torn. I want you to be comfortable, and I crave your company, however I can have it."

She licked his face again, and he stood up. They walked to the barn, her head bumping against his hand until he buried his fingers in the fur he could reach.

When they got to the barn, Derek checked on Sam, and saw she was wearing a gold band with a shiny, black feather on her leg.

"Where did that come from?" he asked. She squawked and fluffed her feathers at him. His enhanced vision, courtesy of the witch, let him see how pleased she was with herself.

"All right, keep your secrets," Derek said with a laugh. "We're leaving tomorrow, anyway."

He reached to stroke her feathers, and she leaned into his touch. A niggle of guilt tried to work its way into his gut, a reminder that he hadn't spent much time with her at all, but she looked happy and healthy, and had obviously kept herself busy while he'd worked.

Violet was already curled up on his blankets, and he laid down next to her.

He woke up with her head on his chest and her cold nose pressed against his chin. With a chuckle, he scratched her behind her ears until she stretched and stood up. She was happy and relaxed, and it struck him how often he'd seen a tinge of anxiety at the corner of her eyes and smile.

A rush of wind outside the barn had him on his feet and moving toward the door. Sam was off her perch and out the door ahead of him, the raven feather clutched in her talons.

A raven the size of the house had landed in the yard and was pecking away at the garden. Sam flew in front of his face and around the beak that Derek was sure could swallow her whole.

With its wings folded behind its back, the raven let out a squawk that sounded like "Yaga."

The old woman opened the door and waved her hands at him. "Give me room, you old buzzard. I'm not the one paying you today."

She slammed the door, and the raven pecked at the roof of the house until Sam flew up into his face, then around the back of his head to grab at the feathers on his back. It spread its wings and tried to knock her away, but she was too small and fast to hit.

Flashes of gold caught his attention as the raven chased his little sister, and Derek realized there were little gold rings around the shaft of the feathers. He looked harder at the raven and saw the faded outline of a man with long, black hair and a mix of features that made his background hard to place.

Gold rings of various sizes covered his talons, too, and Derek suddenly knew who the gold plates were for.

Sam landed on the roof just as the door opened, and the raven pecked at it again.

The house shook and stood. Chicken legs unfolded and scratched at the ground before lashing out and catching the raven across its chest. Several rings fell off and rolled across the ground. Derek picked up the one that landed near his shoe, while the raven squawked and grabbed at the jewelry. It wasn't just a gold band; a deep, green emerald was surrounded by a ring of diamonds which shone enough, Derek was certain it wasn't a piece of cheap costume jewelry.

Two more rings, these ones plain and slightly dirty, rolled against his shoe, and he bent down to grab them and put them in his pocket.

* * *

"Stop it!" the witch shouted. She'd taken an impossibly long step out of the house into the yard and was standing between the two combatants.

The house and the giant bird stopped moving, and she nodded.

"That's better," she said. "Now, leave the baubles where they are. You can look for them later. Serves you right for being impatient, anyway."

The raven squawked but didn't move to argue with her.

"We haven't got much time. The person hunting you has almost found their way into my demesne, and that will not stand. Ivan, take your gear and give the bird his payment for helping."

Derek stepped forward and took the mishmash of armor and questionable weapons, then pulled the gleaming poker chip from his pocket. The raven made to snatch it out of his hand, but Derek closed his fist around it before he could grab it.

"How do I know he won't take it and fly off without helping us?" he asked.

The raven puffed out his chest and fluffed his feathers at him.

"Are you going to refuse to pay him?" the witch asked.

Derek could see the calculating look in her eyes again, but he knew there was pride behind it.

"No, I'll pay him for his help, after he's helped us. I just don't know that he can do what he's supposed to."

The fact that he had no idea what the bird was supposed to do helped, Derek thought wryly.

The raven spread his wings, beating the ground before he pushed into the sky. Dirt and gold flew at him and Violet, who had moved to stand next to him.

"Quickly!" the witch shouted. "Don your armor, take up your weapons, and follow the raven until he makes an opening in the sky!"

There wasn't much to put on, and Derek had the straps buckled while the raven was still gaining altitude. Sam was flying after him, and Violet was chasing after her. In that order, he could see the direction the raven was flying and ran after them.

"She gave me the best armor possible," he muttered to himself. "I can tell, because it's light and shiny, and I can run in it. I just wish the weapons were in better shape for me to use."

The token in his fist heated, and he stumbled as the bow and staff *shifted* in his hands into a modern compound bow with the appropriate arrows, and a weighted bo staff made of carbon fiber with steel bands and tips appeared in his hands.

He recovered from his shock and started running again, faster, his companions just barely in view.

The great black form that was the raven rose into the clouds, its giant wings pushing them away until a beam of sunlight shone through. Violet ran back to him, then took her place at his side while he got closer to the patch of sunlight. Sam rode the currents below the raven, watching the ground for something he couldn't see.

When he stepped into the light, it reflected off his helmet and shield, creating a shining foot path he could almost step onto. Violet jumped ahead of him onto the path. Her first few steps were on the ground, but every step after that took her higher into the air. Sam flew away from the raven and onto the path.

Derek watched as they moved further away on the impossible path, then took the first few steps. They could see something he couldn't, he was sure of that, and when his next step landed on something solid, he knew he had to follow where they led.

Halfway up the path into the clouds, the raven dropped out of where he'd created the opening, and the clouds boiled up behind him. The path beneath his feet felt less solid, and Derek knew they weren't going to make it without the sun.

He held up the poker chip and shouted to the raven. "Keep clearing the clouds, and you can have it! If we fall and die, I'm taking it with me!"

The raven let out an angry *caw* and swooped at him, but Derek put the token in his pocket and notched an arrow in the bow. He let loose an arrow that flew straight into one of the golden rings hanging on his feathers and stuck.

"The next one won't hit your jewelry!" Derek warned. "Clear the clouds!"

With a sullen flap of his wings, the raven moved to the clouds, clearing them again. His armor caught the light, and the path solidified again. As they got to the gloomy, angry clouds, Derek could see the outline of a dark alley that looked familiar.

Sam dove through the clouds into the city, and Violet followed her. Derek was a few steps away when the raven dove for him again. He pulled the token from his pocket and held it out. With the path disintegrating beneath his feet, he dropped the token and jumped. He made it through just in time to dodge the raven coming in behind him, over his head, then skidding to a halt on the dark pavement with a shower of golden rings as his feathers faded into ragged fabric.

A screech of outrage sounded from the raven and the building behind him.

Derek ducked and turned, bringing the shield up just in time for it to catch most of the baelfire that had been thrown at him.

* * *

Violet stumbled through the portal, her legs unsteady after spending several days as a dog. Sam was facedown, her sudden landing a shock she was still trying to recover from.

"No!" a voice shouted down the alley. "Not yet. Damn humans!"

Derek came through the portal as Violet turned to find the source of the shouting. She didn't see what had come through the portal with him, but she did see the sickly green glow that came for her and Sam.

Without a thought, Violet threw herself over the smaller woman, her hands over her head to do what she could to protect herself. It flew over them and splashed against Derek's shield. He dropped his bow and arrow, which looked different from the way she remembered them, and stood up with his fancy staff.

The figure at the end of the alley was muttering, and Violet could see the green glow start up again, then Derek was there, striking him with the end of the staff, and the horrible fire died out.

Violet knew she'd be in the way more than she could help, so she kept herself between the fight and Sam.

"Can you stand?" Violet asked. "We need to get to cover."

"Just give me a minute," Sam snapped. "I've spent the last three days using all my muscles."

"And faceplanted on the sidewalk. Can I help?"

Providing an arm to steady her, Violet helped Sam up, and they stumbled over to the wall together. An alcove shielded them from view while they watched the fight in tense silence.

Derek was quick, but the creature he fought was quicker and using magic. Every time he started muttering, Derek brought the end of the staff down on one of his hands or across his face, ruining his concentration and sending up smoke from the skin that had been struck.

"What is that?" Sam asked.

"Some sort of fairy, I think," Violet answered.

"I thought fairies were tiny, delicate things. That looks like something out of Tolkien."

Violet nodded in agreement, then movement caught her eye. A strange man had been lying in the shadows of the alley and staggered to his feet. His gaze never left the fight at the end of the alley, even as he bent to pick up the bow and arrow Derek had dropped.

He raised it and aimed at the two combatants.

"No!" Violet gasped, then shouted as he shot the arrow into the fight.

The combatants stopped moving and stared at the arrow sticking out of the creature's chest. His mouth opened and closed in shock, his lips moving with words he never spoke, before he stared up at the man who had shot him.

His feet melted first, then his legs, until his entire body dissolved into a smoking pile of goo.

Derek turned and looked at the man who was still holding his bow up and had another arrow ready to let fly.

"My token," the man demanded.

"I threw it to you on my way through the portal."

"You did not."

Violet strained to hear his accent. She couldn't quite place it, though she could swear she'd heard it before.

"I did. And I thank you for your help. Now, if you'll put that down, I'd like to check on my sister."

The man glanced at the two women, then dropped the bow and ran to Sam. He was on his knees in front of her, examining every scrape and bruise she'd suffered coming through the portal.

"Sam, are you okay?" Derek asked, limping over to them.

His opponent may have turned into smoking goo, but Derek hadn't dodged every blow. Violet took note of every injury she could see, and several she suspected but couldn't see behind his clothes.

"I'm fine," Sam said. Her words answered her brother, but her eyes were all for the man in front of her.

"Do you want—" Derek started, and the man stood up.

"I will see to her," he declared, and swung her into his arms like she weighed nothing.

"I don't—" Derek protested.

"It's fine," Sam told him. "I'm fine. I'll call you tomorrow."

The two disappeared around the corner, and Violet turned back to find Derek watching her. "Are you okay? I know you're worried about Sam, but—"

His shield fell to the pavement, and he wrapped his arms around her.

"I'm so sorry," he murmured into her hair. "I'm so very sorry. Thank you for being there for me, and for her. I was so worried."

Violet put her arms around him without a second thought and buried her face against his chest. She loved this man, and she knew he loved her. He'd told her in so many ways, with words he never intended to use that way. Whatever else happened next, she knew exactly how he felt about her, and that was enough.

"You're welcome," she told him, "but I need something right now."

"Anything," he said, and pulled back just enough to look into her face.

"A kiss," she said.

And he did.

* * * * *

C.V. Walter Biography

C.V. Walter, author of *The Alien's Accidental Bride*, is currently working on her alien romance series. She thinks the family you choose is more important than the one you were born into. When she's not on the road, she bounces between Colorado and Texas. To hear more about upcoming releases, sign up for the mailing list at cvwalter.substack.com.

* * * * *

Romancing Some Rock
by Edie Skye
A Titan Mage Story

Orion Havoc sat on his hotel room balcony with beer in hand, swim trunks on butt, and eyes sharp on the vista below. Palm trees and pristine, white sand stretched from the elaborate pool yard of his lodgings into an infinite star-speckled ocean illuminated by the Crystal Moon hanging above. That flawless white celestial body was close and bright enough to be visible even during the day; night made it absolutely radiant, and the sand glowed under its light as if the entire beach was a place of cosmic mystery, or at least ethereal peace.

The light ocean wind rustled the palms, tempting him to fall asleep.

Instead, he took another swig from his bottle.

He knew the true nature of this peace.

That was why he'd come here in the first place.

The glass door behind him slid open, and his roommate wheeled onto the balcony.

The two couldn't have looked more different, but then, titan mages and their engineers usually did. Sevas Lazare sat ramrod straight in his customized wheelchair. While the constant use of his arms had put lean tone on those muscles, the structure beneath them was slight, his skin pale enough to blend in with the sand below, and his expression one that barely showed patience for himself, much less other people—unless those people were Rion, or their objective.

Rion reclined in his chair with a dark bulk that might turn that chair into a lethal weapon at any moment, and flowing black hair that meant he would probably be doing so in defense of a swooning lady.

"What are you doing, still up at this hour?" Sevas grumped.

"Looking for trouble."

"No leads yet?"

"None," Rion replied, then caught sight of the brilliant blue glass perched on Sevas' attached swivel desk. "I know why I'm up, but why are *you* drinking at three in the morning?"

"The bar's open, and I couldn't sleep."

"Legs again?"

"Legs always. Fortunately, tonight's not bad enough to require more than alcohol, and I do like whatever this mermaid thing is." He nibbled some blue-dyed sugar off the rim of his glass. "*You* should sleep, though, so you can wake up early for tomorrow's bounty pool. The best ones are taken at dawn, and you're not going to find any work at this hour."

"On the contrary, this is the *best* hour to find work! Momma always said, nothing good happens after midnight, and even less good happens at the witching hour. And this beach, at this hour, is where I've landed sixty percent of our jobs."

"You did the math?"

"Well, no, but it feels right. Other than bounties, we've taken nineteen jobs since graduation, and eleven of them have come from here."

Sevas took a split second to work the math in his head and chimed, "You're more right than I expected."

"I do occasionally have an intelligent thought." Rion laughed—and then spotted the motion below.

A lone figure crept through the decorated courtyard beneath them, keeping to the palm trees along its edges as if to hide in their shadows. The pool yard had plenty of those. The trees, huge potted plants, and elegant network of dividing walls created the effect of a dark, subtle labyrinth, perfect for sneaking.

Rion caught glimpses of detail when the creeping shape passed in moonlight—a slender, feminine frame, nearly as pale as Sevas, in an opalescent wrap that further reminded him of the sand, and a similarly colored cap that fully obscured her hair. A quick attempt at camouflage, perhaps?

But, no, she wasn't dressed for duplicity.

Another glimpse in the light told him she wore a slight two-piece swimsuit, and she was continually peering toward the next building in the resort complex, as if trying to figure out how to reach it without drawing attention to herself. She crept awkwardly, too, as if bruising bare feet on rough, decorative stone.

"Think she's in trouble?" Sevas murmured. He nibbled another arc of sugar, but leaned toward the holster latched to his chair, which bore both his forearm crutch and a mage rifle. Sevas didn't like feeling vulnerable.

Rion didn't like people who would exploit vulnerability, so he leaned forward and set his beer aside.

The first several jobs they'd landed here had been completely by chance. When he and Sevas had graduated from the Arcane Index Titan Mage and Engineering Academies six months ago, the conditions of their graduation required them to either sign on with an Index-affiliated airship or take a certain number of bounties each month in service of the Index.

Rion hadn't quite found the right airship yet—or rather, he hadn't found the airship that was right for Sevas' situation—so they'd gone the bounty route. Rion was such an adept titan mage, they often filled their quotas fast, which left them time to take auxiliary bounties of their own choosing.

They hadn't even been seeking a bounty when the first job had come to them. They'd been celebrating a good score; Rion had chosen Vasor Beach because Sevas had never been to a beach before, and he'd chosen this hotel because they could afford to splurge for once.

They'd been chatting about titan upgrades by the pool when Rion had spotted the lone woman on the quiet beach—and the two men who'd come out of nowhere to jump her.

Once Rion had pummeled the two men into shallow craters in the sand, the woman had invited him out for drinks—and then offered to hire him as a bodyguard for the duration of her stay. It turned out she'd run afoul of her Vasori family, coming upon some information that could reflect badly on them, and Vasori families were militant—sometimes violent—about maintaining their reputations.

Predictably so, it turned out.

He'd accepted the job as easy money and had barely completed it before the next incident—he'd overheard the violence of a break-in. One Vasori family had been after a significant journal acquired by another, and when he rescued the mousy woman in question from the burglars, he found it was one of those "adventure journals," the ones that were basically treasure maps to lost cities or jewel hoards. She wanted to follow it—but for that, she needed the services of a titan mage.

Lucky for her, Rion was one of the top titan mages in his graduating class.

Over the next few months, he and Sevas discovered that, for whatever reason, this particular stretch of beach, and even this particular hotel, were where Vasori families chose to enact many of their dramas, brutal warnings, or assassination attempts, especially upon targets traveling alone. Just as often, targets *willingly* went there to lure their opposition into the open! He'd lost count of the number of times he'd nearly intervened in an incident, only to find the innocent looking girl in question actually had a gas pellet in her top and a beach wrap reinforced for choking.

The Vasori were, simply put, melodramatic.

But their melodrama meant there were often innocent people who needed to be saved from families who were willing to kill for shitty reasons. The Vasori were used to it, but it grated on Rion's Endpoint City sensibilities, and he hadn't built all this muscle solely to make women swoon. He'd built it because some people deserved to be punched by people who knew how. If he got a job after impressing someone with his punches, all the better.

"There are no guards tonight," Sevas observed.

Rion nodded. "Someone's been paid off."

The hotel knew its role in the dramas, but also contributed. Everything about Vasori territory was a game of greased palms and stabbed backs. The labyrinthine pool yard might have even been *designed* for hiding and sneaking.

Gradually, the woman crossed to the other side of the courtyard. The palms ended, but with a quick sprint, she could make it to the high decorative grasses of the next building's court without being noticed, especially with that sand-pale camouflage.

She was about to begin her sprint when arms sprouted from the giant pots near the palms.

Rion sprang into action.

He swung over the short side of the balustrade onto the decorative brickwork dividing his balcony from the next. It wouldn't have made a ladder for most, but his hands were nimble and practiced, and soon he cleared the lower floor and bounded over the obstacles of the pool yard.

He kept his eyes locked on the scene as he ran.

Not once did the woman scream. In fact, as he wove between pool chairs, pots, and trees, he saw the feet that had stepped tenderly upon the rocks now kicked up in targeted thrusts at the knees, groins, and throats of her black-clad assailants.

But whoever they were, they must have been prepared for her. None of the landed blows had any effect—until she whipped something slim and shiny from within her swimsuit bottom and palm-thrust it into one assailant's neck, between what must've been two pieces of armor.

She couldn't retrieve the weapon, though, before the second assailant snatched her white head covering and the hair beneath it. He yanked her back. The third advanced with what looked like some kind of gas mask.

"Hurry!" the second shouted, and the third scrambled, both fully aware of the elephant of a man barreling toward them.

Number Three didn't hurry fast enough.

Rion bolted over a pool chair and focused the entire weight of his body into one massive punch. It crunched into the man's collarbone with a sickening *pop*, and then popped again when Rion smashed into him. The man screamed, the gas mask tumbled from his fingers, and Rion saw an opportunity. He snatched the mask from the sand and forced it over the man's mouth and nostrils. Whatever gas it was, it certainly wasn't the kind they'd want used on themselves, and within a few screaming breaths, the third man had fallen silent.

Now Rion rounded on the last of the three assailants.

The man had ripped off the woman's cap to reveal a head of conspicuously brilliant red hair, which his fingers currently twisted in a stern grip. The woman tried to kick out his knees, but whatever armor he wore rendered her efforts useless, and each time her blows landed, he yanked her hair in a savage wrench.

"This is no business of yours," the man said to Rion, pinning one of the woman's arms behind her back. "Leave now, and we'll forget you were here."

"You *do* realize I'm a foot taller than you and at least twice your size, right?"

"I realize you're only wearing a pair of swim trunks against whatever I might have hidden—"

Rion bolted forward and landed a punch right in the center of the man's forehead.

"Shit! Ow!" Rion shouted.

Even the man's forehead was armored—but his head still snapped back, and he loosened his grip on the woman's hair and arm.

Rion yanked her away and pulled her close as the man stumbled back, recovered, then drew a knife from his belt—

A hot flash of searing gold split the night and the man's shoulder armor.

Flames burst from the skin beneath the melted metal, and the man collapsed, wailing, to the sandy ground as they consumed his flesh. Rion and the woman had the same idea at the same time and lunged for the gas mask. Rion reached it first and jammed the mask over the wailing man's face until he fell still.

The woman put out the man's skin by kicking sand on it until the flames died.

"Gods damn, I knew the family was pissed, but I didn't expect them to send *ninjas*!"

Rion paused. Hers wasn't the kind of voice he'd expected from a Vasori woman. The Vasori cultivated the most advanced magitek in the world. Their capital city literally floated in the sky, and their people looked down on everyone below with equivalent highfalutin, over-enunciated scorn.

This woman had none of that. She spoke with a charming twang that suggested she'd joined a Vasori family from somewhere significantly less snobbish, and probably even fun.

She kicked sand over her assailant once more, then she looked in the direction the golden bolt had come from.

"What *was* that?"

Lights had begun to come on in the hotel, and in the glow of the surrounding rooms, Rion could see Sevas sitting on their balcony with his cocktail in one hand and a smoking mage rifle in the other.

"That would be my engineer," Rion said.

Sevas raised his glass as if to say, *You're welcome,* then drained it and rolled himself back into their room.

"Your engineer?" The woman crossed to the other side of the burned man—never turning her back on Rion, he noted—and rifled through his armor, as if looting bodies was something she did every morning at three. "Airship pilot, or titan mage?"

"Titan mage."

The woman laughed. "All that body wasn't enough for you? You had to go for the giant suit of armor, too?"

"When you're my size, you struggle to fit into smaller things."

The woman flicked a mischievous look up the length of him. "I'll bet."

She pulled down the assailant's mask to get a good look at his face, then she hurried to the next one to reveal his face and dig through his pockets.

Rion went to examine the other.

"Why'd you help me?" the woman asked, keeping a cautious eye on him.

"Because I hate bad guys, especially those that try to jump—well, I was going to say harmless women, but you're not exactly that harmless, are you?"

"Girl's gotta know how to defend herself."

There was nothing useful in the final man's clothes. Rion pulled off the man's mask. "You sounded like you knew these guys."

"Yeah, they've been in my business from day one."

"Which is?"

"That's *my* business." There was caution in her tone, but also a hint of intrigue, like she *might* let him in on her business in the right circumstances. Her eyes flicked to the next building. "I have places to be. You got a name?"

Rion extended his hand. "Orion Havoc, mage of Titan Ricochet Cavalier."

The woman paused before she shook his hand, like she recognized the name, and then paused afterward as if thinking.

"You can call me Ruby Fi'Renzi. Two-thirteen?"

It took Rion a moment to realize she'd correctly guessed his room number, what with Sevas making the location obvious.

"You're observant."

"Gotta be, in my line of work." Ruby shrugged. "I'll remember you."

Then she scampered into the night like a ghostly fox.

* * *

It was barely an hour before their room's comm buzzed.

The gold candlestick comm between Rion and Sevas' bed vibrated with a soft tinkling noise not unlike that of an expensive music box. Rion set his book aside and lifted the microphone bell from its hook.

"Two-thirteen."

"It's Ruby." Something in the woman's twang made Rion sit up straighter. It wasn't the same playful voice as earlier. There was cold steel in it, ready to stab.

"Did they come for you again?" he asked.

"It's complicated, better discussed in person. That is, if you're looking for work."

"For a lady in need, always."

"Do you know The Siren's Cove?"

"The club on the water?"

"Meet you there in half an hour. Grotto six."

* * *

"She's from a family with money," Sevas observed as he wheeled down the expansive sidewalk. "People don't just *have* grottoes at The Cove."

Rion strode beside him, careful to keep a similar pace. Sevas got so annoyed when anyone tried to push his wheelchair that he'd long since removed the back handles and replaced them with spikes (and his crutch-and-gun holster). The only exception he made was for Rion, but Sevas didn't like to draw attention to himself, and Rion attracted attention by simply existing.

The Vasor Beach streets were bright and busy even at this hour, its hotels and clubs gleaming against the night in radiant arrangements of magelights. Despite the touristy brilliance, there was an air of careful class about it; the Vasori might be snobs, but at the very least, they weren't gaudy.

One hotel across the way had all the appearance of a fairytale castle that belonged to the fairies themselves, perched partway up an architectural beanstalk with enormous magecrafted flowers that either followed passersby with beams of light, or else oscillated in the sky like spotlights. Another floated in the air, its underside glowing a surreal purple from the gravity furnaces its magitek engineers had set up to create the effect. Yet another's exterior seemed to be composed entirely of terraces of timed fountains and other water features, including a huge central waterfall that dumped its mass right over the entry doors—until someone walked within range, which was when an invisible dome pushed up from the purple glow beneath and allowed visitors to pass without getting soaked.

At that display in particular, Rion reflected that the Vasori had very much earned the right to act superior, even if they were insufferable. Wielding gravity magic so precisely required incredibly advanced magitek. He'd be able to do that one day, once his skills and catalyst upgrades were higher, but for now, it was merely an aspiration.

And, looking in that direction, Rion realized his conspicuous size had given someone an advantage.

"I think we've got a tail," he murmured so only Sevas could hear.

The man wasn't dressed conspicuously, but he'd been admiring the architecture across the street at a pace suspiciously similar to theirs.

"Too many people around to do anything about it, though," Sevas replied, as if the crowd alone suppressed the itch in his trigger finger.

"You think we're getting into something too deep?"

"We were going to grab someone's attention eventually, with all the jobs we pull from this area. As far as I'm concerned, it's an opportunity to build our reputation further."

"You're a bit cavalier for someone who can't even walk."

"I've seen nothing on this side of the world that's more terrible than what I came from. Besides, I have good aim and a general disregard for the lives of people who would hurt me."

"Real noble, Sevas."

"You're paladin enough for both of us." Soon a soothing sea-blue light crept onto Sevas' pale face. "Ah, here we are."

Like the rest of the street, The Siren's Cove leaned hard into its chosen aesthetic. The entryway to the club resembled an artful stack of rocks, while the façade behind it crashed three stories into the air in artful, static waves inset with blue magelights that wavered to create the illusion of moving water. Sculpted on either side of the double doors inset in the rocks were two tastefully nude women, with seaweed, coral, and shells woven into their strategically positioned hair and trailing along arms that welcomed customers inside.

Rion spared one last glance for the tailing man—still there, looking like he was waiting for the right moment to follow—and then held the door open for Sevas.

A sultry blast of music swept out to greet them as they came in. A woman's voice slinked along the room's low lighting and atmospheric fog on strange waves of fiddles and flutes, with the occasional drum resonating to add a beat, which the dancers on the central floor swayed to like they were either slow dancing or drunk. To the right sat a well-stocked bar backlit with the same blue, and around its comparatively tamer shape spilled decorative magelit waves similar to those outside, if more subtly lit. The semi-static waves encircled the stage at the back, filled by a small band and a gorgeous singer wrapped in a slinky gown that put Rion in mind of a mermaid.

There were mundane tables and booths all over the place, but the showpiece of the club was the wall of giant imitation coral shaped into subtle nooks of various sizes, and the partially enclosed bubbles that straight-up floated over some of them, again suspended by the glow of gravity magic.

Those weren't seats for casual walk-in customers, yet they were still full.

Rion squinted through the dim lighting, trying to see inside the moodily backlit chambers, and soon saw a hand wave from inside one halfway up the wall. Even in the dark, he recognized the bright red hair above it.

"*Of course* it's one of the high ones," Sevas muttered.

Rion went first, parting the edges of the dancing crowd to make way for Sevas. A small, decorative staircase embedded in the coral wound up to the grotto shelf, so Sevas exchanged his wheelchair for his crutch and led the way, while Rion folded and carried the wheelchair.

Ruby stood at the entrance to greet them.

"You look good for someone who's been running from ninjas," Rion said as Sevas passed her.

She'd traded her bikini for a shimmering sea-green dress befitting both the club's atmosphere and her hair, which was pulled back into a charmingly messy bun. Combined with the teal glasses that sat atop her freckled nose, she presently looked more like a stylish librarian than a damsel in distress, and made Rion glad he'd had the foresight to dress up, too.

Arcane Index magesuits were skintight, but also cut and detailed to look vaguely like uniforms, and the long, slate-black adventurer's coat his parents had given him as a going-off present combined with it to make him look fit for crashing fancy balls. (Sevas had kept his rough engineer shirt and baggy mechanic's pants from earlier, because Sevas simply didn't give a shit. But at least the designs at the neck of the shirt created the illusion of a cravat.)

"You look as good with clothes on as you do with clothes off," Ruby said with a grin.

"Glad you think so," Rion replied, "but you sounded like you had urgent business on the bell."

The mischief in Ruby's face hardened, and she indicated the table behind her, enclosed on one side by a cushioned booth seat.

"We were followed, by the way," Sevas said as he took a seat on the edge.

Rion described the man as he sat in one of the movable chairs on the opposite side.

Ruby nodded. "I'm not surprised."

"What kind of trouble are you in?" Rion asked.

"First things first." Ruby pulled a sailor-knotted cord near the door before she sat. "Let's order some drinks, if only so we don't look out of place."

Soon a green-waistcoated attendant climbed the stairs to take their order. He closed the grotto door behind him as he left, just as the music outside swelled to a vigorous beat, perfect for obscuring their conversation.

While they waited for their drinks, Ruby settled her chin on laced fingers and looked up under long lashes like she was about to flirt.

"I thought I recognized your name," she said, this time all business. "Your reputation precedes you."

"A good one, I hope."

"Depends on who's doing the talking. You've pissed off more than a few families in Vasor since you showed up, but most of those families are made of raging asswits. Those you've saved from the raging asswits, though, find each other, and they *talk*. It seems you're a pleasure to bump into, on multiple fronts."

She raised her eyebrows suggestively. Rion answered with a coy shrug. He didn't take *any* jobs with the intent of romancing the women involved, but when you were a professional adventurer who looked like he did... things sometimes happened. Okay, things *often* happened. He didn't consider himself a man of loose morals, but if a woman he liked made an offer at the right time, he wasn't going to turn her down.

Ruby very much struck him as someone he could like.

"Second things second," she continued, "what are the specs on your titan? I want to be sure you're equipped for my task before I continue."

Rion nodded. "Four gravity catalysts: three Tier One, one Tier Two. The whole thing stands twenty-five feet tall and weighs eighteen tons. What that means in non-mage terms is I can jump real high and punch real hard. I've got an airship I regularly do business with, and my engineer travels with me for field repairs and upgrades." He indicated Sevas.

"What's the most challenging monster you've defeated?"

"Storm drake. I mean, it *was* the hardest I've fought, but even then, it's just upgrade materials in my mech now."

Ruby's eyes lit up. "Perfect."

The waiter knocked to deliver their drinks. Ruby had opted for a glass of bubbly white wine, while Rion had gone for his usual favorite—which was to say, whatever beer on offer had the weirdest name. For tonight, it was Jewel of Denial. Sevas, meanwhile, had gone for some obnoxiously colorful layered thing with fruit around the rim that put Rion in mind of a flamboyant tropical fish.

Ruby smiled. "That's a flashier drink than I'd expect of someone who'd snipe a man like you did earlier."

Sevas shrugged. "I enjoy flavors."

Rion leaned forward with his beer. "So, what kind of business leads a lady to be jumped by ninjas, and then summon a titan mage before sunrise?"

Ruby set her wine aside, her face restored to full business.

"Simply put, my sister's been kidnapped, and I need a titan mage to get her back."

"Oh, we're sold, then!" Sevas plucked a candied fruit off the edge of his glass.

"Sev, we need to hear the rest of the proposal," Rion objected.

"You say that as if you haven't jumped to the aid of *every* damsel in distress who's crossed your path."

"Still, we *do* need to hear the details." He turned back to Ruby. "I assume you know who kidnapped her and why? And what resources they have that require a titan to rescue her?"

"Yes, yes, and... the third is slightly more complicated. It's not the kidnappers who require the titan; it's why they kidnapped her. The Fi'Renzi family is made up of treasure hunters. My sister and I recently came into possession of a map. The family got pissed when they found out we didn't share it with them, so we fled before they could forcibly take it."

Rion nodded. Vasori families viewed anything acquired by a family member as belonging to the family as a whole, especially items as valuable as treasure maps.

"Why not share it with the family?" Rion asked.

"Because we wanted to use what we earn from the treasure—a jewel of considerable value—to leave Vasor. We're only Fi'Renzis by marriage, anyway. Our mom met her current husband after our dad got eaten by a drake, so they've always viewed us as lesser-thans. We came here to meet a contact about an airship, but it turned out that contact tipped the family off to our presence here. After you saved me, I went to my sister's room to find it ransacked, with a note telling me to bring the remaining piece of the map in exchange for her freedom."

Sevas' ears perked at the final half of that. "Remaining piece, you say? It's not, perchance, a P'ettiwing map, is it?"

Ruby smiled. "It is."

Rion punched the air with vigor. "Oh, hells yes, we've done those before!"

P'ettiwing maps were legendary amongst treasure hunters. They were named after an old Vasori royal who'd spent his final years traveling to the most absurd places in the world. No one in his family particularly cared where he went because he, too, was one of the inconvenient ones, and they'd been glad when he'd finally passed.

Until they learned the truth about his travels.

When his coffin returned to the family, it contained not a body, but stacks of incomprehensible maps. It turned out that, in a colossal act of exuberant pettiness, Andreas P'ettiwing had gradually taken many of the family's treasures and hidden them in random places across the world—recorded only in his multi-piece maps, which read like puzzles, requiring ciphers and esoteric knowledge of geography to figure out.

But of course, the family didn't realize this until after they'd dismissed the maps as the ravings of a senile old man. They sold them as art—for they were genuinely beautiful—and by the time a clever treasure hunter put a few relevant pieces together, the maps had been scattered to the winds. These days, they were valuable commodities, as much for the story as for the treasures promised at their ends, and P'ettiwing had drawn enough of them that they were still plentiful, even centuries later.

"Two of our previous jobs have been P'ettiwing treasures," Rion said. "They go to some fun locations. I assume you want to rescue your sister and then follow the map?"

"In reverse order, actually. My sister can take care of herself. I want to find the treasure, *then* give them the map."

"Why?"

"So they can go through the effort of finding it, and then be disappointed when it's already gone! Milly and I *had* talked this over as a possibility."

Rion laughed. "You think a lot like a Vasori for someone who wants to leave them."

"I for one respect the pettiness," Sevas said, "but won't they figure out you're going for the treasure when you don't deliver the map quickly?"

"That's just it. We'd already interpreted the map! The family likely thinks we came to Vasor Beach because we just wanted to mooch off their connections, but it's actually because the map ends right nearby! We pop out, fight some stuff, and grab the stone—and we might even be back before they suspect something's up!"

"Except they already have ninjas tailing us," Rion said. "So, they're going to know when we take off."

"I can take care of that problem once we decide on payment." Sevas nodded subtly toward the dance floor as he took a sip of his drink. The man from outside had taken up the most shadowed end of the bar, trying to look inconspicuous as he watched the stage. "The first shot at the hotel was free."

"Sevas, you can't shoot people in this bar," Rion said. "They'll kick us out, and we do too much business here. Not to mention, he hasn't done anything but watch yet."

"He's not tailing us for fun, and I prefer to shoot first. Besides, we need to get rid of him if we're to buy enough time to make this work."

Ruby took up her drink and looked at Rion. "Does that mean you'll take the job?"

"There are a handful of other details to discuss, but I don't see why not." Rion took a swig of his beer. "Let's work those out, then see what we can do to lose our tail."

* * *

A blinding gold flash illuminated the alley.

"Damn, Sevas, I was just going to punch him!" Rion exclaimed.

"Maybe he shouldn't have underestimated the guy in the wheelchair."

"Is this a regular thing with you?" Ruby asked. "You're not the kind of person I'd expect to—" she looked at the body smoking in the alley "—do *that* twice in one night."

"For the amount you're paying us, I'd do a reasonable number of morally questionable things." Sevas set the safety on his mage rifle, then returned it to his wheelchair holster. "As long as they don't involve a lot of walking, at least. I haven't seen any others tailing us. We should be safe to reach the airship now."

Their usual dock wasn't far, and their usual pilot was a light sleeper. Rion had barely banged on the side of the airship before a tousled head popped up in the bridge window. Not that the sound had far to travel. The *Jet Hawk* was one of those versatile little airships meant to fly small cargo loads fast—or, in the case of this particular ship, one titan and its support equipment.

"Morning, Kierran!" Rion greeted him as the side hatch opened.

Between his captain's chair and the cockpit hatch, the pilot had ruffled his hair into something appropriate for business contacts and put on an eager smile that showed he was used to earning money at weird hours. It was one of the many reasons they continued to hire Kierran Darklight.

In the hand unoccupied by the hatch rested a cocked mage pistol.

"Any pursuers this time?" the pilot asked.

"Not yet, but we might have them soon."

Kierran nodded and yanked a lever near the hatch opening. Elevator mechanisms and a platform slid out of the structure surrounding the door, perfectly sized for Sevas' wheelchair, but Sevas waved it off.

"Lower the hangar door. We'll go straight there."

"On it!" Kierran declared, and soon the lower back of the ship slipped down to form a sturdy ramp.

Rion heard the ship's gravity furnaces hum to life as they walked toward the ramp and saw two purple lights beginning to emanate from the frame—one in the top middle, one at the bottom. The distinctive scent of wood embers and the sharp, fresh tang of burning void essence wafted through the air, and as he breathed it in, Rion felt his enthusiasm for the adventure rise with it.

It was magic—literally the smell of magic, but also the inherent magic of doing the very thing he'd wanted to do since he was a little kid, when he'd seen his first titan and decided he wanted nothing more in the world than to pilot one.

He rounded the curve of the airship, and there it was.

Titans were among the most powerful pieces of magitek in all of Haven. At their hearts throbbed ancient titan cores that processed void essence and materials into energy and equipment enhancements, and around those cores were built suits of complex mechanical armor that stretched over two stories tall, outfitted with honeycomb-patterned catalysts that would allow the titan mage to channel whichever magical elements they had the aptitude for.

Rion's aptitude was for gravity magic, so he and Sevas had outfitted his titan with appropriate catalysts and reinforcements. Though he'd already been its pilot for two and a half years, his heart still swelled when he saw it.

The hangar lights flickered on, and if Ruby's eyes were any indication, her heart did the same.

Titan Ricochet Cavalier gleamed in its docking bay, a slate-black suit of knightly armor that looked every bit as heroic as its pilot aimed to be. Its head nearly scraped the ceiling, and its shape expanded out in powerful metal plating that echoed Rion's own physical shape, except at the forearms and lower legs, the bulk of which were exaggerated in keeping with his preferred fighting style. In each of those broadened sections were long, crystalline rods, transparent in their inert state, but when he channeled his magic, they'd light up in a brilliant purple like the furnaces outside.

"That's an amazing machine," Ruby marveled, admiring its bulk in the same way women tended to admire *him*, "but why only Tier One and Two catalysts? You're an Index graduate, right? I'd have expected your upgrades to be higher after more than two years."

The question made him like Ruby even more; most of their clients didn't ask such targeted questions about his machine.

He was about to answer, but then Sevas rolled by with exactly no sense of awe.

"That's because he breaks them all the time and has to restart his upgrades all over again when I build new ones."

"You say that as if you don't enjoy experimenting with new patterns," Rion teased, and turned back to Ruby. "That's Sevas' thing. Take him outside the hangar, and he's kind of a disaster, but put him in front of a titan or a catalyst crafting station, and he's a genius."

Sevas took another lift to the scaffold at the titan's middle and affixed a large tube to a connection in its back. "I'm not a genius," he grumbled as he funneled liquefied void essence into the mech, "I'm just really good at one thing."

"Well, there's gunslinging as well," Ruby chimed as she followed Rion. "Two things."

Sevas just shrugged. "I don't consider that a genius skill so much as a necessity for survival."

"*Sure.*" Rion chuckled, then opened a tall case on the side of the hangar opposite the titan. Tools and other accessories for titan maintenance generally filled the area, but this particular case was the size of a travel trunk and expanded out into cushioned tiers, tenderly transporting an array of mage rifles, pistols, and shotguns, all of such intricacy that they'd obviously been customized.

Ruby turned to Sevas, then back to the guns, then back to Sevas.

"How do *you* get into enough trouble to merit *this* when you can't even walk?"

Sevas shrugged again, then unlatched the tube from the back. "It's not that I get into trouble; it's that I figure my enemies are less likely to be a problem if I shoot them first."

"This one looks like a beam cannon!"

"That's for big problems."

His absolute nonchalance struck a wider grin across Ruby's face, and she was increasingly satisfied with the hire she'd made.

"We're all warmed up and ready for takeoff!" Kierran shouted down from the pilot's seat. The ship was so small that there was little formal separation between the hangar interior and the bridge, excepting a waist-high wall on the edge of the story-tall rise. "What are we going after today?"

"Some rock," Rion replied as he climbed the ladder to the cockpit.

"Oh, a fun one, then!" This wasn't the first time they'd hired Kierran to go after a shiny rock in an exotic place.

"It's not just some rock!" Ruby followed Rion up, then pulled a sheaf of papers from the bag she'd brought and spread them on the navigational table.

Kierran recognized the stylings of the papers instantly. "Oh, it's a P'ettiwing treasure! Even better!"

"We already know our heading," Rion said.

"Drake Island," Ruby added. "North side."

"Drake Island?" Kierran exclaimed. "That's just a few hours off the coast. How could any treasure stay hidden there for so long?"

"That's what I'm curious about." Rion bore down over the papers. He picked up the centermost two. "This the map?"

They were certainly dotted and lined with the usual map markings, but the lines tracked in no logical direction. They wandered the pages around random landmarks on opposite sides of the island as if drawn by a bored drunk, and there was no clear X Marks the Spot. There were, however, two random slashes of red on each map piece. Those were likely what had clued Ruby and her sister in to the secret of the map, for both pieces were crisscrossed with obvious, fresh folds—some more creased than others.

"I'll show you." Ruby took the two pieces and folded them together. Her fingers moved so deftly, it was as if she were making nothing more complicated than a grade-school fortuneteller, or a paper animal. When she finished, both pieces of the map were combined into the shape of a single distinctive landform—the jagged mountain at the center of the island, shaped like a drake's mouth that had just snapped shut. One dotted line traced up its side and ended at the very peak of the mountain, which was marked by all four of the red slashes, finally joined to form an X.

"There's no way this treasure's at the peak of Drake Mountain," Rion said. "It's too open."

Ruby grinned. "Ah, but see—it's *not*."

She shoved her fingers into the underside of the paper mountain—

And opened it up like a paper fortuneteller.

Now Rion saw the truth of the map. Another dotted line ran down the *inside* of the folded piece, as if tracing a safe path through an inner cave network, and ended in the space between two quadrants, where some of what he'd thought to be random landmark drawings came together to form the shape of a simple castle.

"Ah, so there's a castle hidden in the mountain!" Rion exclaimed.

That made more sense. Haven had a long enough history for some parts of it to be forgotten, and enough of it was weird, mysterious, and dangerous that adventuring had long been a viable career path. As for how a whole castle had been hidden in the first place— all modern Haven history traced back to a period a thousand years ago, when the highly advanced civilization they'd named the Precursors had been snuffed out by what Rion chose to simplify as "some wild shit."

No one knew what precisely had caused the fall, but archaeologists had been busy ever since, rediscovering that society—and its tech—piece by piece. In fact, the cores the titans relied upon were devices from that era, but other discoveries had been even more absurd.

And if the wild shit had contributed to those things, Rion saw no reason it shouldn't be able to bury a castle.

"No further information on what surrounds the castle?" he asked.

"Well, it's on Drake Island." Ruby shrugged. "So, drakes."

"But what kind of drakes? There are tons of different kinds, and Drake Island is named as much for the presence of drakes as the variety."

"That's where this comes in." Ruby produced a well-worn, leatherbound book from her pack and opened it up to a dog-eared page. She beamed at the book as if it contained all the secrets of the universe, but Rion couldn't make sense of it. Much like the map, it was written in incoherent, almost cipher-like scrawl.

The same scrawl, in fact, that appeared on the maps. Rion's heart caught in his throat.

"Gods, is this—is this P'ettiwing's Journal?"

"It's not that special," Ruby said, arranging her remaining papers around it. "I got it from the bargain bin at Fire Stone's Used Books."

"That's not what I mean."

Some historic entrepreneur had published P'ettiwing's journal, not to help hunters find his treasures, but because it was a highly sought-after artifact that every treasure hunter would pay to own, even if it was so incomprehensible that few would be able to make sense of it. The *chance* of solving the cipher was the allure—and that chance had made it a perennial bestseller, even if most people nowadays only purchased it for the novelty.

Official translations were nonexistent, for obvious reasons, but looking at the notes Ruby had gathered, Rion realized that, even after months of hunting P'ettiwing's treasures, he was seeing something he'd never seen before.

"You can *read* the journal?"

"My sister and I have experience crafting our own ciphers and languages. It took some time, but we cracked one of P'ettiwing's ciphers. They change from section to section, you see. And the section that corresponds with this map tells us this—"

* * *

"Hells. *Yes*," Rion exclaimed as he jumped into his titan's open chest hatch and pulled the doors closed. As soon as he was inside the cylindrical chamber, a pliant, watertight ring slid out to seal against his magesuit collar, and the chamber beneath filled with a warm, thick fluid that would both cushion his body against the titan's motion, and transmit his commands to the mage sensors lining the inside of the cockpit.

Ricochet Cavalier's interface flashed into visibility as if overlaid on his very consciousness, and the eye-like visual sensors in the titan's head flickered on, granting him a titan's view of the world outside.

"You ready, Ruby?" he called over his external speakers.

Ruby strode out of one of the hatches in the space beneath the cockpit, now clad in a pair of rugged boots, practical pants, and a tight, sleeveless shirt the same sea green as her club dress. Frankly, it seemed impractical for what they were doing, but Rion wasn't the type to comment on a woman's wardrobe choices. Especially not when they looked that good, and now that he thought of it, *intentional*.

Ruby Fi'Renzi was clearly a woman who knew her own mind. She certainly hadn't been subtle toward him, even before she'd known his name. There was no way she was unaware of how that shirt complemented her figure. Adventure women knew what practical adventure wear looked like, and when they chose the sexy wear, it was for a reason.

But that was something he could explore once their formal business had been completed.

"Approaching the mountain," Kierran reported from the bridge. The shadow of the mountain's peak cut through the early morning sunlight.

Sevas wheeled over to his gun case and pondered his three favorites: a rifle for threats that might board, a pistol for the rare threat that managed to pass his rifle, and a shotgun for the boarders that really pissed him off.

"We're not facing sky pirates, man," Rion said.

"Her family has *ninjas*."

"And your wheelchair holster can only hold so many guns."

"Okay, fair enough." Sevas sighed and selected the rifle. "I topped off your void condensate and did a general tune-up before we checked into the hotel. All indicators still green?"

"Affirmative," Rion said.

Sevas' preparations made him wonder what preparations Ruby had made for her part of the job, and when he looked her way, he noticed pistol holsters and cartridge pockets strapped to both legs, and a shoulder holster that both accentuated her shirt and held a pistol so big, he could've confused it for a small shotgun.

Yeah, she'd be fine.

The peak shadow passed as Kierran centered the back of the airship on the mountain.

"Goal within jumping distance," he reported.

"Then let's do this!" Rion whooped.

His titan's scaffold withdrew to either side as the airship's hangar ramp lowered, and Rion strode forward, feeling every bit of Ricochet Cavalier's power vibrating through his footsteps.

At the edge of the ramp was a wall of solid stone in the exact place the X had marked.

Treasure hunting in the airship age was often a delightfully simple thing. When P'ettiwing had drawn his riddle map, an arduous trek through monster-infested wilderness would've been the only way to reach the spot, and traveling through that wilderness with mage equipment would've proven difficult without the aid of a titan. Even today, most mages had to rely on bulky equipment and void condensate tanks to work their magic.

That considered, Rion wasn't sure how P'ettiwing got a matter mage up here to seal the wall—but that was exactly what had happened. This wasn't a naturally occurring wall of stone; there were wiggles in the striations that suggested a mage who could manipulate physical material had sealed up a small opening.

Well, Rion didn't have matter magic, but he had something just as good.

He sent a mental command to his titan. His catalysts hummed from transparent stasis into glowing purple, a sparkling plume of purple exhaust billowed out of Ricochet Cavalier's shoulder louvers, and he thrust his right fist forward.

Metal clashed with stone in a thunderous *boom*. Shards of rock sprayed out from his blow like splintered flechettes, but the rock didn't break, so he smashed his other fist into the stone. Over and over, he bombarded the stone face with titanic blows. Soon the rock began to crack, and then give, and finally, with a great *crunch*, it shattered into an opening big enough for a titan to walk through.

"I'm in," he reported. "Kierran, keep an eye out for trouble and notify me if any airships show up. Ruby, ready to go?"

"You know it!" Ruby replied, and strode forward to meet him.

Over the years, Rion had grown so accustomed to girls finding reasons to sit on his mech that he'd had Sevas work a subtle cleft and handholds into each shoulder (for when there were two girls).

"Hang on, I've got you."

He channeled another stream of magic into his catalysts. A startled shout from Ruby soon turned into a laugh as she found herself raised through the air in an invisible grip, and then settled onto Ricochet Cavalier's right shoulder cleft. He could have lifted her with his titan's hand, but the way she looked at him made him want to show off.

"There's a belt under the panel to your left and a latch to your right," Rion added. (Sevas had installed seatbelts, too, because no one was more safety-minded than Sevas.) Once Ruby was strapped in, he continued, "Lead the way."

Ruby alternated between the still-folded map and a shortened version of her translated notes. "You see the three cave openings beneath us? Take the middle one, but watch out for the pit."

Rion did, and found the pit barely worth noticing. Again, for someone hiking without a titan, it would have been a rough obstacle, especially with the spikes and what looked like embersnakes at the bottom. But for a titan's stride, it was just a pothole to be stepped over.

The rest of the path was similarly unchallenging, and past a certain point, so open that there was plenty of room for him to swing his fists, should he need to. If his catalysts had been a few tiers higher, he could have even flown the path, but with his upgrades no higher than Tier Two, the closest he could come to true flight was an extended jump or brief hover.

The path was so undemanding, he didn't even have to do much of that. He was actually getting a little bored when an eerie, red-orange light flickered in his sensors. He glanced over to see Ruby sweating at the sudden rise in heat.

"That'll be the chamber," she said, pulling at the neck of her shirt to let the excess heat out… and testing Rion's concentration with the view beneath. Potential danger demanded his concentration, though, so he snapped his gaze back and strode around the ominous corner.

"Ah, now *this* is what I'm here for!" He grinned.

In the center of the chamber before them loomed a tall, crumbling castle, its remaining towers clawing upward like tortured fingers, while the rest of it looked like it might collapse at any moment. Its original color had been blacked over the centuries by the massive moat of lava that oozed around it, but the lava wasn't the only challenge.

No, scattered amidst the lava flow were random islands of volcanic rock that had somehow escaped melting, and on and around those islands lounged twenty lavadrakes.

If Ruby was to reach the jewel inside that castle, he'd have to incapacitate all of them.

Rion had never faced a lavadrake before, but he'd fought their firedrake cousins, and he remembered what he'd learned in his monstrology classes.

"You stay up here," Rion said, then lowered Ruby down. "This ledge is high enough the drakes shouldn't be able to reach you. Do what you can to stay cool, and I'll have these guys cleared out in a jiffy."

It wouldn't be done in a jiffy, but it sounded more impressive to say so. If his plan worked, though, he could manage doing it in a slightly longer jiff.

Ruby gave a thumbs up, and Rion flared his gravity catalysts and super-jumped down into the fiery den. Twenty pairs of slitted, reptilian eyes snapped to him, but he merely punched a giant fist into a giant hand like a challenge, then leapt back into the air.

Lavadrakes didn't look like much in his monster textbooks, not to a titan pilot. Individually, the creatures' alligator-like heads only came up to a titan's knee, and while their salamander bodies stretched nearly as long as his titan was tall, their bellies and tails were weighted with fat that made them seem slow and indolent.

It was a trap.

The first lavadrake sprang at him from within the lava flow, its deceptive shape obscuring a set of muscular legs that rocketed it fifteen feet into the air. The depths of its open mouth glowed as it snarled. A thick flow of red bubbled up, and Rion punched it in the face midair.

Titan Ricochet Cavalier thudded onto a lava island just before the monster crashed into a tilted castle wall. It oozed down with a grunt, then lay there, addled.

It would take more than even a titan punch to do in a lavadrake.

But Rion had more punches to offer.

Two more lavadrakes lunged at him, more aggressive than the first. Thick streams of lava belched toward him out of their throats, their bellies shrinking with the expenditure. Rion dodged to another island, and when he landed, thrust his full gravity sense out toward the pursuing creatures.

The lavadrakes froze in the air—until, with a single thought, Rion shot them a hundred feet across the chamber, straight into an open cave mouth. Even if those drakes weren't addled, they'd still have a difficult time getting down.

There were plenty of cave mouths in this chamber. The way Ruby had spoken of the map and journal, it sounded like P'ettiwing had had his matter mage manipulate tunnels into the mountain to confuse future treasure seekers, and that had given him an idea.

When two more lavadrakes came for him, he picked them up and hurled them into another high cave. Another two he was able to set down gently—he didn't want to kill the creatures, after all, just clear them out so Ruby could explore safely—but soon, the lavadrakes began to move with more caution, sinking beneath the lava until only their eyes were visible, like alligators plotting to roll their next prey.

A gloppy sounding grunt echoed from somewhere in the cave, like an order, and the lavadrakes attacked as one.

Rion leapt up to evade the convergence and landed on another island, right as Kierran's voice crackled over Rion's radio.

"We've got an airship incoming, Boss!"

"What kind—?" he shouted, but cut himself short as the monsters followed, crowding toward the spot where he'd planned to land.

"*Same size as us. Unmarked. Black.*"

"*Probably ninjas,*" he heard Sevas add from a distance.

"Evade them!" he shouted as he thundered down. Lavadrakes scurried toward him, and he leaped into the air once more. "Ruby and I will catch up once we're done here—"

"*Damn, they're fast! They're trying to board!*" Kierran radioed before he could finish. A great muffled *clang* echoed past the receiver before it cut off.

Ricochet Cavalier slammed onto the next closest island—and yellow alerts wailed into his awareness. The last ooze of a wave of lava crashed at his titan's feet, spit from the throats of the attacking lavadrakes. A thick layer splattered up his entire right side, and its heat softened the outside of his armor.

"Dammit!" he huffed as he leapt again, this time dividing his concentration between jumping and working his gravity sense around the lava. He splashed it off as best he could, but his catalysts weren't upgraded enough for such precise handling.

"I can still make this work!" he shouted, as much to reassure himself as the others. He had to do it fast, either way. The heat in his titan had been manageable until this point, but though the machine was generally sealed, its air cycled from the outside, and the volcanic air was bringing in volcanic heat his cooling system struggled to combat. Sweat was already trailing into his eyes.

But he wasn't the only one who'd gained a disadvantage, and he grinned when he saw what was happening below.

The drakes had been glowing red when they launched themselves out of the lava, but now that they'd been out for a bit, the molten rock was cooling into an obsidian-black shell. It wasn't cooling fast enough to fully harden, but it had already cooled enough to gum up their joints, and in some cases, stick them together.

That gave him an idea.

"We're breached!" Kierran's voice shot back over the radio as shots of another sort rang out close by.

"Hold on!" Rion shouted and made his move.

The lavadrakes were surging again, as best they could, but Ricochet Cavalier was on stable footing now, and fully capable of concentrating magic in one precise direction. Rion flung his titan's hands out, and his gravity magic with them, wrapped it around all thirteen lavadrakes, and then *lifted*.

An instant alert flashed in his awareness—not that he needed it. He could feel the buzzing vibrations in his titan's arms and legs as he overtaxed its catalysts.

He folded the mass in on itself.

Cooling but still sludgy lava flowed from the outermost drakes to fill in the gaps between the inner drakes. Another warning pierced his brain, but the lava was hardening. He was close, so close—

The alert flared red, the catalyst in his left arm cracked, and purple smoke jetted out. Tier One gravity catalysts couldn't handle this level of strain, even with the load being shared, and the loss of one increased the load on the remaining three.

Still, he pushed his machine. Soon he'd pressed the entire cluster of drakes into a ball of cooling lava and very confused monsters that towered nearly twice the height of his titan. With a shuddering grunt, he pushed it away, toward a solid ledge of rock and out of easy reach of the castle.

"Ruby!" he shouted, spinning toward the ledge. She was waiting, ready, and he flushed magic into his Tier Two right arm catalyst, still the most stable. He whisked her over to the crumbling castle and followed, stomping on cooled lava islands like stepping stones.

"Kierran, status?" he radioed as she ran inside.

There was no response.

He had to get back to the *Jet Hawk*, but he couldn't just leave Ruby to run the castle on her own.

He swiveled Ricochet Cavalier's head around. There *had* to be something he could do to speed the process along. His eyes landed on the general decrepit state of the castle. If he peered into it from just the right angle, he could see Ruby leaping over various traps and shooting little rat monsters with her pistols. If he nudged himself higher for a better view, he realized he could see something like an elaborate altar through the collapsing ceiling.

It was then that another idea struck—

Before he could voice it, Ruby somersaulted into the room, out of the way of an enormous stone ball covered in spikes and spilling snakes from random holes. One snake landed on her like a scarf, and she flicked it off like it was little more than an errant vine before scaling the altar. She breezed over it for traps, then quickly solved a puzzle he couldn't see to make a panel rise out of the pedestal.

This wasn't her first adventure, it seemed.

The panel finished rising, and on it was…

A rock.

Just a regular old rock, roughly the size of her head, albeit gift-wrapped in a sinister looking bow, as if P'ettiwing had known exactly what he was doing when he'd placed it there.

Ruby just stood and stared at it for a moment.

Which was when Rion saw a shadow move in the space behind the pedestal. A big shadow. He'd originally mistaken it for a huge pile of rubble, but as he watched it unfold from the smoky murk, he realized it was, in fact, solidified volcanic glass sprouting from the back of an enormous lavadrake.

The creature grunted irritably, as if unsure why it had been woken, but then looked down at Ruby and reasoned if it was going to be awake anyway, it might as well have a snack.

It lunged.

"Oh, hells no!" Rion snarled. He focused all his magic toward Ruby and the rock, and yanked both up into the air, then smashed through the wreckage of the castle to punch the giant lavadrake right in its alligator snout. Splinters of volcanic rock showered from the blow. The creature recoiled, snarling and swaying its head in startled pain—but Rion didn't have time to finish the job.

His crash through the castle had rendered the rest of it unstable, and he plucked Ruby and her prize from the air and thundered back as the towers crashed down around him. He super-jumped up to the entry ledge. As he landed, another catalyst popped. Its indicator flashed red, then black.

Dead.

But he couldn't let that stop him, not when his friends needed his help, so he put Ruby on the cooler of his two shoulders and thundered back the way they'd come. His heart clenched in his chest when he saw the light of the entrance, still blocked. Had Kierran not even gotten a chance to take off?

Dread sparked into fury as he ran for his target—

But before it could fully catch, his radio buzzed.

"Rion, you there?"

It was Kierran.

"We're on our way back," Rion replied. "Hold tight!"

"Oh, we handled it."

The easiness in Kierran's voice knocked Rion to a stumbling stop. "What do you mean, you handled it?"

Sevas' voice came next, sounding just as unbothered as Kierran's.

"The sister showed up, leading the family boarding party, but then Darklight and I took some out, and then the sister pulled a double-cross and helped us take out the rest of them. It was a whole drama."

Rion turned his head to Ruby. She hadn't been privy to the radio conversation, so he recounted it and asked.

"Oh, that was one of our backup plans, too." Ruby smirked. "Nothing like a good old double-cross. So, Milly's with them now?"

Ricochet Cavalier reached their entry point to find that, yes, Milly was indeed with them. She had the same bright red hair as her sister, but cut in a wild, indifferent manner, and her muscular physique strained against her tight, rugged clothes. Kierran and Sevas perched to either side of her, Kierran on a cargo trunk, and Sevas in his wheelchair, with legs propped on the shoulders of a tied-up ninja Milly had forced to his knees. Seven others lay around the hangar in various states of perforation.

"*Eight* ninjas?" Rion said as he lowered Ruby beside her sister. "Gods, they must be shitty ninjas if they couldn't handle the three of you."

"The family just got into the ninja business," Milly said. "Thought we should make our escape before they actually got good at it."

"So, what we do with them?" Rion asked.

"Ransom's always an option." Milly shrugged. "I mean, they've got money."

"Would anyone pay for such pathetic ninjas, though?" Sevas asked.

"We can work something out with the family," Milly said. "After all, we've got our own ship now."

"You're keeping their ship, too?" Rion said.

"They attacked us. It's their own fault. And they have good taste in airships."

"Well, at least there's that," Rion said. "Too bad the treasure was a bust."

Ruby turned to face him with a gleam in her eye. "Oh, I wouldn't say that."

* * *

The *Jet Hawk* didn't have prison cells, but it did have cargo containers, so they stuffed the captured ninjas inside for safekeeping.

Once Rion had put the ninjas safely away, he docked his titan and came to join the others, who'd gathered around one of the worktables on Sevas' side of the hangar. Ruby had placed the ribbon-wrapped rock in the center of the table, and Rion settled next to her. She noticed, and he saw mischief gleam in her eyes.

"I'm sorry about your catalyst," she said, shifting to inch closer to him. "I—"

"*What* happened to *what* catalyst?" Sevas snapped, cutting her off.

"Left upper fizzled out," Rion replied, "and then the left lower."

"*How?* They were brand-new!"

"Lifted thirteen drakes and lava-glued them together."

"What the shit, Rion?" Sevas snarled, but he deflated into his chair as quickly as he'd puffed up. "I've shot too many people today to deal with this."

Ruby laughed. "I was about to say, I appreciate the lengths you went to."

"Oh, that's all in a day's work for me," Rion replied, partly because he was showing off, and partly because it was true. But mostly because he, too, had a thought. "I assume your new ship is Vasori?"

"As hells." Milly grinned. "Even the holding cells have plush cushions."

Which meant the ship likely had other conveniences, Rion reflected. Kierran's ship was from Endpoint City, but the modifications he'd made for Sevas were from Vasori kits, meant for standard Vasori ships. The Vasori favored such designs for their convenience, but for Sevas they translated into features that allowed him to function.

"What kind of work do you have planned from here on out?" Rion asked.

"Not sure yet," Ruby replied coyly from behind her drink, "but you sound like you're asking for a reason."

"Maybe. Just wondering if you foresee needing a titan mage. I imagine this won't be the last you see of your family, and broken catalyst aside, this was fun."

"It was, wasn't it?" Ruby inched closer until her tightly clad, holster-bearing thigh was pressed against his. "I think I could go for a little more adventure."

The way she said it reminded him of the first time she'd spoken to him, when she'd… sized him up before even knowing him.

Sevas totally missed the cue. "It's going to be difficult to fund a titan adventure when all you have is this rock. Especially when your mage keeps breaking his catalysts."

"Yes, it would be difficult—*if* this was just a rock." Ruby turned to their prize. "Fortunately, P'ettiwing's Journal suggests otherwise, as does the seam down the middle."

She pulled the ribbon away to reveal a subtle seam in the stone, and turned it over to expose a set of indentations. When she pressed them in just the right pattern, the seam split open, revealing a cushioned interior—and a gleaming red jewel the size of Ruby's fist.

Rion didn't know much about precious stones—finding them was his thing, not appraising them—but it was twice as big as the last P'ettiwing jewel they'd found.

"Let me see!" Milly produced a loupe from her rugged pockets as Ruby passed it to her. She held it to one eye, then handed the stone back. "We can definitely hire a titan mage, and probably a whole engineering team, a cooking staff, and a really good bard for live music nights in the mess."

She passed it to Rion so he could appreciate the product of his efforts, but lacking the proper knowledge, he simply said, "Huh, that really *is* some rock."

"Leave out the bard, and I'll submit my resume, too," Sevas said. "Rion and I are a package deal, anyway."

"You bringin' your guns?" Milly asked, eyes gleaming at the memory of what she'd seen those guns do.

"Of course."

"Then you're hired. Both of you." Ruby's gaze shifted back to Rion in particular. "Now, about that *adventure*."

* * * * *

Edie Skye Biography

Edie Skye wrote *Titan Mage* as a joke and, in doing so, discovered that while she really likes writing smart stuff, she also likes writing smut stuff. Pretty spicy smut stuff, too, 'cause if you're gonna do it, you might as well do it *hard*.

Specifically, she likes to spin fun (and funny) adventure fantasies about badass women with giant robots and giant… plots, and the equally badass dudes who want to do them. There's action, airships, monster-punching, and mech-upgrading galore, with a substantial side of harem and fun-for-all-involved graphic spice. (Which is to say, it's super NSFW. Unless your workplace is, like, really cool.)

* * * * *

Space Mage Secrets
by Daniel M. Hoyt

Neutral Space

"What pairs well with a paladin?" John Collins asked levelly, then chortled, unable to keep his face impassive. The beach fire between them crackled like thunder, spewing savagely hot sparks downwind toward his twin brother.

Tom cocked an eyebrow higher and shifted on a wet log to avoid the sizzling barrage. Eyes stinging from a combination of smoke from the fire and the sea salt from his recent swim, he glared at John. "If you're going to say 'a hot knife,' I may be an only child by morning."

Booming guffaws echoed through the air, pounding at Tom's eardrums worse than a hangover. In the nearby foliage, where the beach gave way to a lush forest, something shifted, and low whines announced predators nearby. In the distance, something howled dangerously.

"Good one, Tommy," John said after regaining his composure. Absentmindedly, he increased the size of the magesphere around them enough to kiss the forest, reinforcing its protective mageweave for good measure. "But I was going to say... um..." He cleared his throat.

Tom raised his other eyebrow and tilted his head questioningly.

"I was going to say..." John shifted uncomfortably.

Tom held up an open hand. "That's what I thought. Do yourself a favor and shut up now." He dropped his hand. "Besides, I'm pretty sure the king's personal guard is *not* what that Earthright hauler pilot meant by the name. They're slippery snakes chasing riches, not— what was it the pilot said?—'honor-bound by a higher calling,' or something equally haughty. Whatever; it was far nobler than they deserve, no matter what King Stupid-head the twenty-something thought, and I refuse to refer to them as the Royal Paladins out of principle."

"*That* sobered me up," John muttered and pouted. "It was just a joke, Tommy."

"Sorry, bro. I get irrational on the subject." Tom reached for another flask of beer. Taking a long swig, he smacked his lips and grinned. "The only recourse is to get drunker."

John swept long blond locks from his face, and lunged for the last flask, toppling dangerously close to the fire, then rolling away smoothly to sit up propped against a slight dune, flask in hand. "I'll drink to that."

He waved his flask around aimlessly, ignoring the hungry growls from the forest. "I like it here."

"So do I. Always good for a restful night. We'll move on in the morning."

* * *

"Ready, John?" Tom yawned wide and stretched, his salt-hardened shorts crackling as the frozen shape broke. He reached down and smoothed the fabric fruitlessly, then joked, "Nice and comfortable."

John chuckled. "We could just do the thing without pants." He pulled his protective magesphere tight, enveloping them and little else.

Whatever was in the forest noticed. Quiet reigned for a moment before several eyes shone in the early morning half-light.

Tom glanced at the forest, then glared at his twin. "You remember where we're going next, right?"

John's grin grew slowly, and boyish mischief shone in his eyes. "Pretty sure it's a harem. Pantsless sounds good to me."

"How does becoming a eunuch sound to you?"

Wincing, John subconsciously bent over protectively, taking the opportunity to grab his provisions, neatly packed by Tom before he'd awakened. "Fine. Pants. We'll only be there for a few seconds, anyway, before I catch you and we're off again." He shook his head and dropped the protective magesphere entirely.

The creatures in the forest noticed that, too, and broke their cover, heading straight for the mages at a run.

Steeling himself for the intense concentration required for what the twins had come to call magecast, Tom ignored them, aligned his mageform with John's bodyform, and magically pushed his twin brother hard toward their next destination while he was still bent over. John's bodyform blinked out, cast along with Tom's molded mageform.

For the thousandth time, Tom wondered if their magecast would work for anyone else. Did it only work for them because they were identical twins, and their mageforms matched each other's bodyforms? What if John gained significant weight? He didn't take very good care of his body, unlike Tom. How much weight difference would it take to break their magecast? How much beer had each of them had last night?

He forced himself *not* to look at the rapidly approaching forest predators. No sense riddling himself with anxiety; John would get him out in time.

Probably.

Tom risked a glance toward the forest as he bent down to grab his own provisions pack.

One of those things is fast!

He launched himself sideways and down just as something large, hairy, and full of teeth and claws sailed over him.

Startled, Tom finally felt the elastic pull from his twin's corresponding catch. As he blinked away, the beach was once again deserted, except for a couple of damp logs flanking a still-smoldering fire and a very disappointed howl splitting the air.

* * *

Messier Frontier

"I'm exhausted," John complained, rubbing his eyes and sweeping his gaze around drunkenly, ignoring the sour stench and dust cloud in the air.

He coughed after taking a deep breath. Scowling, he said drily, "Outpost, right?" and started climbing a nearby ladder without waiting for an answer.

Stifling a cough, Tom muttered, "Yes. Still seems to be abandoned, so we should be safe for some sleep after we reconnoiter." Almost on cue, he heard a twig snap outside the barn door.

He heard John's soft snoring from the hayloft almost immediately. "I'll check it out," Tom mumbled and headed for the door.

The Messier Pool was at war with their home system, the Lactea Ring, whether anyone back home believed it or not. Despite what the instructors had drilled into them at the Space Mage Academy, the Messier Concord was about as two-sided as a lecture from the Academy chancellor. The Messier Pool basically had free rein in neutral space, between the frontiers.

Closer to their own frontier, the Lactean Ring mages were restricted to defensive magic.

The Messier theory held that Lactean magic was too powerful, and offensive magic would be devastating to peaceful Messier vessels wandering too close to the Lactean Frontier—accidentally, of course. The official line in the Ring was that Messier technology was more powerful than magic and would be devastating if the Messiers engaged fully. Officially, there was détente in Neutral Space.

There was a lot of *official* speculation on what it was like out here. In reality, they were as accurate as the location of the Messier Frontier. The Academy's official stance was that the frontiers were fixed in space, but the twins knew better. Entire systems got swallowed up by the Messiers overnight.

Not the outpost—at least, not yet. This had once been the most far-flung colony attempt by Lacteans, yet still considered far enough from the Messier Frontier to be safe from random attacks.

After the colony had been abandoned and was long gone, the Messier had advanced their frontier bit by bit. Tom had no doubt this outpost would be in the Messier Loop soon, considering the noise beyond the door.

Steeling himself with a deep breath, Tom magewove a duplicate of the door, then opened it. The illusion worked, as neither of the heavily armed Pegasun soldiers walking a patrol nearby noticed him standing in the now-open doorway.

They carried powerful weapons, born of their *technology*, but two soldiers were no match for a space mage. Using the techniques developed by The Three—mages who worked together to power alien technology with magic, the foundation of all magic teaching at the Space Mage Academy—Tom turned their technology against its masters, each soldier's weapon quickly dispatching the other. No reinforcements came.

Tom crept up to a dilapidated farmhouse and, hearing no sounds after several minutes, entered cautiously.

No sense wasting magic on an empty house.

A few minutes later—satisfied the guards had merely been a precaution, not guarding an active threat—Tom magewove protection on the door and joined his brother in the hayloft, but a restful sleep failed to claim Tom as quickly as his brother. His racing thoughts kept him awake, knowing they'd have to be more cautious when returning to this outpost again. The presence of the soldiers meant the system likely would be in Pegasus territory soon. Of the Messiers they'd encountered, they were relatively harmless, and very friendly, but they were still the enemy.

Having befriended some hauler pilots on their previous forays into Pegasus territory—the closest system to the Messier Frontier, only a single magecast from the abandoned outpost—they'd learned some of what the Pegasuns referred to as *science*. They said there was something called *gravity* that exerted some kind of *force* on everything around it, even at tremendous distances. Large objects like stars had higher *gravity* and pulled on the planets with enough *force* to make them orbit the star.

It was this revelation that had given the twins the idea for magecast. If they could magically link two mages with an attractive *force* like this *gravity*, and briefly use an *anti-force* to push them apart—anchoring one mage and throwing the other—then anchor the second mage and let the *force* pull them back together again, they might be able to travel a greater distance than was possible with conventional magic. They'd tried it over small distances, increasing slowly until they found themselves magecasting to the other side of the globe. The key to the maneuver was mageseeing the target clearly.

It wasn't long before Tom and John drunkenly tried to magecast between planets—and it worked! The final refinement was for the catching mage to immediately throw the other mage somewhere else, and repeat the process, leapfrogging their way across neutral space between the frontiers in a fraction of the time it would take spaceships to traverse.

Magecast will correct the Lactean disadvantage inherent in the Concord, Tom thought triumphantly, *once we get back and show the Academy.*

This *force* behind magecast had no equivalent in the three basic magical forces Lactean mages used: magesight, used with a magical lens to see across vast distances instantly; mageflow, used to provide magical power; and magetouch, used to shape how mageflow was used. The various mage academies taught students to master all three, but in reality, mages rarely excelled at more than one. Even in the prestigious Space Mage Academy, there were only a handful of mages skilled enough to combine all three in some spectacular display.

Tom remembered hearing of only one such mage at the moment, a prince who'd gone through the Academy with Tom's friend, Osby Trinity—Prince Patrick something-or-other. Allegedly, he'd single-handedly repelled a Pegasun attack on a Lactean outpost—*could it be this one?*—and saved the entire colony.

Couldn't be this one, he thought, *it's abandoned.*

Osby always got this unfocused, haunted look when he talked about this Patrick—*what was it he called him? Pee-pee-wee?*—and said he'd shown him the truth.

That's probably why we got along so well—fellow truth-seekers bucking the world.

By the time of Tom's graduation simulation at the Academy, Osby had revealed secrets that sounded like a load of propaganda, directly contradicting what they'd been taught. That didn't matter to Tom; the Concord was clear in its directive: colonists knew the risks, and their deaths would be a drop in the metaphorical bucket of blood that would be spilled in a full-scale Messier attack if Lacteans failed to put the Concord first.

This PPP—no, it was PP3, I remember now—failed the Academy in disgrace and vanished. Pretty impressive for a prince, actually; they usually manage to hog the spotlight with their sense of self-importance wherever they got. Except for the invisible prince, PP3, apparently.

That didn't change history; Tom had respected the Concord, like a model student, and let the simulated colonists die, not sparing them another thought until now—*could it have been here that they died?*

After graduation, Osby had admitted he'd done the same, and then he'd gotten that haunted look and wandered off in search of a drink.

Having met a few Pegasuns since graduation—the pilots we know are good people, hardly the monsters you'd expect to participate in the kind of attacks they simulated at the Academy. There's always a few bad seeds that might try it, but even they'd think twice if they thought Lactea could retaliate. It'll all be different after we get back.

* * *

Pegasus System

"What are we buying?" John fingered a rough-hewn wooden table at the outdoor market, laden with fish rotting in the sun.

Nearby paced a mouthy merchant, breath reeking from dental decay, and body stinking from months without washing. Without a word, he threw up his hands in frustration and turned to another potential customer, ignoring the twins.

"Nothing," Tom said and pointed his brother toward a tavern at the edge of the market.

John smirked. "Should have known, you drunkard."

"It's not for us. We'll grab something exotic and mage—" he glanced around warily "—and *take* it back."

Nodding his head, John indicated he understood. *Proof. Something unattainable in Lactea.* "I'm thinking the liquor with the Pegasus-drawn, three-wheeled milkmaid cart."

"Sounds good."

They strode on to the tavern, oblivious to the group of rough-looking men nearby who'd perked up at a word that sounded suspiciously like magic.

Gliding into the tavern, Tom strode directly to the bar and grinned. "A bottle of your best milquor. Don't bother opening it; we're in a hurry." He slapped down double the Pegasus credits, barely missing a puddle of weak beer on the bar surface.

The barkeep barely glanced at them as he scooped up the credits and nodded, trundling away for a few moments before returning with the bottle, which he clunked down on the bar top. A moment later, he added a small loaf of tavern bread.

"Keeps the drunk going longer," he croaked with a voice aged by decades of daily liquor rations, and treated the twins to a mostly toothless grin, with only slightly less stench of decay than the fish merchant.

John grinned back and nodded, dragging the bread carelessly through the beer puddle while pulling it off the bar top. Holding up the loaf for a closer inspection, he headed for the door, his brother close behind with the bottle. "Nice. Looks like the stuff made from that big sucker with all the seeds."

Tom glanced at the bread. "I think it's called a 'sunflower.' Heard it came from the Sol System."

"Whatever." John shrugged. "I call it delic—"

Outside the tavern, a greeting committee made itself known by punching John in the face mid-sentence. He crumpled to the ground, somehow managing to keep hold of the bread.

Tom sighed. "It's never easy, is it?"

* * *

Home

Osbourne stared out the bare window, fingers splayed on the cooling glass, tracking the sun's last rays peeking over the horizon. He'd nodded off, waiting for the twins to return after they'd—*What had they called it? Magecast?*—away late the previous night with loud, drunken promises of proof of this amazing new tool they'd developed.

What's taking those guys so long? Maybe I shouldn't have let them leave while so drunk.

Tom blinked into the room, quickly followed by John.

"Hungry?" John asked, tossing a strangely dirty-looking loaf of bread to Osbourne, who caught it with both hands. John slumped onto a couch, reclining. "Might want to dust it off a little first."

Tom thumped the bottle down on the table. "Milquor from Pegasus. Need more proof?" Dropping onto a chair, he rubbed his eyes and yawned.

Osbourne whistled low. "Where'd you get that?"

"Pegasus. Like I said."

Glancing at John for confirmation, he just shrugged. "That was the point, wasn't it?"

"You were gone almost a day," Osbourne countered. "You could have gotten that anywhere within a day's travel."

"Sure thing," John muttered. "Break open that bread, will you? I'm starving and too exhausted for an argument."

Glaring at his friend, Tom said tartly, "Osby, milquor is highly illegal. Just having it could get us executed. Who'd risk keeping that stuff around?"

Osbourne stared at the filthy bread and tossed it to John, who caught it one-handed—easily—then tossed it back.

"Missing the point, Osby," John said tiredly. "Break it open."

Osbourne did so, after wiping off the more obvious grime, and brought the open bread closer to his face, inhaling deeply. "It's still warm," he said, surprised.

"Exactly. Now give me some. I'm starving."

Osbourne tossed the bigger portion to the reclining twin and stared at the nearby bottle while tearing off a clean interior chunk of the bread to chew slowly. "I'm pretty sure this bread is sunflower, from the Sol System. That's in Lactea."

"Forget the bread," Tom said, clearly annoyed. "No, don't forget it; give it to me. I'm starving, too. Magecasting takes it out of you."

Osbourne walked over to Tom and gently placed the remainder of the bread in his outstretched hand, then turned and once again regarded the illegal bottle. "It's really milquor from Pegasus?"

John chuckled. "Open it up. I guarantee you've never tasted anything like it before."

Tom snorted. "Also, we need to dispose of the evidence."

"Don't bother with glasses," John added.

Osbourne struggled, but managed to get it open with a loud *pop*. A small sip burned his tongue and throat, causing him to cough violently.

"Give it here before you break it!" Tom snapped and reached for the bottle, waving his hand around in empty space.

Once again, Osbourne took a few steps over to Tom and handed him the bottle.

Swigging generously, Tom handed off the milquor to his nearby twin, who gulped just as much with just as much ease.

"Oh, yes," John mumbled happily. "Reminds me of this *really* drunk young moth—"

"We get it. Shut up and give it back."

Osbourne watched the two for a few minutes as they passed the bottle back and forth, munching on bread between swallows. They'd completely forgotten about him.

Can it be true? They traveled across the entire neutral space between the Lactea and Messier Frontiers—and back again—in less than a day?

"Much better than that stinky barn," John slurred, his mouth full of sunflower bread.

Tom sighed. "Not as good as the beach."

"Yeah. Except for the pants."

Osbourne stared at John, then Tom, then committed to a hard decision, reminding himself that if he'd learned one thing from his old Academy classmate PP3, it was that sometimes you had to do what was right, despite what the Space Mage Academy dictated.

He remembered the day clearly, when the chancellor had called him in and tasked him with befriending the genius twins she'd called "troubling, possibly dangerous." He'd done so easily enough, but he'd grown to like the boys as they made their way through the Academy. He hadn't found them troubling at all, much less dangerous, but he'd carefully crafted his reports to the chancellor with a sense of mystery and unanswered questions in order to misdirect her attention enough that she wouldn't notice Osbourne's growing friendship with John and Tom.

He hadn't thought about *why* he'd done it; he just did it.

But now he knew why. It was all leading up to this moment.

If the twins had perfected this new magical tool, this planet-spanning, fast *bodyform* travel they called magecast, it would upset the balance of the Concord so much, the Academy would have no choice but to outlaw it.

If *any* pair of mages could magecast in these days of unrest and dissatisfaction, veritable *armies* of mercenary mages would crop up and magecast at the Messier Loop indiscriminately. Messier would have no choice but to declare the Concord void and launch an all-out war. Even if the Lactean officials understood magecast—unlikely; what bureaucrats ever comprehend the subtleties of *any* new invention?—they'd view a full-scale Messier invasion as imminent annihilation.

No, the decision was obvious to Osbourne, hard as it would be on the fun-loving twins he'd soon betray. They'd called on him as a friend and a respected graduate of the Space Mage Academy, unaware of his special relationship with the chancellor, to demonstrate a revolutionary new magic tool they thought could level the playing field in the cold war with the Messier Loop. A fourth magical force, magecast, so powerful that fear of Lactean retribution could finally put a stop to the random attacks by Messier. The twins hoped he'd be able to convince the Academy of the value of magecast.

He'd encourage them, of course, and even try to learn to magecast himself, if he could ever find someone he trusted enough with the secret.

Because it would *be* a secret.

The chancellor would receive the expected report: rumors about the Collins twins were unfounded, a lie, probably drunken boasting. Nothing for the Academy to be concerned with.

Osbourne shook his head and slipped out, unnoticed by the tired twins.

I wonder if this is how PP3 felt when he saved those colonists, knowing he was throwing both his graduation and career away by doing so.

* * *

"Sorry, it's not personal." Trenoway, a space cruiser captain the twins had worked for dozens of times in the past, groaned as he rose from the sticky seats in the bar and trundled off, shaking his sweat-glistening, smooth-shaved head.

John stared at his brother questioningly.

Shrugging, Tom whispered, "That's the third one tonight."

"Why do they keep saying it's not personal? It feels pretty personal to me." John reached out to snag the arm of their passing barmaid; she halted, but glared at the hand on her arm.

"Bring us another round." John dropped his hand.

Turning to face them, she cocked a free arm on her hip and stared at them. "Word is you're no good for credit."

John glanced at Tom, who shrugged.

"Payment in advance," she said, leaning in and extending an open hand.

Tom obliged without a word. After the barmaid retreated, he turned back to his twin. "What word? Have you hear—"

A stranger squeezed himself into the booth next to John. Reeking of a shockingly overdue bath, the pirate's black hair, tied haphazardly behind him, smeared the high seat back, leaving a greasy stain marking his entry. Rotting teeth and decay presaged his opening line, "Heard you boys need a job, bad."

* * *

"You've got some explaining to do, Osby!" John spat at the arrival of the mage at the center of their recent revelations. "Did you know the Academy thinks we're crackpots?"

"And so do most of these fine people," Tom added, waving vaguely around them in the deafening din inside the bar. The other bar patrons, soused and rowdy, took no more notice of the twins than they had Osbourne's quiet entrance.

"Did you know," John said, leaning in as Osbourne slid next to Tom, "we've had three offers from pirates in the last hour? *Pirates!*" He slammed a fist on the table, splashing Tom's beer onto the already-sticky tabletop. "We're *Space Mages!*"

Osbourne held out two hands, palm down, to quiet them and hung his head. "I know."

Tom hissed, "Did you tell the Academy about magecast?"

After a few seconds of silence, John jumped in. "You didn't, did you?"

Still staring at Osbourne, Tom shook his head slowly. "He did tell them."

Osbourne looked up, pain clearly evident in his expression, and nodded.

"He told them it didn't work."

Osbourne's eyes glazed, and he turned to stare somewhere else before answering. "I had no choice."

"What?" John bellowed.

"Do you realize what you've done?" Osbourne asked slowly. "This is basically the fourth force."

"That's ridiculous!" John seethed. "There's a new fourth force boast every few months, with outrageous claims that amount to nothing more than misdirection. Magecast *works!* You've seen it yourself, Osby."

"I *believe* it works," Osbourne admitted, "but it really *is* a fourth force, don't you see? Not a sham, not a wild boast, but a *real* fourth force."

He took a deep breath. "And it would upset the balance of the Concord."

"That's the point!" Tom said through gritted teeth.

Osbourne shook his head. "You don't know the Academy like I do. The Concord comes first; if it upsets the Concord, it upsets the Academy."

John struggled out of the booth and loomed over Osbourne, poking a finger into his chest with enough force to hurt. "It *works!* You saw."

"Sit down, John," Osbourne said quietly. "There's more."

John reseated himself at the edge of the booth, positioning himself for another attack, if needed.

"The chancellor sent me." Osbourne deflated with the admission, but neither twin reacted. He glanced at John, who still fumed, then Tom.

"We figured that out, Osby."

"No, not just today. I mean, from the beginning. She sent me to keep an eye on you two because she thought you were… dangerous."

John opened his mouth, then closed it again without a word. His shocked expression was unmistakable. Opening his mouth again, and still failing to find his voice, he got up and stomped out.

"Osby." Tom placed both palms down flat on the table. "Why did you do it?"

Osbourne tore his gaze from John's retreat. "I was on eggshells after graduation. I told you about the Academy's secret agenda. I needed to keep suspicion off me."

Tom tilted his head and furrowed his brow, his mouth a tight line, as if he were literally biting off a harsh rejoinder.

"I like you guys, Tom, and I consider you friends. What do think would've happened if she'd sent someone else to spy on you?" Osbourne paused for a few seconds to let that sink in. "Think about what an entire force of space mages could do. We can reach them *anywhere*, even their own home worlds, bypassing their blockades, ignoring the Messier Frontier entirely. In mere *hours*, we could effectively destroy the Messier Concord."

Tom nodded. "And we could *win*."

"I think so, too," Osbourne said. "Now look at it from the chancellor's perspective. If she truly believes you're dangerous, and her spy brings her news that magecast is real? That the Concord would be in jeopardy?"

Tom stared, understanding. "That prince you talked about before? He was thrown out of the Academy for less. But John and I are *already* space mages; the Academy can't stop us."

Osbourne sighed. "They already have. You said it yourself; you've had three offers from pirates, not legitimate concerns. You're only alive because I convinced the chancellor that magecast is just another drunken boast about the fourth force."

"But it's not—"

"It doesn't matter; that's how it'll be perceived." He paused. "Do you think you'd be the only… dangerous… space mages to disappear at the chancellor's behest?"

Tom sat in silence for several minutes, thinking. "Magecast really *is* life-changing, just like we thought. And you want us to just *forget* about it?"

"No! Definitely not. I want you to *use* it. I want to learn how to do it myself. I want us to make a difference in the cold war with Messier." Osbourne took a calming breath.

"I just want to do it in secret."

* * *

Pegasus System

"We should've brought Osby along," John said tartly, crouching behind a large stack of smudged and cracked crates in a brightly lit spaceship bay on Pegasus Prime. Huge by Lactean standards, the bay teemed with Pegasun soldiers, each adorned with the same polished and gleaming weapons Tom had encountered at the outpost on their last magecast here. "We could've used him as a distraction."

"Let it go, bro," Tom whispered. "You could've waited for his explanation."

"Your half-baked assurances are only half-convincing."

"Trust me," Tom hissed. "Do you see what's going on here?"

"Yeah. Looks like they're readying an invasion fleet."

"Exactly." Tom peeked around the crates. "And it looks like a squadron is taking off now. Seven, maybe eight."

"Nine," John corrected, glancing over the crates. "We should report back to the traitor. Our puppet master."

"I explai—"

John's abrupt hand between them signaled no interest in debate. "Master Osbourne was pretty clear; no engagement that would attract the attention of the Academy."

Tom sighed and sat down, leaning against the heavy crates, his thighs burning from prolonged squatting.

"You're probably right. We've been gone too long already; last thing we need is for our ship to get tagged as abandoned, and destroyed."

Tom smirked. "Osby's watching it for us, and it's still in Lactean space, inside the frontier."

"Barely."

"Enough. It's not going anywhere. Osby will make sure of that; he owes us, and he knows it."

"Still," John whispered after sitting next to his brother, "we should report back soon. Unless…"

Tom swiveled his head and cocked an eyebrow.

"Unless you're up for some minor mischief, Tommy."

"How minor?"

"I was thinking it would be a shame if the consoles in these ships shorted out."

Tom grinned. "What the Academy doesn't know can't hurt them."

"Or us."

"How many did you see?"

John shrugged. "Maybe a hundred; maybe two."

"It'll take a while."

"Short magecasts. Take us a few seconds between catch and throw to short out the console, then we move on."

Tom screwed up his face. "That's still a lot of magecasts, and we'll need to cast an illusion in case anyone happens to see us in the cockpits, even for only a moment. That's a lot of magical energy. What if we get tired?"

John pointed in front of them. "Looks like lockers there. We'll change into Pegasus uniforms. One less drain on our magic."

Tom looked pensive. "Those timepieces the soldiers carry on their wrists? They have timers on them. I think I could mageform a standard sequence to short out the consoles; they're all the same."

"Yeah, that's good. Make it so it grabs a little mageflow from the magecast catch and starts the sequence, and we don't even need to take those few seconds in the cockpit."

"In and out, shorting as we go."

"Tommy?"

"What?"

"Maybe we *are* dangerous." John stifled a cackle. "Spying behind the Academy's back might be fun!"

* * *

Neutral Space, Just Past the Lactea Frontier

Osbourne's mageform ran interference down the Earthform freighter corridor, spinning out explosive balls wildly as lines from Pegasun weapons sizzled dangerously close. The bodyform of his old classmate, Prince Patrick Peterson the Third—PP3—ran behind him with hastily formed magical shields blazing.

Less than an hour earlier, Osbourne had heard a very curious distress call.

"Space mage down. Space mage down."

It wasn't the right form, but if a space mage was in trouble, he was obligated to respond as best he could. Then he got the shock of his life, hearing words over shipvoice he'd never anticipated in all his years as a space mage. A name and rank that couldn't be.

"This is Phoenix 12, Space Mage Patrick Peterson."

Without thinking, he'd blurted out, "PP3? A space mage?"

Then he shut off his comms, embarrassed, confused, and conflicted, stewing in his own thoughts for too long. In the end, Osbourne had decided he still felt the same obligation to his old school nemesis as he did for any other space mage, even if PP3 wasn't really one.

Couldn't be one, since PP3 had washed out of the Academy after a disastrous final simulation—the one that had convinced Osbourne of a dangerous secret being kept from the students, a secret that haunted him even now.

Osbourne owed the prince a debt, even if PP3 didn't know it. But what could he do? Osbourne was too far away to help any more than he was already.

Unless...

"Ever heard of the Collins twins?" he blurted out, instantly regretting it, but knowing it was the right thing to do.

"*No. Should I?*" The shipvoice, of course, didn't sound at all like the prince's voice, rather like the mountain lilt of the simple folk in the ice regions, Osbourne's favorite setting.

"They came through a couple years ago. Claimed they could move bodyform, not just mageform."

A grunt came through the shipvoice, as if PP3 had fallen. "*That's impossible.*"

They continued down the corridor with minimal banter, lines sizzling all around them until the prince skidded to a halt near a cargo hold Osbourne had already scouted with his mageform and found to be empty. PP3 assured him there was a hiding place.

Jumping as he spied two Pegasun soldiers taking aim, Osbourne twisted his mageform around, letting loose a wall of fire.

Taking advantage of the cover fire, the prince slipped around the corner and into another empty cargo hold, just as a line from somewhere else sizzled against the wall by the closing door.

Osbourne's mageform followed him, unaffected.

"*I won't survive this.*"

"Hide anyway."

* * *

Osbourne concentrated harder than he'd ever expected was possible, light-headed from the effort, and wheezing from his previous failed attempts.

What was it Tom said? Focus your magesight on the target like you normally do, and move your mageform there, anchoring it with mageflow, but with a line back to a second mageform that you align with your partner's bodyform. Then use your magetouch to make a giant hand with as much mageflow as you can muster, and use that to throw your mageform here as hard as you can toward your other mageform there. If you do it right, your partner's bodyform goes with it.

But the twins had never done it alone. Why should he expect he'd be able to?

Still, he had to try. Again.

He formed two mageforms again—one aligned with his bodyform through magetouch, and a duplicate a few feet away—formed the hand, and threw himself as hard as he could...

... and found himself a few feet away.

The euphoria from his success clouded the next few minutes of his memory, but Osbourne managed to stay on task, eventually finding himself in an empty cargo hold with a sizzle line scoring one side of the door. Spinning around, he found the smuggler's door and opened it. Inside the cramped space was PP3, slumped to the floor, unconscious.

Osbourne squatted in front of him, thighs burning and eyes drooping. He shook the prince awake and smiled at him.

"I guess we do it the hard way," he managed just before crumpling to the floor, exhausted.

* * *

Near the Lactea Frontier

Patrick looked between the twins. "Collins, I presume?" He extended an open hand. "Your push-pull thing is *amazing*. I've never done anything like that before!"

John stared at the dirty, disheveled pilot standing next to Osbourne, who appeared just as disheveled. He dropped his hand. Behind them stood the mageform of a young, slightly plump redheaded woman with brilliant blue eyes. She nodded once when Osbourne glanced back, then blinked out.

"My sister, Lizzie."

"I thought she wasn't a mage," Tom said.

"I mageformed her using my own," the stranger said. "I got the idea from your push-pull. You know, wrapping your own mageform around someone else and—"

"We know how *magecast* works," John interrupted.

"Sorry."

Osbourne's attention snapped back to the twins. "Sorry, I'd like to introduce Prince Patr—"

"PP3." Patrick glared at Osbourne, but his expression showed amusement.

"Aren't you dead?" John blurted out.

"Thought I was." Patrick glanced at Osbourne, who nodded an acknowledgement.

"I magecast alone," Osbourne stated flatly, as if everybody did that.

"Alone?" Tom challenged. "How?"

Osbourne shrugged. "Concentration? It took me a few tries to get it right."

John's mouth gaped.

"And then he—what did you call it?—magecast me out of danger." PP3 shrugged. "I figured it out and pulled him with me."

"That's the catch," John said absentmindedly. "We usually then throw the other to the next target." He turned back to Osbourne. "Are you saying we don't concentrate?"

"That sounds handy," Patrick muttered, thinking about the ramifications of prolonged leapfrogging with magecast.

"Well, you're usually drunk," Osbourne teased.

"Enough," Tom admonished. "Think about what you just did. And you think *we're* dangerous!"

Osbourne looked offended. "The *Academy* thinks you're dangerous; *I* don't!"

John waggled a finger between Osbourne and Patrick. "Then you two are *twice* as dangerous." He glanced at his twin. "Maybe we should turn them in. Do you think there's a reward?"

Tom chuckled and scratched his chin. "If only we knew someone with the chancellor's ear…"

Osbourne shook his head. "Funny. And it was an emergency; PP3 was in Neutral Space, under attack by five Pegasun ships. I had to do *something*."

"Yeah," John teased with a smirk, "something *dangerous*."

"Fine, I deserve that. But it worked."

"I'm glad you see it that way," Tom said, "especially after what we just did on Pegasus Prime."

After a quick recounting, John added, "There are still nine ships on the way."

"That explains why the five that attacked me were so heavily armed and keen to board me," Patrick said. "Scouts."

"Fourteen heavily armed warships can still do a lot of damage," Osbourne admitted, "but they might give it up once they figure out no reinforcements are behind them."

Patrick scowled. "Not in my experience. They'll still try."

"Unless—" Tom started.

"—we stop them before they get to the Lactean Frontier," John finished.

"It'll take them quite some time to get there," Osbourne noted, "but we can intercept them in hours."

"Or," Patrick said, "you could take a tour of the five hanging around the Frontier and destroy their life support. Leave the derelicts there as a warning."

John guffawed. "I like this guy."

"Before we go," Patrick said cautiously, "you never asked me if I wanted to join you. I'm kind of like the plague."

"Seriously? A few days ago, a handful of *pirates* offered us jobs, because *this* guy knifed us in the back at the Academy." John jerked a thumb at Osbourne. "We're not afraid of the plague, Princess."

PP3 laughed at the new nickname. "I'm in, if you'll have me."

"The four of us right here," Tom pointed out, "are they the only ones who ever need to know about any of this. We've got a lot of spying in our futures."

"Right," John agreed.

Osbourne hesitated. "I was thinking about that…"

Tom groaned. "No. Just the four of us."

"Seriously," Osbourne said. "There may be more like us out there. Space mages who are tired of the imbalance with the Concord. We know it's not just you two that can magecast. PP3 and I did it."

"*You* did it alone," Patrick added.

"So maybe others can be trained."

Patrick nodded. "We start with space mages with relatives on the colonies. Once they know the Academy's secret, most of them will join us."

"We can fix that imbalance with the Concord," Osbourne added, nodding toward the twins. "Just like you wanted to."

"From the shadows," Tom clarified. "Unbeholden to the Academy or anyone else."

"The Star Guard," Patrick offered.

Tom grinned. "Sworn to a higher purpose, survival of the Lactean Ring, despite the bureaucrats. What could be more noble?"

John smirked. "Sounds to me like pala—"

"Don't say it," Tom warned, waggling a finger at him, "or I swear I'll be an only child by morning."

* * * * *

Daniel M. Hoyt Biography

Daniel M. Hoyt is a systems architect for trajectory physics software, when not writing or wrangling royalty calculations. Dan has appeared in premier magazines like *Analog* and several anthologies, notably *Bonds of Valor* with another Space Mage story, Baen's *Founder Effect* and *Stellaris*, and Dr. Mike Brotherton's *Diamonds in the Sky* online anthology, funded by the National Science Foundation. Dan also edited *Fate Fantastic* and *Better Off Undead* for DAW. Having published in several genres, Dan turned to his science fiction roots for his debut novel, space opera *Ninth Euclid's Prince*. Catch up with him at danielmhoyt.com.

* * * * *

The Oaths That Bind
by H.Y. Gregor
and David Shadoin
A Milesian Accords Story

Darwin Hayes stumbled through the darkened forest. His soaked, tattered clothes snagged on bushes and brambles he couldn't make out through the pouring rain and moonless night. His flashlight was on its last leg, and the dim arc of light it produced hindered his progress more than helped. He'd been on the run for several weeks, making his way by whatever means he could to get to the forested hills just outside of Portland.

Running ahead of his own reputation.

He couldn't understand how it had gone so wrong. They'd set up the ritual just so, followed every instruction to the letter.

He only wanted one answer: who was his father?

When they'd called beyond the veil of life, what had answered was not his mother. There was no explanation for what had gone wrong, nor could he identify the being who'd answered the call. The only thing Darwin knew was what answered had been powerful and bloodthirsty.

Weighed down by his mud-caked, tattered shoes and the vegetation clinging to his threadbare pants, he could barely start up the incline away from the Columbia River. His animal instincts drove him toward a cave up the slope, a promise of protection from the elements. He slogged uphill, slipping several times on ground where he couldn't find purchase, but ever so slowly making progress.

Finally, the dim light flickered on a rock outcropping poking out from the dense foliage. Behind it was a pitch-black opening in the side of the hill. He managed to get one good sweep of the mouth of the cave before his flashlight succumbed to the cold and wet, leaving him with nothing.

A breeze ruffled the remains of his shirt, sending shivers down his spine as he approached the gaping maw. He squinted into the darkness. Darwin shivered again, this time sensing a presence in the cave his faded flashlight hadn't revealed. Caught between a rock and the continuous onslaught of the rain and cold, he stepped inside.

Instant relief washed over him once he was out of the bone-chilling rain, yet his gut told him to be wary. He reached out with his senses, hampered as they were by struggling through the freezing rain for so long, and strained to hear or see a whisper of what was with him. He didn't think bears were common around Portland, but what did he know? He'd been in the area for all of a week.

Then something spoke to him.

"*Watashi wa anata no shujinda. Watashi no ishi ni yudane, watashi no chi kara o ukeirenasai.*"

"W-w-what... Who was that?" Darwin sensed rather than heard the presence.

"*Eigo hanashimasu.* Come to me, my child. Come to me, and bow down before your king." The voice came from everywhere and nowhere, and for a fleeting second, Darwin thought he was hallucinating it. He stepped further into the abyss, but remained silent, drawing his Ka-Bar, feeling outward for the direction of the attack—in case his hallucinations turned into a real presence.

"Do not be afraid, my child, for I am the King of the Destitute and the Damned. You will serve me to atone for your sins."

Darwin felt that last sentence imbued with the power of command. A tingling shock went through his body. His skin crawled; his vision blurred. Suddenly, the pain of a thousand needles wrapped his body. His muscles bulged in response. He doubled over, his knees striking the stone beneath him as his knife clattered away. His weathered shoes trapped his feet. Three sharp points dug into his skull.

As Darwin's vision faded, the voice penetrated his conscience. "You will serve me well."

* * *

Seth Bradley stalked his quarry as his masters had taught him. He'd arrived in Portland several days before and been forced to don the local attire in place of his saffron monk's robes when he kept catching looks.

As the one bestowed with the gifts of Nga Phee, and as the newest knight of the Bagan Order, his abbot had chosen him for this task. Seth had practically jumped at the chance. What better way to prove his oath than to stop a mass murderer? There were even rumors floating around that these murders were spiritually related. His predecessors barely even remembered the tales of when the worlds were open to each other.

Then a few weeks ago, the other world had revealed itself.

Despite the lessons he'd been taught, Seth's mind had refused to believe myths and legends had come to life. In recent years, his cohorts had discussed an uptick in unexplainable phenomena. The other knights had also been taken aback by the revelation of magic and otherworldly beings, but all agreed training harder and studying their potential adversaries was the smart thing to do.

With the supernatural being the simplest explanation for a spate of grisly murders around Portland, Seth knew DHS would have someone on the ground to investigate.

That's what Kyansittha hinted, at least, he thought.

Sure enough, some suit-wearing busybody and his young, eager, ignorant protégé flew in and declared the crime scenes "federal jurisdiction."

At the first two scenes, Seth did his best not to get in the way. He tried to do his own investigation, leaving the mundane evidence he found in plain sight, and intending to hide any evidence of the supernatural from the suits.

The task proved tedious, especially when the body count mounted, as he'd attempted to go unnoticed and still complete his mission. He was the knight of Stamina, not the knight of Small Details, and while the bodies had been mauled and sometimes dismembered, no evidence existed of a powerful being the suits couldn't handle.

He'd combed the woods for almost a week, searching for any sign that something bigger was in play. On the verge of giving up hope that there was anything involved from the otherworld at all, he'd found a tree ripped from its trunk. No bear possessed the ability to do this. Here at the top of the waterfall, leaning on his *khakkhara*, he surveyed the area for further evidence.

The Feds showed up shortly after, revisiting the scene of the quadruple homicide. Seth, aware they'd spotted him a few times previously, moved into the woods to make himself scarce.

Son of a dog eater, Ksanti save me... the suits have the worst timing.

He circled them as they hiked to the stump he'd discovered. Unfamiliar with his surroundings, Seth found himself against the sheer drop of the cliff. If the Feds decided to investigate, he had nowhere to go... except down.

He needed to get out of sight. Seth sheathed his staff on his back and started his descent. The grips were slick from the mist of the falls. A bush sprouted from the rock face just below his foot. Seth put his foot on it, testing his weight. It bent, but he remained balanced.

For a second.

He fell before he could re-grip the rock, and the rock face flashed by. He grasped the brush at the last second and swung into an underhang, smacking the cliff hard. The blow knocked the air from his lungs as he struggled to hang on with his feet.

Then his toes found purchase on something solid. He lowered himself, never letting go of the bush that had betrayed him. This ledge held. It was a few feet wide, but there was no clear way to climb back out.

Several minutes passed while he caught his breath and examined his predicament. His best route was to follow the ledge sideways and find a better spot to climb back up. That took another set of minutes he had not planned to waste.

A faint tinge of putrid stench fell on the air. During his climb, he heard a distant roar. Once he mantled the top, he found himself alone. No sign of either of the suits.

Gunshots rang out.

Seth chanted a simple protection mantra, reaching out with his will toward the gunshots. Silence, punctured by the occasional distant shout, settled on the mountain. Seth hesitated.

Then a feral bellow echoed through the forest.

The younger hotshot agent scrambled by, unaware of Seth's presence. The agent was injured, but mobile.

The older Fed was nowhere to be seen.

Seth heard the crashing of underbrush further up the hillside. He drew his staff and prepared for a fight.

* * *

Ryan Fortner had thought the road driving up the Columbia River Gorge was bad. He'd been wrong. He'd spent the better part of an hour hiking up an increasingly narrow, mud-slicked trail. Right angles trapped him in on either side: a mossy canyon wall to his left, a deadly plummet into the river more than twenty feet below to his right.

He toed the edge and pretended he wasn't afraid of heights.

"You can't say it's not worth the effort." Artem Collins, Ryan's training officer and partner at the Department of Homeland Security, stopped in his tracks at a curve in the trail. Ryan tore his gaze away from the churning water below and joined his partner. The waterfall they sought spouted from the cliffs ahead of them.

"Remind me why we ruled out this death trap?" Ryan asked. It was no Niagara Falls, but a drop into the canyon was more than enough to kill someone. Water plummeted into a cauldron of churning white water in the ravine below.

Everything about these mountains screamed, *accidents happen.*

Artem's lips thinned into a nearly imperceptible line as he surveyed the jungle-like terrain surrounding them. He'd been Ryan's training officer for several months now, but Ryan still had a hard time getting a read on the dark-eyed man. Based on the amount of actual talking Artem did, Ryan was either a prodigy or completely hopeless.

Maybe rehashing the facts of the case out loud would prompt Artem into conversation—or at least confirm that there wasn't anything to see here. "So. Four guys come up here, and the only reason we know that is because their fifth buddy was too hungover to join them on the hike. The incident happened over a week ago. If the search and rescue guys were going to find something, they'd have done it already, right?"

Artem grunted.

Undeterred, Ryan continued, "Time goes by when they should have returned, but the fifth guy gets crickets. He spends one more night alone at their campsite before hiking out and alerting the authorities."

"Four men don't just fall at the same time. That stream's way too shallow for cliff jumping. You'd have to be a special kind of stupid to want to give that a try." Artem's eyes were still fixed on the waterfall ahead.

"I've met some pretty stupid people."

Artem rolled his eyes. "Even then, you get one guy too scared to jump, or at least hesitant enough to look down and see the splat from one of the first three guys."

This wasn't the first group of hikers to go missing outside Portland in recent weeks. If there was any chance these guys had just fallen to their deaths, nobody would have called Crypto Division to begin with.

No, whatever was going on out here definitely wasn't normal. They'd already spotted one guy lurking around their investigations—some weirdo with a shaved head wearing orange robes, with a staff topped with jingling gold rings strapped to his back. He stuck out like a sore thumb. Not to mention nine disappearances just in the last few weeks. That many people missing so close to a major city would've raised eyebrows even under normal circumstances.

And circumstances were anything but normal.

It had only been a few weeks since some guy calling himself the First Druid had gone on the news claiming magic had come back into the world. The Crypto Division of the Department of Homeland Security had been buried in copycats and false alarms ever since. Ryan thought he'd chased down just about every kind of idiot claiming every imaginable power.

It's better than a desk job, he reminded himself.

DHS was supposed to be exciting. If he hadn't expected that to include hiking up a muddy Oregon trail in the rain, well, that was his own fault. After a disagreement with a supervisor, he'd been shunted sideways out of training for the Secret Service. One argument had landed him in Crypto Division—where they stuck all the losers, weirdos, and washouts. At least his supervisor, Miriam, knew her stuff.

Now he was all the way across the country, clomping through the forest and chasing a ghost.

Ryan laughed despite himself. A few people who'd made recent reports to Crypto actually believed in ghosts.

"Get it together, Fortner," Artem said.

The incline evened out, and the trail veered away from the falls and into the forest. What little sunlight they had was scattered beneath the canopy of trees.

"Say our men ran into something they weren't exactly expecting." Artem pointed ahead.

Ryan's steps fell short as he caught sight of the destruction his partner pointed out.

Something had torn a tree up from the roots, but even a city kid like Ryan could tell it hadn't been like that for long. The leaves were all still green—though the trunk had been ripped in half. Jagged splinters of white wood stuck out from the tree's core like spikes from a porcupine. Ryan circled the base of the tree, edging around the network of roots sticking up out of the ground.

"That could be anything." Ryan didn't see any supernatural evidence—just weird evidence. "What about a bear?"

"I think Fish and Wildlife would know about bear activity in the area, especially if they were this aggressive." Artem almost sounded amused, though his stony expression rarely betrayed emotion. "Bears don't just attack people out of nowhere."

"Polar bears do," Ryan said, remembering a documentary he'd seen at the dentist once.

"Okay. If you see a polar bear in the Cascades, you be sure to let me know."

They followed a path of destruction that led them further away from the river. Ryan grimaced at the mud and uneven ground, but did his best to keep up. His hunches about natural disasters or animals faded as he took in more of the damage.

Artem held up a hand. "Do you hear that?"

Ryan stopped scraping his shoe against a rock in a fruitless attempt to get the mud off his sneakers and looked around. He strained his ears, but couldn't hear anything above the roar of the waterfall and the occasional whisper of wind through the trees.

A tense moment passed before Artem lowered his hand. "Might be nothing... but keep your eyes peeled. I don't like this."

Ryan frowned at the broken earth surrounding the uprooted tree. Most of the time, the worst thing their investigations turned up was a nutjob with a bad case of Bigfoot fever.

Bigfoot—that was a popular cryptid in Oregon. *So it's not a bear. It's Bigfoot. Case closed.*

The look on Artem's face stopped Ryan from laughing again. A deep frown line creased his partner's forehead. Artem wasn't exactly the most lighthearted guy Ryan had ever worked with, but he'd never been this tense before. The sudden change sent a shiver down Ryan's spine.

Focus. That many people *didn't* just go missing out of nowhere, and they didn't just fall off cliffs en masse. If local law enforcement couldn't figure it out, and the regular Feds had passed up the job, something strange really was going on. This was Ryan's first serious Crypto case.

Time to start taking it seriously.

Ryan shook himself and kept his head on a swivel as they tromped deeper into the undergrowth. A moment later, Artem raised his hand for silence again. Ryan closed his eyes and listened for any unexpected sounds. The wind rustled gently through the trees.

Not just the wind. The sound was deeper. Guttural.

Almost like an exhale.

Ryan opened his eyes. Then a warm breeze swept across his face, carrying with it a fetid taint that made the contents of his stomach curdle. He gagged and threw his hands over his mouth and nose.

"It's coming from up here." Artem took off at a run.

Fighting his gag reflex—and his better instincts—Ryan followed. It was his job, he reminded himself, but he also didn't think he could find the trail again by himself.

It was probably something totally normal for the middle of nowhere, the wind picking up the scent off the carcass of some animal that had died a perfectly natural death... a scent that grew steadily in the air around them. Soon, Ryan could taste the rot even with his nose plugged.

Another gust breathed through their surroundings. Ryan gagged, though by some witchcraft, Artem didn't even seem fazed. Just when Ryan knew he was about to lose his lunch, the strange exhalations stopped.

It's just the wind.

The sudden absence of the strange, heated wind proved even more unnerving than its unexplained presence.

We're close, Ryan thought, though close to *what* was anybody's guess. An animal attack, maybe? Crazy hillbillies in the woods?

No, that made even less sense. The cannibals were all in West Virginia. Ryan had that on pretty good authority.

So what was going on?

"Run." Artem turned to Ryan, his face white as a sheet. He grabbed the collar of Ryan's jacket and shoved him back the way they'd come. "Run *now.*"

The force of their collision slammed Ryan's back into a tree trunk. He grabbed Artem's arm and tried to get his bearings. Run from what? Even the smell had died off.

But it had been a direct order—and a scared one. That was enough.

Ryan lurched forward and was rewarded with a face full of pine needles. Artem dragged him on, clutching Ryan's arm like a mother clutching her wayward toddler near a busy street.

Putrid air ruffled Ryan's hair and slipped down the collar of his jacket. A crackle of bursting wood tore through the trees around them. Then a low, haunting growl reached Ryan's ears.

Whatever was tearing up the forest had found them—and it was gaining ground.

There's no way we can outrun it.

Artem must have come to the same conclusion. He yanked Ryan to a halt. "Give me your gun."

Bewildered, Ryan handed over the weapon. His mouth dropped open as he watched Artem eject the magazine and the chambered round from his government-issued 9mm Glock 19.

"Hey!" Ryan reached out to swipe the gun back. Artem reloaded it with another mag from his own pocket and chambered a round before returning it.

"I need you to use these—" Artem shoved another full mag into Ryan's hand "—if it comes to it."

"What the hell?"

"I'll explain later. Get back to the trail and wait for me there."

Then Artem was gone—running straight *toward* the bestial sounds.

Blood pounded in Ryan's head. The scent of decay grew stronger by the second, so heavy in the air now, his eyes were watering. A small, desperate part of him wanted nothing more than to run back to the trail.

Hell, he wanted to run all the way to the parking lot where they'd left their car, then drive straight back to DC without stopping.

What the hell is Artem thinking?

Another animal grunt filled the air. Ryan's head snapped up, searching for a sign of Artem—or their stalker. Gunfire broke out over the noise. Then silence.

Shit.

Ryan traced Artem's path as best he could through the dense undergrowth. His instincts screamed that he was moving in the wrong direction, but that was the job—running toward danger.

He jumped over an uprooted sapling blocking his path. Dark liquid glistened on the tree's trunk.

Ryan forced his gaze away. "Artem?"

Fetid air rushed into his lungs. Ryan choked and covered his mouth with one hand. He brandished his pistol with the other, loaded with whatever ammunition Artem had decided was better than Ryan's own. He skirted a mossy boulder as a feral screech confirmed he was still headed in the right direction.

Ryan rounded the boulder and stumbled upon a scene he couldn't have conjured in his worst nightmares.

Artem sat with his back against a tree trunk, his gun clasped tightly in both hands. Somehow, he was still alive, though with that much blood, Ryan had no idea how.

Artem caught sight of Ryan and shook his head, then mouthed something inaudible.

A hulking figure loomed over Artem, its back to Ryan. The man had to be at least seven feet tall, wearing torn denim jeans and the shredded remains of a shirt hanging around his waist. He turned slowly, following Artem's gaze until he faced Ryan.

The thing had mangy black hair and a leering gash of a mouth—a mouth larger than it had any right to be. Wide-set eyes blinked down at Ryan from a greenish-yellow face. Gnarled hands matched wrinkled and pockmarked skin.

No way that thing's human, right?

At least Ryan had finally found the source of the pervasive stench—a mix of death and despair.

Ryan didn't know the first thing about bears, but he'd been to enough zoos to know that wasn't what they were dealing with. It paused in front of Artem, then settled its murderous gaze on Ryan. A broken-toothed snarl split its lips.

Then it charged.

Ryan lifted his Glock and summoned just enough sense to make sure Artem wasn't in his line of fire before squeezing the trigger. He hit his attacker center mass once, twice. Three times.

The bullets punched into the thing's chest, eliciting an animalistic roar of rage and pain.

The creature slowed and looked down at its torso, peppered with bullet holes and trailing dark specks of blood. When it looked back up at Ryan, something disturbingly close to curiosity lit its features.

What the hell? It should be dead. Ryan backed toward the cover of the boulder, firing again, again, until—

Click.

Empty. Ryan ejected the mag and fumbled for the spare Artem had given him. The creature let out another growl—and advanced, faster than Ryan had ever seen a man move. It slammed into him with inhuman strength.

The spare magazine flew from Ryan's hand and vanished into the undergrowth.

"Down!" Artem shouted.

Ryan flopped onto his stomach without a thought. Gunfire rang through the forest. The thing screeched, slowed, but didn't stop. Instead it whirled, changing direction and turning its back to Artem.

Artem shouted something in a language Ryan had never heard before. Then he dragged himself to his feet. Ryan crawled into the bushes where the magazine had fallen, frantically digging through the plants and mud in search of it.

No luck.

"Call Miriam." Artem's voice trembled. "*Go*. Go get help."

Artem dropped his gun. They'd unloaded countless rounds into that thing… and not only did it refuse to die, it seemed fine.

To Ryan's disbelief, Artem launched himself at the creature. They collided. The thing grabbed Artem by one arm and threw him back against the tree like he was made of straw.

Ryan blinked.

Artem's arm stiffened and darkened to shades of mottled gray. The bear—thing—slammed him against the tree again. Artem drew a knife with his normal hand and stabbed it down into the meaty juncture where his assailant's neck met its shoulders.

"Run—"

The beast's savage roar drowned out the rest of Artem's words.

Ignoring the knife sticking out of its shoulder completely, the creature grabbed Artem's arm and slammed him back against the tree. Blood spurted from Artem's shoulder joint.

Ryan's stomach curdled as he stared at the gray, torn limb in the creature's hand. Artem dropped bonelessly to the ground, and his head flopped onto his chest. He might have been sleeping if it weren't for all the blood.

Run.

The spare mag was nowhere in sight, but Ryan's gun had proven useless before ammo had been removed from the equation.

Call Miriam. Get help. Run.

And to Ryan's great shame, he ran.

* * *

Seth was no longer hunting the forest for a serial killer. He was of two minds. According to his order, he should continue to work behind the scenes, but it was unlikely the junior suit who'd survived would wait for backup, thus requiring Seth's protection.

He'd been unable to find the senior agent—until a search party had pulled his body from the forest, mangled and limp. He'd also failed to find whatever had attacked them. It had disappeared like smoke on the wind.

The stench of decay dragged at Seth's senses, the only further clue he'd found.

So, here Seth sat, in the brilliant white and green waiting room of the hospital, hoping to catch the young suit before he did anything rash.

A soft chime announced the elevator, and the disheveled agent stepped out. His thick, dark hair was mussed as though he'd run his hands through it repeatedly. His face was partially swollen underneath a few shallow cuts marring his skin.

What stood out the most, though, was the haunted, sunken look of a man who'd faced his own mortality and insignificance.

The young agent hobbled up to the sliding pane. As the automation kicked in, it seemed to jumpstart his brain, and he shambled back toward the front desk. From his position, Seth could hear parts of the mumbled conversation between the agent and a nurse at the desk, words like "notification" and "arrangements," along with a list of items that probably belonged to his partner.

The monk breathed a heavy sigh. It seemed callous to approach the young man during this time of grief. However, whatever was terrorizing the campsites outside Portland needed to be stopped before the body count got too high.

It's already too high, he thought.

Seth arose from his post and placed himself between the desk and the door. When the young agent went to leave, he said, "Good evening, sir. Let me start by offering my condolences for your loss. I'm—"

The man's eyes narrowed. "You're the guy who's been following us."

"Sir, if you'd just let me explain—"

"Just, no. This is a federal investigation. No need for civilian involvement. Get out of my face before I arrest you for impeding an officer in pursuit of justice." The suit attempted to push by him but recoiled when Seth refused to move.

"First, that's not even a real charge. Second, do you even know what you're up against?"

The suit rolled his shoulder and scowled. "That's not a question the DHS is at liberty to answer. However, I've contacted my supervisors—"

"You're with the Department of Homeland Security? And you're willing to let the death count rise while you wait on an answer from DC?"

"Well, I… we can't just…"

The suit was off balance. Seth pressed his advantage. "You're right. We can't just sit here. Someone should do something about it.

Why don't we go get you an ice pack and some coffee, and we'll talk about what you saw."

"Hold on. I can't divulge information to a civilian."

Seth leaned in and whispered, "What attacked you wasn't human, was it?"

He watched the reactions dance across the agent's face. First there was confusion, followed swiftly by scrutiny as he scanned his memories. Then realization dawned. Finally, true fear lit up his eyes, the remnants of how he'd felt during the episode.

"What do you know about what we faced?"

"Let's find a place to talk." Seth gestured to the door. After several minutes of hesitation, the younger man stumped that way. Seth followed him out into the afternoon sunlight.

After a brief, awkward conversation where Seth explained he'd been using public transportation, and an even more awkward, silent car ride, they ended up seated at a nearby diner.

The waitress eyed them wearily when they first walked in, but delivered two cups of coffee and a full breakfast for the suit.

"So, I guess we should start with the basics: what's your name? I can't just keep calling you Agent Sir."

"Ryan. Ryan Fortner." The suit took a moment to look up from his eggs and bacon. "And you are?"

"Nga Phee, at your service."

"Well, if we're just using made-up names and aliases, you can call me Agent Smith."

"That *is* my name. I'm a knight of the Bagan Order. Once we've chosen our name from the original four, we cease to use our given names to live up to the ideals they represent."

"Whatever." Agent Fortner shoveled another forkful of egg into his mouth. "So, what does the Order of the Gibbons think they can do about a serial murderer?"

It took all Seth's willpower not to roll his eyes. "First, the Knights of Bagan vow to protect all mortals from beings more powerful than they are. Second, are you telling me a simple serial murderer killed your partner and roughed you up like a ragamuffin?"

"You know, for a monk, you sure do talk a lot." He grew misty-eyed and cleared his throat before he continued. "It can't have been much bigger than you or me. It had two big fangs, sharp nails, and dark-colored skin. It… didn't really seem human. I almost thought it wanted to eat me."

Seth let the sizzle of the griddles and the clinking of silverware from satisfied patrons fill the silence while he considered this.

"Did your attacker have any distinguishing marks? Were there any other sounds not natural to the area?"

The agent scratched the stubble on his chin. "I don't remember any marks, but its clothes were torn up and muddy. I *do* remember we smelled it before we saw it. And it grunted like a pig when it moved."

"Well, that sounds… intriguing." Seth stood and threw some cash on the table for their meal. "Thank you, Agent Fortner. This has been most enlightening."

"Where do you think you're going? You can't just take off with this information. At the very least, we—"

"*We* aren't doing anything. *You* are going to finish your breakfast and go rest, while I consult some books on how to deal with this malevolent spirit." Seth put a gentle but firm hand on the agent's shoulder to keep him from standing. "You're hurt and need to recover. You'd be a liability to me."

The suit opened his mouth to argue, and Seth held out a conciliatory hand. He recognized obstinacy when he saw it. "If you must, meet me at the Bridge of the Gods at dusk."

* * *

A short Uber ride later, Seth entered the gate for the River Lotus Temple, the closest library with the texts he sought. Despite the lack of advance notice, the monk who greeted him did so with a cup of tea and a small vegetarian lunch, escorting him to a study. Relevant manuscripts littered the table.

Seth sat, took a drink of the delicious warm tea, and began skimming for clues. He needed a restless or malevolent spirit that could physically manifest and was often found near bodies of water. Memories of his previous studies provided no immediate answers.

Time slipped by as he read. The possibilities of what could be haunting the forests narrowed. His studies absorbed him such that he didn't even notice somebody refilling the teapot.

Without proof that a greater deity had crossed over, a *rakshasa*, a *yaksha*-turned-*bhuta*, or a *kappa* seemed most likely. There weren't very many land-dwelling, purely malevolent spirits in Buddhist, Hindu, Jainist, Taoist, or Shinto scripture. *Yokai* or *oni* weren't out of the question, but based on the agent's description, were unlikely. A simple banishing technique or even a forced negotiation should work to quell such a creature. Seth found himself wondering what all the victims had done to draw the wrath of the Ether.

Not the Ether, Seth reminded himself. The creatures from across the Rift. It had been called the Glaswold in the article he'd read. He wasn't sure how it all worked, but that was a problem for a later time. Right now, the people of Portland needed a protector, and that's what he was here to do.

The sky was glowing with the early evening sunset by the time Seth had memorized the barrier symbols he'd need. About an hour and a half remained until the appointed time to meet the suit. He finished his tea and walked the temple grounds as he waited for his ride share. Peace reigned, despite the chaos of the city around it.

By my oath, I will protect them all.

* * *

The so-called monk was waiting for Ryan when he pulled into the agreed-upon lot near Bridge of the Gods.

"Ryan, did you hear me?" Miriam Caspar's voice crackled over the Bluetooth connection in his rental truck.

"He's here," Ryan said.

"The monk?"

"Yep." Ryan waved at the man, then held his hand up to his ear, miming that he was on a phone call.

"If the bullets Artem gave you didn't work against the thing that attacked you, take extra precautions." Miriam's voice lilted with a slight accent Ryan had never quite been able to place.

"You ever going to tell me about that?"

"It's need-to-know."

"I watched a ten-foot ogre pull my partner's arm off."

"You said seven feet."

"Not sure the difference matters when you're getting ripped apart. And you still haven't explained the arm."

Silence. Ryan bit down on another question—it sounded too much like an accusation, and he was too on edge, but...

But the search and rescue guys had brought back more than just Artem's body. Part of their recovery had included a marble statue of an arm... the same limb Artem was missing.

Miriam's sigh was as impressive as it was long. "I'll fill you in when I get there in a few days. Keep a close eye on this monk, and keep me updated."

The line went dead.

Ryan huffed out a sigh of his own and got out of the truck. The monk—Nag Something, he couldn't remember the guy's name—was on top of him before he could even shut the door.

"Greetings and well met again, Agent Fortner. I've already prepared the trap, so if you could show me where you met this creature, we can end this and move on."

"Trap? You're not going to just kill it?" Ryan asked. Miriam had told him to avoid killing it if possible, but had been vague on the reasons why. *Need-to-know basis, my ass.*

Seth patted his satchel. "If you'll just show me the specific spot where you first encountered it, and then retreat back here, I'll signal when it's safe for you to come in."

Ryan shook his head. "I call the shots. You're just advising me."

"All right, sir. It's your show. I'll help where I can." Seth nodded again, his face devoid of expression.

"Tell me what you found, and describe your trap, then."

"I believe you ran into a rakshasa. They're the more aggressive, goblin-like versions of the even-keeled yaksha, or environmental spirits. One of those can be dangerous at the best of times. I've placed three wards about half a kilometer away. I have the final warding paper here to complete the barrier once the creature's inside the space."

Environmental spirits? Wards? Ryan had to fight back a laugh, since the guy was serious. What was worse, Miriam had seemed to take him seriously, too.

"Is there any possibility you're wrong and these wards won't work?" *Because this is crazy?*

"It's possible that I'm wrong, but these will work on almost anything we could face."

"So, there is no Plan B."

"Ah. Plan B is 'I'm wrong and we need to run.'"

So basically the exact same as my Plan A.

"Do you have a better Plan B?" the monk pressed when Ryan didn't reply.

"The standard Plan B is to hunker down and wait for backup."

"Do we *have* backup, Agent Fortner?" The monk raised one eyebrow.

Ryan clamped his jaw down on a slew of arguments. Each of them made less sense than the last—how could he argue logically when nothing about the situation made any sense in the first place? Without waiting for an answer, the monk turned toward the hiking trail where the whole mess had started.

Here we go again.

"Since this particular rakshasa is aggressive enough to kill people, I'll be live bait. I'll lead it here and place the last barrier to trap it." The monk pointed at a trio of trees with strange markings on them.

"And what then? We just have a raging spirit trapped in a box in the forest?" Ryan leaned in to examine the symbols carved into one of the trees. An Asian script he couldn't read, or the nonsense scribblings of a crazy guy?

"Then we have a conversation. We determine why it's here and what it wants, see if we can put the rakshasa at ease. Hopefully— *watch where you're stepping.*" Seth's hand shot out like a snake and grabbed Ryan's shoulder, stopping him dead.

Ryan looked down. A circle of bowls full of colored, powdery substances lay inside the triangle of marked trees. He stepped back, a wash of embarrassment raising heat on the back of his neck.

"As I was saying, hopefully it'll be something as simple as providing it with what it wants," the monk finished.

"Yeah, simple. Right."

"As long as you don't break the components of the barrier before I place the last piece, it really will be that simple." The monk started off up the hill. "Now, can you guide me to where you first met the creature?"

"Unfortunately, yeah, I can." Ryan described the path, the waterfall, and the first signs of the giant creature that had torn through the woods like a tornado. "Once you get to the patch of ruined trees, you can't miss where Artem died."

"Then, Agent Ryan, I'll leave you here and go on alone." Seth raised a hand. "I'll bring it back here, so be ready. Remember, your bullets won't really hurt it, but they'll distract it. I'll need that time to close the trap."

Ryan opened his mouth to argue, then closed it. "I'll initiate Plan B if you're not back by sundown."

The monk cracked a grin. "Make it sunrise. These mountains are no joke."

* * *

Seth didn't linger over the spot where the agent's partner had died. The damage was obvious enough, and it didn't take supernatural insight to interpret the smears of blood and damaged foliage.

He moved on, hiking well into the evening.

Rock formations jutted out of the earth, the stoic minders of the underbrush and trees of the Pacific Northwest jungle. As the light faded, he began to despair of ever finding the rakshasa's hideout.

He was just contemplating turning back to find the suit when a dull grumble and heavy panting interrupted his thoughts.

Seth stopped, still as the rock formation next to him.

The sound echoed from just around the next bend. Either he'd stumbled upon a homeless camp, or he'd found the hideaway he sought. He drew his *khakkhara*, a monk's staff, from his back sheath and crept forward.

The stench hit him first. The unholy mix of feces, body odor, and decay staggered him as if he'd walked into a wall. Seth fought through his gag reflex and found the outcropping in front of the granite and stone gaping maw of the spirit's lair.

Beast, he self-corrected.

The scant light from the moon failed to penetrate the darkness of the cave. Seth squinted, determined to make out his target in the dark. He stared until his eyes watered, itching to blink.

Just as he was about to give in, it moved.

And it was much, *much* bigger than he'd imagined.

A hulking mass stepped out of the cave, grumbling and sniffing the air. Then another sound filled Seth's heart with dread. The sound of people enjoying themselves. Laughter.

The creature heard it as well and turned toward the sound, still sniffing.

It no longer mattered what the creature was. If he didn't get its attention now, it would hunt—and kill.

Seth tapped his staff against the rock face as he stepped into the open. "Hello, there. You seem a bit lost. Welcome to Earth. Why don't you come with me, and let's have a chat and some tea?"

A rumbling basso answered. "Existence is pain. Pain shall be the cure."

A chill crept down Seth's spine, invoking images of torture and corruption. This was no yaksha or rakshasa.

"This sounds like an interesting conversation. You know, the way to enlightenment has pain as well. I'm sure we could—"

"I will cure you of your pain." The creature charged.

Seth took a drop step with his left foot, pivoted, and sprinted behind the rock he'd come out from. He'd only taken a few steps when he heard it smash against the rock behind him. The beast was fast, but clumsy. It crashed through the trees behind Seth, unable to keep up with his changes in direction. That was the only advantage he had.

Seth's concentration strayed for too long. He planted his foot to change direction, and it skidded out from under him. Going down in a jumble of legs and arms, he struck his knee on something solid and unforgiving. Unable to control his momentum, he rolled through the underbrush toward the river.

The misstep saved his life. A few moments later, while he attempted to regain his breath, the creature stalked by, taking no notice of Seth. He did his best to bite his tongue against the rising pain in his knee. He remained prone until the sounds of crashing brush and breaking sticks faded away. Even then, he counted another thirty seconds before he stood.

With the beast now ahead of him, Seth mentally mapped out a route that would keep him away from the creature's path. He moved as quickly as his knee would allow. From time to time, he could hear his opponent stomping around, searching for him.

He made it back to the path and was met with eerie silence.

He picked up a branch and started banging it on the nearest trees. "Come on, big fella, I know you're out there. Come have a chat with me."

Twigs snapped to his left.

His instincts screamed, and he dodged the lunging creature. He rolled to his left, popped up, and took off running. His knee protested the sudden surge of energy. It was a nearly half mile race through the forest to return to where the agent waited with the trap.

"Stop running. You'll only die tired." The tortured voice sent another chill through Seth's body.

Seth slowed enough to let the creature catch up as he approached the trap. Seth called out, "Agent, now!" as he dodged to the side.

The rakshasa's momentum carried him past Seth.

"Over here, ugly!" the agent bellowed. The suit fired two rounds into the creature.

Seth spared a glance in his direction to ensure the creature took the bait.

"You!" The monster roared and charged at its new target.

Seth scrambled to place the last barrier. One last race, this one with Agent Fortner's life on the line. The timing had to be perfect.

The suit stepped backward, gun still sighted. He passed through the center of the trapped area, drawing the beast closer. In a few more steps, he'd be safely through.

Lungs burning and knee in agony, Seth sprinted.

The suit backed clear of the barriers, but tripped on a root and fell, the pistol disappearing from his hand.

The creature crossed the front threshold of the trap just as Seth reached the fourth corner. His fingers found the parchment holding the final barrier symbol, and he slammed it up against the tree. He spoke the name of the barrier and willed it to hold.

Gasping for breath, Seth looked up to see a blank piece of parchment staring back at him. A sinking feeling filled him as the beast bore down on Agent Fortner.

An iridescent glow illuminated the area. The barrier flared to life and stopped the creature in its tracks within feet of the suit.

Seth's whole body melted in relief. Devanagari script glowed from the side of the parchment facing the tree. He let go, and it held its place as if it had always existed there.

Once he was satisfied that it wasn't a trick, Seth made his way around to where the agent was collecting himself, careful not to step across the barrier lines.

"Glad that worked. Well done, Monk." The suit picked up his firearm.

"I am, too. I wasn't entirely certain it would." Seth turned back toward the trapped creature. Two enormous white eyes with pinprick pupils like black holes watched Seth from within the barrier.

"You mean you used me as bait in a trap you weren't sure was even going to work?" The suit stepped up to Seth and pointed a finger at the side of his face. "I'll throw you in the darkest hole I can—"

Seth threw out a hand to stop him dancing around. "Don't cross the barrier line. It works a lot like summoning circles: if you're half-in and half-out of the barrier, and the creature touches you, it'll break free."

The creature's eyes blinked once.

Seth turned to the creature. "All right, friend. I said we'd talk, so let's talk. How about we start with names? I'm Nga Phee, a knight of the Bagan Order. And you are?" Seth grasped his left wrist in front of him and bowed his head. It was a greeting to show deference to a creature that thought itself above mortals.

"My name is Agony and Anguish and Death." The creature touched the space where the barrier glowed. "And this cage will not hold me forever."

In the glow, Seth could make out the face of the monster. Its skin was an eerie yellowish-green in the light, bumpy and wrinkled. The eyes stared out from the sunken depths of its face. Dark hair, thinning and mangy, parted around three distinct horns.

I now understand you, Seth thought.

"Yeah? Going to break out of a cage you can't see? You may as well just give up there, freak. We got you right where we want you." The agent was all confidence and no understanding.

Seth decided discretion was the better part of valor.

"Of course we do. So, Agent Fortner, let's leave him alone a bit while he ponders the futility of his plight, shall we? Maybe when we come back, he'll be more amenable to negotiation." It took most of Seth's willpower to turn his back on the barrier—and the demon it held—and walk off.

"But we have him right here." The suit wasn't catching on.

Seth resisted the urge to drag the agent away and kept walking. "You heard him. He wants to be anguish and agony. Let him wallow in anguish, then."

The agent huffed his annoyance, but Seth heard his footsteps as he hastened to catch up.

"Monk, need I remind you that this... *thing*... has killed at least nine people in the last few weeks?"

"Don't stop yelling at me, but keep walking. We have to leave *now*." Seth ignored the suit until they were well down the trail, leaving the creature behind them little more than a myth in the darkness.

"What's going on?"

"That wasn't a rakshasa. It was no yaksha, either. That, Agent Fortner, was an oni. A torture demon."

"What does that even matter? It's trapped. You said it would hold most things."

"Yes, I did. *Most* being the operative word. That won't hold an oni. We may have minutes at best. We need to be clear of this place before it breaks out. I'm not equipped to handle it right now."

"So, it escapes—and what? Kills more people?" The suit glanced back as if debating whether or not he should return.

Despite himself, Seth was impressed.

"That's a possible outcome. Hopefully, our barrier trick draws it to us. From what I remember about Shintoism scriptures, most oni are usually harmless to the living. They're meant to torture sinners who've died. Every great once in a while, however, a malevolent one will form out of a living human who's done terrible things."

The agent's eyes narrowed, but he checked over his shoulder once more.

"They don't like to be tricked, and they typically maintain most of their original personality, at least in the beginning. It hasn't happened in recent memory, so we only have Japanese folktales to go by. Didn't you say DHS sent you here because you were chasing a murderer? From..." Seth's memory failed him.

"Illinois." The fed's brow furrowed. "Yeah. There was a string of brutal murders there. The suspect was, allegedly, the illegitimate child of a serial killer, the Bonecrusher."

"What was the suspect's name?"

"Darwin Hayes. Are you implying *he's* the creature?"

"Yes, Agent Fortner. Your suspect has become a demon on Earth. *We* need to find the tools to stop it. Lucky for us, the Portland Japanese Garden has a library."

* * *

They arrived at the garden sometime near midnight. An elderly Japanese man met them at the door to the building.

"I am informed you seek answers on the oni. We have very few scripts on that subject, and even fewer on defeating them." He ushered them inside.

"That'll have to be enough, then. My knowledge of Shinto folklore is severely lacking," Seth stated as they passed a closed gift shop and climbed the stairs leading to the library.

"Folklore is an interesting word choice, considering you're here because you've seen one."

The librarian showed them into a room where books and manuscripts on shelves filled one wall. A panoramic window view of the garden filled the other. "The writings you will need to study the oni are stored here." The librarian reached behind him and pushed a button on the side of a bookshelf. The seamless wood panel design on the wall next to him revealed the outlines of a door. It opened inward with a gentle push.

"Well, that's not something you see every day. I'm not on an episode of *Punk'd*, am I?" the suit asked with an incredulous look on his face.

"Well, it's not every day you have to take down an oni, either. I'm surprised the DHS didn't teach you about hidden doors," Seth responded, deadpan.

"They teach us real things, like gathering evidence. Not this Hollywood thriller crap."

"If you need anything further, just call for assistance," the librarian interrupted with a smile and a bow of his head.

"Thank you, Mr.—uh—what did you say your name was again?" Seth asked.

"Minamoto. It has been my pleasure to serve." He disappeared back into the hallway.

Seth pointed at a stack of scripts on the first table "You can help by familiarizing yourself with the associated folk tales. Call out anything that'll help us defeat it."

The suit picked up one of the manuscripts and scowled. "Are they all unreadable?"

"They're not unreadable, they're in Japanese." When the agent didn't reply, Seth pushed. "Are you telling me the government neglected to teach you kanji?"

"I'm telling you I've never learned Japanese, or any oriental language, for that matter."

Seth rubbed his temples. "Tell me, Agent Fortner, what do you know?"

"I took four years of Spanish in high school. *El burro sabe mas que tu.*"

Seth bit back a retort that would have been unknightly of him. "Let's divide and conquer, then. The demon will have broken out of the barrier by now and is hunting us. Find it and draw its attention from everything else." He pulled his phone out of his pocket and tossed it to the agent. "Put your number in there, and I'll call you when I have a plan."

Suit raised one eyebrow and turned the phone over in his hands. "You're full of surprises, Monk."

"We strive to become enlightened, not Luddites." Seth turned to the table of parchment in the back room. He heard the suit chuckle as he walked out the door.

Two hours of skimming later, Seth thought he had a solid plan. There were only three ways to deal with an oni: negotiate, seal it away, or lop off its head with a Tenka Goken—one of the five legendary swords under heaven. Since the demon wouldn't negotiate, and Seth was confident that all five swords were securely tucked away in Japan, he focused on the sealing techniques. A Buddhist sealing ritual combined with a *mamori* provided the only surefire solution.

However, there was one catch. He needed a magically sensitive area big enough to keep the oni busy while they finished the sealing ritual. Seth glanced out a window and caught sight of the torii gate.

"Mr. Minamoto!" he called out for the librarian. "I have some questions about the gardens."

The suit wasn't going to like his new plan.

* * *

"What in the actual hell?" Ryan stared at his cell phone in disbelief. He'd been driving up and down back roads in the Columbia River Gorge—first searching for the creature, then desperately regretting success at that particular venture. He glanced in the truck's rearview mirror. He'd lost the oni again, but probably not for long.

"You want me to drag a murder-crazed demon through downtown Portland because you *think* you know how to capture it?"

"Yes, that about sums it up," Seth said. "Besides, we'll have help this time, even if we die."

"What help?" Ryan already regretted the need to rely on the monk. The idea of letting more innocents in on this monster hunt twisted his gut. "More civilians?"

"Recruits," the monk said matter-of-factly. "It's handled."

"It's a crap plan." Ryan drummed his fingers on the steering wheel. "Explain it to me again, except this time, like I'm dumb."

"You'll lure the oni to the gardens. Once inside, the monks will activate the sealing barrier from each of the four cardinal directions, trapping you, me, and the oni in place. You need to lead it to me a short time later so I can finish the sealing. How is our big friend, anyway?"

As though summoned by the monk's question, a roar tore through the mountain air. Ryan swore. "Well, you were right about one thing: it's definitely hunting me."

The towering creature burst from the forest lining the roadside.

Here we go again. Ryan glanced at his GPS. *Because this isn't the craziest thing I've ever tried.*

"How much time do you need?" Ryan slammed on the brakes, skidding the rental into a fishtail and narrowly avoiding the demon in the road. It swiped at the truck as it passed, its claws eliciting an earsplitting screech as they scraped the vehicle's side.

"With beings this powerful, you must seal its essence a little bit at a time, weakening it gradually until you can trap the whole being."

"What?" Ryan gagged as a whiff of decay breached the cab of the truck.

"Think of it like chopping down a tree."

"How much time do you need?" Ryan asked again.

"Make sure you take at least twenty minutes to get here, and do your best to take the most direct route once you enter the city limits. Are you up for this?"

Ryan's thoughts flashed back to Artem's final moments. His partner's last acts had saved his life.

A debt he'd never be able to settle.

Driving around for another half hour with a demon on his tail was the least he could do.

Ryan put on a burst of speed, then brake-checked the oni as soon as the beast broke into a full run. "I got this."

* * *

Seth stood in the Flat Garden sometime later, meditating on the simple, stylistic patterns that had been raked into the gravel. Moss-covered boulders and Japanese maples encircled this patch of dry garden. His preparations were complete, his wait almost over.

A distant roar interrupted his meditation. Ryan had reached the gardens with the oni in tow. It was time.

A sizzle of energy filled the air. Seth spared a glance to notice the shimmering across the sky.

The barriers are up. No turning back.

Another roar proved the oni found this barrier much stronger than his previous cage. Seth checked the *mamori*—a charm to Enma, the Lord of *Jigoku* and Master of all oni, encased in a silk pouch. While typically used as good luck or protection charms, Seth had placed a symbol for locking inside. The purple and gold silk-covered *mamori* provided a channel for whatever energy Enma would give to seal his rampaging servant.

With the *vajra* from the tip of his staff and a *ghanta* bell the monks had graciously provided him, he faced the standing stone he'd chosen, then began to chant a centuries-old version of the *Kilaya* mantra.

As he chanted, the buzz of energy grew around him. He reached his will out toward the darker energy and siphoned it off as quickly as he could, redirecting it to the boulder in front of him. He had to be careful not to take too much at once, or the creature might notice him. The final sealing event would be a contest of his will against what remained of the fiend's life force.

Every time Seth reached the end of the verse, he hit the *ghanta* with the *vajra*, filling the air with a clear ring. It was a summons directed at the oni. Maybe it was the adrenaline, but the ring sounded purer than his normal mantra rites and tugged on his own psyche. Each subsequent chime of the bell pulled a little harder. Soon, the energy contained by the stone forced Seth to draw in his focus and pinpoint his target.

Sweat beaded on his brow despite the chilly morning breeze. Birds chirped their rising songs, and the leaves of the trees rustled. They joined the sound of his voice and the ringing of the *ghanta*. It was peaceful.

It shouldn't have been.

Seth inhaled to restart the verse when his intuition shrieked at him. He crouched in place. A massive, clawed hand swept overhead, grazing his hair. He rolled toward his *khakkhara* and sprang up to deflect another incoming blow.

"Incoming!" the suit screamed.

A warning would have been nice before *it nearly took my head off.* Seth jammed the *vajra* into its slot and attached the *ghanta* bell to his belt.

The oni brought both hands down toward his head. Seth raised his staff crossways, willing it to hold.

The staff bowed, but it held.

The oni staggered. "I feel what you are doing, Knight. Stop your incessant chanting and die."

A clamor of gunfire drowned out the oni's rumbling. Bullets slammed into the demon's chest. The creature snarled as the rounds pierced its skin. The projectiles might have been flies, for all the good they did, but they served to distract the creature.

It changed targets again, whirling now on the suit.

The agent's gun clicked empty.

There wasn't even time for Seth to shout out a warning. The agent turned to run, but what man could outrun an oni? The beast's claws slashed the back of the suit's neck, and the power behind the blow sent him sprawling against a bank of mossy boulders. Agent Fortner didn't stir.

Seth centered himself and took a deep breath, then picked up his verse.

The demon fixed its attention back on Seth.

Unlike the unfortunate agent, Seth was ready for it. Warding off every other blow and dodging the rest, he finished the chant. He flipped his staff, and with a flourish of one redirected swing, tapped the *vajra* against the bell again. The oni wavered in response to the direct call of the summons.

Almost. Too far away to finish the seal.

The monster roared, forcing Seth to sidestep and twirl back toward the torii gate, away from the standing stone.

Can't keep going like this.

His knee ached, slowing his reactions. Every time he tried to use his footwork to open a path, the oni contained him.

Time to improvise.

"You're too weak to withstand me now," Seth huffed.

"You're a small man with a stick. At my weakest, I am stronger than you. Note how you may only defend, while I do as I please."

"The *vajra* is the enlightened warrior's second greatest weapon." Seth ducked the next attack, stepped into the monster, and stabbed upward into its ribs. He planted the butt of the staff in the ground for leverage.

The creature roared in pain, then laughed. "I will grant you, that stings a little, but it can't kill me." One of the oni's meaty paws grabbed Seth around his bicep.

One moment Seth felt his arm being ripped out of its socket, and the next he was hurtling through the air toward the pavilion near the Flat Garden. He crashed through the sliding panel doors and landed in a pile of exhibits.

He sat up slowly, his face scrunched uncontrollably against the pain. His whole body hurt, especially the arm he'd been thrown with. He winced as he inhaled. *Just a broken rib.*

The oni stalked him, reaching the edge of the Flat Garden.

Seth pushed himself up and hobbled down the steps toward the creature.

"You have quite the pitch there, big fella, but I said the *vajra* was only our second greatest weapon. You forgot to ask what the first was." He raised the unadorned end of his staff in front of him. He gripped the *vajra* this time and started the final verse of the mantra.

Quick as a lightning bolt, the oni grabbed his staff, flinging Seth away. He crashed against his standing stone and crumpled to the ground, the wind leaving his body, his back screaming in agony.

He gasped for air, but continued his chant as he dragged himself back up.

The demon threw the staff halfway across the gardens, well out of reach. It took the few steps between them and picked up the monk, holding him by his neck. "Answer it yourself then, Knight. What is the greatest weapon of the enlightened warriors?"

"Our minds." Seth calmed himself as he had so many times before during training, slowing his heart rate. He closed his eyes for a moment as he felt the demon take hold of his arm again.

"Yours was not quick enough, Knight. Now you will suffer the torment of being ripped limb from limb." The oni's putrid breath was hot on his face, cutting off his next words.

Gunshots rang out, announcing the suit's return. The oni turned its massive head, and the momentary distraction was enough.

Seth took a deep breath and finished, "Darwin Hayes, I summon you to stay in this place. I call upon your Lord Enma to revoke your power and seal you in your prison." He rang the *ghanta* with the *vajra* he'd palmed when his staff was wrenched away.

He pushed his will into the tone and mentally grasped the remainder of the fiend's dark energy. The oni turned back to face Seth, first showing anger at this new battle of wills, and then fear as it slowly lost control of its hands.

It released Seth, who landed off balance and fell against the standing stone.

He warred against the dark power, summoning it to reside forevermore in this garden. He warred against the summons of the bell himself, fighting to keep from being trapped in the same prison. The oni shrank in front of him as its life force energy seeped into the stone, dragging its physical form with it this time.

The oni swiped at Seth's knee. Searing pain clouded his senses, but he maintained his willpower on the creature's dark energy. Then it smashed him in the stomach.

Seth doubled over—and his will slipped.

The oni reared up, its hulking mass returning. Another hail of bullets hammered into the demon. It staggered.

Seth warred against oblivion and seized the demon's energy once more to finish the seal.

He willed the life force of the struggling creature inside.

"This will not hold me forever, Knight." The oni's physical form dissolved into a hazy black smoke, which streamed into the stone.

Seth battled against the summons, his own energy exhausted. He tried to finish the sealing, but couldn't get his hand to grasp the *mamori* and place it in its proper place. The tone of the bell pealed in his ears, compelling him into the prison he'd created.

He did the only thing he could think of—sank into full meditation as his body slid down the face of the stone.

Time froze. The tone ceased, and he stared down at himself, slumped against the base of the stone prison. Gray fog obscured everything else.

He turned in a full circle, and when he finished, his body and the rock were gone. In its place stood a man with a wiry, muscled frame, wearing a white- and gold-hooded robe, and grasping a *khakkhara* identical to his own. A long, dark mane with a beard to match framed the man's golden eyes.

"You have done well, Nga Phee. Now calm your mind once more, and still your raging heart. Take up your name in full and finish the seal." The man smiled at Seth.

"I'm doing my best. The pull is much stronger than I anticipated." Seth felt its silent tug even now.

"The pull is strong because you are of two minds. You have been named Nga Phee, and yet you still refer to yourself as Seth." The man's smile didn't waver, but his eyes lit with a fierce gaze. "You have proven your oaths. All except one. That you will become one of the Four Paladins. You fight yourself with your doubt, as if you have tied one arm behind your back. This gives the summons power over you. Fulfill your oath, Knight, or you will fail to finish the seal, and the demon will escape."

Seth's eyes widened with this fresh fear.

The man reached out a hand and brushed his fingertips lightly over his eyelids, closing them as if he was a *samanera*. Eyes now closed, the monk knight slowed his breathing and reached deep into his own heart, his own mind.

That's me.

His life passed before him. All the times he'd been Seth. All the work to be more. *No! I will not throw it all away! I am Nga Phee. I was Seth, but no more.*

"Who are you?" the figure asked.

"I am your namesake."

"Who *are* you?" demanded the apparition.

The monk squared his shoulders. "I am Nga Phee."

"Who are *you?*" asked the spirit once more.

"I am what you were: Nga Phee, the paladin."

"Then finish the seal, Paladin."

Nga Phee's trance broke, and he opened his eyes. The tone of the bell returned slowly. Its pull was a wind unable to shake the mountain.

"You who were Nga Phee—I, who am Nga Phee, thank you for your guidance."

He grasped the *mamori* and faced the rock. Placing the charm against the standing stone, he imbued it with his will. It glowed, wrapping the rock in chains of ether for an instant. The light faded, and the silk bag fixed into the stone's face, a permanent reminder of the monolith's new purpose.

Nga Phee heard a shout of celebration and saw the suit, blood staining his shoulders, hobbling toward him. "Way to go, monk! You got the bastard!"

"*We* got him, Agent Fortner," Nga Phee said and collapsed as his world faded to black exhaustion.

* * * * *

H.Y. Gregor Biography

H.Y. Gregor was born in Portland, Oregon, but will always call the mountains of Colorado home. She holds a bachelor's degree in political science, but put it down often enough to narrowly avoid law school. Now she spends as much free time as possible weaving fantasy tales and battling plot gremlins.

Her short fiction is recipient of Silver Honorable Mention awards from the Writers of the Future contest and has been published in a number of anthologies. These include contributions to Chris Kennedy Publishing's 4HU, William Alan Webb's Last Brigade, and a multi-genre spread of stories with Knight Writing Press, CKP, and Three Ravens Publishing. Her debut novel, *Stonewhisper*, was released in June 2023 by Eldros Legacy Press. You can find her online at hygregor.com.

Upcoming projects include a spinoff trilogy in Jon R. Osborne's Milesian Accords world. Keep an eye out for the Black God trilogy, coming soon!

* * *

David Shadoin Biography

David "Shady" Shadoin is a troublemaking, corn-fed Nebraska boy the United States Air Force managed to turn into a somewhat decent pilot of whirly birds.

An avid reader from a young age, he has always found inspiration listening to rock music, consuming arts/entertainment content in as many ways as possible, travelling the globe, and drinking single malt scotch. This love of written adventure set up Shady to moonlight as a new author trying to find a good outlet for creative ideas that start with nothing more than a misplaced pop culture reference and some D&D dungeons.

For more Shady dealings, visit www.davidshadoin.com/home.

* * * * *

Valor's Wirth
by Jon R. Osborne
A Milesian Accords Story

The air hung still, as though the night held its breath. The hushed chanting of four witches competed with the soft, glass-like tinkling from the quicksilver distortion hanging over the summit of the small hillock. Candlelight flickered over the shimmering membrane in the air.

Darwin's hand itched to reach out and touch it. His other hand clutched his mother's suicide note. He'd made copies, although his mother's last words remained seared in his memory.

Darwin –

I prayed if I brought you up right, you wouldn't turn out like your father. Maybe I should have known better. I had no business bringing a child into this world, and the evil ran deep in your father's blood. I don't know why he spared me, but now I wish he hadn't.

When I found your bloodied clothes, I knew what you had done. Those women's deaths are on my hands as much as yours. I brought a monster into this world, and you are truly your father's son. I can't bear the guilt. I see those faces from the news every night when I try to sleep. Worse yet, I can't bring myself to turn you in.

Maybe this will jar you to get help, find God, or... find another way to make sure you don't hurt anyone else.

Goodbye, Darwin.

Mother

Darwin stuffed the note in his jacket pocket, swapping it out for a photocopy. He didn't want to burn the last words from his mother in the cauldron smoldering on the ground in front of the silver ripple. He'd dripped his own blood on the copy—the witches insisted he needed to burn something with a personal connection.

His mind wandered as the witches called to spirits and invoked goddesses' names, waiting for his cue from the woman in charge, their priestess. The matronly woman read an incantation from a book, calling out each line with a theatric flourish, as though to compensate for invoking the dead with English instead of Latin or Ancient Greek.

Darwin's eyes flicked to the younger witches, and he nervously licked his lips. One reminded him of—no, he mustn't get distracted. The priestess insisted her coven could call forth the shade of his mother from the spirit-world.

He'd have scratched her off as crazy. Then last month, supernatural monsters had spilled into the streets of a nearby town, followed by a guy calling himself the First Druid vanishing into thin air during a television broadcast. While Darwin could chalk those events up to special effects trickery, when the third woman he killed vanished at his feet, he couldn't deny it.

Magic was real.

The priestess repeated a line, the urgency in her tone snapping Darwin back to the present. He dropped the faux note into the cauldron. The paper darkened before bursting into a fitful flame. An orange line spread from the point of ignition, devouring the paper in its path. When it reached the red motes of blood, the fire sparked and spat.

The constant breaking glass tinkle from the otherworldly aperture changed tone and grew discordant, as though music played in reverse. The quicksilver shimmer warbled and darkened to a glassy, obsidian sheen. A smear darkened the center of the distortion, spreading like oil in water until it grew into a human silhouette.

"We did it!" the priestess whispered.

A pale hand emerged, reaching from the black membrane. As the arm reached the elbow, a foot clad in a polished black leather shoe appeared.

Darwin took a step back. Something wasn't right. That wasn't his mother, ghostly or otherwise.

"Don't break the circle!" the priestess warned.

A tall, slender man stepped from the otherworldly portal, his footfall silent. He stood half a head taller than Darwin, wearing a dark suit two centuries out of date. His pale skin gleamed in the candlelight, but the bright blue sparks in the shadowed pits of his eyes burned with a light of their own. Silver streaked the thin, slicked back hair, but despite his slender build, the man betrayed no sign of frailty from age.

"Are... are you my father?" Darwin stammered.

The man's arm stretched out, and his long, slender fingers clasped Darwin's shoulder. Without a step, the new arrival stood a foot away from Darwin, staring down with those glowing blue eyes. A smile too wide split his face as he regarded Darwin, revealing a glimpse of sharp, predatory teeth.

"What is he?" one of the younger witches whimpered.

"I left no get on this world." The man tilted his head, his smile growing feral as he regarded the witch behind Darwin. "I have many names—Seoc Dhu, Black Jock, Jacky Du…"

His gaze snapped back to Darwin. "I am not your father, though I sense a shared darkness in you. Yes, your hands have dipped in blood. It would be a shame to kill a kindred spirit."

The priestess muttered a curse as she leafed through the book. She held her lamp close and peered at the page. "We need to send him back!"

"How?" one of the other witches cried.

"Take up this chant." The priestess faltered over the first words, squinting. As she repeated the phrase, her cadence quickened, and the other women echoed her words.

The pale man's over-broad mouth twisted in a sneer. "Harlots. I'd make a bow of their entrails if not for this circle. I guess you'll have to do, lad."

Darwin's blood turned to ice as the stranger held out his long arm, fingernails turning into obsidian blades. "Wait! What if you could get out?"

The soft tinkle of the portal warbled as ripples ran from its perimeter to the middle. A breeze tugged at the man's clothes, drawing his jacket tails in the direction of the aperture.

"You'd turn me loose on these women, on your world, to save your own skin?" The man's lips peeled back in wicked glee.

Darwin scooped up the small cauldron by the handle and pitched it at the priestess. Trailing incense smoke, it impacted the stump in front of her, and sparks erupted. Her cry broke the chant. Darwin stepped to the nearest candle marking the perimeter of the summoning circle and kicked it into the darkness, catching a clod of earth with his boot toe for good measure.

"No!" one of the women shouted.

"I like you, lad. Care to join me in some fun?"

Darwin shook his head, equally terrified, and intrigued. "Um, all yours."

"Good luck finding your father."

The priestess resumed the chant, but before she could complete the verse, the man stood in front of her with a single unnaturally long stride. He backhanded the book from her grip, the pages fluttering as it arced into the night. He lashed out with his ebony talons.

Darwin fled, the witches' screams ringing in his ears.

* * *

Gavin Wirth drew a deep breath of night air. People avoided the Forest Park Preserve at night, the poor illumination, lack of traffic, and shadow-filled woods rendering it "creepy." Gavin found the quiet, only punctuated by the occasional insect rasp, peaceful. Light pollution from Peoria still occluded half the stars, but Gavin leaned back against the picnic table and stared into the night sky.

Zeus shifted next to his feet, the German Shepherd's nose flaring and ears perking up. A pair of cars sat empty at the far end of the parking lot, but there'd been no sign of the owners, and the A-framed Rec Center sat dark.

Maybe a couple on an illicit tryst? As long as they didn't disturb him.

A strange bird cry caught Gavin's ear from deep in the preserve. No—coyotes? Zeus rose, alert and watching the closest trail. A light bobbed between the trees, bouncing drunkenly, and blinking as it passed behind tree trunks. One of Zeus' ears twitched as he moved between Gavin and the trailhead.

"What is it, boy?" Gavin stood and brushed off his jeans. His gun was in the car thirty yards away.

A woman burst from the trail, a small flashlight in her hand. She wheeled as she cleared the woods, flaring her torn peasant skirt. Great, a tryst gone wrong. Some jerk must have accosted her.

Now Gavin really wished he had his gun. No—he should stay out of it. His life was complicated enough. If the asshole wasn't around, Gavin didn't need to play white knight.

Her eyes fixed on the cars, and she dashed across the pavement. She tugged frantically on the doors. "Dammit!"

Gavin sighed. He could at least call her a ride, and if necessary, the police. "Miss? Do you need a hand?"

She spun at the sound of his voice. "Please! Help me!"

Zeus growled, glaring into the woods.

Great, the asshole in this drama.

Gavin almost missed the tall, slender man, despite his pale face. He ignored Gavin and Zeus until the dog gave a single bark. His head twisted, like a predator spotting a fresh victim. Gavin clenched his left fist, rasping metal muffled by the glove he wore over the prosthesis.

"Hey, asshole! Leave the lady alone!" Gavin strode toward the halfway point between the woman and the slender man. Old instincts hewn in the Sandbox kicked in, and time slowed, while simultaneously playing out impossibly fast. One moment the stranger stood at the edge of the woods, his black suit blending with the shadows. A step, and he closed a third of the distance.

The back of Gavin's mind screamed danger even as he broke into a run. This wasn't some insurgent or desert fighter. This wasn't even of this world.

Another step, and the man was already at the two-thirds mark. Gavin's artificial left hand tingled. Another step, and the man stood on the other side of the car from the wide-eyed woman. The static buzz in Gavin's hand spread throughout his body.

"Going somewhere, little bird?" the man cooed in a weird Irish accent. He splayed his fingers, glinting black blades where his fingernails should be. Blood dripped from the scalpel-like talons.

The black-clad stranger wasn't the only one with a supernatural edge. In the blink of an eye, Gavin seized the outstretched arm and hurled the man into the parking lot. Gangly limbs flailed as the man tumbled across the pavement. Zeus caught up, barking and snarling from the other side of the sprawled man.

The man gathered his limbs and rolled to his feet, stretching as he rose. A smile spread across his pale face and kept going almost to his ears. He bared sharp, feral teeth as he spoke. "What's this? A protector? Usually, I avoid your sort. There's no joy in killing a warrior. Not like snuffing dainty fireflies."

Glowing blue eyes glanced at the woman, frozen behind the car. Running either direction would leave her in the open.

"You want to eff around and find out, freak?" *Yup, should've brought the gun.*

The man cocked his head, the grin fixed. "I don't recognize you. Maybe I'll peel you apart and find out how you caught Seoc Dhu, let alone hurt me... after I skin the witch and her fellow birdies."

One moment he was fifteen feet away; the next he was in Gavin's face. Gavin drove his left fist into the man's chin. Something cracked in the too-wide mouth before the man stumbled back, the blow lifting him off his feet.

The slender man spat out a shattered fang and a glob of blood. "You're full of surprises. Fine. I'll flay the other birdies, then come back for this one." A step carried him ten yards, and a few more took him back to the concealing shadows of the forest.

"Well, this is effing great," Gavin muttered. He turned to the woman. "You okay, miss?"

"How did you... who are you? *What* are you?"

"My name's Gavin, and I'm the idiot who saved your hide and stepped into another pile of spooky shit." He called Zeus to heel. The dog gave one last glance at the woods before trotting to Gavin's side. "I take it these ain't your cars?"

The woman shook her head. "I rode with Caroline. He killed her."

"Let's get out of here, before he comes around again. My car is over here."

"He'll come back for me."

"Yeah, he said as much. First things first, we need breathing space so I can make some calls." If he could get a hold of the Druid or a Champion, Gavin could pass her and the problem wearing an antique suit off to folk better suited for dealing with them.

"He'll come back. I can feel it."

"Not where we're going." Gavin opened the back door of his car for Zeus. "Sorry, buddy, you need to ride in the back."

The dog snorted once before hopping in.

"Are you a K-9 officer?" the woman asked as she circled the car. The memory of Gavin's grandma chided him for not opening the door for a lady.

"Naw. Zeus is a retired police dog, but I'm only a cop if you pay by the hour." Gavin half expected the pale man to appear in the rearview mirror as he whipped the car out of the parking lot.

"What do you mean?"

"I'm a security guard. I'll take you to my work. We should be safe there. I didn't get your name."

"Olivia." She watched the road behind them in the side mirror.

"What were you doing in the forest preserve in the dark?"

"This guy asked my priestess to help him contact his dead mother. He wanted to ask her about his father." Olivia turned to Gavin, studying his face for a reaction before continuing. "Our coven used an obscure, prehistoric mound as the ritual site. My priestess claimed it would make contacting the spirit world easier. Unfortunately, she was right, but whatever came through, it wasn't the guy's mother."

Gavin hissed through his teeth. "They need to fence it off to keep people from mucking around with shit they don't understand."

"You know about the mound? Is that why you were in the park?"

Gavin shook his head as he followed the Peoria River south, back into the city. "I like the peace and quiet when there's no one around. I don't care for a bunch of ruckus, or crowds. I ain't had no problem with the wold-ford on the mound, but I heard others tell different."

"Wold-ford? I've heard the term before. Isn't that a portal to the Otherworld?"

"So they say. People shouldn't mess with it."

It only took a few minutes before he wheeled through an open gate in a concrete wall. A pair of gargoyles flanked the entrance. The squat, stone building beyond lacked any signage other than Private Property – No Parking posted in the lot.

"This isn't far from the preserve." Olivia eyed the parking lot, her gaze jumping from shadow to shadow. "What if Jacky Du—Seoc Dhu—can walk through walls like a ghost?"

Gavin opened the car door for Zeus. "He ain't walking through *these* walls. That's why I brought you here. It's spook-proof."

"I don't think it matters how thick—whoa."

Gavin paused at the trunk, Zeus at his side. "What?"

"The building has a weird aura. I've never seen anything like it."

Gavin popped the trunk, retrieving the 12-gauge and the holstered .45. "I'll take your word for it."

Olivia jumped when he slammed the trunk, tearing her gaze away from the building.

"Sorry. Let's get inside."

Olivia rushed to fall in step on the opposite side of Zeus. "Do you think a gun will do anything to the dark fae psycho?"

"These might. They're loaded with elf-shot."

"Sounds like you know more about this stuff than I do." Olivia scanned the shadowed perimeter of the parking lot while he unlocked the heavy wooden door.

Gavin stepped aside to let her in. "Not as much as I should. I hoped I could stay out of all this spooky crap. I guess fate has other plans."

"You sure this door will hold?" Olivia asked. "It's ancient."

"You'd be surprised. Replacing it with a modern door was a mistake—that broke whatever magic protects this building."

"What is this place?" Olivia peered into the darkened rooms on either side of the empty corridor. Her voice echoed off the marble floor and walls.

"It was some sort of Masonic hall. Now it's more of a private museum." Gavin checked the monitors in the small security office next to the entrance. *Nothing unusual, but will the creep show up on cameras?* "This way."

Zeus' claws clicked on the stone floor as they followed the corridor, turning into a small break room. Olivia shivered as she sank into one of the cheap plastic chairs.

"You want coffee?" Gavin rooted through the cupboard before she replied. Even with his nerves on edge, a cup of normal sounded good.

"You said you could call someone. People who know more about this than us?"

Gavin nodded as he filled the carafe from the sink. "Yeah. There's this guy called the First Druid; he's the expert on magic and supernatural shit. And a woman who works for him—well, maybe that's not quite right, but she fights supernatural baddies and monsters that cross over into our world. Also, we need to call the police."

"I dropped my phone back in the park."

"I know a deputy. He's dealt with the weird crap before. I'll start with him." The coffee brewing, Gavin fished out his phone and dialed.

"Deputy Dahler," came the answer.

"Hey, Luke, it's Gavin Wirth. You remember me?"

"I do. The guy with the silver hand. You calling now can't be a coincidence."

"'Fraid not. I picked up a woman who was attacked in the Forest Park Preserve by a spooky-world psycho with blades for fingernails. He ain't right. I've never seen anyone move so fast. If it wasn't for my left hook, he'd have carved us both up. Before he slunk off, he said he'd come back to finish her after he killed her coven."

"Shit. There was a call to a house on the west side of those woods. A woman stumbled onto the back porch, screaming and bleeding. There's an ambulance and a unit on the way now."

"You need to make sure no one else goes into the park."

"What if there's more survivors?" the deputy countered. "Bad time for Grace to be out of town."

"She was my next call. I'll try the Druid. Maybe his ex is in town, or he can do his Gandalf shit and deal with this freak."

"I'll call those Crypto Division agents from Homeland Security." Luke paused to talk to someone. "Tell them we got a killer loose in those woods. Any idea where the attack happened?"

"The old mound with the ford on it. You know, the gate?"

"I know where it is. There's no easy access for EMTs. I guess we'll figure it out when we cross that bridge. Can you call Knox while I deal with things here?"

"Yeah, I have the Druid's number. What about Olivia—the woman I picked up."

"Keep her there for now. Once we've sorted out the scene at the preserve, I or another officer will get her statement."

Gavin nodded before remembering Luke couldn't see him. "Right. We'll sit tight here."

"What did he say?" Olivia fidgeted in her seat.

"Another woman got away from your attacker. An ambulance is taking her to the hospital." Gavin scrolled through his contacts until he found Druid Knox.

Olivia perked up. "Did he say who? Which hospital?"

"He didn't say." He held up a finger as the phone rang in his ear. After three more rings, the voicemail message kicked in. "Great. He's not home, either."

"The First Druid?" Olivia collected two mugs from the cupboard and poured the steaming coffee.

Gavin accepted a mug and blew on it. "Yeah. I don't suppose you know anyone?"

"There's a priestess in another coven who's supposed to be tight with him, but I don't know how to get a hold of her." She returned to her seat, cradling the mug in her hands. "If that asshole hadn't interrupted the spell, we might have sent Seoc Dhu, Jacky Du, back to the spirit world."

"What do you mean?" The bitter coffee burnt his tongue.

"When Mist Raven—I mean, Caroline—realized we'd called something else, she started a spell to banish him. The protective circle kept him trapped, and the gate drew him in."

"What happened?"

"The guy who hired us chucked a cauldron at Caroline and broke the circle. As soon as the chant stopped, the spell collapsed, and with the circle broken, Jacky Du got loose and attacked Caroline to keep her from casting the spell."

"Where'd the asshole who set him free go?" The second sip was less scalding, but just as bitter.

"He bolted. He was only worried about his own hide." Olivia shuddered and drew her mug closer. "Based on what Jacky Du said, the guy was a scumbag. Called him a kindred spirit—when a nightmare killer calls you kindred, it's not a good thing. Anyway, he ran off into the dark."

"The best bet is for you to stay put here while the cops do their job. If you need to lie down, there's a couch in Mr. Argus' office. Maybe once the sun rises, I can drive you home."

Gavin paced until Zeus brushed against his leg. Taking a cue, Gavin pulled out another chair.

Olivia broke the silence. "How did you catch him? You covered half the parking lot in a split second."

Gavin bit his lip in thought before relenting and peeling off the glove over his left hand. He flexed the metal prosthesis. Whorls and knotwork etched into the silver plates glinted in the harsh light of the overhead fluorescents.

"I wound up with this during a scuffle with a pack of little murder-hobo dwarves. They came to steal it, and in the fight, my regular prosthetic hand got torn off. This attached itself. Supposedly, it belonged to an old Irish king." Gavin drummed his artificial fingertips on the table. "I have no clue how it moves, or why it hasn't fallen apart, if it's so old. During times of stress, it acts like it has a mind of its own, and pulls me along for the ride."

"Both useful and eerie."

"Once the dust settled, I decided I didn't want anything to do with spooky shit, but..." Gavin gestured toward the door. "Supernatural stuff keeps turning up. Once I found out magic was real, I couldn't keep from seeing it."

They both jumped when the phone rang. Zeus rose to a sitting position, leaning against Gavin.

"It's all right, boy." Gavin answered the phone.

"They're taking the woman to Proctor Hospital," Luke said after exchanging pleasantries. "She's cut up pretty bad, and lost a lot of blood, but she's stable. Her name is Kim Hooper."

"You going to post a guard on her in case the freak comes after her?"

"Yeah. Any idea what we're dealing with? Those Homeland Security agents are on their way, but it'll be an hour before they get here."

"I only work in a museum. If Mr. Argus were here, I could ask him. He might have something in one of his old books. If you run into this 'Jacky Du,' try shooting him with silver bullets or elf-shot."

Luke lowered his voice. "How am I going to explain why they need silver bullets, let alone why I carry them?"

"If this crap is going to keep happening, they should be ready. Between the Battle of Bloomington and the First Druid pulling his disappearing act on the evening news, folk can't say you're crazy for suggesting something weird is going on."

"What about Olivia? Is she still there?"

"Yeah. I reckon I can drive her home in the morning, or you all can come get her." Gavin glanced at Olivia, who stared into her mug. "I've done my good deed. I want to stay out of weird-world."

"I don't think you have much choice. I'll let you know when I learn anything new."

Gavin set the phone on the table. "Your friend Kim is going to Proctor Hospital. I reckon you figured out the rest."

"What if the police get killed trying to protect her?" Olivia asked without looking up.

"That's kinda their job."

"I need to go back." She shivered. "Back to the preserve. I need to cast the spell to send him back."

"Are you crazy? What if he's lurking out there?"

Olivia set down her mug and wrapped her arms around herself. "He'll go after Kim, and sooner or later, he'll come after me. I think because we summoned him, it has to be us, at least one of us, to send him back."

"You don't even know what he is."

"It doesn't matter. This feels right. That's why he wants to kill all of us. If killing only one broke the magic binding him to our calling, he could saunter off anywhere." Olivia leaned forward on the table. "I need to do this before he finds Kim."

"Do you even know the spell? Don't you need more witches?"

"I don't know if I have enough magic on my own, but I have to try. Besides, even if I could get ahold of other witches, I don't want to put them in danger. I remember the basic chant, and Caroline's Book of Shadows is still at the mound."

"Which is now a crime scene. How do we explain this to the police?" Gavin ran his right hand through his hair.

"Can't your deputy friend pull some strings?"

"Maybe."

"I know you don't want to get involved in magic, but will you at least drive me back to the park?"

Gavin sighed and stood. "You really want to do this?"

"No. I'm terrified." Olivia rose to her feet. "But what choice do I have?"

"All right. I'll call Luke on the way." Gavin collected his shotgun on the way out and double-checked the holstered .45. He half expected Jacky Du to appear as soon as he opened the door.

Gavin scanned the parking lot from the doorway, Zeus at his side. "All clear. Let's go."

They crossed the lot briskly, starting at every night sound. Once they reached the car, Gavin peered through the glass, checking the interior, before leading Olivia around to the passenger side, and standing guard while she climbed in, then let Zeus into the back seat.

The call to the deputy went the way Gavin expected. "You can't go traipsing into a crime scene. Besides, what if the monster is still lurking in the woods?"

"Olivia insists she has to be the one to cast the spell to send this creature back where it came from," Gavin countered. "Otherwise, it's going to hunt her and Kim down to make sure no one can do the job."

"I am so getting fired. Fine, I'll call Sergeant Felcher and tell him to let you in."

"Any word from the Homeland Crypto Division agents?"

"They're still a ways out, last I heard," Luke replied. "Even odds, if they pull the jurisdiction card, it might make our guys dig in their heels. You sure this can't wait?"

Gavin glanced at Olivia. She stared straight ahead into the night, her face pale in the dashboard light. "Naw. The freak could appear at the hospital any time."

"So much for you staying out of this," Luke remarked.

Another glance at the woman sitting next to him. "Reckon I ain't got a choice."

Retracing the route north only took a few minutes. Gavin swung the car onto the road leading back toward the park when a dark shape appeared in the road. The tires squealed as Gavin hit the brakes and jerked the wheel out of reflex. Olivia cried out, and Zeus barked.

Gavin fought the wheel and reversed the skid before they reached the opposite shoulder. Whatever was in the road wasn't the slender man. A lump of shadow coalesced into a crude, bear-like mass, rising. Red motes glared back in the headlights' illumination.

"This can't be good," Gavin muttered.

The creature lumbered forward, and Gavin gunned the engine, trying to swerve around it. He gripped the wheel in anticipation of the impact when the shadow-bear lunged into the car's path. The bumper and right fender passed through the inky bulk.

Olivia screamed and ducked as the passenger window erupted in a spray of shattering glass. Metal crumpled.

The jeep swerved on the sandy road, tipping on its side from the force of the explosion. Smoke, glass, and screams filled the air. The Jeep's driver's side door vanished, and the vehicle rolled.

Gavin's hand slipped off the steering wheel, and he instinctively grabbed for purchase. Metal shrieked on pavement, drowning out Gavin's cry as his hand was crushed between the metal frame of the Jeep and the cement of the road before the appendage tore free.

"Sarge! Sergeant Wirth!" Someone shook him.

Gavin shook his head, blood pounding in his ears.

"Gavin!" Olivia shook him. Zeus barked from the back seat.

Gavin blinked. Night's darkness replaced the desert sun. The car's engine revved, but the front wheels spun with no purchase. The car had nosed into a shallow ditch along the road.

"What? Where are—the bear!"

The driver's side window shattered under ebon claws. A gaping, abyssal maw clamped on Gavin's left arm. Icy pain shot up from the flesh above the prosthesis. The bear yanked, hauling him against his seat belt. By reflex, Gavin snatched the pistol out of the holster and fired it point blank into the shadow-bear's right eye.

The creature fell away, its roar of pain echoing out of a dark well. Gavin freed himself and threw the door open. He snatched the shotgun from behind his seat, while Zeus scrabbled to climb out of the back, snarling. The bear rose, its remaining eye a red ember of hatred. Gavin levelled the 12-gauge.

BOOM!

Gavin pumped another round. *BOOM!*

Through the smoke, the shadowy hulk wavered.

Pump. *BOOM!*

The bear sagged to the ground as though its bones had melted. The dark mass collapsed in on itself.

Gavin spun when a touch brushed his shoulder. He snapped the barrel skyward in the split second it took him to recognize Olivia.

"Are you okay?"

Gavin flexed his left arm and checked to make sure the bear wasn't reforming. "It's a flesh wound. The artificial limb took most of the bite."

Olivia stepped back. "I don't mean the arm. You, well, went away for a second."

"Yeah, I did. Sorry about that. It hasn't happened in a while." He scanned their surroundings. They were short of the entrance to the parking lot by half a mile. A streetlight cast a feeble pool of illumination at the entry. The trees on both sides of the road faded into the darkness.

Gavin took a deep breath. There were no insurgents with AKs and RPGs hiding in the trees, only a dark fairy version of Jack the Ripper and whatever other monsters lurked in the shadows.

"Where the hell did the bear come from?" Gavin returned to the car and killed the engine. Calling a tow truck could wait. He opened the back door. Zeus pressed against him, watching Gavin's face. "I'm all right, boy."

"Will the gun shots bring the police?" Olivia asked.

"Shit. Probably." Gavin debated leaving the shotgun in the trunk, but one glance at the melting blob in the road put paid to the idea. "When they get here, do what they say. I don't know if Luke got through to them."

A gunshot popped in the woods, followed by two more. "What now?"

"The bear. If it came through the wold-ford, it might have friends."

"You sure you want to do this?" Gavin asked, ashamed of the part of him that hoped she'd say no. "This keeps getting worse."

"Which is why I can't wait." Her voice cracked. "Can you—"

"I'll be fine." Gavin marched toward the Nature Center beyond the streetlight's glow. "This isn't the Sandbox."

"That's where you lost your hand?"

"Yeah. Our patrol was ambushed. At least most of me made it out. That's more than I can say for others in my squad." Gavin slowed as he spotted the outline of another car in the parking lot—a police car. The vehicle sat dark, with no sign of movement around it.

"Shouldn't there be more than one squad car?" Olivia whispered. "Where are the police?"

"The entrance by the Missionary Center to the east is closer to the mound. Maybe most of them went there," Gavin replied.

"Why'd you bring us back here?"

Gavin shrugged, studying the woods as they approached. "Habit. There's nowhere to sit at the east entrance."

The trees muffled a distant shout. Gavin handed Olivia a small flashlight. "Hold the light. I don't want to stick it on the gun in case we run across any police."

She clicked it on and aimed it at the ground ahead of them, sweeping toward the trailhead. "Do you think he's in there?"

"Maybe. With any luck, he's walking around the city, wishing he had a car instead of those lanky legs." Zeus sniffed the ground, but gave no sign of alarm as they entered the woods. "Head north and west at the fork."

"I don't have a compass," Olivia retorted. "I can call quarters if I know which way is north, but I'm not a boy scout."

"Straight, then left when the trail splits." Several faint cries carried from the east, followed by the report of gunfire. Gavin shivered, and Zeus whined next to him. Gavin patted the dog. "I'm good."

"Shouldn't you be telling him he's a good boy?"

"Zeus reacts when I get stressed. He can tell if I'm about to—well, if something's wrong before I even know."

"Oh. Gods, I'm sorry, I didn't mean—"

"Don't sweat it." They followed the fork west, starting at every sound. The path curved back north. A light glinted through the trees. "Good. Looks like they're still at the mound. I hope I can convince the cops to help me keep watch while you do the witchy work."

Olivia froze on the trail. Gavin scanned ahead, peering where the flashlight's glow faded into the woods. Zeus sniffed the air but didn't signal any danger.

"What's wrong?"

"They're—my friends. Their bodies are there."

"Probably. The police need to document everything before they take the bodies away."

Olivia squared her shoulders and marched forward. Gavin divided his attention between the woods around them and the lights ahead. Nothing moved to block either of the sources of illumination.

"I don't think the police are still there," Gavin whispered as the trail split into a t-intersection. A faded wooden sign identified the mound beyond. "Hello?"

No one answered.

"The bear might have chased them off." Olivia found a deer path, now trodden, to the left of the sign.

"Let me go first." Gavin kept the shotgun low. The path led to a circular ditch surrounding the hill. A pair of lights mounted on stands glowed from the crest. Gavin crossed a crude bridge of parallel logs. "Hello? Anyone there?"

"Do you think Jacky Du will answer?" Olivia hissed, following Zeus across the bridge.

"If he's here, he knows where we are. I don't want to startle any jumpy cops." At the summit of the hill, shredded yellow tape decorated the trees. A gurney lay on its side next to a woman's corpse. Two floodlights on stands threw bright beams across the scene. A third light, fallen over, illuminated the tree branches overhead. At the center, a rippling pool of obsidian hovered in the air.

"The portal?"

Olivia nodded, her eyes fixed on the partially covered corpse, blood staining the visible clothing.

"Something must have chased the cops off." Zeus followed Gavin as he circled the hill, peering into the dark woods. "At least it looks like they all got away."

"I can't find—wait, there it is." Olivia retrieved a blood-stained notebook from the bushes. "Shit, there's pages missing."

Gavin glanced over her shoulder. The scribblings on the tattered, blood-smeared pages might as well have been high school poetry. "How did Jack know which ones to pull out?"

"He must have started with the pages open and ripped out a few more for good measure."

"Do you remember the chant without the notes?" Gavin froze when Zeus' ears perked up. A raccoon scuttled up a tree.

"I think so." She poked in the weeds around the summit, righting fallen candles and retrieving one from the edge of the ditch. "I can't cast a circle. He'd be stuck outside of it—the opposite of what we want."

"A circle of candles can stop him?"

"There's more to a protective circle than lighting candles. You channel energy into it with intent."

"Does your circle have to surround the portal?" Gavin twitched at a snapping twig.

"I guess not. We used it to contain whatever we called forth, for all the good it did us." Olivia's gaze swept the circle of candles. "I could put the candles around us. That would keep him away. I don't know if I'm powerful enough to drag him through with the banishing, though."

"Once he's through, can you close it?" Gavin asked.

"That's the easy part."

"Cast the circle around yourself and chant the banishing spell." Gavin eyed the shimmering blackness. "I'll make sure he goes through."

"What if he kills you?"

Gavin replied, "Then keep the circle going until the cops come back."

Zeus whimpered, loud against the deathly silence of the night. "We're out of time. Make with the magic."

Olivia arranged the four candles around her and the priestess' corpse. She lit each one with a spark from her fingertip. Gavin couldn't make out the words of her soft chant, but the light of the four candles flickered in unison. Drawing a breath, she chanted a new verse, haltingly at first. The liquid darkness of the portal emitted a dissonant *hum*. Gavin swept his gaze across the shadowed trees. His eyes followed one of the beams from the lamps until it faded.

"Sarge, what's out there?"

"I can't see anything beyond our headlights. Keep your eyes open. A convoy got hit last week."

Something fluttered alongside the road ahead. An insurgent, lying in wait?

"What's that?"

"I don't see—wait, there's a tarp."

The Humvee slowed. Everyone sat up, alert. The gunner panned the floodlight. A ragged tent fluttered in the desert wind. The hairs on the back of Gavin's neck stood up. In slow motion, he turned toward the other side of the road. A glint over a low wall of brick and rubble. Why were there two glowing blue eyes? They weren't part of this memory.

Zeus' bark snapped Gavin back. A pale face blossomed around the two blue pinpricks as they surged out of the night. Gavin levelled the shotgun, praying he wasn't shooting at a cop's flashlight painted over by his jumbled recollections.

BOOM!

The grin splitting the inhuman face wavered into a grimace before veering behind a tree. "Oh, that stings! I guess ole Jacky will have to flay you after all. Maybe I'll carve your arm off and take it as a prize."

Olivia's yelp of surprise interrupted her chant. Gavin couldn't tell if the portal had fallen silent over his ringing ears. Zeus snarled, watching the tree Jacky Du vanished behind. After a moment, Olivia renewed the chant.

Gavin fought to keep the post-flashback waver out of his voice. Shit, this was worse than a guy hiding in the scrub with an RPG. "I'm guessing it hurt more than you let on if you're hiding. The shadow-bear I gunned down didn't care for it one bit."

"I'm not some umbra-spawned brute, boy. Give me the witch, and I'll let you go. The last lad was reasonable enough."

"He must've been a real asshole. I'm not giving you anything except a face full of tungsten." Gavin watched the shadows, trying to keep Zeus in his peripheral vision in case the dog spotted the freak.

The portal hummed after a minute. "Oh, my. Is that all the magic you can muster, little witch? Maybe I should have finished the one in the hospital instead of hurrying back here. You can utter your incantation until your voice goes hoarse, little bird. You can't send ole Jacky Du back on your lonesome."

A blur flashed between trees, but Gavin stayed his trigger finger. His eyes flicked from tree to tree… window to window. No, trees. Another memory bubbled at the edge of his mind, but he shoved it down. His magic hand might make him fast and strong, but it couldn't carry his baggage. He had to muscle that on his own.

"You could always go back where you came from," Gavin said.

"And wait another century or two for some silly witch to open a door for me?"

Speaking of witches, Olivia had fallen silent. Gavin spared her a quick glance. She rifled through the notebook.

"What are you doing? Send this asshole back to Hell or whatever."

"He's right—I can't do this alone." She stopped at a page, running a finger across it.

Zeus' bark saved him. Gavin blocked the swipe of black talons with the shotgun. Long fingers closed around the gun, and Jacky Du wrenched it. The report rang Gavin's ears, but the pellets burst harmlessly skyward. Zeus snapped at the spooky man's long coat, to no avail.

Gavin shoved the gun, smacking Jacky across the face with the steel barrel. In a step, the man vanished back into the trees.

As Gavin's hearing recovered, Olivia's chant returned. No, this was different. The portal remained quiescent. He wanted to ask what she had in mind, but answering would break her spell.

Another blur. "What are you doing, little bird? Your song sounds familiar. I should know, I followed it from the Umbra to the world of the living."

Gavin sidled to his left. If Olivia's banishing sans coven didn't work, would her protective circle hold? Gavin didn't intend to let Jacky Du test the theory. A glimmer tugged at Gavin's peripheral vision. A ghostly duplicate of the woman on the ground hovered over her corpse.

"Caroline! I need your help." Olivia flipped back through the notebook. "The page is missing, and I can't get the chant right."

The apparition nodded. She held out a translucent hand to Olivia. The women clasped hands. As Olivia took up the spell again, another voice joined her, soft and distant, as though carried on the wind. The hum returned to the portal, reminding Gavin of vibrating glass.

Zeus bared his teeth and gave a low growl. A pair of red eyes appeared a split-second before a pitch-black mastiff hurtled out of the shadows. Zeus intercepted the new threat, blocking Gavin's line of fire. The two canines snarled and snapped at each other.

Gavin spun and levelled the shotgun. Jacky Du's pale face, his lips peeled back from sharp teeth in a rictus grin, loomed from the darkness, ducking behind a tree as a spray of tungsten-carbide bearings blasted bark from the trunk.

"You're a clever one, lad. Must be why you wear Nuada's Hand. It needs you as much as you need it," the slender man crooned from behind a tree.

"What are you going on about? This lump of metal doesn't have a mind of its own."

The hum of the portal grew with the witches' chant. The black surface rippled in concentric circles collapsing to the middle.

"You think not? How do you move as fast as a jack-spriggan? Does it act before you even realize what it's doing? There's ancient power in the relic you wear, lad. Or maybe I should say the relic riding you. I could tell you more. Call off the witches. I can find my entertainment elsewhere, and before I go, I can tell you of Nuada and the god-wrought hand you bear."

"Nice try, asshole. I don't trust you." Zeus and the black dog circled each other, barking and lunging, but neither committing to the fight. "How about you jump into the portal and go back to where you came from?"

"Wait another century in the Umbra? No, Jacky Du has tasted freedom and blood, and craves more of both." He snapped a command, and the black dog lunged at Gavin. Zeus slammed into the hound, trying to grab hold with his jaws, turning the pounce into a collision.

As Gavin fell, Jacky Du bolted from behind the tree, covering the intervening space in a step. Gavin twisted, landing on his side. The shotgun shredded the pants and pale skin of Jacky Du's right shin. Black blood welled from the pocked flesh.

As Jacky Du fell, he grabbed for the shotgun barrel, hissing as his slender fingers wrapped around it. Instead of trying to yank it away, he pinned it to the ground as he levered himself onto his good knee and jabbed with his other hand. Razor-sharp nails pierced Gavin's jacket, and he winced in pain before seizing Jacky's wrist and extracting the scalpel-like blades.

"Good thing I wore my vest." Gavin released the shotgun and punched the man. Lacking the hardness and heft of the silver fist, the blow still snapped Jacky's head aside. Before Jacky could recover, Gavin grabbed the other arm.

"You'll tire before I do, lad." Jacky locked his ice-blue eyes on Gavin's. "Aren't you tired? Weary of being a broken man with a broken soul? Yes—war has left its mark on you in more ways than one."

"Shut up, asshole!" Gavin pulled his knees under himself and planted one boot on the earth. Jacky Du tried to wrench his arm free of Gavin's flesh and blood grip.

The dogs split apart from their snarling, whirling dance. The hound's fur rippled as though blown by a wind toward the portal. Its outline wavered as a ghostly shadow of the dog stretched toward the humming obsidian pool. The black dog fell back a step toward the portal, then another. A warble in the hum accompanied another shadow tugged away, and the dog grew translucent. Gavin stood and dragged Jacky Du in the direction of the otherworldly doorway.

"No!" The slender man twisted, and Gavin's grip slipped. He slashed with his free hand, the sharp talons slicing into Gavin's forearm.

Blood ran down Gavin's sleeve as he wrenched Jacky another yard closer. The man tried to plant his feet in the dirt, faltering as his wounded leg bore weight. Gavin snagged another swipe. The claws split his jacket open and raked across the vest underneath before Gavin could lock the arm against his body.

The black dog yelped in reverse before the faded image was sucked into the portal, as a cloud of dust beset by a vacuum cleaner. Gavin dragged the writhing man closer.

Jacky Du spewed curses in a mix of English and a foreign tongue. At the edge of the portal, Jacky spat at Gavin. "Stupid Dunwold get. I'm not a phantom of shadow. Even two witches lack the magic to draw me into my prison. As soon as I'm free—"

Gavin punched Jacky Du square in the face with the silver hand. Grabbing Jacky's flailing hand before he could recover, Gavin shoved Jacky Du bodily through the rippling blackness. His blood turned to ice where his flesh met the magical prosthesis.

"CLOSE IT!" Gavin shouted.

"But you're part way—"

Jacky Du twisted in his grip on the other side of the gateway. "DO IT!"

He'd left part of himself on a battlefield before.

Olivia held a stone aloft, called a phrase, and squinted in concentration. The humming of the portal collapsed with its perimeter, as though it sucked the sound into the otherworld. Darkness blossomed in Gavin's vision, and he fell for a second stretched out to minutes. Had Jacky yanked him through at the last minute? Maybe the gate had pulled him through, since he was in contact with it.

He expected to awaken in the desert, a soldier soon to die shaking him to his senses. Instead, grass tickled the back of his head and neck, and he drew in the scent of earth and loam.

"Gavin?" Olivia shook his shoulder softly. Instead of snapping awake in panic, he drew a calming breath, interrupted when Zeus licked his face.

"Are you okay?" the witch asked.

Gavin sat up, steadying himself with his hands against the ground. A black patina of tarnish covered the metal surfaces of his prosthetic hand. His stump still burned as though frostbitten, but the pain ebbed.

"I take it he's gone?" The space at the summit of the hill stood empty, the shimmering portal absent.

"Yeah. How did you know you wouldn't get sucked in, or that closing the wold-ford wouldn't cut off your arm?" Olivia asked.

"I didn't." Gavin patted Zeus with his right hand. "I figured if it lopped off the prosthesis, I'd be no worse than before—a small price to get rid of that asshole."

Gavin's phone chimed, loud in the quiet following Jacky Du's banishment. This time Gavin didn't jump. "It's the deputy. Hey, Luke."

"I got word shadow-monsters chased the officers from the crime scene. You might want to stay away."

Gavin chuckled. "I appreciate the heads up, but I'm pretty sure the crisis is over. We shoved Jacky Du—the dark fairy killer—back where he came from and closed the door. I'd be obliged if you'd tell your police pals coming back not to arrest us."

"Shit. I'm on my way; I'll call them. They might make you sit tight, if for no other reason than to get your statement, but I'll be there soon."

Gavin collected the shotgun and leaned it against a tree. He turned and found himself face-to-face with the ghostly witch.

"She said, 'Thank you.' He can't hear you, Caroline," Olivia said.

The spectre nodded. She took Olivia's hands one more time in an obvious farewell.

"I will, I promise." The witch choked on the words and sniffled. "I wish I could—"

Caroline shook her head and put a single finger to Olivia's lips. The ghost nodded her head toward Gavin.

"I just met him." A sob dampened Olivia's laugh. "You're still playing matchmaker, even if it's literally the last thing you do?"

The ghost shrugged, then embraced Olivia. After a moment, Olivia was hugging empty air.

"She didn't need the wold-ford to go wherever?"

"Caroline didn't need a wold-ford to pass on." Olivia wiped a tear from her eye. "She asked me not to give up on magic or life because of this."

"It can be a struggle—not giving up, I mean." Gavin flexed his fake hand.

"Does it get easier if you have help?" Olivia scratched Zeus behind the ears. "Maybe we could help each other. If nothing else, we know we're not crazy—this really happened."

"I've got Zeus to help me." He quickly added, "But it might be nice to talk to someone who can talk back. Plus, you seem to know more about this weird life I've landed in."

"Yeah. I heard what he said, about your hand and Nuada. I know a bit of the story, and we can research the rest together."

"I've avoided digging into the legends. Maybe I was a little afraid of what I'd find," Gavin said. "Maybe I can be brave with a little help."

* * * * *

Jon R. Osborne Biography

Jon R. Osborne turned a journalism education and a passion for role-playing games into writing science fiction and fantasy. His second book in The Milesian Accords modern fantasy series, A Tempered Warrior, was a 2018 Dragon Awards finalist for Best Fantasy Novel. Jon is a core author in the military science fiction Four Horseman Universe, where he was first published in 2017. He now has eight novels and numerous stories published in multiple languages.

Jon resides in Indianapolis, where he plays role-playing games, writes science fiction and fantasy, and extols the virtues of beer. You can find out more at jonrosborne.com and at https://www.facebook.com/jonrosborne.

* * * * *

Welcome to Detroit
by Nathan Balyeat
A Powers of the Night Story

"Good for you. Welcome to Detroit. Now go home." The massive bouncer crossed his arms.

Every time I visit this city, it never takes long for someone to tell me I'm not welcome. It's a badge of pride for the residents of a city sliding into darkness. It's their way of telling you you're not tough enough to live here. It's a cry of desperation from people slowly losing their souls as the city feeds.

"Listen, buddy, I'm telling you for the last time. There's a private event, and the doors are closed for the night. Go home. Go somewhere else. I don't care. Just go."

"Do you know who I am?" I asked pleasantly, but channeling the coldest stare I could. I'd gotten very good at it over many years.

"No." He was either too dumb or too confident to realize the trouble he was in.

"People call me Tony, but I used to be someone else."

"I don't care if your last name is Stark. You're not getting in."

"My parents named me Athanasios." I said it the way they'd said it, with my native, Ancient Greek accent.

"So?"

"It means immortal."

He laughed. "So what?"

"In the legions, I was known as Atrox. The Horror."

"Legions?"

He was getting confused. That was what I was going for.

"The Roman Legions. History remembers me as Longinus."

Longinus had always been more myth than reality, and it was a myth mostly forgotten now. I wasn't surprised he didn't get the reference. My banter had distracted him long enough for me to retrieve a useful tool from my pockets. I might have a couple thousand years of experience on him, but he *was* twice my size, and that made him *really* big.

I have three rules for fighting. The third rule applied here.

Don't fight fair.

I stepped in with a snap-kick to the groin, and didn't get a clean hit, but made him flinch. He responded with a big overhand right. I obliged his predictability with a left-handed jab to his armpit.

His arm hung limp. There's a lot of nerves in the armpit.

I'll give him credit, he didn't back down. I didn't want to permanently harm the guy. He was just doing his job, but if I didn't close things out quickly, one of us would end up hurt badly.

So, I covered his face with the pepper spray I'd retrieved from my pocket.

With him blinded, it was the work of a handful of seconds and a few more carefully placed punches to position him so I could choke him out.

It's not like the movies, where someone stays knocked out forever. I quickly wrestled his wrists and ankles into zip ties from yet another pocket.

This is why you bring duct tape, Tony.

He stirred as I removed his compact pistol, one of the newer Glocks, from the concealed holster on his hip. He blinked his eyes, tears running down his face—pepper spray burns like a son of a bitch—and struggled against his bonds. I removed the magazine from the pistol, and though he probably couldn't see what I was doing, the sound of me racking the slide to remove the chambered round caused him to freeze.

"Don't kill me."

"Don't worry. I don't want to hurt you any more than I already have. I'm just unloading the gun. I'm also not a thief." I stuffed the empty gun back into his holster. "I've given you back your gun, but you might have to look for the magazine."

I threw the full magazine into the parking lot and heard the crash of a window breaking.

Oops.

"Do me a favor, and stay still. Don't shout for help." I powered down his cell phone to stop any voice-activated shenanigans and took a cheap two-way radio from his belt. I threw the radio battery into the parking lot, careful not to hit a car this time, and set it down next to him. I felt bad about leaving him there, unable to see, face soaked with irritants, but I was on a mission.

* * *

On a previous visit to the city, I'd learned that the hotel that housed the club had been built in the twenties. As far as I could tell, it had been a significant nexus of despair from the beginning. It still was. Given the general darkness consuming this city, that said a lot.

The Purple Gang had used the building as a headquarters during Prohibition. It was one of the last places Jimmy Hoffa had been seen, and one of the first places the police had raided when looking for him. When the Mob left in the sixties, the desperate, destitute, and helpless moved in. Now only the destitute and hopeless stayed in the hotel.

Then they died inside, and sometimes on the outside, as the city sucked them dry.

The club in the old hotel ballroom had gone by different names over the years, but since the '80s, the crowd had been "goth-lite," and the decor matched.

On a normal night, the patrons were a wide mix of people from different backgrounds gathered to drink and dance. The last time I'd been there, the decor of the big wall across from the bar had consisted of chalk drawings from that stop-motion Halloween-Christmas movie. Creepy usually wasn't my thing, but I liked the jack-o-lantern lead.

The poster on the door advertised tonight's invite-only Nain Rouge party. Only in Detroit would they celebrate a harbinger of doom.

Nain Rouge, the legendary "Red Devil" of Detroit, was unlikely to be here himself. He was usually only seen before a major disaster, often of the personal kind, but sometimes a city-wide one. Before opening the door to the club, I checked the encrypted Network app on my phone to refresh my memory of the girl I was here to find.

Cassandra, goes by Cassie. Twenty-two years old. Five foot two, eyes of blue—an instant ear worm. Damnit. Her hair color varied, but in every picture, she had a thin, tasteful nose ring in the left nostril, and big hoop earrings. Height wouldn't be reliable, given the crowd's penchant for platform boots, but I'd found less remarkable people in bigger crowds with less information.

I stuck the mostly empty pepper spray and my phone back into my pockets. I had to hope I wouldn't need it in the club. The only other tool I had left was the knife. I certainly didn't want to have to use that.

I hated using the knife.

As soon as I opened the door to the club, I cursed in seven different languages, four of them no longer spoken by anyone but me and other, usually awful, immortals. The concentrated hunger of the city itself tried to feed on me as I pushed my way into the building. The foulness here meant dark rituals I'd come to associate with the Fallen. I needed to make this quick.

There wasn't another bouncer inside, and I ascended the stairs to the club. With every step, the thump and boom of electronic dance music grew louder. At the top of the stairs, a red-lit bar stocked with bottom shelf liquor supplied dim, bloody illumination. The pumpkin-headed skeleton art I remembered was gone, replaced by lesser art that didn't infringe copyright and wasn't nearly as charming.

Many of the human patrons, and not everyone here tonight was human, wore the red devil masks associated with the Nain Rouge. Others were in elaborate makeup instead. I wasn't the only person unmasked or unmarked, and fortunately, I wasn't too out of place in my black jeans and t-shirt.

I scanned for Cassie.

For such a crowded club, with such powerful music, the atmosphere was dull. Something was feeding well tonight, though everyone would probably remember having a wonderful time.

I slipped cleanly through the crowd toward the dance floor, but still ended up brushing against people who felt empty. They didn't feel like people anymore.

I'm going to need a shower. A long one.

The masks and makeup made my search difficult, but after a few moments, I was confident Cassie wasn't in the bar area. I moved to the dance floor next. It was a riot of flashing lights filled with the spastic dancing of the lost. Maybe on an ordinary night, they'd be losing themselves in the lights and noise, dancing to escape their demons.

Tonight, they danced *because* of the demons.

Demons, plural. I saw at least two of the lesser Fallen on the dance floor. Fortunately, they weren't heavy hitters, but they weren't powerful enough for what I was sensing. There had to be someone—or something—I couldn't see.

Two thousand years ago, I saw the divine in a way that forever changed me, leaving me blessed and cursed. After that happened, I always see the world as it is. No illusions.

Behind their glamours, the demons were androgynously, gloriously beautiful. The Fallen were fallen *angels*, after all. Forget what the paintings of Hieronymus Bosch depict. Forget what Hollywood shows on screen. The Fallen Host, what most people think of as demons, can be every bit as beautiful as the Celestial Host when manifesting in this realm.

They aren't the only dark forces, though. The really dark ones, the most powerful of the Fallen, make Bosch's depictions look like puppies. Their manifestations are always terrifying.

And, doing what you'd expect demons to do, the Fallen here tonight fed.

I found Cassie.

She was right where I didn't want to find her. Between the two Fallen. The demons were doing the nightclub, fallen angel version of the frat boy grind, one in front, one behind. She was moving with them, but in a daze. A casual observer might think she was drunk or high, but it was a supernatural compulsion that kept her dancing.

I moved across the dance floor in a way that could charitably be called dancing toward the center of the room. I bounced roughly in time to the bump and boom, drawing and concealing the small, straight-edged knife from the hidden sheath near my belt buckle.

The thumb-sized blade didn't seem like much, but like me, it was more than it appeared. It was a fragment of a much more powerful weapon I was no longer worthy of wielding.

Even though I was ready for it, the surge of divine power made me stumble. Two thousand years passed in less than an instant. I said I see the world as it really is. Seeing the world in that way, without illusion, isn't just for the present. I relived every moment of my life in a flash, without filters. Every action I'd ever taken, seen without self-delusion. Every selfish choice. Every harm inflicted on others. Every moment of anger, and the agony of every loss. Everything. All at once. My brutalization of the bouncer tonight was another straw added to my spiritual load. Enough straws, and I'll break.

Soon, but not tonight.

My stagger wasn't too different from my dancing, and I kept the knife hidden as I finished my approach. "Can I cut in?"

Up close, the vibrant face from Cassie's photos remained, but supernatural torpor softened and dulled it. She barely glanced in my direction and continued to dance as her hellish partners walled me off from her.

The demons looked at me in contempt, like I was an ordinary club patron.

"Buzz off," the one on the right said, straightening the vest on its otherwise bare chest.

"She's with us," the one on the left added, tugging at the ruffled cuffs of its shirt.

I stepped in close, touching the tip of the knife to the hip of the one I decided to think of as Lefty.

"Not anymore."

Lefty hissed and recoiled. I don't know what the Fallen feel when touched by the fragment, but the lightest contact seemed to hurt like hell.

Right Said Fred—because that's who its shirtless attire reminded me of—stepped close, not quite certain what was going on. It hadn't seen or felt the knife. Yet.

I slipped into the opening the retreating Lefty made and grabbed Cassie by the arm. She wasn't aware enough to resist.

I flashed the knife at Fred. "She's coming with me. Feeding time is over."

Fred quickly stepped away from the knife and stood next to Lefty. Both kept their distance, apparently unwilling to put their immortality at risk.

"We *will* find you, mortal," Lefty said.

"Our master won't let you get away with this," Fred added.

As satisfying as it would be to end the two of them right here and now, the odds weren't in my favor. There was still something powerful I hadn't seen. That meant it was time to follow my second rule of fighting: *Don't fight if you don't have to.*

I smiled and led a submissive Cassie to the door clearly marked Emergency Exit Only behind the stage. I took satisfaction in ruining the rest of the evening for the demon pair as the fire alarm blared.

* * *

With every step, Cassie became more animated. By the time I got to the edge of the parking lot along Cass Avenue, she was back to herself. She shook herself free from my grasp.

Cassie saw the little knife still in my hand and took a dramatic three steps back. "Get away from me!"

I made a deliberate show of taking another step away from her and putting the knife back into its hidden sheath.

"Relax, Cassie. Your cousin Matt sent me. He wanted me to tell you you're overdue for lobster and a visit to Maine."

"You know Matt?"

"We've never met in person, but we've been talking online for years. He and I belong to the same network. When your parents posted you were missing a few days ago, he set it in motion to find you."

"How *did* you find me? And I haven't been missing!"

I looked back at the club. A number of patrons, mostly in the red of the Nain and the black of the goth, were gathering nearby in the parking lot.

"Look, I'll explain as we move, but we can't stay here." I was worried about what sort of reinforcements Lefty and Fred might be reaching out to, especially since Lefty was on the phone.

"Not until you tell me your name."

"Call me Tony. Tony Long." That *was* the name on my current ID.

"Okay, *Tony*." Her tone said she didn't trust me, but she was willing to give me a chance.

"We really need to move."

I heard shouts. It sounded like someone had seen the bouncer.

"Matt told me, if you weren't sure you could trust me, to say, 'cantaloupe.'"

She burst out laughing. "That goofball. Okay. He did send you."

"You going to tell me what's so funny?"

"No." She flushed red as soon as I asked.

It wasn't as important as getting her moving.

"Fine. Just come with me. We need to get to Woodward as quickly as possible."

"Woodward? Why?"

"Cameras. Lots of cameras." I put my arm around her shoulders and forced her to jaywalk across the street.

"I don't understand," she said, struggling to keep up in her platform boots.

I looked back over my shoulder. A pair of human clubbers were following us. Physically, they didn't look like a threat, but anyone with a cell phone could make sure threats could find us.

"What day is it, Cassie?"

"Wednesday?" She sounded uncertain.

"You've been missing for three days. It's Friday."

"What?"

"Check your phone."

She patted her skirt. "I don't have it."

"No surprise they'd take it from you."

"Who are *they*? Where is my phone? Can you slow down?"

I eased up a bit. "Your last social media post was Tuesday night, with you and your friend Lindsey in a picture at a house party. Wednesday, you didn't come home, and your parents started to worry. They reached out to your friends to find you. Thursday, Matt found out you were missing and got the network involved. The tech nerds—don't ask me how they do this—hacked the city cameras around the last location of your phone and followed things forward until they saw you go into the club tonight with Lefty and Fred."

"Who?"

"The pair that probably kidnapped you."

"Did they drug me?"

I said nothing and let her assume what she needed to.

She patted her skirt again. "They took my wallet, too!"

"Wait, does your skirt have pockets?"

"Yes!"

In other circumstances, her enthusiasm would've been delightful. Right now, I was annoyed that she slowed down to show them to me.

"Keep moving." I didn't look back, because I didn't want to see the disappointment at not sharing her enthusiasm for pockets. They were cool, but now wasn't the time to stop and admire them. Her boots thumped as she caught up to me.

"Where are we going after Woodward?"

"Greektown."

"What's in Greektown?"

"My car."

"Why did you park all the way over there?" she asked. "Were you gambling?" I sighed. I wasn't sure how to explain to her that Greektown was one of the "safe" places in Detroit. It's an area where a binding agreement between a local real estate billionaire and the resident powers prevent them from working overtly in the areas he controls. The fiction that he'd sold his interests in the district didn't affect the agreement in the least.

I didn't know what price he paid—or was continuing to pay—to the powers and to the spirit of Detroit itself, but it certainly wasn't money.

I don't lie. So, as I had with the bouncer, I misdirected with the truth. "It's the safest place to park."

"That's like a mile away."

She made a statement, not a complaint. Interesting. I'd probably complain if I had to walk just one block in the clunky things she was wearing.

"Yup. Just about."

"Okay." She sounded almost cheerful.

* * *

By the time we were on the third floor of the Greektown parking structure, some of that cheer was gone. There was no sign of anyone still following us.

"Which car is yours?" she asked, trying to catch her breath from the pace I'd pushed.

"That one." I pointed.

"Ooh. That's nice."

"Not the sports car. The Jeep."

"Oh."

Technically, a Jeep Liberty is a Jeep. It says so.

I liked it because it was small, inconspicuous, and had a tremendous amount of room for gear in the back, while being small enough to travel in dense cities. I also went through a lot of cars and wouldn't care if I lost it.

"Where are we going now?"

"I'm taking you home," I said.

"That's it?"

"Yep. The goons are gone, and you're safe. My work here is done."

I paid the parking fee, and we pulled out of the garage and got onto I-75, headed north.

We'd just passed under Gratiot when the blue and red lights of a Detroit police cruiser flashed behind us. I hadn't been speeding, so it should've driven past us. I slowed down and hoped it wasn't what I thought.

No such luck.

Normally, the Fallen would cut their losses if someone escaped their clutches. There was an endless supply of victims. More people disappeared every day than anyone could possibly rescue.

They had to be after me. I shouldn't have used the knife. It never ended well, and using it had probably alerted every power in the city that I was in town. Now someone had sicced a pet cop on me. If I tried to run, he'd call for support and I wouldn't be able to get Cassie home. The items under the surplus blanket in the back would be more than enough to get me arrested by normal cops.

"Listen carefully. I made some powerful individuals—" I purposely didn't say people "—angry tonight. This is one of their bought-and-paid-for cops. When we pull over, I'm going to get out and greet the officer. That's going to make him nervous, and he's probably going to draw his gun on me. I'll let him cuff me, and while he's doing that, I want you to drive away as fast as you can. Stick to the expressway, and don't stop for anything until you're past Eight Mile. If other police come after you, you can let them catch you. But *only* after you're past the *boundary*. Past Eight Mile."

"Boundary?"

She'd picked up the subtle emphasis I'd put on the word. That was a mistake.

Am I nervous?

"Past Eight Mile. If you get pulled over by a cop in another city, tell them you were fleeing from your kidnappers. They'll find things in this car that'll make it seem like I'm a bad guy, and that I was one of those kidnappers. It'll make it easy for them to believe you and protect you from the Detroit cops."

"But you'll go to jail!"

"Maybe." I'd escaped from cuffs and squad cars before. If I couldn't, well, it would suck. They'd want me to suffer instead of killing me. Being mostly immortal has its downsides.

"If you can, go straight home. If you have to stop, don't stop until you're north of Eight Mile. Do. You. Understand?"

She nodded, tears in her eyes. She'd been brave after being rescued from the club, but something in my manner scared her. There was no way she understood what was going on.

She didn't need to.

I took as much time pulling over as I thought I could get away with and used the time to remove the little knife and its sheath from my belt. It fit neatly into a gap in the dashboard under the steering wheel. Over the years, I'd found if I hid the weapon or any of its pieces, they couldn't be found by anyone but me. I've always known where to find them, even after decades separated from them.

I handed my phone to Cassie. "This is your phone now. Pass code is 5150, like the Van Halen album title."

She looked at me, obviously not familiar with the band. *Talk about making an immortal* feel *old.*

"When you're safe, open the Network app in the upper left. Contact Matt to let him know you're okay. Call whoever you need to."

We pulled to a stop. I undid my seatbelt and got out, hands in the air. Slowly, I walked toward the cruiser's blinding lights. The spotlight was trained on me, as well. I couldn't see a thing, and my eyes were watering.

The loudspeaker roared to life, the harsh voice of the officer booming out over the sounds of passing traffic. "Put your hands on your head! Get on your knees!"

The debris on the shoulder dug painfully into my knees. I was there for long seconds before I caught the shadow of the driver's door opening.

A massive shape crossed the spotlight, and I swore, a single word in English. It's overused to the point of meaninglessness—until it isn't.

"Fuck."

The police officer wasn't an officer. Behind the glamour, it was one of the soldiers of Hell, probably trained by Michael himself before the Fall. One of the big-name Fallen. It hadn't bothered to draw its gun or reach for his cuffs. It didn't need to.

"Hello, Longinus."

"Hello, Eligor. Haven't seen you since Cherbourg. How's the knee?"

It enthusiastically showed me how well its knee had recovered by stomping me into the pavement with the leg it was attached to. My head bounced off the ground, and I gasped for air with bruised ribs.

"Glad—" wheeze "—to see you again."

I was waiting to hear the sound of the Jeep pulling away, but all I heard was the rush of passing traffic and the slow exhaust of the idling Jeep.

Eligor picked me up by the throat as if I weighed nothing and gave me the real version of the stare I'd tried on the bouncer earlier. Unlike the bouncer, I knew enough to be afraid.

"No escape for you this time. Just lots of suffering." He emphasized the word suffering by tossing me into the push bar of the cruiser. Ouch.

The Jeep still wasn't leaving. Worse, the passenger door was opening.

"Cassie, get out of here!"

Eligor turned to greet the girl.

"Let him go." She pointed one of my pistols at Eligor.

"What are you doing? Run!"

Eligor laughed. "Wait right there, little one. I'll be with you in a moment." He turned back to reach for me and staggered to the *crack-crack-crack* of the 9mm bullets slamming into him.

Reflexively, I clung to the ground as bullets continued to fly. A headlight blew out, and I heard the distinctive sound of windshield hits. There was a satisfyingly meaty *thwack* as a bullet took Eligor in the back of the knee I hadn't wrecked the last time we met.

It stumbled to the ground in front of me and turned to growl at Cassie.

The retention holsters police use are supposed to prevent the people they're arresting from lifting their gun easily. I don't like being prevented from doing anything and was familiar with the design. Three rounds to the back of Eligor's head sent the Fallen sprawling forward, unmoving.

"What the hell, Tony!"

Despite her recent, desperate spray of bullets to save me, my callous apparent execution of the officer appalled Cassie.

"Get back in the Jeep. We need to leave. Now."

I tucked Eligor's pistol and a spare magazine into my waistband. A phone started ringing from a case on Eligor's belt. I grabbed it and checked the caller ID as I slid into the driver's seat.

The screen displayed Red.

The Nain himself.

I handed the phone to Cassie. "Answer it on speaker."

I slammed the accelerator to the floor of the little SUV and left the speed limit way behind as I hauled ass toward Eight Mile and the boundary. I wasn't stopping again.

The Nain's voice came from the phone. "Hello, Tony. That *is* what you're going by these days, is it not?"

I responded in French. He'd been serving the spirit of the city for centuries, at least as far back as when it was a French possession. The important part was that Cassie likely didn't understand it.

He gracefully continued the conversation in French. "You disrupted a very important ritual tonight. I'll be direct. I want the girl. Tonight."

"Not happening, you sadistic midget."

"Fine. Then here's what'll happen."

He switched to English.

"I still have Cassie's friend, Lindsey, in my possession, along with eleven other young men and women."

Cassie gasped and looked at me in desperation. She *and* her friend had last been seen together, but Lindsey wasn't my mission.

"So?"

"The city can feed on twelve innocents tonight, or on one. If I remember correctly, sacrificing for others is the way your side does things."

"You're twisting and misrepresenting things, like your kind always do."

"The city will feed tonight. It's your choice whether it's one or many."

"Tony!" she cried. "I can't let them hurt Lindsey!"

"Ah, she *can* hear me."

I hated his laugh.

He said, "Girl, I propose a binding agreement with you. If you surrender yourself to me tonight, I'll free your friend Lindsey and the eleven others. Because I know the person with you is familiar with our ways, I'll save you both time. Neither I, my agents, nor the powers in the service of the City of Detroit and their agents will take any further actions against those freed, including indirect actions to manipulate others to harm them."

"Hang up," I said.

She looked at me.

"Hang up!"

"Call me back. Soon." He hung up for me.

Cassie looked at me. "What's going on?"

* * *

I stayed silent until we slipped underneath the Eight Mile overpass, out of the supernatural reach of the city's spirit. I let off the accelerator and parked in an empty shopping plaza parking lot off the next exit.

I slumped back into my seat as I cut the ignition. She deserved the truth.

"My real name is Athanasios. I was born in a small village near Athens, Greece in the summer of the first year A.D." Without looking at her to see her response, I continued. "When I came of age, I joined the Roman Legions and served with the Tenth Legion, Fretensis. By the age of thirty-three, I was a centurion stationed in the Roman province of Syria. My troops called me Atrox, The Horror, because I was a vicious bastard."

I looked over at her, and she stared at me, but not like most would. She didn't show any sign of disbelief. It was like she already knew.

"What about being called 'Longinus?'"

I looked at her for a long moment. I hadn't mentioned Longinus. "That came many years after. People want to make legends about unnamed individuals from their sacred stories. Most of what they say about me, about Longinus, isn't true."

"But that was your spear? The Spear of Destiny?"

I nodded.

"Holy shit! It's all real!"

"What's real?" I asked.

"God. Angels. Demons. Monsters. What I saw when I touched the knife."

"Yes." It took a second to process what she'd said.

"You *touched* the knife?"

"I've always known there was something more out there. I mean, I believe in God, but I knew the other things were there, too. The evil." She tugged at a cord around her neck to reveal a small, stainless steel cross tucked into her bodice. "And the *good*. I've always had faith."

She presented the cheap necklace as if it meant something. To her, maybe it did.

"That must be nice," I said with a calm I didn't feel. Faith hadn't been enough for others.

"What do you mean? Don't you believe? After what you saw? After what you lived through?"

"Oh, I *believe*, but that's a far cry from having faith like you. That, I don't have." I took a deep breath. "When you've seen what I have, up close, you don't need faith. You don't have a choice but to believe."

She nodded sagely. "What does that have to do with tonight and me?"

"I'm still trying to figure out the details, but you believe—have faith—that angels and demons can act in this world?"

"Yes."

"That's good, because the Fallen have taken an interest in you. The cop wasn't a cop. He was a fallen angel, a demon soldier I've run into in the past, using glamour to look like a cop."

"But he's dead now."

I snorted. "Hardly. He'll be ugly for a while, what with needing to regenerate his face and half his skull, but there's only one way I'm aware of to end one of them permanently."

She nodded as if she knew.

Of course she knew. She saw it through the knife.

"Okay. What about the Red guy on the phone?"

"He's different. He was once a mortal who sold his soul for more power. I'm not sure whether he's a native, or a French explorer, but he calls himself the Nain Rouge. Regardless, he found the dark nexus here and made a bargain with its spirit. He pledged service to its hunger, and for his service, he gained immortality. He and the spirit of the city are contained by the river on the east and south, plus a Boundary of Belief at Eight Mile Road in the north. The west is... more complicated. It has power and reach farther than that, but it has the most power and greatest freedom of action within the city limits. We're safe from him and it here."

She huddled in her seat, hugging her knees to her chest, silent for long moments.

"What does this have to do with me? Why am I so important?"

"I'm not sure," I deflected. She had to be special if she could touch the knife and not go insane. "But you're certainly special somehow."

"What about my friend Lindsey and the others the Nain mentioned? He said he'd make a binding agreement to let them go?"

"Yeah. Binding agreements. There are rules that govern how the supernatural world works. You've heard of people making pacts with the devil, right?"

She nodded, looking very small, curled up in her seat.

"Then you know they always turn out badly for the person who makes them, right?" I asked.

"I guess."

"Trust me. Nothing good comes from those agreements. The forces of Heaven and Hell both *have* to keep to the exact terms of the agreement they make when they state it's binding, or put it in writing. They literally cannot violate or knowingly allow others to violate a binding agreement. Evil will either find loopholes or, if they close the loopholes like the Nain offered to do, create misery elsewhere out of proportion to what they've given up in their agreement."

"But they'll..." She swallowed hard, tears forming at the corners of her eyes. "They'll kill Lindsey and other people if we don't do anything."

"Look. I'm not a bad guy, but I'm not a nice guy. Sometimes you have to let bad things happen to prevent worse things."

I had to believe that was true.

"Lindsey and the others might have to be sacrificed. Whatever the Nain is up to can't be good for anyone. For each person he spares tonight—which won't include you, if you accept his bargain—many more will suffer from whatever his scheme is. Everyone freed will live a seemingly blessed life, but every day they live will multiply the suffering for others."

The more I said, the more upset she got, until tears were flowing freely down her face. "I don't accept that. There's always something you can do."

"I used to think that, too."

She glared at me for a long moment before bursting from her seat and fleeing into the parking lot. I let her go to give her space for a bit.

My body hurt from Eligor's beating, and my soul twisted inside my chest as I allowed myself to accept that there were lives I couldn't save. Again.

One more straw added to my load.

I sat, listening to the open-door chime for a long while. I was about to get up and go find Cassie when she sat back down in the passenger seat and closed the door.

"Okay, I have the address pulled up in GPS."

I started the car. "I know where you live."

"Not my address, the address of the Nain."

"*What?*"

She wiggled Eligor's phone in front of my face. "I called the Nain and negotiated a binding agreement. I said I'd bring you and the Spear of Destiny to him. In exchange, he'll release me, Lindsey, and the others without future threats. The same agreement he was going to make if I turned myself in." She was looking very smug.

"So you're going to give me up to save your own skin?"

"No."

My confusion must've shown on my face.

"I said I'd bring you, but I was clear that I couldn't force your surrender. He didn't seem so concerned. His only condition was that you couldn't have the Spear or the knife fragment in your possession when you arrived."

"So, I show up without meaningful weapons, and I'm somehow supposed to escape?"

"Yes."

She held up the knife I'd stashed in the dashboard. "You know how to be sneaky, and I picked up some of your tricks."

She crawled between the seats and rummaged under the blanket in the back, coming out with a steel-bladed short sword, missing its tip.

It had been centuries since *I'd* been able to wield the reforged Spear. Saints and sinners couldn't carry the spiritual weight of it, of what I'd done. The broken tip, made into my knife, was all I could manage anymore.

She looked at me with a malicious grin. "I bring you and the Spear, and they can't harm me, right? You can't have it, but they aren't expecting me to use it, either."

The knot in my chest from earlier, thinking we'd be sacrificing her friend and others to win a small victory, loosened a little. Maybe we *could* save everyone.

It was a flawed plan, and I told her so, but it felt right. I fleshed out what she had in mind. It still wouldn't work, but she and the others would live, even if I didn't.

For the first time in a long time, I felt at peace.

* * *

The Jeep wouldn't transport everyone we needed to rescue, so we "borrowed" her dad's pickup. It had a cap on the bed, which meant we could cram the people we rescued inside without drawing too much attention.

Cassie had snuck in and grabbed the keys, along with a change of clothes. She'd found her parents asleep in the living room, and her mother holding a family photo. As we pulled out of her driveway onto the quiet neighborhood streets, she said, "I should've left a note at least."

"It was your decision."

"I know." She pulled her knees to her chest again. "If this doesn't work, I don't want them to think they've lost me a second time."

I couldn't think of anything useful to say. She looked much smaller and more vulnerable in the pale blue tracksuit she now wore, plus missing the extra six inches of boots. Chuck Taylors just weren't as intimidating.

"So why do you do what you do, Athanasios?" She said my name with the correct accent.

"I go by Tony now."

"You aren't Tony."

I ignored her. "Why do you help people? You don't have to."

"I don't know anymore. Habit, I guess? Because I can?"

"You used to have better reasons."

I turned on her as we stopped at the traffic light, angry. "What do you know about my reasons? How can you possibly understand what I—"

She held up the backpack with the reforged weapon. "I've lived your life, too, though not as deeply. When I touched the knife, I knew…"

Touching the knife had literally given her knowledge beyond her years. She knew me better than anyone.

I sagged back into the seat. I also felt uncomfortably vulnerable, with all my innermost secrets and failures exposed to a girl with a tiny fraction of my life experience. "You shouldn't have had to feel that."

"Earlier tonight, you said you weren't a bad man."

"I'm not."

"I agree. You're a *good* man."

I laughed darkly. "You can say that after you saw everything I've done? The reasons my fellow legionnaires called me Atrox? I was the most brutal of a brutal brotherhood."

"*Was.*"

"You saw Cherbourg, then. All the people I let die when I fled?"

"I saw your dick move."

"See?"

"See what? That your remorse for abandoning those people has eaten at you for hundreds of years? You sometimes wake up screaming because you left them to—"

"To a fate worse than death?"

She nodded. "That's when it started, becoming harder to use the spear."

"And now it's impossible. I can barely manage the knife."

"Remember, I've seen your life, too. You thought you had to flee to save some people, or stand and lose everyone. You didn't leave to save yourself. You tried to save those you could. You might have been a dick, but your heart was in the right place. You're a good man, Athanasios."

The rest of the trip passed in silence.

As I parked the truck, Cassie looked at me and said, "I have faith in you."

* * *

Abandoned neighborhoods fill the east side of Detroit. In places, a single standing home is the only one left on entire blocks.

The address the Nain had provided led to one of those. I stepped out of the truck, breaking my first rule of fighting: *Don't go where you might have to fight.*

Cassie got out of the passenger side and gave me a nervous glance.

"Hey, runt! We're here!" I shouted at the single, darkened home on the block.

A moment later, the door opened. A thrall in a Nain mask held the door open for twelve other thralls, each leading an unresisting youth into the yard. I recognized Cassie's friend Lindsey from the pictures.

Last to appear was the Nain himself. He looked nothing like the devil masks his followers wore. He was recognizably human, his face red with eczema and acne. His diminutive stature, twisted limp, and hunched back made it almost painful to watch him move.

"You're even uglier than you were in '83." *1883*.

He ignored me. I'd have ignored an insult that weak, too.

Cassie called out, "I brought him, like you asked."

"And the spear?" the Nain asked. Someone so evil shouldn't have such a pleasant voice.

Cassie held up a bag to show both the sword and knife.

"Very well." He motioned to a spot in the yard. "Set the bag down there, and the binding agreement will be sealed. You and your friends will be safe from direct and indirect action, per our discussion earlier."

He and Cassie went back and forth, reviewing the precise language for a few minutes. It was a solid bargain, and I nodded my approval.

She nodded back and strode forward. She took the sword and knife from the bag before setting it down. "Our bargain is complete. I was to *bring* the spear, not let you keep it."

The Nain began clapping. "Well played, girl. I underestimated you. Our bargain is binding. Of course, if there were an independent power present, not serving any party or bound to our agreement…"

He stopped clapping and gestured to the sky.

"Eligor, our visitors want to leave with your sacrifices. Per our agreement, I have all thirteen of them present for you."

A giant, winged shadow crashed to the ground in front of Cassie. Eligor had given up any pretense of hiding its nature, instead embracing all the power available to it on this plane. It had manifested as an ebon-skinned angel, wielding an archaic greatsword. The still-healing ruin I'd made of its face and a slight limp from where Cassie had shot him marred his unearthly grace.

Cassie made a desperate, unskilled attempt to stab Eligor with the Spear. It contemptuously slapped her to the ground instead.

The weapon tumbled across the lawn to land a step away from me.

Eligor leered at me from its ruined face. The exit wounds from the shots I'd fired had left its face a mess, and without its right eye.

"You don't get to flee this time, *Tony*. Not like Cherbourg." He made a pointed glance to the sword on the ground in front of me. "You ran, but I got what I wanted. I got stronger. It seems you've gotten weaker. You can no longer wield the Spear. That saddens me. I'd get so much more out of this victory if you could." He stepped toward me, sword raised. "What's your third rule again?"

I had nowhere to run.

He stepped forward. "There is no escape. Tonight, you finally die."

"Don't fight fair!" Cassie cried and sliced his calf with the knife. Black ichor sprayed from the wound.

Eligor roared in agony, as the brave young woman it kept ignoring had hurt it for the second time tonight. His rage at the affront had become a tangible thing.

He spun on Cassie and raised his unearthly blade. "I will make you suffer, girl."

I just reacted. I rolled forward to sweep up the reforged Spear of Destiny, ready to suffer the crushing weight of my awful life to save this girl. My past was full of failures, of cruelty, and of pain.

But this time, I relived my life through the filters of Cassie's words. *You're a good man, Athanasios. I have faith in you.*

The Spear hadn't rejected me because I wasn't a good man. *I'd* rejected the *Spear* because it showed me I'd stopped trying to be a *better* one. I'd let guilt consume me, shame me into doing the bare minimum. To essentially do nothing.

All that is required for evil to triumph is for good men to do nothing.

I rolled to my feet and roared with centuries of suppressed anger, slicing across Eligor's folded wings, ripping them savagely. My attack carried me past him, and I interposed myself between him and Cassie.

The stories say the Spear of Destiny made its wielder invincible. That isn't true, but it's close enough. Spiritual energy manifested around me, taking the shape of the segmented plates I'd worn as a legionary with an open-faced, crested helmet. I shed the fiction of Tony Long and embraced who I'd been.

Athanasios Atrox.

Horror to my enemies.

"It looks like I'm not the one who needs to escape, Eligor." I jabbed with the blade. "Cassie! Get everyone out of here. I'll keep him busy."

A ghostly shield in the form of a legionary scutum manifested, and I raised it just enough to absorb Eligor's wicked overhand blow.

Despite his wounds, he *was* stronger than when I'd fought him at Cherbourg all those years ago. Even though I could wield the Spear of Destiny again, it had been centuries since I'd fought like this.

I thrust. And missed.

Eligor rained blow after blow upon my shield. Any mortal construct would've been shattered in the exchange.

I dashed inside, trying to be clever with a slashing blow, but was turned aside by Eligor's raw power.

He tried to use his greater size and longer weapon to control the range, but his footwork was poor from his damaged knee.

I took advantage of that and kept him off balance by circling to his blind side.

His wounds against my lack of recent experience. It was a poor balance, but it was *a* balance. All it would take was for something to change that balance, and one of us would die.

After several furious exchanges, I heard tires slip on the pavement and caught the taillights of the truck as it drove away.

Eligor noticed, as well, becoming distracted enough for me to disengage enough to speak. He looked just as tired as I was.

Manifesting took energy, and so did healing. If he spent too much now, he'd have to return to the other side, and it'd be a while before he could come back. I wasn't sure I could win, but he wasn't sure, either.

"You lost your victims, Eligor. You might win this fight. You might not."

"Your second rule?"

"Don't fight if you don't have to. Binding agreement. No direct or indirect hostilities between us or our agents for thirty days. The same goes for Cassie and her friends."

"You're not bargaining for more on her behalf?"

"You wouldn't agree to more."

He smiled. "No, I wouldn't. Agreed, and done."

* * *

Later that afternoon, I sat on Cassie's front porch. Her grateful parents had gone inside to let us speak in private. We'd told them I'd saved her from kidnappers. That was true enough, but it was easier to let them assume human traffickers than to explain what had really happened.

She sat down next to me. "The memories from the Spear are fading."

"That's probably for the best."

"Maybe. So, what's next?"

"First, I need to make the Spear whole again."

"After that?"

"In order to beat Eligor, it won't be enough for me to be good. I need to be *better*."

She put her hand on mine. "I have faith in you, Athanasios."

* * * * *

Nathan Balyeat Biography

Nathan is the author of fantasy short stories in the Fellblade and Powers of the Night settings, and the upcoming science fiction novel, *Knight Unbroken*. He's a United States Marine Corps veteran with a degree in history and a day job in project management. His hobbies include weightlifting, travel, martial arts, miniature painting, and both tabletop and computer gaming. He currently resides in Michigan with his cats.

* * * * *

Those Who Went Before
by Glen Cook
The Black Company on the Long Run

So there we were, in the bedamned primeval forest still, following the ghost of a memory of a road that only sometimes trended in the direction we wanted to go. It meandered from one glade in the woods to another, those likely once camping stations along a trade route back in the time before the Lady rose up and the world changed forever.

Those clearings were inconvenient.

In the forest, we were hidden from eyes in the air. The open spaces forced us out, where our enemies might spot us.

Those places were potential killing zones.

* * *

I shared breakfast with the command staff and inner circle of those who make the Black Company go. This blessing, the road we'd been on for more than a hundred miles now, seemed to have struck some of us with a black-smoke paranoid fever.

One-Eye said it. "It's been too damned long since somebody tried to kill some of us."

Goblin echoed, "What he said."

I asked, "You *want* people trying to kill you?"

That started several minutes of crazy, half the gathering trying to make the argument that when we're not in contact with our enemies, we got careless and might stroll into an ambush that could take us all out.

Neither side of the argument made much sense to me but, after all the time I'd spent with this mob, no amount of conspiracy theory or plain crazy completely surprised me.

At the foundational level, there lies a granite-hard conviction: There were people who were out to get us. Always. And these days, there was no doubt about that. But some among us took that truth almost to the point of making it a Company religion.

* * *

As ever, Elmo was in charge of the advance party making the road passable. He came back to report, "Road's getting better again."

Ever paranoid, Candy asked, "Maintained?"

"No. Just less weeds and brush."

The condition of the road varied considerably, probably according to who'd built a particular section. The only thing that mattered was that, for a while, we'd been able to move along a little faster while doing a little less work.

"We" in the sense of the Company. I don't do manual labor.

Candy and the Lieutenant headed off to check it out. I stayed where I was, not being a glutton for unnecessary exercise. Besides, Darling was signing me a story about something that had happened while she was away from the Company with Raven. She hardly ever wanted to recall those times. They made her remember Raven, her first love, who was gone now.

Then Elmo had to go and say, "I've got one of my feelings."

"Stay away from me if it's catching."

"Wiseass."

Darling signed, "What feeling?" She's deaf, but she's a genius at reading lips.

"You know. The feeling I get when something bad is about to happen."

I'd known Elmo for twenty years. This hadn't come up before, ever. "Who are you? What have you done with my friend Elmo?"

"Hey!"

"You don't…" Well, maybe he did get premonitions, but had never told anybody before. In this mob, offering any prophecy later found wanting could get you mocked for years. That could get you a nickname like Skunkbugger. "So. What is it?"

"We stopped kicking up game."

Half the advance party was out there as hunters. As time rolled on, and our effort to escape the Lady's empire proceeded far more sluggishly than we'd hoped when we scooted out of Chimney, we were trying more and more to live off the land.

Following a pause, Elmo said, "I don't mean just deer and wild pigs. I mean everything. Squirrels. Rabbits. Turkeys. Every kind of animal that doesn't fly much. There are still birds in the treetops."

That did seem unusual, but on this long run, unusual has gotten more usual by the day.

* * *

Elmo was spot-on about the road getting better. By the time we stopped for the night—*not* in one of the open spaces—our leading elements were on solid pavement that needed no grooming at all.

But now there wasn't even any bird talk in the treetops, and our animals seemed extremely reluctant to move forward.

Elmo had gotten glummer by the hour all day.

That was his habit when he thought things were going too well. In his eye, that was a sure sign a major shitstorm was about to blow in.

* * *

I fell asleep easily, slept long and well, and didn't have to empty my bladder but once all night. Insofar as I could remember, the Lady never wandered through my dreams, either.

Some of the men, rabble-style, were up and moving forward early. Evidently, there was something ahead that was worth getting excited about. Show Boy and his clique had decided to push ahead of the vanguard, then had brought back word that we were about to run into something weird.

Again.

Rabble-style. Yes. Discipline had been getting steadily worse since we left Chimney. The complaining worsened every day. We were just marching, fighting nature, hiding from the Taken, being eaten by bugs, day after day, week after week—and now, month after month. We've actually had some guys desert. In the middle of the damned forest!

A big part of the morale problem is, nobody really knows where we're going. It's all just get away from the Taken and the Lady's empire. Get out of somewhere we're no longer welcome, and try to do that while staying alive.

Eventually, I got off my butt, got my mare into the traces, and my medical wagon rolling.

* * *

It was actually hard to tell what we'd run into because the next clearing lay behind a ten-foot-high berm that began yards outside the woods. The road turned left, hugging the base of the berm. The woods ended sword-stroke suddenly. The berm ran in both directions, as far as I could see, which was not very far.

I left my wagon and joined the command staff in time to hear the Lieutenant ask, "Goblin? One-Eye? Thoughts on this geometer's boundary line?"

Something about the precise end to the forest troubled everyone. Not one of the rowdiest rowdies had yet dared leave the cover of the woods.

One-Eye announced, "It's magic."

"And that just answers it all, doesn't it?" the Lieutenant snarked back. "With all that wisdom and a Rosean silver half star, I could get myself jumped at Missus Hattie's House of Happy next time we find ourselves in Roses. Or I could probably get better service with just the half star."

Which was a really windy way of telling One-Eye that he wasn't helping.

One-Eye stared at the Lieutenant in disbelief. Around about, within hearing distance, mouths hung open.

The Lieutenant had to be seriously stressed. That might have been the longest speech anyone had ever heard from the man. Even One-Eye, rarely at a loss for something to say, even if it was something stupid, was taken aback.

Remarkable. Hardly anything can impact the felonious little shit.

Goblin saw a chance to stick a needle into his fellow runty wizard. "I'll go scope it out, Boss." He comic opera goose-stepped to the berm, and then climbed it. And then, once up top, he froze, staring, like he couldn't believe what he was seeing.

Darling—woman-child Company mascot and most valuable Company secret weapon—was next to find balls enough to leave the woods and scramble up the berm.

You know it. Not one guy she left behind was going to let a girl show up his courage. There was a general surge. The Annalist—me, Croaker—was part of it, but I was very nearly the last guy up because I was ninety percent sure that, before I got there, I'd be screaming that the Taken were coming.

The Taken didn't come, however. I wasted several firkins of apprehension right there.

The view from the top of the berm was amazing. It was stunning. And it was thoroughly disquieting.

The first thing that registered with me was the berm that encircled the clearing completely just yards inside the surgically precise edge of the woods. Second thing was this clearing was larger than any we'd seen before.

The road turned alongside the earthwork to the left a quarter of the way round the circle, to a break in the berm. It turned in there and ran straight across the heart of the enclosure to another break in the berm and, I supposed, from there ran along the outside again until it headed its original direction again.

Then I finally registered what had captivated everyone else immediately.

Almost the entirety of the grounds was given over to what was, almost certainly, some kind of military cemetery.

There were *thousands* of pristine white posts, each one five feet tall, triangular, six inches to the face, pointed at the top, and spread out in mathematical precision, so much so that it was mesmerizing to the onlooker.

Once I was able to tear myself away from a view that, no matter what direction I looked, the white posts swept away in rigidly straight lines, I noted a building complex opposite us, across the vast, round field. That complex could be approached only along a ring road pressed up against the inside of the berm, which ran all the way around the field.

Most everyone else had noticed already, and the Lieutenant had Elmo's bunch down on the inside road, already headed toward those structures.

"Ah, shit! The fucking livestock!"

I have no idea who yelled that, but he for sure had a point.

With nobody there to keep control, our animals had taken the opportunity to get away from a place they had no desire to go.

* * *

The only partly successful roundup cost us a day and a half that we should have spent putting miles behind us. The Lieutenant was in a constant blistering rage because every minute of that time, some of our guys were out in the open, exposed to anyone who happened to be flying by.

Fate was kind. It spared us that taste of pain.

By the time the roundup ended, I'd begun to wonder if the Lady and the Taken were just not interested anymore.

Some of the livestock were never recovered.

The Lieutenant called a general assembly. Speaking from the berm, and from the heart, he left no doubt in even the thickest head that indiscipline was a now thing of the past. Ancient history. There would be no tolerance. And anyone who didn't like that could hand in their weapons and head on back to Chimney and the Lady.

Not one man chose to seize the day.

This particular man was sure there'd have to be examples made.

Nobody would be able to claim ignorance. The Lieutenant was loud, and he was clear, and he had the backing of the majority of the men, even including most of those who'd joined us after the old hands had managed to escape from Juniper.

* * *

While the roundup was still under way, I, having gotten my mare back because she was too lazy to drag my medical wagon around very far on her own, climbed over the berm to go snooping. I was always too damned nosy for my own good. Otto, Hagop, and Goblin went with me.

Goblin said, "I strongly recommend we stay on the road. No cutting across. There's something way off about all that out there." He waved at what I was convinced was a graveyard.

I was inclined to heed his suggestion.

Goblin was right about there being something seriously off in this place.

The worry trigger for me was the condition of the whole. It was better kempt than any graveyard I ever saw, but Elmo and his guys had found no sign of active groundskeepers or a maintenance crew. There was no evidence anyone had been there in decades. I even got a feeling it might be always summer inside the berm.

Everything suggested that, yes, yet again, we'd blundered into a locus of serious ancient magic. The great forest was infested with spooky shit from ancient times.

Goblin kept talking to himself, having what he claims was an intelligent conversation. I didn't catch everything he said, but I caught enough to understand he was trying to talk himself out of the notion that we'd stumbled across the border into the realm of the fey. Because that would be the kind of thing that, for him, would be a blessing too good to be true. That would be a lifelong dream achieved.

We stuck to the long way around, which showed how powerful the aura of the place was. Lazy me, for sure, any other time, would have taken the straight-line course to avoid having to take a few hundred extra steps.

Elmo and his gang were camped on the portico of the complex. Elmo told me, "There isn't much that's interesting in there. It's completely empty, but it's huge. If you're a big fan of echoes, that's the place for you to go crazy."

I looked around at a perfectly maintained structure built using perfectly dressed, first-grade limestone, with the outer columns and some of the facing done in white marble.

Somebody had made a serious investment.

Elmo said, "This is pretty obviously a monument to fallen heroes, made by somebody who had a shitload of magical power to make sure the place would, basically, be frozen in time as soon as it was finished and was still perfect."

That was an amazingly long speech for Elmo, not known for his thinking outside the moment, but probably to the point, here.

I didn't say much back. I wasn't focused. I felt like the place was doing something to me. Or trying to do something with me. What, I couldn't guess.

Elmo told me, "If you don't concentrate, you remember things that never happened to you. Especially when you go to sleep. Last night was crazy; my dreams were so real. I don't usually remember them. Not even the ones where I watch you getting frisky with the Lady, who, I got to say, is Woo! Boom-chicka-boom, bow-wow!"

I messed with his shit by saying, "You got that right! She's all that and more! You can't even begin to imagine how much!"

I stopped, a little ashamed of myself, but actually concerned She might be listening.

She does stuff like that.

I should worry about her feelings when her minions have been trying to murder me for half a year? I should worry about making sure she's respected?

Maybe I did love the woman, as she existed in my fantasies, but I didn't love her enough to defend her in the face of men she'd been hunting for so long. Men she couldn't just let go away.

There was never a time, any time after my prisoner passage in the Tower, when I wasn't confused about my relationship with the great devil of the age.

On the one hand, I was sure the woman was the core of all evil; on the other, she was the heart of my heart, and the only woman who, if I should live a thousand years, would be my dearest.

And having written that, I should maybe hope nobody reads these Annals until after I'm gone.

I shook my head, like that would clear the developing fog. I told Elmo, "We should probably get out of here if there's nothing to find. Go let the Lieutenant know about the road layout."

"Yeah. That's kind of weird, the way it wraps around one side, cuts across the cemetery, then hugs the berm again, then heads on out straight, just like it came in on the west side."

"It does that?"

"It does. I checked. You're probably right. We should get out of here. I don't know if I could take another night like last night, dreaming other people's nightmares."

His weathered old face turned all vacant as he went back to wherever he'd gone through during the night. He murmured, "Those people out there, I think they died fighting the Dominator. Very early on."

"These woods seem like they're chock full of stuff left over from those days."

He grunted agreement.

I noted that, despite my suggestion and his agreement, neither he nor I nor anyone else had gotten to their feet and started moving.

A glance around showed most everyone with the same vacant expression.

"Where's Goblin?" I wondered.

Nobody knew.

I managed to conjure up enough ambition to get to my feet and shamble around, looking for the little toad.

* * *

The runt wizard had gone inside the main structure.

Elmo was right about the echoes.

Goblin was having a great time singing (an overly generous description), making a song up as he went, about how One-Eye had a face like the northern end of a southbound mule. He kept interrupting himself with giggles over his own creativity.

He spotted me. "Hey, man! This's great!"

Great? Maybe. Grand, certainly. Everything stone, everything polished white, some massive, glazed windows way up high to let in light.

In olden times, someone had gone to massive pains and expense. But to what end? I understood the monument concept, but this just seemed like way too much.

I told Goblin, "We're going to get back out of here. There's something too spooky about this place."

He grunted. "Twice ten thousand spooky. You go on ahead. I'll catch up. This's too much fun not to sing a few more verses."

"I'll let One-Eye know where you are. He can come over, and you guys can sing rounds."

Small scowl followed by another big grin. "Yeah. Send Silent, too. We could do some three-part harmony."

The man was in one of his nonsense phases.

I did snicker at the notion of Silent singing.

That man won't talk, even in his sleep.

* * *

Elmo and the others hadn't moved while I was being entertained by the toad-face boy songsmith.

"How about you guys turn to?" I barked. My visit inside the structure seemed to have cured my lassitude.

I turned Elmo's sergeanting philosophy back on him: If you yell loud enough and long enough, using language that's foul enough, you can get anybody to do anything.

I got them onto their feet and shuffling, not back toward the rest of the Company, but in where Goblin was still failing to harmonize with himself. If the space had broken the spell on me, maybe the others could be shaken loose, too.

It worked.

So there we were, a bunch of guys standing around, looking sheepish, listening to Goblin's cat in heat caterwaul… until somebody told him to shut the fuck up or they'd make him eat One-Eye's louse-ridden black hat.

"There's a deadly threat," Elmo reckoned.

One-Eye's hat was ancient and unbelievably filthy.

One-Eye himself was ancient and unbelievably filthy.

Goblin joined us for our brief journey.

* * *

The Lieutenant had questions. "Will that sleepy business hit us all if we stay on the road going through?"

Shrugs all 'round. Nobody knew. Not even Goblin had a guess, and he, like One-Eye, willingly admits he's the world's foremost authority, and thinks you should agree.

Second-in-command man Candy said, "I hate the thought of being out in the open that much."

Someday we'd come to the end of the forest. After that, we'd be out in the open all the time.

Elmo pointed out, "We haven't had a run-in since back when Croaker was plooking that Leta woman."

Croaker pointed out, "Croaker wasn't the only one doing some plooking."

Somebody sighed. "Ah, yeah. Too bad we couldn't have just stayed there."

Now the Lieutenant shared in the pointing out. "Staying there as long as we did was why Whisper found us."

Candy added, "We just have to keep on heading east until we get out of the empire."

Somebody grumbled, "We been doing that for half my life already."

A slight exaggeration, but not an unfounded complaint. It earned the rejoinder, "And if you stop moving, it'll have been for the rest of your life."

The Lieutenant and Candy like to worried themselves into a case of the ulcers while we waited for the last reclaimed animals to be brought in.

One-Eye said, "I'm thinking maybe the Taken are still recuperating from the ass-kicking they got the last time they tried us on."

That was a hope I'd been nurturing privately, myself, keeping it private because I was pretty sure it was just whistling past the graveyard. Pun not deliberate, despite what lay just a hundred yards from where I was brooding.

Coming from a right angle to reality, Goblin announced, "I just had a thought."

One-Eye, naturally, had to counter. "Kill it quick, before it gets out and bites somebody, and gives them rabies."

Goblin ignored him, which is usually the safest course with the old black wizard. Besides, it makes him nuts.

Goblin said, "Ever since we started this march to Hell, every time we run into a situation, there's a bunch of naked-ass hot women around. I'm starting to wonder when they're going to turn up here."

"Runt's got a point," One-Eye conceded, he being an even smaller runt than the toad, if anybody was counting.

It might be coming up on that time of the year when some daring secret cabal got One-Eye blind drunk, then made him suffer a bath.

* * *

The passing of the clearing cemetery started smoothly enough, and continued to go well while everyone stayed on the road. But then, one of the dumbest of dumbass Chimney-born FNGs, Rusty, thought he saw something shiny between two white posts and just had to go get it. He grabbed a post to maintain his balance as he bent over…

Screaming!

"Don't!" Elmo barked as a couple of guys started to go help. "Let's scope it out first. You don't want that to happen to you, too."

The column stopped moving. Everybody had the same mixed feelings. Nobody liked Rusty. He was a confirmed bully, and a suspected thief. But he was also one of us, and we stick together.

Rusty passed out. When he did that, he let go of the post.

Elmo said, "Now get him. Drag him by the feet. Don't touch anything out there. Croaker. Time to do your stuff."

I looked around for my apprentices. I had two, teenagers from Chimney, both amazingly skilled at turning invisible when my work threatened to get bloody. I didn't see either one now.

The column began to move again, past my wagon. I dropped the tailgate and had Rusty laid out there. His lower legs hung over.

His pulse was the most rapid I've ever felt. It was a wonder his heart hadn't burst. His breathing was rapid and shallow, too. His face was all sweaty. I told Elmo, "I don't think he's going to make it. Get the word spread. Nobody touches—"

Screaming from up ahead.

I said, "Go clean that up. And if you see Butterbutt or Spangler, tell them I want their skating asses over here now."

Butterbutt was Butterbutt because he'd had a huge behind when we pulled out of Chimney. Our trek had worked that off, but he'd be Butterbutt until he shamed himself enough to earn a new name.

Then here came One-Eye and Goblin, side by side, bickering about something that had happened twenty years before I was born.

"You two. Take a look at this guy."

One-Eye asked, "Was that him yelling a while ago?"

"Yeah. He touched one of those white posts."

"Heart rate is elevated. Breathing fast and shallow."

"I did notice that."

More usefully, Goblin said, "Something tried to possess him."

Oh, boy. "Tried? Did it take?"

"I don't think so, but you'll have to wait for him to wake up to find out for sure."

And here came a couple of guys dragging the limp body of my apprentice, Spangler.

"Same story with this one," Goblin told me before I could ask.

I did ask, "Where's Darling? I think it might be handy to have her here while I'm dealing with this."

"Couldn't hurt," One-Eye said, just before another shriek of agony sounded. "How blessed are we with stupid? Some dumbass just, I'll bet, grabbed one of those posts to find out if that was what the screaming before was all about."

I had six idiots to work on before the stupid storm completely passed. I told the Lieutenant, "On the plus side, they were all Fucking New Guys we picked up in Chimney."

Most of those were runaways and wanted criminals, men of a sort seldom lauded for their formidable brainpower or inspired life choices.

Darling and Silent turned up, but they seriously didn't want to stay in the middle of the graveyard. The mystic climate was too harsh for the girl. Silent signed, "We'll help if you'll move outside the berm."

I told Elmo, "How about you round up a dozen swinging dicks and get these morons out of here?"

Fifteen minutes later, me and my wagon and my patients were on the roadside, up against the woods, outside the southern exit from the confined area, and a few yards on up the road. A very uncomfortable Darling stood surrounded by outstretched, unconscious men. She rocked back and forth constantly, left foot fifteen inches in front of her right.

Silent signed, "Even here, you can feel it, strong. That's why the animals didn't want to come close."

He didn't explain "it."

I didn't feel much, myself, maybe because I'd gone into that big, empty space where Goblin had done his singing.

Darling signed, "It's working," meaning that her presence was having a positive effect on the half dozen idiots.

Darling was the first thing Rusty saw when he opened his eyes. His face darkened with pure, lustful evil. Then he saw something else: Silent. And Silent wasn't smiling.

Then Rusty saw a third and a fourth thing, Goblin and One-Eye.

They weren't smiling, either.

The fool scaled back his ambitions.

One-Eye settled into a squat beside Rusty. "Tell us what happened." Watching closely to see if Rusty wasn't Rusty anymore, despite his very Rusty reaction to Darling.

"When I touched that white post, I got blasted with somebody's memories. All of them, all at once. A whole life that ended really bad. All I could understand was stuff that he saw, because whatever lingo he talked wasn't like nothing I ever heard before."

Goblin said, "I reckon he's clean and can head on out as soon as he can walk."

Still weak, Rusty began whining and lobbying to ride with me.

Darling poked my arm.

Another idiot was coming around.

His report matched Rusty's, except for adding that he thought what he'd run into wanted to take him over, but couldn't because they had no common language.

I thought that sounded a bit strange. I looked at the wizards. None had an opinion.

The Lieutenant turned up. "How much longer are you going to be? We're burning daylight."

"No clue, Boss. I've got two awake, but can't tell how able they are to move on their own."

"Shit. And we had to leave three wagons behind because we couldn't get the teams back. I'll find out if there's any room in the wagons we kept. I'll send stretcher bearers if there's room."

* * *

Long story short, I was sitting in the same spot when darkness came. Two men, one my apprentice Spangler, remained unconscious. One of the ones who'd recovered was completely mad. He never stopped weeping and babbled continuously, obviously terrified, in a language nobody recognized. The Lieutenant found only enough space for two men to ride. The rest might have to be hauled on stretchers until they could walk—if they had somebody willing to carry them.

One-Eye opined, "This is not good."

Goblin agreed. "We might have to put that one down, for our own safety."

Not a happy thought, but one I understood.

The man was possessed. We had no way to tell by what. It could be something seriously dangerous, or it could be just plain crazy.

I thought Rusty might get left behind. He had no friends, but he got lucky. He recovered enough to move himself at a slow walk.

* * *

Asleep under my wagon, I was startled awake when my hobbled mare got excited. I still had two patients and no assistants. I had orders to catch up when I could. I didn't see how the whole mob heading out and leaving me made any sense.

"Hey, you'll be fine," Candy had told me. "Your woman isn't going to let Whisper do anything serious if she does find you."

He might actually believe that shit.

"Thank you, Candy." There was going to be some fun had the next time his ass needed some doctoring.

But he and the Lieutenant really were that spooked. And likewise, almost everyone else who'd passed through without visiting the empty space.

I couldn't blame them after the incidents we'd survived to get this far.

I might be calmer than most, but I was, for sure, not confident that the grand monument wasn't a bad place. The testimonies of my recovered idiots did nothing to convince me that we were just misunderstanding the nature of a memorial to those who'd gone before.

Because I still had patients down and no way to move them, I'd remained fixed in place since I came out. I was still exposed. But, as noted, I'd slept under my wagon until the mare awakened me.

* * *

Age has begun to stalk me more closely. There's almost no night, anymore, when I don't have to get up to relieve myself a time or two, and the Night of the Fallen Dumbasses was no different. That was the first thing I took care of when the mare stirred me out, before I turned to consider the Grand Memorial to Our Honored Dead.

I have no idea how that got into my head.

So there I was, at the edge of the woods, in the moonlight, draining the snake and trying to figure out what had the mare agitated, when two things captured my attention.

First, I spotted a firefly perched on a twig off to my right, not far from the horse, then I heard one of my patients start mumbling to himself in no language I recognized as he got to his feet and, in a zombie-shamble, headed toward the break in the berm.

He wanted to go back inside?

I wasn't certain, at the time, which of those things troubled me more. Whenever I spot a lightning bug close by, I know there's a strong chance that the Lady's watching. However, on the other hand, Spangler, barely more than a child, was stumbling back to the place where his own stupidity had taken him down.

I'd chosen him as my apprentice because I thought he was one of the smartest Chimney kids.

Either I was wrong, or I was pretty dumb myself.

Six of one, half a dozen of the other, likely.

I've been with the Company since I was only a little older than Spangler. I've had numerous apprentices. They never seem to last. Maybe it's me.

I hope it's not me.

I went after Spangler.

* * *

The idiot was headed back to the post that bit him. He couldn't move as fast as I could. I caught him before he got there. I took hold of his left shoulder.

He twisted away and faced me, looking puzzled. Then conflicted. Then, finally, puzzled again, but asked, "Croaker?" in a small child voice.

"That's right. And you're Spangler. Don't forget that. Put that right up in the front of your brain and hold on tight. You're Spangler from Packer's Lane in Chimney, fifteen years old, almost sixteen, and you're my leading apprentice."

And my only apprentice, as far as I knew. I hadn't yet seen or heard from Butterbutt. I'd heard nothing concerning his welfare, good or bad, either.

I had an idea.

"Come with me." All balls and no brains, guiding Spangler by gripping his left elbow, I headed straight for the building complex, taking the direct route through the white posts. Where I caught remote, obscure whiffs of countless lives, none of which had had a happy ending.

We'd walked along maybe a hundred yards when I saw a pulse of light in Spangler's hair.

"Ah, shit!"

I let go of the kid's elbow and flicked a forefinger at the bug. It wobbled away, sparking weakly a couple of times, then landed on the tip of a white post.

Big spark!

Small crackle!

A feeling like a sudden earthquake ambush, and a harsh gust of anger wind...

The firefly was down, crisped.

Shit! And Great Shit! I probably just called down the lightning! If that was really her, the sky would soon crawl with any Taken still capable of action.

"Let's go, kid. We need to keep moving."

Shit warmed up and redoubled! He wanted to turn around and go back the other way.

Spangler wasn't handling the internal traces anymore. He hadn't kept himself at the forefront of his mind.

Apprentice Spangler wasn't as strong as his master. I grabbed hold and forced him to go in the direction I wanted.

Whatever was going on inside Spangler shifted again as we neared the fancy buildings. He came back out and was very cooperative. And contrite. He knew what had been going on with his body. While he was back in charge, he wanted me to know that when he touched the white post, back when, he'd gotten blasted by the being of someone who'd perished centuries ago, in a no-mercy war with the Domination. This particular one who'd gone before belonged to a people facing total extermination, but who were determined to fight on until there was no one left to fight.

The shades of the fallen were imprinted into the posts. They weren't intended to attack a living being who came into contact, but that was the practical result. The intent had been a memorial to the life of one who'd fallen. Someone who cared could come to a post, touch it, and be with a hero or a loved one for a time.

The physical property remained flawless—the memorials, not so much. An unknown force had slowly turned them askew across the centuries.

Spangler and I made it to the building complex, mounting the steps by moonlight. Inside we went.

The grand space where Goblin had sung was still a den of echoes. And it was lit, I don't know how. The light was almost painful when we first went in, and the echoes seemed far fiercer than earlier.

Spangler had him a few moments where he tried to shake my control, but his efforts were feeble. Then whatever it was about the place broke the possession, and he was just plain young Spangler from Packer's Lane, a kid who resented having his life so much controlled by the Annalist and physician of the Black Company.

He wasn't my apprentice in the Annalist trade. When I had one of those, it was somebody we thought should be groomed for an officer's role.

I *wanted* one of those. An assistant Annalist. I was getting sourer by the month, ever more certain that my time was running out. But the prospects for acquiring an assistant were grim. The only men in the Company that I knew could read and write were One-Eye and Goblin, either of whom would be a disaster as Annalist, guaranteed.

Anyone else who was sufficiently literate was keeping it secret. Annalist wasn't a job many people wanted.

* * *

The big, empty space cleaned Spangler up just fine.

We got back to my wagon before dawn, me with a serious case of the cobblies, but the expected swarm of Taken never materialized.

I did watch a lone flying carpet slowly transit the setting moon.

* * *

My other patient had gone missing. What became of him, I have no idea. Like Butterbutt and several others, he just disappeared.

I thought they might be in that cemetery somewhere, dead, or lost in a mental wilderness. The Lieutenant wouldn't let anyone go look. No way was he going to lose any more men.

The missing were all recruits from Chimney. The Lieutenant was seriously regretting having let most of those people attach themselves.

* * *

As soon as there was light enough, Spangler and I got the mare into the traces, and we started moving, me certain that the shit would start raining down any minute.

I walked, leading the mare. I had Spangler ride and nap. He'd take over leading later in the day. I probably wouldn't be able to nap when it was my turn because I was so sure the Lady was going to bring the hammer down.

We walked away from that whole unsatisfactory and confusing encounter without suffering any attention from our enemies. Maybe there was stuff going on somewhere else. Or maybe Whisper just wasn't recovered enough for another round.

Maybe the Lady would cool down a little, I wishfully thought, knowing there'd always be a reckoning on the books. That debt would get called someday.

Spangler and I caught up with the main body two days later. Right away, I got put to work on a backlog of minor injuries that probably should have been handled by One-Eye in my absence.

Elmo's gang had found the end of the road.

Now it would be back to making our own.

* * *

And then came the hard news.

A strange little man called Whittle, one of the guys who'd headed into the woods while we were on the road to the memorial cemetery, came huffing and puffing from back down the road to warn us that an imperial infantry regiment was on the road behind us, and was gaining fast, because we'd cleared the road so they could travel more easily.

So. That wicked woman did have another bolt in her quiver.

Well, the troops would have to get past those who'd gone before, too. Maybe they wouldn't be as lucky as we were. Maybe they'd do something stupid, like try to fight back.

More graveyard whistling, Croaker.

More graveyard whistling.

* * * * *

Glen Cook Biography

Glen Cook is the perpetrator of several story collections and more than fifty fantasy and SF novels. He's best known for his Black Company series, which has been continuously in print, in more than a dozen languages, for more than thirty years. Sometimes credited with being the godfather of the Grimdark sub-genre, he's been both Guest of Honor and Special Guest at The World Fantasy Convention. His most recent books are *Port of Shadows* for Tor and *The Best of Glen Cook* from Nightshade.

Glen was born in New York City in 1944, grew up in Northern California, served as Walt Disney's gopher at the 1960 Winter Olympics, joined the Navy after high school, then went to work for General Motors after discharge. Most of his earlier novels were written on the assembly line. In 1969 and 1970, he attended the Clarion Writers' Workshop, and it was there that he met his wife of fifty years, Carol Ann Fritz. He (and she) have three sons. The eldest, Christian, commands 2nd Battalion, 7th Cavalry (in the footsteps of G. A. Custer & G. S. Patton). Second son Michael is an architect specializing in airport renovations. Third son Justin is just wrapping up his doctorate in music. Glen has a whole herd of grandchildren, almost all of them female. He hopes to live long enough to finish the thirty-some novels still racketing around inside his head.

* * * * *

The Muses Darling
by Sarah A. Hoyt
A Tale of The Muses Darling

I'm not a paladin. In fact, I'm famously not a paladin. My name is Christopher Marlowe. Kit Marlowe. You might have heard of me, somewhere. I was once a playwright, once a poet, but now I'm... not quite human. Mostly a Muse. Though also a detective.

It's complicated. You'll come to understand, as I tell the tale, such as it can be told.

You want paladins? My friend Will could fit the mold. He risked all to save a friend, and not a friend anyone would say was worth the trouble. It wasn't his fault saving me also changed me into what I am.

He overflowed with the milk of human kindness. He believed.

I've never believed in anything much, or when I did, I could trade those beliefs again for others that presented. So long as they were interesting, or amusing. And mostly I looked out for Kit.

Which makes this story quite the strangest I could tell you.

It started with the boy. Okay, not a boy in the time I was born. I judged he was twenty or so, and he'd be a man grown then, with a passel of children around his table. But that wasn't the way of the twenty-first century.

In the twenty-first century, he was a boy, skin soft and unlined, and the look of a child untried by life. He stood by my bed as I woke up. For a moment, in that space before fully waking, I thought he was a dream, a scrap of memory or thought wandering free in my tiny apartment in Imago.

But as I woke fully and opened my eyes, taking in the space between my single bed and the wall, he became more solid, and his appearance more alarming. Wide eyes in a face smeared with blood. Just slightly overlong hair in a mahogany color. White t-shirt and jeans. All of it dripping with blood. My wakening senses smelled the tinge of iron in the air.

I opened my eyes fully and sat up. *Vampire?* Sure, I lived in the Noir section of Imago, but if you think that kept vampires and other fantasy creatures out of it, you haven't fully comprehended the shamelessness of fantasy writers. I quailed the first time I saw an elf drinking in the Mermaid, in the Elizabethan section of Imago, but now they were everywhere. Elves in Noir might not be immediately obvious because they could hide the pointy ears with a fedora. And vampires were often not identifiable till they opened their mouths and tried to sip you like a malted milk.

Slowly through my still-sleep-fogged brain, the thought percolated that if this was a vampire, he'd wasted more than he'd eaten. And then reason, limping behind the panic, bid fair to slow my racing heart with some home talk: *Listen, stupid, you have protections in this place. And even if you didn't, vampires can't come into a place uninvited, and though he's purty, I don't think you invited him. Not unless they spiked the milk you had with your ham sandwich last night.*

When my reason gets insulting, I listen to it. Well, sometimes I do.

So I looked at the protections I'd woven into my spartan living quarters. It was small, maybe all of two hundred square feet, into which space it crammed a single bed—cheap, but I dare say more comfortable than the queen commanded in my time—an armchair, and a small table piled high with books. There was a radio on the bedside table, because in Noir, news and announcements often came through it.

A door on the wall at the foot of the bed led to a closet-sized kitchen, and next to it, a closet-sized bathroom with a toilet, a sink, and a shower. They all looked like they would in a noir novel, hard-beaten and chipped. But in an old-style noir novel, the water would only work sometimes, and there'd be no refrigerator.

Fortunately, most current writers of noir weren't that accurate, and were convinced refrigerators had existed in pre-history, somehow humming away in a corner of the old cave. So I had a working refrigerator, and the water poured from the shower in cascades when the faucet was turned. Hot and cold, too.

Thing is, I'd woven protections into this space, into which I never invited anyone, not even what passed for friends, much less what passed for honeys. I hadn't invited any of those anywhere in probably going on a century, and likely more.

The protections—well, in Imago, land of muses, magic of a sort works. It's not the magic that works in the fantasy quarter. I can't speak bad Latin, wave a wand, and get what I want. Frankly, if bad Latin had that power, I'd have been a wealthy sorcerer in my own time.

Manifestatum, and there'd be a pile of gold.

In Noir, the power of bad Latin was less impressive than even in the Urban sections. There, a large part had been claimed by Urban

Fantasy and Paranormal, and you could trip over shape shifters while going out for bacon and eggs, and amorous werewolves if you took the wrong turn in an alley, finding out for yourself the meaning of doggie-style.

But Imago… it's a place of the mind, isn't it? And therefore, it's a place not fully of reason. Because the human mind is built of layers upon layers, from dinosaur to ape to smarter ape. And those apes afraid of lightning, afraid of the things that moved in the dark, convinced of the power of the fire in their hands, the power of hammer and lance and word, had built Imago so that atavistic magic was part of the thing.

I'd set wards in my space, with will and mind, with my intent certainty that this place was mine, my own private domain. And with a bit of my hair and a bit of my blood over the transom and every window.

I could see the door to my left from the bed, and the window on the wall at my right, next to the armchair. The ancient sigils I'd drawn into the whitewashed plaster still glowed to my slightly unfocused eyes.

And yet, the boy was still there, staring at me. He'd jumped back, as I sat up, and pressed himself against the wall. His chest rose and fell fast, fast as though he were the one who'd woken up to find someone in his bedroom.

There was something familiar about his too-large eyes, something that echoed a known face, but in a disturbing way I couldn't quite pin down. I reached for the Smith and Wesson under my pillow—just because no one had ever come in here, that didn't mean they couldn't—and I pointed it at him and barked, "Who are you? What do you want?"

He threw his hands up by reflex. If his clothes hadn't told me he came from present day in the human world, that gesture would have done it, the immediate, thoughtless raising of the hands when faced with a weapon. From the look in his eyes, showing way too much white, he was either hurt or in shock, so no thought was involved, only the training of thousands of movies watched from earliest infancy. See a gun, and if you mean no harm, throw your hands up. That'll protect you.

I didn't laugh, but I did relax fractionally. No hardened criminal would do that, but I remained ready to fill him with holes should it become needed. I'm paranoid that way.

"Who are you?" I asked. "How did you get in?"

"Per. Per Merlin."

"Merlin let you in?" Damned Fantasy Writers. Was nothing safe from them?

He shook his head. His teeth clacked together so loudly, I could barely understand him as he said, "No. My name. Per. Per Merlin."

"Peter?"

"No. Per. It's short for Percival. Percival Merlin, okay? It's Mom's fault."

I blinked. Well, yes. Such things usually were Mom's fault. Someone's mom, at least.

"Right, Percival," I said, and I might have dripped unfair sarcasm into the word. "What are you doing here?"

Now he shook. His body did a little shake shake whole-body dance to go with the castanets music of his knocking-together teeth. He was sweating, too, and the blood on his face mixed with beads of sweat.

"I don't know," he said. "I don't know!"

The second was almost a scream, and strangely, I believed he was telling the truth. And a lie. He might not know how he'd landed in my room particularly, but he knew something.

I was trying to think of a way to get him to tell, because I was fresh out of thumb screws, and there wasn't an iron maiden in sight, and if I went to the medieval section to borrow a cup of either, likely I'd run into an elf. Or a werewolf. Or a magical talking squirrel or something. And it would take far too long.

But before I could speak, he did.

"Y-Y-You."

So, okay, he stuttered, and his teeth clacked when he spoke. Assume that, because transcribing it gets tiring.

"You're Kit Marlowe!" he said. And accusingly, "You look like him."

I sighed. Look, I thought I was a big deal when I used my first ill-gotten gains—from spying, not whatever your gutter-bound mind is telling you, though sometimes the difference was one of intent, not action—to have my portrait painted in the very first fashionable garment I'd ever bought. A doublet in dark velvet, the sleeves slashed through to show satin in the color known as Harlot's Leg, with very expensive gold buttons. And my hair hennaed to hide the fact that it was, like my father's, mouse brown.

I was young and stupid, but if I'd known it would be rediscovered in the twentieth century and printed in a million books, then set free to haunt the internet, I'd never have done it. I was stupid. Barely seventeen. Really. What did I know? But there it was. My too-pretty countenance at seventeen would haunt me for eternity. And the number of people who recognized me never failed to surprise me.

"Guilty as charged." I raised my eyebrows at him. "Are you charging?"

He moved his right hand, then, from where it remained raised against the wall—surely his arms must be aching, no?—and touched his left eye. "You—you have an eye patch."

I gave him my best disquieting grin. "No, I have several eye patches. I'm just wearing only one. That's the eye the knife went into, pulling my brains out as it exited. The slicing edge of death and all that."

None of this was the precise truth, but it would serve.

It served. He made a sound like "Eep," his hand went back up, and he swallowed, Adam's Apple bobbing in his skinny neck. The stutter came back. "You're dead."

I shrugged. "Not particularly. Do I look dead to you?"

"You're undead!" he wailed.

Damn Fantasy Writers.

"I am *not*," I said. "I'm neither vampire nor werewolf, lych nor graveyard haunting. I—"

I almost segued into *I am myself alone,* because my friend Will, the earnest scribbler I'd helped get a handle on iambic pentameter, had become woven into the culture, a part of everyone's back brain, even mine.

"I did briefly die, but I'm alive. I mean you no harm." Except for holding the gun trained on him ready to fill him full of lead, should he mean me harm. "You're the one who broke into my room. What do you want?"

He slid down the wall, as if his legs had lost the power to carry him. His eyes still stared at me. At me, not the gun. Which was interesting.

"My girlfriend said I looked like you."

"Women say a lot of things," I said, though suddenly the familiarity of his features clicked into place. He did look like the face I saw in the mirror over the sink every morning while shaving. How much he looked like me was a matter for discussion, and I wasn't about to discuss it, or clear his face of blood to have a better look.

"Why are you here, kid?"

"I don't know!"

"Where did you get all over blood?"

He was now squatting against the wall. The light of streetlights coming through my window blinds painted stripes across his features, as he looked up and stared, pole-axed. "My muse. I… I was really angry."

I didn't say, *Oh, shit,* but I thought it. And there might have been an echo of *oh shit* in my tone as I said, "Your muse? You beat your muse?"

He nodded. "I thought I'd killed him. But then he got up, and he came toward me, and—"

Yeah, yeah, he would. Muses aren't as easy to kill as all that, or I'd no longer be alive.

"And I was scared, and I saw… There was a place behind him. There was a portal. Like, a jagged cut in the world? And I went through it, and there were… things. And then I wished to be safe."

And "safe" had brought him here? I had no idea what that even meant. Unless…

Well, he did look like me. If there was a familial bond, a congruence of genes… I did tell you Imago worked by resonance, did I not? By things older than reason and logic? By the scraps of lizard left in the smart ape brain?

I know you're thinking the man famous for saying he liked boys—meaning men, I never had much use for the infantry—and tobacco would've left no descendants. You'd be right. And wrong.

Look, I was a roaring boy, grasping life with both hands and whatever else I could use to get a foothold in an unkind world. I was a cobbler's son from Canterbury, catapulted to Cambridge on the strength of my brain and bravura. A scholarship boy, laughed at by the better born, but holding my own, by the fact my thoughts and my learning could beat theirs with half my brain tied behind my back.

I didn't know how long I could hold on to that sliver of learning, that bit of wealth, that ability to consort—in any way—with the best of the society I was born to, but I knew as long as I could, I was going to make it count. Not limit myself to one half of the human race, to the meager food served in the refectory, to the monk-like discipline of the colleges in those days.

Sooner or later, I thought, I'd fall all the way down, back to Canterbury, where I'd been a very bad apprentice to my father's trade. And I'd take over the old homestead and the old shop, marry a fat wife, and produce a passel of brats. But by the mass, when I did so, I'd take with me the memory of forbidden adventures, of tumbles in taverns and clinches in alleys—and yeah, in the perfumed beds of the nobility, too. So there'd been sweet Tom Walsingham, but also a never end of women. Mostly wealthy and married, and hungry for a pretty boy with a daring tongue.

I hadn't tumbled any human—male or female—since I became a Muse. And the people of Imago... It was different. But though I hadn't thought I'd sown any unauthorized crop, I'd been a profligate sower. Heaven only knew it could have happened.

And that—four hundred and some years later—things might have aligned so my genes came up in a random blind shuffle, as though from an expert gambler in a rigged game. And the boy might be close enough to me in genes that my protections read him as me. Or close enough.

"You have to clean yourself," I said.

He looked down at himself, as if surprised at seeing all the blood. Then dumbly at me.

And I lost patience. Look, yes, I have a shower, and other things to cater to the necessities of the body, but while I have a body, Imago is not... the real world. I like showers with lots of hot water, but it's not a necessity. And I keep suits in my closet, but they're also not a necessity.

I don't know if other people work the same way in Imago. I really don't have close friends, though I have people with whom I play a friendly game of poker, now and then. Perhaps my powers came to me because I'd once been an author—well, a storyteller—and was now a Muse. But I'd never seen anyone use money in Imago, unless it was as a token piece of himself, or unless—Well, there are things for which you need drachmas or sesterce, and damn hard to come by.

But I had powers. I waved a hand, and the blood on the boy disappeared. His clothes transformed into something that would pass unnoticed in Imago: a grey suit, a white shirt, a red tie. A fedora tilted over his brow.

Then I waved a hand again, and I was dressed in my usual suit, my own fedora tilted over my eyes.

He made a sound like "Gleep," or perhaps "Eep" again, but other than his rabbit-like alarm, the resemblance was uncanny. With him wearing what I'd worn for well-nigh the last hundred years, it was very much like looking in the mirror on the back of the door in the bathroom. His hair was redder and darker, with no hint of mouse. But then again, the 21st had far better dyes than henna.

I holstered my gun and got my silver cigarette case—a gift from a grateful client—out of my pocket. I extracted a cigarette and lit it with my silver lighter—ditto. The first drawn-in puff of smoke steadied me. Say what you will about cigarettes, but they're much better than the sweepings of a tobacco warehouse, which was all I could afford back in Elizabethan England. And though there's a place for the ceremony and pomp of a pipe, you can't beat a cigarette for convenience.

Belatedly, I realized I'd been rude and fished out the case again, and offered it to the kid. "I'm sorry, do you want—"

Paint me red and call me a barn if he didn't try to knit himself tighter to the wall, and if his eyes didn't manage to get even larger. "B-b-boys and tobacco."

Damn me. If I'd known I was going to live this long and be this well known, I'd have been more careful about the stupid things I said, wouldn't I? I laughed before I could stop it, and put the case back, while still laughing.

Then I waved the idea away. "You're safe from me, kid. I've never been one for unwilling partners."

Quite the contrary. Being a handsome lad in a rough age, sometimes *I'd* been unwilling and had to fight groping hands off my body. "And I don't partake in the fascination of Narcissus."

"Narcisus?" He frowned at me.

Right. I walked toward the bathroom. "Come with me. Come. Stop acting like a hunted rabbit, damn me."

It took a moment, but he got up and followed. A slight balk at the bathroom door as though, were I an infamous seducer, I'd have dragged him from the proximity of a relatively comfortable bed or even the spacious floor to get him into a bathroom that was all of seven feet by seven feet, and half of it taken up by a clawfoot tub. Okay, so my pronouncements when young and stupid might have justifiably given him the impression I was lecherous, but did they give him the impression I was that dumb?

Eventually he came to stand by me, back against the sink, and leaving me barely enough room to close the door. I reached up for the hanging cord and turned on the light.

In the mirror, side by side, we appeared revealed as twins. Oval face and wide, light-brown eyes, arched eyebrow, and too soft a mouth, limber body, mine more muscular than bulky. His—well, he could have worked out a bit. Would need to, if he was going to survive.

The strangest thing in all this was that he'd managed to beat his muse till his muse bled freely.

He touched the mirror as if he thought that would change the image. Then he looked at me. "You're my father?"

I shook my head. "Unlikely. And your name isn't Luke."

He didn't laugh. Tough crowd.

"Look, kid, I haven't laid a honey, not a real, human one, since... well, not in four hundred and some years." It occurred to me— where do these thoughts come from?—that perhaps the creatures available in Imago, muses and scene-setting actors, creatures of dream and imagination as much part of the place as the buildings and the stores and the food, could catch and increase.

A thought to make me abstemious for the rest of eternity.

But the kid was human. I'd swear to it. I could smell his bewildered humanity, see the bedewing of sweat on his upper lip, barely marked by the appearance of facial hair.

He swallowed hard, staring at the mirror. "Mom said my father was—she said his last name was Merlin. I always thought—"

I raised my eyebrows at his reflection. In the free spelling—and sounding—Renaissance, my name had been written Marlowe and Marlon, Marlin, and, yes, Merlin, though that only when I was feeling fanciful.

"It's a way to write my last name," I said.

"I know. When my girlfriend said I looked like you—"

"Right. And you do. And yes, though I never married anyone, it's possible I have descendants, and it's possible even one or more of them has taken my name, or a variant of it." I laughed. "All my sins remembered!"

He looked confused—I mean, more confused than his baseline confusion. So I dragged him out of the bathroom and to the bedroom. This time he didn't balk. Perhaps our resemblance had reassured him.

"Look," I said. "I must know. Why did you beat your muse? How did all this happen? How do you even know you have a muse? You're awfully young."

He frowned, and the fear and the confusion melted as anger took their place. "I know I have a muse because I started seeing the bastard when I was seven. And he's... insane. He invades my dreams. He whispers stories to me in class. He won't leave me time to eat or sleep, or—he brings me visions of blood and stories about serial killers. He'll drive me to the madhouse."

I shook the ash growing on my cigarette into the ashtray perched precariously on the stack of books on the table by my chair. Then I took another puff of smoke down into my lungs and exhaled slowly. The genes I could see, but was it a family curse?

"Your muse sounds much like mine."

"I couldn't take it anymore. He's destroying my life. When he woke me up and insisted I write—" He shook his head. "I just started beating him with my desk lamp, then with my fists, then I kicked him. He bled all over, and I thought he was dead, but then he stood up and came at me."

Oh, I knew this story well.

"They—we, perhaps—No, it's too complex to explain. Look, Muses don't die. Yes, they can be killed, but not that easily. And they keep coming. And here, in Imago—" I shrugged. "Kid, you jumped from the frying pan into the raging fire."

At that moment, the room exploded. Or at least my door and the wall around it did, blowing up like overheated glass, taking my protection sigil with it.

Through the gap came... creatures. They looked like werewolves wrapped in shrouds. A muse's creatures coming for vengeance against the muse's errant writer.

I'm not a paladin. I should have shoved the kid into the creatures and run.

So explain to me why I shoved him behind me and fired away at the creatures, blowing them to bloody pieces.

One, two, three, four, five, and six, and damn it, they were still coming. And the boy behind me was making sounds that might be "Gleep, gleep, gleep," like a giant, scared gerbil.

I took a deep breath and used my weapon. No. My other weapon. No, not that one. Where did you get the idea—never mind.

You see, when my muse stabbed me through the eye, in the Hell of the Forgotten, my friend Will—who'd plunged in after me, for reasons only he'd have been able to explain—had stabbed the muse through the eye with his own quill.

And at that moment, by the ancient magic of the place, an eye for an eye, a soul for a soul, I realized I could leave my dying body for the Muse's living one. So I did, and he got caught and pulled into my body. He took days to die, too, as he was catapulted back to Deptford and a small room where the great reckoning had started.

They say he—well, they say I, but it wasn't me—cursed fearfully and took days to die. Which is not how a human dies who's been stabbed through the eye and into the brain. But it *is* how a Muse would die, trapped in a human body.

I was glad that a church tower had been built over where his body was buried. I wouldn't trust the bastard not to come back.

On waking up in the Hell of the Forgotten, with Will trying to make me come to my senses, I'd found that this body—well, muses don't die, but they don't heal normally, either. The eye, lost to the sharpness of Will Shakespeare's well-sharpened quill, had been gone, but in its place was left a vortex to the center of what it was to be a muse: to half-formed thoughts and ungelled words, to stories with no words, to the chaos at the heart of the universe.

I wear a patch for the world's protection. Oh, I have some volition, and can keep my eye closed. But if I don't, if I forget—

I pulled my patch up, opened my eye, and *looked* at the creatures. They got sucked into the eye, one by one, screaming and dissolving. It shouldn't work, because they were human-sized, and my eye is only eye-sized, but it did, because they whirled and turned into some kind of unrefined substance, matter primordial with a glimmer of stars and the cold of space.

They felt cold, too, rushing past my orbit, but they were gone. All of them.

Which was good and bad. They were gone, and not a threat. But on the other hand, I'd now taken this muse's substance into myself. He was connected to me. If he could break through my sigil in pursuit of his writer before, now—

"We have to go," I said, grabbed the kid around the forearm, and pulled him out to the narrow hallway that had become one with my foyer. I looked at and dismissed the elevator. Lots of fun in movies, but I wasn't going to be trapped in a box with whatever the bastard was going to send after us next.

I opened the metal door to the stairs, instead, and ran down the narrow winding stairway, marked by the soles of countless climbers, and smelling faintly of vomit and piss.

From the sounds, the kid hesitated only a second, then ran after me. Note, after me. He made no effort to overtake me. Considering what he'd seen me do, I wouldn't either, to be fair.

Down and down and down, and on the first stair landing, three women dressed in dark shrouds, and—

No, they had the bodies of serpents, and fangs.

Damn it and holy hell, I hated to give the bastard more of a link to me, but even though I could have reloaded my heater with an effort of will and blasted them with that, it would have slowed us down, and my logic told me speed was of the essence. The patch was still flipped toward my forehead. I opened my eye. Which swallowed them whole while they howled and shrieked their outrage.

We ran on.

"Where are we going?" he asked. "He's going to keep sending them after me. These are... The things he wants me to write. I don't even *like* horror."

"Yeah," I said. "Sounds like my own muse, way back. I wanted to write long-form narrative poems and erudite epigrams. He wanted me to write blood-soaked plays. Which, to be fair, sold quite well, but gave me nightmares and left me sleepless."

"Why?"

"Why what?"

"What are muses, and why do they do that?"

"Most muses don't do that," I said. "Ours happen to be insane."

I opened the door to the street, a normal Noir street, which you know as well as I do, from an archetypal New York City described in a million noir books, and seen in a thousand noir movies. Or you know, an archetypal Chicago, or Detroit. Or Gotham, for that matter. It didn't make much difference, because it wasn't any of those cities, not really.

Though, having visited those places, I sometimes recognized a landmark when walking—or in this case, running—past it. It was night, it was raining, and the streets were deserted. But by the Empire State Building, incongruously situated next to what looked like an opera house of nineteenth-century vintage, three walking skeletons waited. I vacuumed them up with my eye, feeling my bond to the kid's bastard muse grow tighter.

"What are we doing?" he asked. "I can feel him closer. He's going to—"

"Yeah, he is, but we need something."

I'm not a paladin. Where do plans and ideas come from, fully formed, before I've had time to think them through, before I and my mind could discuss the matter, and agree to it or reject it like a sane being?

I should have let the kid go. Many writers have horrible muses. There's a man who, for some reason, crosses over to Imago now and then—it's not common, but some writers can do it—hides in bars and markets, and his muse, a tall, dark woman, powerfully built and dressed all in leather, pursues him. She'll erupt into movie theaters and taverns, screaming for "John." It's a joke all over Imago, and we all shake our heads at the poor bastard. But I understand he's had a lot of success in the human world.

If the kid cut his cloth to fit his—

But I couldn't. Look, it's as easy as that. Perhaps it was the fact that he looked like me. Not my son, certs, but almost for sure my son's son's son, with a few more sons in between.

And the poor bastard—I speak advisedly, for at least his ancestor got by me in some darkened and flea-infested Elizabethan bedroom, was one. I never married—had drawn a genetic hand that amounted to being myself come again. Impossible to deny that it spoke to that lizard brain. Aye, and the ape brain, too. And perhaps the human one.

After all, if living beings didn't fight for their get, how would any species survive?

But more than that: I'd been there. Like the kid, I'd had a muse I couldn't escape, a creature so ill fitted to me, one of us was going to kill the other. Sometimes, like bad marriages, bad muse-writer relationships can't help but end in tragedy.

I didn't want to help. No, that's not true. I'd become a PI just so I could help people in this situation, so humans would have someone who fought for them in Muse world. But I didn't want to risk my life.

And this was going to involve risking my life.

I didn't want to die. Every century it delayed, I wanted it less.

But Will had risked it for me. Risked it without a thought when we were both barely twenty-nine.

"Ah, hell, I've lived enough. If this is the end..." I said.

"What?" he said, alarmed. "What do you mean?"

"Nothing. Come. We need the price."

Finding places in Imago isn't straightforward. The landscape changes and moves with the latest creation, the most commonly read story. You keep your destination in mind and aim...

My destination was a little door between a Chinese restaurant and an undertaker's. I almost missed it.

But the light shone through the panel of hammered glass in it, even though this was, supposedly, the middle of the night. I opened it, and a bell jangled. I stepped in, grabbed back at the kid, and dragged him in with me.

Inside, it was dusty and cramped, most of the space taken up by a counter, and behind the counter floor-to-ceiling niches in which were half-glimpsed shapes. Urns, it looked like, and dark bottles, jars filled with things that moved and flapped, or else swirled.

A cough turned my eyes toward the man who'd either been sitting in the corner, or had just materialized there. I don't know which. He was old. I mean, really old. He looked a hundred, with skin like parchment, and a few wisps of hair on a mostly bare cranium, but something gave off the sense he was much older than that, and his dark, lightless eyes looked like they were peering at us from the dawn of humanity.

"Drachmae," I said. "Four."

He raised his eyebrows. "It'll cost you."

"Doesn't it always?"

He provided the dish. It was ceramic, and looking old enough to come from my birthplace. Much like, in fact, the dish in which my mother had mixed oil and spices for seasoning meat. For all I knew, it was the same dish. It would fit. He provided the knife, small and wicked sharp.

I cut into my arm, careful not to slice so deep it would run uncontrolled. A rivulet flowed onto the plate, red and smelling of iron and life. I let it flow till it covered the bottom. Then I concentrated, and the wound closed.

Nicodemus, the shop owner, sniffed at the blood, then dipped a finger in it and tasted it. He grinned, showing yellow teeth. "A rare vintage."

Behind me, the boy made a sound, and I wanted to tell him, *in the end, the price is always blood and life.* They're always and forever the only real things.

Nicodemus' claw-like hand dipped behind the counter, and then tossed four coins on the counter.

These were no modern Greek drachmae, but ancient ones, so flattened by use and passage through many hands, you couldn't see the figures on them. They'd do. They were proper.

I scooped them into my pocket and turned around to find a pale kid looking confused again. Why was I bothering? But I grabbed his arm and pulled him to the sidewalk.

There was a group of dark somethings approaching from the left, but I didn't wait. I didn't need to take more of his damn muse's being into mine. Instead, I raised my hand in the ancient sign.

A taxi, black and yellow, glided up to stop next to us. I opened the door and got in. These conveyances take the shape of where they appear. The taxi was cleaner than any real taxi in the world of humans, but it smelled faintly of fish, and felt cold, with a damp frigidity.

And the man driving looked very Greek, a dark and roughhewn man such as you'd find, say, plying a boat across the river of the dead.

He grinned at us. The name on the license clipped next to the wheel was Charon.

I leaned back against the upholstery. "The Hell of the Forgotten."

Charon raised his eyebrows, but started the car. We glided quietly through the rain-soaked streets of Noir.

"Don't look back," I said. "Whatever you do, don't look back."

"Or I'll turn into a pillar of salt?" the kid asked.

"Worse. Far worse." I must have conveyed my seriousness, because he sat next to me, looking rigidly forward.

"But where are we? What are muses? And where are we going?"

"You're in Imago," I said. I knew I'd have to explain. It had taken me months to figure it out, and I'd almost gotten ended a hundred times, when it was me. And back then, Imago was much, much smaller, and far less dangerous.

"It's a place made of all the fiction in the world. When writers write it, and people read it, it... Things come into being. It's like the energy of all those minds, picturing the places and thinking about them, give them life and solid existence. Well, mostly solid. We're on the edge of the created worlds."

"Worlds?"

"Right, so—" I took a deep breath. "You know how you think of the universe. Except there's not one universe, but many, all separated by—"

"Something like pieces of glass, existing side by side and never touching," he said, sounding vaguely offended. "Yes, I do understand the concept of parallel worlds and the multi-verse. I know some universes will be almost the same as the one I live in, except my shirt will be blue instead of red, and I'll have a cat instead of a dog. And that we, mere humans, never cross over."

"Bless comic books," I said in great amusement. The things humans think they know because some writer wrote about them. "But some things are wrong, you know. It's not sheets of glass, but *thin* sheets of *barely hardened* glass. And humans do cross over now and then. If you make it back to your world, look up the Mandela effect."

"Oh, but that's just people misremembering stuff, and—"

"Sure it is, kid. You tell yourself that. And you're just having an unusually vivid dream is all, right?"

He shut up.

"Credit me with some knowledge, since I've lived here for hundreds of years, and have crossed to the real worlds, and seen them change," I said. "Your idea was right, save for those sheets of glass. It's wax—it's permeable. And some humans are born with... Well, call them circuits in their head that allow them to glimpse all the other worlds. Stories, ideas, images, thoughts not theirs bombard them from their earliest moments."

"Writers," he said as though it were a curse.

"Well, storytellers," I said, "but not all. And not just. Imago is a place created by storytellers and their muses, but I understand it's possible to live in places shaped by musicians and painters."

"Picasso must be a treat there," he said, showing that as well as the looks, he'd inherited some spirit.

"Shouldn't he just, but here's the thing, I understand most such people destroy themselves. It's hard to know which voice is yours when there's so many of them. And supposedly that's why muses are assigned to writers: to control the flow of ideas into their brain, to make them able to live and perform in the world of humans."

"Supposedly?"

Oh, sharp, too. Good. I'd hate to be risking myself for a dunce.

"Yeah. When should you just trust the advert on the can? I suspect—have for some time—the muses are a sort of parasitical species who attach to such humans. It might make them sane as a side effect, or at least most of the time. But the muses, in return, get a world spun for them, and they can shape it to the one they prefer."

There was a moment of silence. "My muse *wants* the worlds he sends to me?"

"Probably. Mine did. He wanted a world of blood, revenge, and cannibalism."

"Charming."

"Some muses are psychopaths, just like some humans are. They seem to imitate us, largely."

"So," he said, "where are we going? And why does it keep changing?"

We'd driven out of Noir by then, and the landscape outside the window had changed into contemporary, either Romance or—

shudder—Literary, but it looked too clean and well kept to be Literary.

"So, we're going through different parts of Imago. It tracks, more or less, to genres of stories."

As I spoke, we were driving, tilting and bumping through what looked like a path through a forest. From lights blinking on either side, and the hazy pink fog, I took it to be an enchanted forest.

"Ignore it. Soon, we'll be going back and back, back before words and before... Before everything. Think of it as going back into the mind of humans before humans were human. Back to the place of power we've forgotten at the very root of human thought, of human stories. Just don't look back."

We were then driving through a foggy land. The beginning of the Hells. Along the edge, things formed and disappeared. Dark carriages seemingly in hot pursuit. For a moment, three Roman chariots, and then just a pack of half-naked savages, riding horses.

The trees were hung with moss, then there were no trees, but just what the impression of trees would be before humans had a word for trees. And then just flickers in what seemed like endless dark.

I felt cold, which was stupid, because there was nothing here. Nothing to feel cold about.

Charon stopped the taxi. "You get out here. I will wait."

I handed him two coins, one for each of us. And maybe he'd be there when we needed him. And maybe he wouldn't. Maybe we had to be lost.

We got out. The ground was spongy and shifting underfoot.

"Why hells?" Percival asked.

"The Hells of the Forgotten. I don't know. Because it's shadowy and shifting, and it's so far back that humans have consciously forgotten it. Like paying for things in blood, it's the only thing that works. This is the only place a muse can die."

At his look, I gave him a laugh. "Yes, me too, but I'm hoping not. I'll try to make sure not."

At that moment, a man overtook us. He was wearing what the kid had worn—jeans and a t-shirt—and he ran to overtake us.

"You, dog of an uncertain mother," he said. "You are balking of my righteous prey."

I refused to turn to him and said dismissively, "What? You're going to bite your thumb at me?"

He jumped me.

I moved and wasn't there.

He picked himself up from the spongy ground and stood in the side-stance position of a fighting man. "Swords," he said. "Swords."

He looked like me. Or the kid. Look, it's something I don't fully understand, but when a muse is the same sex as the writer, they tend to look like twins. It's a miracle the kid didn't try to beat *me* when he first came into my bedroom. But then, probably being half naked and asleep, I didn't look like the insane bastard now brandishing a sword and howling at us.

"Swords. Fight me!"

I'm not a paladin. I'm not even particularly honorable. I reached for my heater. Of course, it wasn't there. See what comes of taking some of the wild muse into me and giving him power over me? Fine. There was a sword at my waist, and I drew it.

I don't know what the muse thought he was doing. Perhaps he mistook me for someone like the kid, with the same upbringing?

His sword fighting was all show and no bite, the sort of thing you see in movies. Mine was... Look, I grew up where swords were regularly plied in self-defense, and having gotten my degree, I was entitled to wear a sword. Which means I learned how to use it. And I wasn't fighting pretty.

But he was strong, and he was insane. There's something to be said for the strength of the insane, their inability to know they've been cut.

So he came at me, dancing and flourishing his sword like it was some kind of fairy wand, you know, making it look pretty for the non-existent cameras. I dove low and slashed my sword across his chest. He howled, but didn't flinch, and with me that close, he clawed at my face and grabbed me by the shoulder.

I cut frantically at him, slicing a piece off his shoulder. He didn't even flinch and started to bring his sword down, point toward my heart.

I wriggled away, and screamed, and dove, and managed to stab him next to his heart, because he was no longer where I'd thought.

He moved fast, for a man pouring blood. Muses were like that. And insane muses worst of all.

I could smell sweat and blood, so vividly I could taste them, and I didn't know whether it was mine or his.

I cut him, and cut him again, and he was losing and bleeding, his blood falling and sparkling in the spongy ground. But he could do for me well before he died.

And I could use my eye on him, but look, you, he was a muse. I'd already taken too much of the bastard into me through his creations. I didn't want us to integrate into one being.

He came running at me. As I lifted my sword to parry his, he lunged past me. I thought he'd missed, then heard the kid scream.

Damn it and hell. I'd told the kid not to look back, but not that he should stay well away. My fault, and my damn fault, and I'd pay for it.

I grabbed the bastard muse and spun him around and said, "At me, sirrah!" then rushed in and under his arm.

His sword gave me a glancing cut to the shoulder, but mine sank to the hilt in his chest. He fell, and I turned to where the kid stood, a pale image over his own body. And I reached and grabbed his immaterial arm, and pushed him into the muse, who was gasping and struggling.

The muse fought. Not with his body, which was prone and bleeding. But his… for lack of a better term, the soul of the creature fought like the possessed. Or those who feared death. I grabbed the kid and shoved him right in, and the muse clawed at both of us and screamed.

His talons had grown knife-long, and they sliced at us.

They couldn't cut our physical bodies, but it felt as though they were needles of ice penetrating. Where they grabbed my arms, they went numb.

And where they touched the kid's soul, they left dark pinpricks.

The kid tried to scramble backward, but I wouldn't let him. I kept pushing.

I remembered all too well, this felt like dying, and now the kid fought me, too, seeking to escape me, but he *had* to go into the muse's body.

Or die.

I grabbed with my other hand at his neck and shoved the boy into the muse's body, pushing as hard as I could. Inch by inch, I forced him in.

As I pushed him into the muse, the muse was forced, like recoiling elastic, into the kid's body.

It gasped and stood still.

I removed the sword from the kid's chest—the muse's chest, now with the kid in it—and willed the wound closed and repaired.

He sat up, shivering, and looked at his own dead body, and then at me.

"You're bleeding," he said.

And then I felt the blood running down my arm. A thought, a word, and it stopped, but I was weak. What a ridiculous thing, to do this for a child I'd barely met. Even if he looked like me.

But he was human. Had been human. And I had chosen to fight for humans.

"Sounds much like a paladin to me," the kid said wryly. And I realized I'd spoken aloud and added that I was no paladin.

I made a sound like spitting, but he only laughed at me.

Then he grew somber. "I guess… I guess I can't go back?"

The body that had been his had disappeared.

"Nah. It went to the last place you were. And it will definitely be identified as you. You're dead in your world. Sorry, kid. I was trying to avoid that."

"Well, Mom will be sad, but it's been hard on her, ever since Dad left, and—eh. She'll find a way. Call me Per, not kid. But… I can't see my girlfriend again?"

"How about Val?" I said. "That's easier to say. And you can, but I wouldn't advise it. It can be… fraught, to visit our loved ones in the world of the living."

He weighed it. "All right. Val will do, if I'm not going to run into anyone I know."

He was taking it amazingly well. I remembered the relief of being free of a crazed muse.

"You can visit the world now and then. But I wouldn't advise visiting those you know. Trust me. I tried. It hurts too much." So much that I'd run back into Imago, and stayed away from humans for a hundred years.

"What do I do here, though?"

"I don't know. I'm a detective. I could use someone to do the filing. And an assistant."

He weighed that a moment, too. "Maybe. To start."

We walked through the shifting landscape and found Charon waiting for us. The ride back was uneventful. I paid him the drachmae as we left.

I took the kid to The Heartbreak, the corner bar, for ham sandwiches and glasses of milk. Later, Pinky and Baltazar showed up, and we beat them at poker for enough drachmae to pay the rent and get the kid his own apartment.

It's a living.

* * * * *

Sarah A. Hoyt Biography

Sarah A. Hoyt was born and raised near Porto Portugal, where after six years of a blameless life, she conceived the eccentric notion that when she grew up, she was going to live in Colorado and be a writer. Though this objective took her another 21 years to achieve—and imagine her surprise when she realized that Denver wasn't by the sea. Apparently, her mental viewer was behind the times by a few million years—she did end up spending most of her life and career in Colorado, where she raised two sons and mumble mumble mumble cats.

Recently, she and her husband have come down from the heights to a more manageable altitude, where she continues to write Science Fiction, Fantasy, Mystery, Historical novels, recently scripts for a revived *Barbarella* comic series, and whatever she very well pleases.

Her husband has been instructed to warn you that no genre is safe from her. This story gave her an opportunity to revisit the obsession with Elizabethan poets that first gave her entrance into the industry, with *Ill Met By Moonlight*, a Mythopoeic Award finalist. She's also won the Prometheus Award for her novel *Darkship Thieves*, and the Dragon Award for her alternate history *Uncharted* (in collaboration with Kevin J. Anderson).

* * * * *

End of Book 5
Libri Valoris

Find the rest of the Libri Valoris here:

amazon.com/dp/B089LX1988

* * *

And join the New Mythology Press mailing list to find out all about our new books here:

chriskennedypublishing.com/fantasy-mailer/

* * * * *

About the Editor

Rob Howell is the publisher of New Mythology Press, including his work as editor of the *Libri Valoris* anthologies of heroic fantasy. He's the creator of the Firehall Sagas and an author in the Four Horsemen Universe. He writes epic fantasy, space opera, military science fiction, alternate history, and whatever else seems fun. He also writes for Luke Gygax in the Okkorim RPG setting.

He's a reformed medieval academic, a former IT professional, and a retired soda jerk.

His parents quickly discovered books were the only way to keep Rob quiet. He latched onto the Hardy Boys series first, and then anything he could reach. Without books, it's unlikely all three would have survived.

You can find him online here:
- His Blog: robhowell.org/blog.
- Firehall Sagas: firehallsagas.com
- Amazon: amazon.com/-/e/B00X95LBB0
- Twitter: @Rhodri2112

* * * * *

Excerpt from
A Reluctant Druid

Book One of The Milesian Accords

Jon R. Osborne

Now Available from New Mythology Press

eBook, Hardcover, Paperback, and Audio

Excerpt from A Reluctant Druid:

"**D**on't crank on it; you'll strip it."

Liam paused from trying to loosen the stubborn bolt holding the oil filter housing on his Yamaha motorcycle, looking for the source of the unsolicited advice. The voice was gruff, with an accent and cadence that made Liam think of the Swedish Chef from the Muppets. The garage door was open for air circulation, and two figures were standing in the driveway, illuminated by the setting sun. As they approached and stepped into the shadows of the house, Liam could see they were Pixel and a short, stout man with a graying beard that would do ZZ Top proud. The breeze blowing into the garage carried a hint of flowers.

Liam experienced a moment of double vision as he looked at the pair. Pixel's eyes took on the violet glow he thought he'd seen before, while her companion lost six inches in height, until he was only as tall as Pixel. What the short man lacked in height, he made up for in physique; he was built like a fireplug. He was packed into blue jeans and a biker's leather jacket, and goggles were perched over the bandana covering his salt and pepper hair. Leather biker boots crunched the gravel as he walked toward the garage. Pixel followed him, having traded her workout clothes for black jeans and a pink t-shirt that left her midriff exposed. A pair of sunglasses dangled from the neckline of her t-shirt.

"He's seeing through the glamour," the short, bearded man grumbled to Pixel, his bushy eyebrows furrowing.

"Well duh. We're on his home turf, and this is his place of power" Pixel replied nonchalantly. "He was pushing back against my glamour yesterday, and I'm not adding two hands to my height."

Liam set down the socket wrench and ran through the mental inventory of items in the garage that were weapons or could be used as them. The back half of the garage was a workshop, which included the results of his dabbling with blacksmithing and sword-crafting, so the list was considerable. But the most suitable were also the farthest away.

"Can I help you?" Liam stood and brushed off his jeans; a crowbar was three steps away. Where had they come from? Liam hadn't heard a car or motorcycle outside, and the house was a mile and a half outside of town.

"Ja, you can." The stout man stopped at the threshold of the garage. His steel-gray eyes flicked from Liam to the workbench and back. He held his hands out, palms down. The hands were larger than his and weren't strangers to hard work and possibly violence. "And there's no need to be unhospitable; we come as friends. My name is Einar, and you've already met Pixel."

"Hi, Liam." Pixel was as bubbly as yesterday. While she didn't seem to be making the same connection as Einar regarding the workbench, her eyes darted about the cluttered garage and the dim workshop behind it. "Wow, you have a lot of junk."

"What's this about?" Liam sidled a half step toward the workbench, regretting he hadn't kept up on his martial arts. He had three brown belts, a year of kendo, and some miscellaneous weapons training scattered over two decades but not much experience in the way of real fighting. He could probably hold his own in a brawl as long as his opponent didn't have serious skills. He suspected Einar was more than a Friday night brawler in the local watering hole. "Is she your daughter?"

Einar turned to the purple-haired girl, his caterpillar-like eyebrows gathering. "What did you do?"

"What? I only asked him a few questions and checked him out," Pixel protested, her hands going to her hips as she squared off with

Einar. "It's not as if I tried to jump his bones right there in the store or something."

"Look mister, if you think something untoward happened between me and your daughter –" Liam began.

"She's not my pocking daughter, and I don't give a troll's ass if you diddled her," Einar interrupted, his accent thickening with his agitation. He took a deep breath, his barrel chest heaving. "Now, will you hear me out without you trying to brain me with that tire iron you've been eyeing?"

"You said diddle." Pixel giggled.

"Can you be serious for five minutes, you pocking faerie?" Einar glowered, his leather jacket creaking as he crossed his arms.

"Remember 'dwarf,' you're here as an 'advisor.'" Pixel included air quotes with the last word, her eyes turning magenta. "The Nine Realms are only involved out of politeness."

"Politeness! If you pocking Tuatha and Tylwyth Teg hadn't folded up when the Milesians came at you, maybe we wouldn't be here to begin with!" Spittle accompanied Einar's protest. "Tylwyth? More like Toothless!"

"Like your jarls didn't roll over and show their bellies when the Avramites showed up with their One God and their gold!" Pixel rose up on her toes. "Your people took their god and took their gold and then attacked our ancestral lands!"

"Guys!" Liam had stepped over to the workbench but hadn't picked up the crowbar. "Are you playing one of those live-action role playing games or something? Because if you are, I'm calling my garage out of bounds. Take your LARP somewhere else."

"We've come a long way to speak to you," Einar replied, looking away from Pixel. "I'm from Asgard."

"Asgard? You mean like Thor and Odin? What kind of game are you playing?" Liam hadn't moved from the workbench, but he'd mapped in his mind the steps he'd need to take to reach a stout pole which would serve as a staff while he back-pedaled to his workshop, where a half-dozen half-finished sword prototypes rested. From where he stood, though, he didn't feel as threatened. He knew a bit about gamers because there were a fair number of them among the pagan community, and he'd absorbed bits and pieces of it. Maybe someone had pointed Liam out to Pixel as research about druids for one of these games—an over-enthusiastic player who wanted to more convincingly roleplay one.

"Gods I hate those pocking things," Einar grumbled, rubbing his forehead while Pixel stifled another giggle. "Look, can we sit down and talk to you? This is much more serious than some pocking games you folk play with your costumes and your toy weapons."

"This isn't a game, and we aren't hippies with New Age books and a need for self-validation." Pixel added. Her eyes had faded to a lavender color. "Liam, we need your help."

* * *

Get "*A Reluctant Druid*" at:
amazon.com/dp/B07716V2RN

Find out more about Jon R. Osborne and *A Reluctant Druid* at: chriskennedypublishing.com/imprints-authors/jon-r-osborne.

* * * * *

Excerpt from
The Chimera Coup

Book One of the Heirs of Cataclysm

Christopher G. Nuttall

Available from New Mythology Press

eBook, and Paperback, and, coming soon, Audio

Excerpt from *The Chimera Coup*

Greyshade smiled thinly. "Where will you go after you pack?"

"I don't know." John tried to think, but he was too dazed to think straight. Where could he go? There was no way he could go back home. He had some money saved from summer work experience, enough to get him across the Free States, and... and go where? Where could he go? "I don't know, sir."

"I have a suggestion," Greyshade said, a hint of warmth entering his voice. "You're a clever young man with a magical talent. You have astonishing potential, and I don't want to see it wasted. I know people who might be interested in hiring you. There will be a certain element of risk involved, and it will mean travelling beyond the Free States, but it may offer you the best chance of either redeeming yourself or building a new life."

"The Frontier," John said. He'd be lying if he claimed he hadn't considered making his way there after he graduated. The Free States were too well established, even now, for a complete newcomer to make his mark. "You think there are people who'll hire me?"

"Yes." Greyshade met his eyes evenly. "I know a group that will. They've been looking for a magician, and you fit the bill."

John blinked. "They'll take me?"

He thought he saw a hint of irritation cross the headmaster's face, but it was gone before he could be sure. "They'll give you a chance," Greyshade said. His eyes narrowed in warning. "They're a band of travelling adventurers, which means 'mercenaries.' They do all sorts of jobs along the Frontier and the Wildlands beyond. They'll give you a chance—one. If you prove yourself, they'll be loyal to you as long as you are loyal to them. If you don't, you can probably find other employment along the Frontier."

"I..." John forced himself to think. There was nothing left for him in the Free States. He had nowhere to go, even if Katrina's family didn't send assassins after him. Katrina herself certainly wouldn't want anything to do with him after he'd destroyed her future beyond repair. He'd be lucky if she didn't curse him on the spot should they ever meet again. "If they'll take me..."

"I'll give you a letter of introduction," Greyshade said, "and also a travel pass. You'll take the slider to Lucasville, a ramshackle town on the edge of the Frontier, and meet up with the team there. If they don't want you, you should be able to find something else to do there until you find your footing."

John nodded slowly. A travel pass would be very helpful. If nothing else, it would keep him from having to spend his own money on the journey.

A question nagged at his mind. "Sir, why are you helping me?"

Greyshade shrugged. "Which answer would you like? I could give you several."

"The truth," John said.

"They'd all be true." Greyshade smiled as if he'd thought of a private joke. "Suffice it to say, I dislike parents contacting me and throwing their weight around, trying to bully me into forgoing proper procedure and doing what they want. You might well have been expelled anyway, after we carried out a formal inquiry, but they wanted you expelled yesterday. And so I must, yet I can give you at least a chance to make something of yourself. Anyway..."

He looked past John. The door opened behind him. "The Grey Men will escort you to your bedroom, then out of the school," he said. "Don't speak to anyone along the way. Your letters and a couple of other things will be waiting for you in the entrance hall. Once you're gone, don't come back. And don't try to visit your girlfriend. It might hurt her chances of making a full recovery."

"Yes, sir," John said reluctantly. He disliked the idea of owing Greyshade anything, particularly a debt he had little hope of repaying, but he had no choice. "And thank you."

"If it works out, you can thank me then," Greyshade said. "Now, go."

John turned and walked out. The Grey Men followed him soundlessly. John felt as if he was caught in a dream as he made his way down the corridors, passing students who stared at him and his escorts as if they were tigers or weirdlings, or something—anything—that shouldn't be anywhere near the school.

He spotted a number of familiar faces—a couple gloating at his fall, a couple shocked—but didn't dare speak to them. If he saw his friends... he suspected they wouldn't be friendly any longer. They probably wouldn't dare. Katrina's family wouldn't hesitate to destroy anyone who showed the slightest hint of sympathy for the boy who'd ruined their daughter's life.

I didn't mean to, he thought. I didn't!

Really? His thoughts mocked him. So what?

Tears prickled in his eyes as he reached his bedroom door and peered inside. The room was a mess. The bed was scorched, ruined; his wardrobe and bookshelves were drenched, water pooling around his feet.

He felt his heart twist as he eyed the spellbooks—he'd spent much of his allowance on them over the last few years—and then he picked them up, trying to brush the water off. The protective charms on the books, and the clothes, had failed. He guessed his desperate attempts to save Katrina had accidentally cancelled those charms, too.

The Grey Men watched soundlessly as John opened his trunk, then transferred the money and a handful of prized possessions into a knapsack. There was no point in trying to take the trunk. He'd bought it fifth-hand, and the charms had been fraying to the point that he was mildly surprised someone hadn't broken into it long ago. The notebooks at the bottom made him hesitate before he shoved them into the knapsack, too. He might not sit his exams, let alone try to gain accreditation, but he could study on his own. No one cared about formal qualifications on the Frontier. They just cared about results.

He brushed water off the desk, then sat on the soggy chair and tried to work out what he could say to Katrina. She'd hate him when—if—she recovered.

He wanted to put his feelings into words, and he didn't know how. He forced himself to write a few lines, trying to convey how sorry he was, and promising to write again when he reached safe harbor. He hoped she'd get the letters. Greyshade might be willing to pass them on to her, but Katrina's family would have other ideas.

There were all sorts of stories about wealthy families who treated their daughters as chattel, practically locking them up until they could be married off. Katrina was too powerful for that to happen to her—no, she'd been too powerful. Who knew what would happen to her now? Her family, deprived of her talent, might just sell her to the highest bidder.

If they do, he promised himself, *I'll rescue her. Whatever the cost.*

He took a quick shower, then changed into simple journeyman's clothes before slinging his knapsack over his shoulder, taking one last look at the room, and then walked out. The corridors were clear, somewhat to his surprise, as he walked down the stairs and into the entrance hall, his escort dogging his heels.

Greyshade's secretary—a sour-faced woman who was cordially loathed by everyone else—was waiting, holding a folder in one bony hand. She looked John up and down, disdain clearly visible on her face, then passed him the folder and turned away.

John had no time to inspect the contents. The Grey Men were already motioning to the exit.

John took a long breath, then turned and walked out of the school.

* * *

Get *The Chimera Coup* at:

amazon.com/dp/B0BFLV4TH8

Find out more about Christopher G. Nuttall and *The Chimera Coup* at: chriskennedypublishing.com.

* * * * *

Made in the USA
Middletown, DE
13 May 2024